'Yet again the author proves herself to be among the leaders of contemporary British crime fiction'
forwinternights.wordpress.com

'A masterclass in pace and plot'   **joanne-sheppard.com**

'An outstanding read'
cleopatralovesbooks.wordpress.com

Praise for *No Other Darkness*:

'Riveting . . . Sarah Hilary delivers in this enthralling tale of a haunted detective, terrible crime, and the secrets all of us try to keep'   **Lisa Gardner**

'At the centre is a queasily equivocal moral tone that forces the reader into a constant rejigging of their attitude to the characters. And did I mention the plotting? Hilary's ace in the hole – as it is in the best crime thrillers'
Financial Times

'Sarah Hilary cements her position as one of Britain's most exciting and accomplished new writers. Complex, polished and utterly gripping, this is a book to make your heart pound'
Eva Dolan

'The skill of the prose produces a deft and disturbing thriller'
Sunday Mirror

'Truly mesmerising from its opening page to its thunderous denouement. A haunting, potent novel from a bleakly sublime new voice'   **David Mark**

'Heart-breaking . . . I can't recommend this highly enough'
SJI Holliday

By Sarah Hilary and available from Headline

Someone Else's Skin
No Other Darkness
Tastes Like Fear

TASTES
LIKE FEAR

SARAH HILARY

headline

First published in 2016 by
HEADLINE PUBLISHING GROUP

First published in paperback in 2016 by
HEADLINE PUBLISHING GROUP

1

Cataloguing in Publication Data is available from the British Library

ISBN 978 1 4722 2643 3

Typeset in Meridien by Palimpsest Book Production Limited,
Falkirk, Stirlingshire

Printed and bound in Great Britain by
Clays Ltd, St Ives plc

Headline's policy is to use papers that are natural, renewable and recyclable
products and made from wood grown in sustainable forests. The logging
and manufacturing processes are expected to conform to the environmental
regulations of the country of origin.

HEADLINE PUBLISHING GROUP
An Hachette UK Company
Carmelite House
50 Victoria Embankment
London EC4Y 0DZ

www.headline.co.uk
www.hachette.co.uk

For Francis,
for being one of the brave ones

Two years ago

Rain had blunted all of London's spires, flattened her high-rises, buried her tower blocks in puddles of mud. Even the chimneys at Battersea Power Station were laid low, their long reflections boiling in the water. Not just days, weeks of rain. Pillars of it coming down, stirring up a stink, shifting the ground under your feet, not letting you forget that this city was built on burial pits.

The rain found its way into everything, bleeding through brickwork, shaking the glass from broken windows, filling the empty can Christie put out for the rush hour. She ran her finger around its ragged lip, inviting blood – proof that she was still here. A Guinness can, its top taken off with a blunt knife, stones weighting the bottom. Coins did the same trick, but it'd been days since anyone dropped coins. She sucked at her finger, tasting meat and copper. Raw inside, an empty ache, but *I'm still here*, she thought. She wished she had better proof than a bloody finger in her mouth.

The world was a wall of umbrellas. She knew the

1

commuters on this route, had seen them sweating in their summer dresses and shirtsleeves. Scowling now, heads down, shoulders up. Angry at her for taking up space on their pavement, sticking her dirty feet in the half-shut door of their conscience. The rain was an excuse to hate her more than they already did.

When she was new to this game – how long ago? Months? – she'd searched the crowd for kind faces. But she'd quickly learned it wasn't kindness that gave coin. People threw change at her the way they'd toss it at a toll-gate basket. To get past, away. Soon, they wouldn't have to pretend not to notice her. She'd be see-through. The rain was washing her away.

'Do you mind?' a woman demanded, meaning Christie's feet, which were in her way apparently, even though they weren't. She'd made herself so small, no part of her was in anyone's way. 'For God's sake find yourself somewhere to go.' Thin and furious, her fist fierce with rings, clenched around the handle of a yellow umbrella.

Christie had tucked herself into a doorway where it was almost dry, but the rain still found her. Pricking through old bricks, a trickle and then a stream. She felt its fingers tickling her neck.

'There are *places*, you know.'

She didn't know. She wished she did. She was scared of the rain, the way it ruined everything, her clothes, her sleeping bag – everything she had. Rain scared her worse than fire.

When she was new to this, a young couple would come with leaflets. They'd stop and crouch, faces working hard. Talking about Our Lord and what was coming and 'Are you ready?' Christie expected it from old people, though most shook their heads as if beggars hadn't existed back in their day. Only once did anyone over the age of sixty give her a second glance. The young couple had pamphlets with pictures of grinning people. The colours ran, making her hands dirtier. When she asked for money, they got mad. They pretended they weren't – 'We're on your side' – but she saw it under the surface of their skin like a swallowing of snakes.

Worse than the snakes was the little man who came and sat beside her. He never spoke, just sat dropping change into her can, one penny at a time, so she couldn't get up and go or tell him to piss off even though he was freaking her out. He smelt funny. Not poor-funny. Rich-funny. Being rich didn't help, the young couple said, it was about being ready for what was coming. Death or Jesus, she didn't know, but there was a whole moment when she thought she could do it – pretend to be religious so they'd save her from this. Being nobody, nothing, invisible.

When the rain started, they stopped coming.

Everyone stopped, except the little man. In a plastic cape that ran the wet off him into her doorway. Splashing coppers into her can, and she knew she couldn't afford to be picky but when he went, she shoved her hand in and scooped out his coins, flinging them away from her, sucking rusty blood from her knuckles. He'd be back for more tomorrow. She should move, somewhere he couldn't find her. Her whole body hurt like it was being squeezed.

Where would she go?

Who should she be?

She could make herself smaller for the woman with the rings, pretend to believe in Jesus for the religious couple. Go with the creep in the cape and be . . . whatever he wanted her to be. Just to get out of the rain for a day, an hour. It was washing her away, all her colours, everything. She wasn't *her* any more. Empty inside, scraped out. Missing.

That was when he found her, *where* he found her . . .

Right on the brink of being lost.

He wasn't like the little man. He was tall and fair and he smelt of the rain that was bluing the shoulders of his shirt. He didn't have pamphlets, or questions. He wasn't angry with her.

His hands were empty and open, like his face.

When he stood in her doorway, he blocked the umbrellas and the hiss and spit of tyres in the street. His shoulders stopped the rain from reaching her.

Strong fingers, wet like hers, but his palms were dry and warm.

Safe, he was safe.

There are places, *you know.*

She hadn't believed it, until then.

1

Now

Noah Jake was running late. He grabbed a bagel for breakfast, leaving the house with it held between his teeth, hands free to search for his Oyster card and keys and his phone, which was playing the theme tune from *The Sweeney* . . .

'Jake.' Remove the bagel, try again. 'DS Jake.'

'Shit, mate.' Ron Carling laughed. 'You sound like a dirty phone call. What've I interrupted?'

'Breakfast. What's up?'

'Not *you*, by the sound of it. Late night?'

'The late nights I can handle. It's the early mornings that're killing me.' No luck finding the Oyster card. He had a nasty feeling his kid brother Sol had swiped it. 'I'm on my way.'

'The boss wants you in Battersea.'

'Where, exactly?'

Ron supplied an address Noah recognised. 'When?'

'Ten minutes ago. Better get your roller-disco skates on.'

*

5

Forty minutes later, the traffic on York Road was being diverted by police accident signs. A snarl of cars ate the streets to either side of Battersea Power Station. Noah walked in its wide shadow, the tilt of its chimneys like stained fingers flipped at a blue sky. Out of commission for years, the power station was sometimes home to film shoots or exhibitions, but empty for the most part. Dan had worked here when it was an art venue, said it made the Tate look like a maiden aunt's curio cabinet. Now it was being hauled into a new shape, one chimney gone, hobbling the building like an upturned table. Penthouses were on sale at six million, and there was talk of private clubs and restaurants. Noah was going to miss the old power station. Sunset Boulevard with a savage facelift, still slyly smoking sixty a day . . .

He heard the police tape before he saw it, switching back and forth.

Black smell of scorch marks from the smash site. An SUV had hit an Audi, the impact piling both cars into a concrete wall, taking a lamp post along for good measure.

DI Marnie Rome was with a traffic officer, her red hair tied back from her face, her neat suit the same shade as the gunmetal Audi, bits of which were still being removed. The SUV was gone, just the shape of its shoulder in the wall. 'DS Jake. Good morning.'

'Sorry I'm late.'

'Everyone's late,' the traffic officer said, 'because of this.'

'How bad is it?' Noah asked Marnie. 'Ron said no one died.'

'Not yet. Four in hospital, two critical. Our eyewitness says a girl walked out into the road.'

No mention of a girl in the early reports online. 'She's one of the critical ones?'

'She walked away. Not a scratch on her, or not from this. The driver of the Audi was lucky. His wife wasn't. Nor was the passenger in the SUV.'

'Which two are critical?'

'Ruth Eaton from the Audi. Logan Marsh from the SUV. He's eighteen. His dad was driving him home from a friend's house. Head injuries. It doesn't look good.'

'But the girl doesn't have a scratch? Where is she?'

'I wish I knew.'

'So when you said she walked away . . .'

'I meant it literally. We need to find her. From the description, she's at risk of harm. Half-dressed, covered in scratches. In shock.' Marnie was studying the scars left by the crash. 'The Audi's driver is our only eyewitness. Joe Eaton. He's at St Thomas's with his wife.'

'How old was the girl?'

'Sixteen, seventeen?' She pre-empted Noah's next question. 'Red hair, not blonde. It doesn't sound like May Beswick.'

Twelve weeks they'd been looking for May. Noah had hoped . . .

'This girl's skinny,' Marnie said, 'and half-dressed. No one in Missing Persons matches her description.'

'It's not much of a description.' Twelve weeks was long enough for May to be skinny, and to have dyed her hair. 'Didn't he notice anything else about her?'

'He was trying not to run her down.'

'I was in a near-miss accident once. A kid ran into the road, after a ball. I hit the brakes in time, just. He got his ball, vanished like that.' Noah snapped his fingers. 'I only saw him for a second, but I can still see the freckles on his nose, scabs on his knees. Like a photo. It happened two years ago.'

'Flashback memory . . .' Marnie's eyes darkened to ink-blue. 'Perhaps Mr Eaton remembers more than he realises. Let's find out.'

2

St Thomas's smelt the same as always, a squeaky top layer of clean with sour base notes of bodies. Noah breathed through his mouth from force of habit. He and Marnie walked down a corridor where trolleys had left skid marks on the walls, and the floors had a frantic shine, to the room where Joe Eaton was waiting for news of his wife.

Eaton was in his mid thirties, could've passed for twenty-eight. Darkish hair. Grey eyes, the left spoilt by a subconjunctival haemorrhage, bleeding into the white. Natty suit ruined by a neck brace for whiplash. A shade over six feet tall. Blank fright on his face when he saw Marnie and Noah.

'Mr Eaton, I'm Detective Inspector Rome, this is Detective Sergeant Jake. How are you?'

'Fine.' He brought his shoulders up. 'I'm fine. Ruth's in surgery. They think a ruptured spleen.'

'I'm sorry,' Marnie said, 'but we need to ask some questions.'

'How's Logan? I spoke with his dad last night.' Joe put a hand across his mouth. 'It sounded bad, worse than Ruth. And he's just a kid.'

'We haven't spoken with Mr Marsh yet. Shall we sit down?' Marnie drew up a chair, settling her slim frame to face the man.

Joe nodded, following her lead. Noah could smell his stress: stale sweat under CK1; green hand gel from one of the hospital's dispensers.

'I was hoping you could tell us about the young woman you saw last night.'

'She stepped right in front of me. I didn't have any choice but to swerve. I'd have killed her otherwise.' He pushed a hand through his hair. Winced. 'Has she told you what she was doing?'

'She's missing,' Marnie said. 'We're looking for her.'

'You mean she ran off? After the crash?' He looked stricken, scared rather than angry. 'She did *that* and then she ran?'

'We're looking for her. You thought she was injured?'

'She was covered in scratches. But she's okay, she must be, otherwise how did she run off?'

'We'd like to go over your description from last night. In case we missed anything.'

'There's not a scratch on *me*, that's what I don't get. Just this thing for the whiplash.' Joe touched the neck brace then put out his hands and stared at them. 'Even Logan's dad . . . We walked away, both of us. But I'm the only one without a scratch to show for it, and I caused the bloody thing.'

Marnie and Noah waited, not speaking.

'She walked right in front of us. If I'd hit her, she'd be dead. I was doing thirty tops, but that's enough to kill someone. I *had* to swerve.'

'Which direction was she coming from?' Marnie asked.

'My left. I suppose that's . . . west?'

'And she was walking east.'

'There's an estate on that side of York Road, maybe she lives there? They breath-tested me, I wasn't over the limit. I'd had a glass of wine with Ruth, but we were eating spaghetti. I was stuffed full of carbs and I'd had two coffees. We've got *kids*. They're with Ruth's sister, too little to understand what's going on with their mum.'

'How old are they?' Noah asked.

'Sorcha's two. Liam's ten months. Carrie's great with them. They love their auntie.' Joe wiped his eyes, settled his hands on the lip of the table. 'Okay. The girl, last night? She looked seventeen, maybe a bit younger. Hard to tell because she wasn't dressed properly, just a man's shirt, too big for her, white. And her skin was really pale, except for the scratches. She was moving like a wind-up toy. Not fast, but like she wouldn't . . . *couldn't* stop. Her face was . . . scary.' He blinked. 'She wasn't going to stop.'

'Was she calling for help?'

'No, but her face . . . It was like she was screaming.' He grimaced, moving his head as if he wanted to get rid of the image he'd conjured.

'Mr Eaton.' Marnie held out a photograph. 'Was this the girl you saw?'

'Isn't this . . . Mary Beswick?' He held the photo by its edges. 'The missing schoolgirl?'

'May Beswick. Yes, it is.'

Noah held his breath as Joe studied May's face, but . . .

'It wasn't her.' Joe handed back the photo. 'Sorry.'

'Are you sure? She could have lost weight since this was taken. Dyed her hair, changed her appearance. How tall was the girl you saw?'

'Shorter than Ruth. Five foot? Not much more than that. Just a kid, a teenager. Maybe she's nearer to fifteen.

11

And really skinny. Bony knees. Red hair.' A glance at
Marnie. 'Not like yours. Red red, like paint.' His eyes
flicked back, frowning, to the photograph. 'It *was* dyed.'

'Long hair, or short?'

'To her shoulders. But it was crazy, like she'd back-
combed it. Really wiry and wild.'

May Beswick was five foot one, not skinny but not
fat. In the photo, her blonde hair was waist-length,
brushed smooth. She wore a green jumper over a white
blouse, and she was smiling, her top lip coming away
from her front teeth, soft brown eyes crinkled at the
corners. Noah didn't need to look at the photo to be sure
of those details. He'd been seeing her face in his sleep
for twelve weeks.

'What else was she wearing,' Marnie asked, 'apart from
the shirt?'

'Nothing. Knickers, I think.' Joe flushed. 'No trousers,
no shoes. No bra. Maybe she was seventeen. I can't tell.
She should've been wearing a bra.'

Somewhere a door slammed open. Joe turned his head
towards the sound. His hands were clenched on the table,
his neck red inside the brace.

Marnie said, 'Tell us about the scratches.'

'All . . . all over her. Her legs, her stomach, her chest.'
He grimaced. 'Everywhere.'

In the photograph, May's face was smooth, like her
hair. Round cheeks, a wide forehead, no acne. Not a mark
on her, twelve weeks ago.

'Was her face scratched?'

'Not her face. But everywhere else, from what I could
see.'

'Were the scratches recent?' Noah asked.

'I don't think so. Hard to tell in the headlights, and I
only saw her for a second. They looked black, not red,

12

not like fresh blood.' He drew a breath. Held it in his chest. Let it go. 'Ruth got a better look than I did. The girl came from the left, her side of the car. If . . .' He pushed his hands at his eyes. '*When* she wakes up, she'll be able to give you a better description. Ruth always notices stuff. She's brilliant like that.'

He pushed harder with his hands, knuckles bleaching under the pressure. 'I can't forget her face. Maybe it *was* May Beswick, I don't know. She didn't look like her, but she didn't look like *anyone*. Whatever happened to her . . . she looked . . . *terrorised*.'

He dropped his hands and looked up at Marnie and Noah. 'She wasn't making a sound, not a sound, but her whole face was *screaming*.'

3

Aimee

Three months ago, I thought I was safe. Home and dry, off the streets. And not just me. All of us thinking the same thing, that we'd landed on our feet. Like cats. He took us all in.

He called the new place home, but not the way you'd think. 'It's wide open,' he said.

Open-plan, the estate agent called it, but Harm meant something different, the sort of place where you're over-looked, where you disappear even if you don't mean to. London's full of places like that. Dead spaces, dazzle spots. Empty doorways, gaps between buildings. Places no one thinks of looking because they don't *see*, not properly. Maybe they did once, but they've trained themselves to stop. Even when you're right where they walk every morning, when your hand's out and you're asking for a little help, even when you've got a fucking *dog*. A thing could be right in front of your face, Harm said, and you still wouldn't see it. Some things are just . . . invisible.

Grace wouldn't be invisible. She'd started answering

back. She wasn't playing by the rules and I wanted her to shut up. Too much fizz in her, making her skip, making that crazy red hair stick out like she'd rubbed a balloon the wrong way. She wouldn't sit still and she wouldn't shut up, and I thought there was something wrong with her. Something was wrong with each of us, that was how he chose us. The noisy ones like Grace and the ones like me who were disappearing – burning up like fireworks until nothing was left.

Harm would keep us safe, he said. We just had to listen to him, let him help us. Grace should've shut up. At least she had a roof over her head.

A new roof. The house where he'd been keeping us was getting too small, too much like a squat. We were spilling over, making mess. This new place was better. 'Great potential,' Harm said.

The estate agent liked that. 'Some people just see dead space, but I can tell you're one of the smart guys.'

Harm nodded, and turned his back. He thought the man was a cocksucker, I could see it in his face. Harm hates cocksuckers; it was one of the first things I found out about him.

The new place was a flat, but on two floors. Split-level, the estate agent said, *loft living*. One room higher than the others, up a flight of stairs. My room. Unfinished when we saw it that first time. Raw walls with fist-sized holes for wiring, and the estate agent was full of crap about uplighting and underfloor heating, but you could see the money they'd have to pour into the place just to get it fit to live in. No wonder it ran out. It looked good, though, back then. The cocksucker left us to appreciate the view. All of London dazzling under us. 'I'll give you a minute,' he said.

Harm turned his back.

15

So you know, that's when he's dangerous – when his back's turned. It means he can't stand looking at you any longer. You've made him sick, angry. So sick and angry he won't look at you. He wants you to stop talking, stop looking, stop *being*. We all knew this, even Grace, but the estate agent didn't. He was the sort of man who used to sidestep me when I was begging on the streets, so I suppose I wanted him to stop talking and stop *being*, just the same as Harm did.

In the end, Harm shook the man's hand, making his eyes light up, smelling a sale. That was back before the money ran out, when they still believed the uplighting and underfloor heating would happen. Back before Grace stopped fizzing. Before he made her stop.

I remember exactly how it felt, that first day in the new place.

The others followed Harm and Christie outside, but I stayed, wanting to get my bearings, needing to know what I was up against.

Harm doubled back. I didn't hear him on the stairs, but I saw dust smoke up from the floor when his feet moved across it, not making a sound.

Then the heat of him behind me . . .

The damp weight of his shadow across my shoulders, at the back of my neck.

He kept my hair cut short. I could feel his stare sharp on my skin.

Not touching. He never touched. It was worse than that.

His stare was hotter than fingers, or a tongue.

I could smell him, smiling.

He was so heavy behind me.

'This is it,' he whispered. 'This is home.'

4

Like Joe Eaton, Calum Marsh had a neck brace and a sling for his right arm, taking the strain off a badly bruised collarbone. He was sitting on the end of the hospital bed, trying to push his left foot into a leather shoe. Whoever had removed his shoes hadn't untied the laces, and he was struggling, his face fisted in concentration. Wearing chinos and a half-buttoned shirt, wanting to be dressed so he could go and check on his son. All his panic and pain was there in the struggle with the shoe.

'Mr Marsh, I'm DI Rome and this is DS Jake.' Marnie crouched and took the shoe, freeing the laces from the stranglehold of a knot. 'We're here to find out what happened.'

Calum peered at her in confusion. 'Have you seen him? Logan?' His feet and face jumped with stress. 'I was *asleep*. Is his mum here?' Looking away from Marnie, concentrating on Noah. 'Is he okay? What's happening?'

'We're waiting to speak with the doctor. Logan's in surgery.' Marnie stayed crouched, the unlaced shoe in her hands. 'I've asked someone to speak with you as soon as there's news.'

'There's nothing I can do. That's what they said in the ambulance. And here. The nurses said the same.' Calum wiped his hand on the sheet, leaving a rust stain where his sweat had brought dried blood back to life. 'There's *nothing*.' He was in his early forties, well-built, greying temples and stubbled skin, blood in the lines under his eyes. Unless the shirt was hiding damage that Noah couldn't see, the blood was his son's.

'There should be news soon.' Marnie put the shoe down and straightened, stepping back. She nodded at Noah, who moved a chair to the side of the bed.

'We were talking with Joe Eaton about how it happened,' he said. 'We're trying to find the girl.'

'The girl.' Calum's face was empty. He blinked, focused. 'What girl?'

'The girl who walked out into the road. That's why Joe Eaton swerved.'

'He came right at me.' Calum put his hand up, palm out. '*Right* at me.' His hand was broader than Joe's, and scarred in places, twitching with shock like the rest of him.

'Joe says a girl walked in front of the Audi.' Noah took care not to crowd the man. 'That's why he swerved. To avoid hitting her.'

'That's what he said? The other driver . . . He said there was a *girl* . . .?'

'You didn't see her?'

'No girl, just the Audi coming at us, and . . . the wall. Then Logan hitting the windscreen, making this *noise*.' Punishing his injured arm with his left hand. 'His head made this noise like something *bursting*. He broke the windscreen with his *head* . . .' Putting his hand out, blindly. 'Don't let him die. Not like this. Not my fault, don't let it be my fault, he's just a kid. *My* kid.'

'All right.' Noah took the man's hand, chilled and sticky with his son's blood, aftershocks locking and unlocking the fingers. 'Mr Marsh? Calum. It's all right.'

Marnie left, coming back with a nurse, who helped Logan's dad back into the bed. Noah waited until he was lying down before easing his hand free from the man's grip.

'Sorry,' Calum kept saying, to the nurse, to Noah. 'I'm sorry.'

Marnie was in the corridor, waiting.

'He didn't see a girl,' Noah said. 'Do you think Joe Eaton got it wrong?'

'Something made Joe swerve. He wasn't drunk and it wasn't raining. Traffic conditions were good. Why invent a girl? Especially a half-dressed girl covered in scratches.'

She took out her phone. 'We need to know who else was on that road. DC Tanner's looking at CCTV. Whether or not she's May Beswick, this girl's in trouble.' She dialled a number, held the phone to her ear. 'Ed, call me when you get this. I need to pick your brains.'

Ed Belloc was a victim care officer, one of the best. He and Marnie had been together six months, maybe a little longer.

'Whether or not she's May Beswick,' Noah repeated. 'You think there's a chance it's her?'

'I don't know. I'd like to hope so. At least . . . This girl was running from someone. Injured by the sound of it. She didn't stop after causing the crash. I'm wondering whether she's gone to ground, in a refuge if she was lucky enough to find one. Ed will know the ones around Battersea, how easy or otherwise it is to find a safe place in that part of town when you're desperate.'

'She could be desperate because she caused the crash.

19

If Logan dies, or Ruth does . . . She could be scared of *us*.'

Behind them, through the wall, the thin sound of Calum Marsh's distress.

'Let's find her,' Marnie said.

5

Aimee

Nails scratched at the door. 'Food's ready. He wants you with us.'

I didn't want to eat, so I didn't answer. Ashleigh came into the room, fighting the door. Harm had fitted a weighted hinge; it banged shut if you weren't careful. 'You can eat with us, he says.'

'I'm not hungry.'

'Don't be stupid.' She looked around. 'And don't land me in the shit. Again.' Her eyes were greedy, going everywhere. I'd got too much stuff.

Harm was always giving me presents. The hairbrush was the latest, real silver, hallmarked. Ashleigh walked to where it sat on a joke of a dressing table with light bulbs round the mirror like I was the star in a soft porn movie. 'Nice.' Her voice was ironed flat. She hated me. She didn't touch the brush, though. She didn't dare. The light bulbs gave her a rash.

'You need to come and eat with us.' She walked to the door. 'Get up.'

I lay on the bed a bit longer before I did as I was told. She hated me, but she was right. I couldn't land her in the shit again, not so soon after the last time.

Downstairs, the others were waiting around the table. No Gracie, which meant she was in trouble again, confined to her room. Ashleigh had started calling her *Dis*gracie. It was funny, except it wasn't. I felt sick for her. Not that I was doing any better. I was worse off than any of them, no amount of silver hairbrushes changed that.

The kitchen smelt hot and brown and I wanted to puke at the thought of whatever was cooking on the stove. Tins, always out of tins. I'd rather starve, except of course I wouldn't. I'd spent enough nights starving on the streets. Starving's for rich kids who're never more than an arm's reach from a decent meal. I'd eat this shit, whatever it was, and be grateful for it.

May smiled at me, sitting very straight in her chair, her hair brushed neat, all of her covered with the school uniform. The tights made her legs itch, like mine. Neither one of us dared to scratch, though, not at the table. Ashleigh took her place, pulling a napkin into her lap, hiding all trace of the bitch she was upstairs.

At the stove, Harm was serving brown food on to grey plates. He was moving more slowly than usual, as if he needed to remind us how this worked – marking our places. My fingers twitched, until I stopped them. Anything different, any change to the rhythm made me nervous.

Everything must always, *always* be the same.

That's what he'd taught us, what he kept teaching us. I hated how slowly he was moving. The candles sucked at his shadow, pulling it on to the table. I moved my hands out of its reach.

Christie was helping Harm, holding two plates in each

hand like a waitress. She was tall and solid, more real than the rest of us. Blonde hair down her back, the way he liked it. A cotton dress that stopped at her knees, showing off her calves. She had some serious muscles. Next to Harm, though, she was nothing. She glanced at me, nodding her approval. I'd been allowed downstairs and I'd come without a fuss. Good girl. Good dog. I pulled out a chair and sat next to May, who sneaked her hand into mine under the table. Her hand was warm, or mine was cold. My room never got warm, not properly. That underfloor heating was a lie, like everything else.

Ashleigh scuffed her feet on the floor, then stopped, sitting quietly.

Three of us in our white blouses, black skirts and tights, faces washed with soap and water, hair brushed neat. Mouths like butter wouldn't melt, not that butter was on offer.

Christie brought the plates to the table. Harm was a good cook, she said. As if you needed a Michelin star to cook the crap we lived off, food so full of preservatives it could serve itself. May tried to plant vegetables once, but he wouldn't let her. Everything had to be long-life. Slimy slices of reconstituted aubergine like the tongue from someone's boot died on the side of my plate.

We ate in silence, the only sound the squawking of forks on tin plates. We drank water from tin cups. Nothing at our table was breakable, unless you counted the high-strung silence of teenage girls in the thrall of a handsome and bountiful middle-aged man. I really, *really* wanted to puke.

'We are what we are,' Christie always said.

I'd seen a horror film with that title, but I kept it to myself.

We are what we are.

If you'd looked through the window, what would you have seen? A father and his youngish wife sitting with their family of photo-booth-ready dolls, smooth hair down to their waists, new tits under neat shirts. And me – the odd-looking one at the end, with a flat chest and short black hair that was wasted on his fat silver hairbrush.

It was all lies. Christie wasn't his wife. We weren't his daughters, not even sisters. Of course you couldn't have seen through the window. There were blackout blinds for one thing.

Harm refilled my cup with water, a pinch of concern on his face. 'Don't dehydrate.'

Ashleigh risked an eye roll, turning it into a blink before Harm could catch her.

The water tasted of coins, the way my hands used to smell at the end of a good day's begging on the streets. 'Thank you.' My voice cracked on the last word.

Ashleigh was the first to clear her plate. 'That was yummy.' She licked her lips, shooting a white smile across at Harm, eyes as shiny bright as her teeth. She'd put something on her lids.

Fuck . . .

She'd smeared Vaseline on her eyelids, and her mouth. No make-up in the house. One of his rules. The Vaseline made her mouth wet. She didn't look like a schoolgirl. She looked grown-up, and slutty. Stupid, *stupid* cow . . .

Harm hated grown-up. He hated *slutty* more than anything. We were meant to be his perfect dolls, sexless, chaste. She *knew* this. Ashleigh knew. She was sitting too far forward, her hands pulling at the hem of her shirt, skin-tight at the front. He was going to notice. She'd been trying to get his attention for weeks. *Fuck.* How could he *not* notice her tits when she sat like that?

24

Christie put back her chair. 'Ashleigh, it's your turn to help clear the table.'

Ashleigh stood, hips rolling like a slinky toy coming down the stairs. I felt the slap in Christie's stare as hard as if she'd hit me.

The air got tight, the way it does in a storm. I could taste the buzz of static on my tongue. At my side, May was taut with waiting, to see what he'd do. We were dressed right, sitting where we were told, eating his crappy food, but it wasn't enough. Nothing was ever enough.

'Ashleigh.' His voice was soft, like it'd been chalked, the way a weightlifter chalks his hands before a big lift. 'Ashleigh.'

She turned, not smiling now. She'd tried to lick the Vaseline off her lips, but it was still there at the edges of her mouth, winking at him.

'Come here.'

Under the table, May squeezed my fingers.

Don't don't don't . . .

'Come here,' Harm repeated.

Ashleigh walked back to the table, not slinking now, jerking like she was on a leash. He looked into her face. He was so close she must've felt his breath. He was the only one breathing; the rest of us didn't dare. Even Christie was holding her breath. The candles burned straight up to the ceiling in the sudden scooped-out silence.

'Did you hurt your mouth?' His voice stayed chalky soft.

Ashleigh jerked her head from side to side. Her tits swelled under her shirt and she tried to stop them, tried to hold it together, but she couldn't. He wouldn't let her.

'Did you hurt your eyes?'

She jerked her head.

'Are they dry? Cracked?'

25

And again.

'Then why is there petroleum jelly on your face?'

'I . . . no. Yes. P-please. Sorry.' She hit each word in turn, hoping to land on the safe one.

Harm wasn't listening. He held out a hand to Christie, who picked up her paper napkin and passed it across the table, making the candles crouch and shudder.

He spat on to the napkin. Straightened to his full height.

The whole room tilted away, dragging our shadows towards him like he was swallowing us up.

Ashleigh hadn't moved. She was very little now, with him standing over her.

He rubbed at her mouth with the napkin. Spat again. Rubbed at her eyelids. Like he was trying to scrub her out. She let him do it. She had that much sense, at least. She was hunching to make her tits look smaller. *Good*. Spat. And rubbed.

When he was done, Harm dropped the balled-up napkin on the table.

Then he picked up a candle.

My fingers twitched under the table. May stroked her thumb across my knuckles, trying to keep me quiet. It should've been the other way around, *me* looking out for her. I was the only one he wouldn't touch, the only one with any power, but I was scared, I was always too scared.

Ashleigh was standing stone-still, her shadow squirming at her feet like she'd wet herself.

Harm held the candle so close, the whole side of her face was yellow.

I took a pinch of air through my nose because I couldn't not-breathe any longer but I didn't want to pull the flame into her hair.

He looked at her. 'Better.' His voice hadn't stopped

being soft. He never shouted. He never had to. 'Now, what do you say?'

'Th-thank you.'

'No, not that.' Each word made the flame flap closer to her face. 'What do you say?'

'S-sorry.'

'Say it to everyone.'

She had to turn towards the table to do as he said, putting her face into the flame. He held the candle steady and I could smell her skin scalding like milk, his spit drying on her face . . .

I could smell his spit on her.

'Sorry. I'm s-sorry.'

'For what?' Harm said.

'Spoiling this.' She was crying. The flame licked at her face, finding her tears, making them sizzle. 'I'm sorry for spoiling this.'

'That's better.' Harm put the candle down. He opened his arms and she fell into them, landing on his chest with a howl. 'Good girl.' He stroked her hair, petting her. 'Good girl.'

He was looking right at me.

After a bit, he eased Ashleigh to arm's length and let her go.

Don't, don't *let him turn his back* . . .

He'd turned his back on Grace, last night.

Christie started to clear the plates from the table, breaking the silence, jerking sound back into the room. Harm smiled at Ashleigh and pointed her towards the sink. Her face had sunk in on itself, still shiny with his spit. All because she wanted to be his special one. I could've told her . . .

You don't want to be his special one, you really don't.

All she saw was the gifts, the giving. She didn't see the taking away.

27

Harm was back at the head of the table. 'Aimee, finish your food.' He moved his eyes to May. 'You too.' Like nothing had happened.

Everything must always, *always* be the same.

Food was a privilege. I shovelled it in as if I was filling a ditch, edgy with adrenalin. It made me brave, and stupid. I hated it when he looked at May. *Hated* it. 'Where's Grace?' I reached for my cup, listening to the new silence. Different to before, because he was fixed on me, but better than him fixing on May. Through a mouthful, I repeated the dangerous question. 'Where's Grace?'

I had his attention. All of it. Like we were the only two in the room. His stare made me dance, but I wanted to hear him say it. I wanted proof.

Grace was gone.

I could feel the hole. I knew all the spaces in there, wide open or otherwise. One of them was empty. Dead space. She was gone, and I wanted him to admit there was a way out. Away from his gifts and the hard leash of his attention, the fear of what'd happen when his patience ran out, or the food did. His family was fake, and toxic. We were toxic. He'd made us safe, and he'd made us sick. Living by his rules, wanting his attention and not wanting it. Hating each other, hating *him* because we needed him, because there was nothing else and we were *scared*. Living like whipped dogs.

Grace was gone. She'd got away.

I wanted to hear him say it.

My hand was cold, and empty.

May was on her feet.

Not like the others. She didn't need Harm's attention, but she got it. She got everyone's attention when she said, 'I'm pregnant.'

6

Marnie stood at the scarred side of the road under the fixed stare of a CCTV camera. London was littered with these cameras. Her team had hours of footage to search for the girl who might be May Beswick. House-to-house was quicker but had its own complications, chiefly that not-noticing was most Londoners' superpower.

Joe Eaton's description had been vivid enough for Marnie to see the girl in her mind's eye. Dyed red hair wild around her face, black scratches on her skin. Bare feet. Walking out into the traffic like a wind-up toy. Who wound her up? And from where?

She turned to where the housing estate was sprouting still more CCTV cameras. One for every six people in the city. Tim Welland, her boss, was fond of quoting the figures. The average Londoner was filmed four hundred times a day, yet only three per cent of crimes were solved using surveillance footage. Perhaps she was wrong about not-noticing. Perhaps the city's superpower was paranoia. She walked in the direction of the estate, away from the tyre burns, thinking of the girl's bare feet. She was running, injured, searching for a safe place. So why didn't she stop?

Twelve weeks ago, May Beswick had been a bright, quiet teenager. No mood swings, no anxiety, or none that her friends and family had witnessed. Joe Eaton's girl had been screaming.

Noah was waiting at the corner. 'Ron's on house-to-house.' He nodded across his shoulder to the Garrett estate. 'He says he was due here this morning in any case.'

'Emma Tarvin,' Marnie remembered. 'She was complaining about kids setting fires.'

'And making threats.' Noah nodded. 'Ron says she's an old battleaxe, not the kind to take fright easily. Any word from Ed?'

'He's still making phone calls, but he spoke with the nearest refuge and no girls were admitted last night. She couldn't have walked in off the street in any case. She'd have needed to call ahead, and to know which number to ring. If she had access to a phone, she could have called the police. We're checking emergency calls either side of the time of the crash. Nothing so far.'

They walked on to the Garrett. 'Joe Eaton said bare feet.' Noah eyed the pavement. 'I wouldn't take my chances on these streets.'

'Or any London street. It's getting cold, too. She'll have wanted to find somewhere warm.'

'Assuming she's on her own. That whoever she was running from didn't catch up with her.'

'Assuming that,' Marnie conceded.

The Garrett had been built as four tower blocks joined by a system of shared walkways. *Deck access* was the architect's term. The towers were brutal concrete pyres housing London's poor in squat boxes with savagely sparkling views across the river. Communal living, but it reeked of anonymity at best, isolation at worst. Boarded doors and windows said paranoia was thriving here, just about the only thing that was; the flower beds were cement troughs flooded with litter and worse. The grass growing between the flagstones was starved, more grey than green. Even the graffiti was dead, sandblasted to pastel pockmarks on the walls.

The mobile unit was setting up outside the first of the towers, Ron Carling briefing the house-to-house team on their likely reception on the estate. 'We're about as popular as Ebola round here, so keep it pally. We want scores on the doors, as Larry Grayson liked to say. Oh, hello.' He cracked a grin at Noah. 'Speak of the devil.'

'Emma Tarvin,' Marnie said. 'Which flat is hers?'

'Seven four six. She stays up all night sometimes, keeping an eye out for what's coming. It's got so she's scared of her own shadow, poor cow.'

'I thought she was a battleaxe,' Noah said.

'Doesn't mean she doesn't get scared.'

'She keeps an eye out,' Marnie said. 'From which window?'

'Was she watching when our girl came past last night?' Ron pointed towards a row of windows halfway up the first tower block. 'Bird's-eye view, and she's a nosy old bird. Needs to be, to survive round here. Welcome to what's left of Lambeth. Gotham's got nothing on this shithole.'

'Cheer up, Bruce. You've got this covered.'

'Bruce?' Ron peered at Noah. 'Oh, right. Bruce Wayne.'

'Or Forsyth. I was going for Forsyth. It's the moustache.'

Ron snorted, but he was grinning. 'Let's sort the scores on the doors, then.'

On the south side of the estate, two kids were kicking a fire-damaged wheelie bin. Seeing the police, they kicked harder until one of the uniforms moved in their direction,

31

then they disappeared fast between the blocks, soaked up by the long shadow of the towers.

'Terror is a normal reaction to social living.' Noah fell into step at Marnie's side. 'Isn't that what they say?'

'They didn't look very terrified to me. Bored, maybe.'

'My dad would call it Thatcher's legacy. No such thing as society, just families and individuals. *Competitive* individuals. Everyone's a competitor, so everyone's a threat. We're pretending to be social, but really we're scared out of our wits.' Noah scratched at his cheek. 'My dad's actually a lot cooler than I just made him sound. But he likes to bang on about the old days, circa 1987.'

'You were born in 1987, weren't you?'

'In a place like this.' He craned his neck at the walkway above them. 'My dad called it the gulag. Among other things.'

A hundred feet away, a black boy of about ten was circling on a bike, beanie pulled down to the bridge of his nose. The bike was too small for him, and pink nylon ribbons were trailing from the handlebars. He was a caricature of boredom, circling aimlessly, but Noah said, 'He's the lookout. That means someone's dealing drugs here, or selling stolen goods. Or both.'

He knew what he was talking about. Marnie heard it in his tone, saw it in the watchful way he moved. 'Do you think he might've seen anything useful last night?'

'Maybe, but would he share it with us?' The boy peeled away, cycling between two of the towers. 'Unlikely.' Noah didn't turn his head after the boy, keeping his shoulders and spine loose, eyes in the back of his skull. 'If we asked him, he'd get his social worker on our case. Kids like that know every trick in the book.'

Ron looked at everyone on the estate in the same way, but Noah was smarter. He wouldn't make the mistake of assuming that familiarity was the only thing breeding contempt around here. Marnie was glad to have him on her team.

They'd reached the entrance to the block where Emma Tarvin lived.

'Come on, love.' Ron was waiting with his finger on the buzzer, his mouth close to the intercom panel. 'You know me by now. Open up.'

An elderly voice, snippy with static: 'There's a whole crowd of you out there. Where were you when those girls were sneaking all sorts through my letter box? No bloody where.'

'Well we're here now. Buzz us in, I'll make you a cuppa. We need your help with something.'

'Like what? Figuring out your arses from your elbows?' But she pressed the buzzer, letting them into the lobby of the building.

Ron nodded towards the stairs. 'Or there's the lift if you like the stink of piss.' He led the way up the stairs, tramping heavily.

Marnie and Noah followed, seeing signs of fire damage everywhere, black on the walls, melted plastic on the railings. Marnie had been inside burnt buildings before; she knew this was nothing – kids playing with matches. Which didn't mean they wouldn't graduate to lighter fuel or petrol. It might not matter that people were living here. Not so long ago, and not far from here, a teenager had burned down a dogs' home, killing dozens of animals. Arsonists had hard hearts. And fire was quick. Too quick for second thoughts.

'Next floor,' Ron said, still climbing.

No one came up or down the stairs as they climbed. No sign of life from the flats, just the occasional scrabble of sound from a TV. How many residents were home?

33

How many had jobs to go to? The statistics for this part of London were depressing. Joe Eaton and Calum Marsh had been passing through in their nice cars to better lives elsewhere. Until this happened.

Emma Tarvin lived on the seventh floor.

Marnie paused on the walkway to look out to where the mobile unit was setting up. The kids were back, kicking at the wheelie bin, bumping it across the concrete waste-land between the flats and the main road. Further back, the building site at Battersea Power Station lay wide open like a wound. *Places of exile . . .*

The words came unwilled into her head. She'd paid to have them inked on her left hip when she was eighteen, fancying herself a clever rebel. She read the words on her skin whenever she dressed and undressed. Ed Belloc had read them too, the first person she'd trusted to do that. And Stephen Keele had read them, as a teenager in the house where she'd grown up. Her foster-brother. Her parents' killer. *Places of exile* was the reason he'd given for what he did, as if the words had incited him to murder. As if her skin had been an instruction, or a plea.

A thud from below. The kids had succeeded in felling the wheelie bin. It lay on its side, spilling its guts of litter. Marnie blinked. Refocused.

The girl who might be May Beswick had been headed this way last night. The seventh floor had a clear view of the crash site, and Emma Tarvin was a watcher. Had she seen something?

Ron was at the door of number 746. 'Open up, love. You know me. Sick of the sight of me, probably. But we need your help.'

'Badges.' Mrs Tarvin's voice was sharp. Her front door was reinforced with metal sheeting, full of footprints where kids had kicked. Brown stains around the lock and letter box, fire damage at the foot of the door, spreading the entire length of her flat. She was living under siege.

Ron held his ID to the viewer in the door. 'Come on, I'm dying for a cuppa.'

'Who's with you?' Her eye at the peephole, sharp like her voice.

'My boss, Detective Inspector Rome. She wants to meet you. I told her you'd like to give her a piece of your mind.'

Open Sesame.

7

'About bloody time. Thought I'd be long dead before you lot got your act together. Burnt to a crisp in my bed most likely.' Emma Tarvin was a big woman, her broad shoulders making the mean hall look meaner, in a purple dress and tan tights, salt-and-pepper hair cropped close to a square face with indoor skin, no make-up, red threads everywhere. Brown eyes, hard as pellets, fixed on Marnie's face before shifting to Noah. 'Who's the pin-up?'

Ron said, 'This is DS Jake. He makes a mean cuppa.'

'*You* can make the tea. The pin-up,' giving Noah a smile tough enough to take the skin off his face, 'can come with me.' She jerked her head at Marnie. 'You too.'

Noah and Marnie followed her into the sitting room, a box painted the colour of jaundice. Sooty streaks up the walls and around the window filling the south-facing wall. Net curtains that looked like they'd been tie-dyed in strong tea, an aggressively nylon carpet, furniture straight out of the Festival of Britain, everything Formicaed to within an inch of its life. It reminded Noah of his gran's flat, down to the antimacassars and sunburst mirror. The only things missing were family photos. His gran's place was full of photos of him and Sol. Emma was seventy-six. Either she didn't have any grandchildren, or she kept their photos in another room. No ornaments, not even a vase of flowers. Bookcases, mostly filled with video cassettes and DVDs. Widescreen television. Desk by the window, covered in magazines and papers. More like a student's flat than a pensioner's home. It smelt like a student's flat, male and stale.

'You can sit here.' Emma settled herself on the sofa, nodding at Noah to join her.

He did as he was told, Marnie taking one of the two armchairs opposite. Ron came back from the kitchen with four mugs of tea on a battered tin tray.

'Who's paying for those?' A snort. 'I'm Tarvin, not bloody Tetley.'

'I'll bring a box of tea bags next time.' Ron sat in the other armchair. 'And biscuits, if you like.'

'If she lets you,' jerking her head at Marnie. 'Doesn't look like she eats biscuits. Me, I'm partial to a chocolate finger.' Another skin-stripping smile for Noah. 'Sorry about the fuss with the door, but I get all sorts trying to get in here. Old dear downstairs left hers open for Social Services, can you believe that? Cleaned her out, of course. Round here, if it's not nailed shut it's as good as gone.' She reached for a mug of tea. 'So you want to hear about my arsonists. Finally taking it seriously after thirteen fires. Unless you're going to give me a lecture like the last lot they sent round. "Arson is a cry for help." Too much bloody crying round here. No one gets heard. I don't. Can't remember the last time I slept through the night. When they're not setting fires, they're making threats, nicking all sorts. Kick and run, isn't that what you lot call it? What we used to call burglary. Or shouting all hours. I don't bother going to bed now. Sit up and watch for them.' She nodded at the window, chewing on her lip. 'They're less frightening when you can see them.'

'And you keep notes,' Marnie said.

Noah followed her gaze, seeing the notepad on the table next to the window, half tucked under a copy of the *Radio Times*. He hadn't noticed it until now.

Emma reappraised Marnie. 'I'm thorough. Someone round here's got to be.'

'Go on, please. You were saying you sit up and watch for them.'

'Every night. They're bold as bloody brass. The girls are the worst of it.'

'Natalie Filton and Abigail Gull. Those were the names you gave to DS Carling.' Marnie drank a mouthful of tea. 'Are there any others?'

'Plenty, but those two are the ringleaders.' A pause, then, 'You're young to be his boss.' She jerked her chin towards Ron. Looked at Noah. 'Positive discrimination, is it?' She had the jaw of a middleweight boxer. Noah could see bristles on her chin.

'Thirteen fires. In how many months?' Marnie matched her tone to the other woman's, as if they were trading blows.

It was the right tactic for Emma. Noah caught the appreciative gleam in the woman's eye. 'Less than a year. Not that it's ever been flaming Frensham round here.'

'Frensham?' Ron echoed.

'The quietest village in England. Or one of them. Do you know Frensham, Mrs Tarvin?'

'Only from the telly.' Sucking at her tea, holding the mug in a hand twice as big as one of Marnie's and wider than Noah's. She wore a wedding band under an engagement ring knuckled with stones too dull to be diamonds.

38

'You told DS Carling you believe the same girls are responsible for all thirteen fires.'

'They are. Just because you lot failed to find any evidence.'

'Did you see them starting the fires?'

'Of course I didn't. They're not stupid, just little savages. I've had them threatening me, throwing stones, shoving stuff through my letter box. I wrote it all down, gave it to him.'

Ron said, 'We've spoken with the girls, and their mums. No dads around to speak with.'

Emma snorted. 'Course not. Pair of bastards, both of them.'

'What were they threatening?' Noah asked.

'To report me to the police for spying on them. Yes, I thought you'd like that. The kids *rule* this estate and they're a bunch of bloody savages.' She looked Noah up and down. 'You're lucky you don't live round here. They hate blacks, even the good-looking ones. Mrs Singh, next floor down? Her boy's in hospital after they decided he was a jihadist. I'm sticking my neck out standing up to them and I'm doing it with no bloody help from anyone. You lot won't touch anything with brown people, and you're scared of little girls after Savile and the rest of the perverts. Scared to do your job, so people like me end up doing it for you. At my age. Sitting up all night keeping watch.' Her hand trembled, catching the light in its fake diamonds. She stilled it, clicking at her teeth with her tongue. She was older than Noah's gran and she looked it, just at this minute. Repeated arson attempts, and she was a long way from the ground floor. What was it like waking up to the smell of smoke coming in under the front door, knowing there was no way out?

'Were you sitting up last night?' Marnie asked.

'Every bloody night. And most of the day, too.'

'And you make a note of anything out of the ordinary?'

'No, love.' Dripping with sarcasm. 'Because round here *ordinary* is setting fires and battering Muslim boys. As I've explained.'

'Can we take a look?' Marnie nodded at the notepad. A shrug. 'Please yourself.'

Marnie got to her feet and so did Noah, glad of the excuse to escape the clutches of the sofa. The carpet by the window was worn. How many hours each day did she stand here looking out? Keeping watch on the girls who kept her prisoner. Girls younger than May Beswick. Girls who saw an irascible old-age pensioner as an easy target for their bravado, or boredom. Noah had grown up around gangs like that. Kids who strutted their way through adolescence, fretting their fear into something else, big enough and loud enough to be mistaken for courage. Sol still ran with some of the gangs they'd known back then.

Rescuing the notepad from under the *Radio Times*, he and Marnie stood looking through its pages while Ron made small talk with Emma. Her handwriting was cramped but legible. In emphatic blue ballpoint she'd written dates, times and incidents. Most of the incidents concerned the girls whose names she'd given to Ron: *NF and AG smoking. AG kicking cans. NF littering.* Page after page of it, occasionally enlivened by reports of verbal abuse, or a punch-up involving other kids, bravado between gangs: *AG pushing UBF up against the wall, hands on her throat.* That had happened more than once in the last fortnight.

'Who's UBF?' Noah asked.

'Unknown black female,' Emma said.

'So UWF is unknown white female?' Marnie touched her thumb to last night's report.

'It's not rocket science, love.' Rolling her eyes at Ron, who grinned back at her.

'The unknown white female you saw last night. Can you describe her?'

'What's it say there?'

Marnie read from the notepad: '"UWF. New. Trouble?" You've put a question mark at the end, and you've underlined "New".'

'*Her*. I remember. Prossy, probably.'

'Prostitute,' Ron interpreted. 'Why'd you think that?'

'Way she was dressed, or wasn't. Flashing her knockers, and that's not all.' Nursing her mug in her big hands. 'Proper mess, she was. Red hair all over the shop, staggering about. Drunk, I suppose. Not seen her before.'

'She was alone?'

'When I saw her, yes.'

'Which direction was she coming from?'

'Off York Road.'

'Did you see where she went?'

'What's she done?' Looking at the three of them in turn. 'If she's trouble, I've a right to know.'

'You thought she was trouble last night,' Marnie said. 'It's written down here.'

'The last thing this dump needs is more people like that. We're not Knightsbridge, love. The whores round here don't shop in Harrods and drip with diamonds. Most of them are doing it to pay for drugs. They leave used rubbers in the corridor, and God knows what else. So yes. I saw *her*, I saw *trouble*. From the look on your faces, I was right too. What's she done?'

'You heard the crash last night?' Ron said. 'That was her walking out in front of a car.'

Marnie's teeth tapped together. 'DS Carling, would you like to do the washing-up?'

41

Emma chuckled. 'You're for it now, Loose Lips.'

Ron collected the mugs in silence.

'Did you see where the girl went?' Marnie asked.

'She was coming this way, but when they get near the entrance I lose them. Angle's wrong.'

'So she was coming *into* the flats?'

'Maybe. She doesn't live here, not that I've seen. And I've seen them all, one time or another.'

'Did you notice anything else about her?'

'Just that she was drunk, and half-dressed. She'll fit right in round here.'

Noah checked the angle of the view from the window. He calculated the girl had been eight feet from the main entrance when Emma lost sight of her. Almost certainly coming into the block.

Marnie was at his side, also looking, but not down at the dead space under the window. Across to where the kids had kicked the wheelie bin on to its side, spilling its contents on to the concrete. She'd seen something; her attention was fixed on the bin. Noah could only see crushed boxes, the broken ribs of an old shelving unit, flashes of white from empty carrier bags.

'Would you recognise this girl,' Marnie asked Emma, 'if you saw her again?'

'Oh yes. I've got a memory for faces.' A stony smile for Noah. 'You don't need to be a pin-up for me to remember you.'

'Re-brief the team,' Marnie said, when they were back in the open air.

'You think she's here?' Ron asked. 'In one of the flats?'

'I know she's changed her clothes.' Marnie walked towards the wheelie bin. She was pulling on crime-scene gloves. 'Unless that's a coincidence.' She pointed.

In the spill of litter from the capsized bin was a white shirt. Noah had mistaken it for a carrier bag.

Marnie extracted it from the wreckage of the shelving unit, shaking it loose from plastic bottles, crisp packets and pizza boxes.

A man's shirt.

Stained on the inside with what looked like blood.

8

Aimee

Someone was knocking at the door. Downstairs, the *front* door. Someone out there, trying to get in.

I sat up in bed, listening until my ears ached. Nothing. I was going crazy. No one ever came; why would they? On the streets you think the *next* person will notice you, the *next* one will help, but you're kidding yourself. No one ever helps, no one ever comes. Except Harm.

'I'm pregnant.' May held her head up when she said it, as if he couldn't touch her now. As if *pregnant* made a difference. She had a little sister she loved more than anything, and she'd always wanted a baby. I'd hoped I'd meet her sister one day. But right that minute all I could see was him, the way he buried her with his stare.

'Go to your room.'

After all his lectures, his rules . . .

I'm pregnant.

What had she done?

May's room was directly under mine. She shared it with Ashleigh and with the plastic water barrels, crates

44

of toilet rolls, cleaning products, batteries. Self-sufficiency, Harm said, survival. Everything was right there. No need to worry ever again about being cold or wet or hungry. No need to leave, ever. We were all we needed, Harm said, and I'd thought we were safe.

Go to your room.

No one was knocking at the door. Even if they were, Harm would get rid of them; securing the perimeter wasn't something you did once and then forgot about. You had to stay on your guard, on your toes, frosty and alert.

I'm pregnant.

I saw his face, when he sent us to our rooms. He looked in pain. As if there was a storm inside his head and he heard it crying, like a baby. May's baby. Standing by the blacked-out window, his fingers touching the glass, and it was like I could see inside him, hot and red. He *hurt*. I thought . . .

We were like pain to him. Pushing our noise through the walls, needing to be held, having to be fed. If he was a woman, he'd be leaking, his whole body pulled by the pain, unable to resist. But he was a man and so he held the pain at bay, hoping it would settle, fearing what would happen if it didn't. Christie and Ashleigh and May . . .

All of us within reaching distance, grabbing distance.

Standing by the window, kissing the ends of his fingers to taste the grey of the glass.

It made me ache with fear.

When May said, 'I'm pregnant,' before I could stop myself, just for a second, I'd thought:

You're dead.

9

At the station, OCU Commander Welland said, 'Traffic called. They want their crime scene back. Something about a bloodstained shirt in a skip?'

'It was in a wheelie bin.'

'Well, it's got their knickers in a twist. They want to know why our major incident team is investigating their skid marks.' Welland eyed Marnie and Noah. His face had a toehold on his temper, his brow heavy. 'They've got a point. Even if this turns fatal, it's Traffic's.'

'We're looking for the girl from the crash,' Marnie said. 'We think she's at risk of harm.'

'Because of the bloodstained shirt? Where're you up to with it?'

'Fran Lennox has the shirt. We're searching the estate where we found it. This girl's not the first teenager to go missing in that part of London in the last twelve weeks. She might even *be* May Beswick. If there's the slightest chance of that . . .'

Welland gave a slow nod. 'This is the Garrett estate. DS Carling's favourite vacation spot, the arsonist's Algarve. But someone was sober enough to see this girl last night?'

'Emma Tarvin,' Noah said. 'She confirmed what Joe Eaton told us about the girl looking like she's in trouble, probably traumatised.'

'Tarvin.' Welland pulled at his upper lip. 'She's the nosy neighbour?'

'She keeps a record,' Marnie said, 'of everyone who comes within eight feet of her front door.'

'That's a lot of wasted paper.'

'Faster than processing CCTV.'

'So's a striking snail, but I wouldn't put one forward as a witness for the CPS. You're doing house-to-house?'

Marnie nodded. 'But not everyone's as keen to talk to us as Mrs Tarvin.'

'You astound me.' Welland snorted. 'Communal living at its finest. Last time I was on the Garrett, I'd have lit a fire just to keep the chill away. No one knows anyone else, or cares. Security's a joke. Don't bother checking the CCTV. It packed up years ago. No expense spent . . . From what DS Carling tells me, it's got worse recently.'

'Mrs Tarvin agrees. She has a particular problem with a group of teenage girls.'

'Kids,' Welland said disgustedly. 'They lowered the age of criminal responsibility for a reason, but most of the time we can't arrest them, never mind prosecute. They know it, too. I've seen six- and seven-year-olds working their patch, popping out to pick up Mum's prescription from whichever lowlife's dealing her a day's oblivion. If this girl's gone to ground on the Garrett, good luck finding her.' He tapped his teeth with his thumbnail, shaking his head. 'May Beswick has more sense than to set foot in that shithole.'

'As far as we know,' Noah said.

Welland cocked an eyebrow at him. 'Your pessimism

does you credit, Detective.' He nodded at Marnie. 'Buy DS Jake a large coffee to go with that.'

Marnie did as she was told, standing in the street outside the police station to drink coffee with Noah. 'We should speak with the Beswicks.'

'It's been weeks since we had any news for them.' Noah shielded his eyes from the glare coming off the station's windows. 'What if we're raising their hopes for nothing?'

Marnie worked the lid off her coffee. 'When the press get hold of the story from last night, May's parents will be on the phone wanting news. I'd rather call them before they do that.'

'You still think it might be May? Mrs Tarvin mistook her for a prostitute, or a drunk.' Noah frowned. 'Assuming she *was* mistaken. Without a proper ID, how much can we tell them?'

Marnie drank a mouthful of coffee before she answered. 'They'll see a connection because that's what they need. *This* girl is alive. They'll want to believe she's May. I would, in their place.'

'I wonder how Loz is coping.' Noah felt a pang for the Beswicks' younger daughter. 'Poor kid.'

Loz was thirteen, prickly with intelligence. Living in a house that was cracking apart under the stress of her sister's disappearance. May was sixteen, with no good reason to leave home, or none Marnie and Noah had uncovered. Fearing the worst was easy. The hard part was hoping for the best.

'Any news from the hospital about Logan Marsh or Ruth Eaton?' he asked.

'Logan's condition remains critical. Ruth's stable, for now.'

'If we find this girl . . . will Traffic want to charge her?'

'With what? A public order offence?' Marnie's blue eyes

were dark, serious. 'They'll go after Joe Eaton if they can. They'll want to know why he swerved instead of braking, how he ended up on the wrong side of the road while going fast enough for a smash on that scale. He said she wasn't running, so why wasn't there time to brake, or slow down? He'll have to answer some hard questions, especially if no one else witnessed what happened.'

'Do you think Mrs Tarvin was right about her being drunk, or drugged?'

'Trouble, that was the word she used. New, and trouble. I don't think Mrs Tarvin has much time for kids of any description.'

'No family photos. Odd for someone of her generation not to have kids, or grandkids.'

'Families fall out. And split up.'

'She's living alone up there. I wouldn't want that for my gran, would you?'

'I think she's making a decent fist of it.' A dry tinge to her voice. 'But no, I wouldn't.'

'We did house-to-house on the Garrett after May first went missing. Same part of Lambeth. No one saw anything, not even Mrs Tarvin.'

'No,' Marnie agreed. 'This girl's found a change of clothes from somewhere. It's possible she lives on the Garrett, or knows someone who does.'

Not May Beswick, in other words.

'D'you think she knows Natalie Filton or Abi Gull, our friendly neighbourhood arsonists?'

'Let's not take Mrs Tarvin's word for everything.' Marnie dropped her empty coffee cup into a litter bin. 'And let's see the Beswicks before this story breaks.'

Sean and Katrina Beswick lived in a terraced house on Taybridge Road, not far from Clapham Common. The house was bay-windowed, clinging to its original features the way a pensioner clung to her handbag on pension day. The neighbours had put up a pierced cement wall, but the Beswicks had a privet hedge that until recently had been kept trim. In the last three months, it had grown a shaggy fringe.

May's father opened the door, face falling when he saw Noah and Marnie.

'No news,' Marnie said, knowing the news he feared. 'We're still looking for May.'

'Come through.' He held the door wide.

They followed him to the sitting room. At six foot four, Sean was the only one on eye-level with the pictures he'd hung too high up the walls. Inoffensive landscapes, the kind Dan described as middle-class graffiti. A rack of wine bottles filled the gutted fireplace. No books. Flatscreen TV and shelves of glassware, sticky with dust. White walls, lots of empty space. An estate agent would've called the house bright and sunny. But it wasn't, bent double under the weight of its missing child.

'How's Katrina?' Marnie asked. 'And Loz?'

'On their way back from work, and school.' Sean pushed his fists into the pockets of his jeans. He had a tall man's stoop, fair head down, broad shoulders hunching. Not dressed for work, and he hadn't shaved. A laptop was open on the low table by the sofa. He flicked a glance in its direction. 'I've been registering with websites that search for missing kids, forums where kids can leave messages. Not that May was into computers, didn't even use the phone we got her. Well, you know that . . . Loz is different, she lives on the internet.' He flinched, backtracked. 'We're careful, of course. We have parental controls on the worst of the websites.'

'She's at school.' Marnie gave the man her steady smile. 'How's that going?'

'Questions, sympathy, you know. Some of the kids are cruel, maybe they mean to be, maybe they don't, speculating as to whether May's alive or dead, if she ran off or someone snatched her. The school deals with it, then they start up again. I wish we could keep Loz home, but we can't. We agreed to try and carry on as usual.' He blinked across the room at nothing, his brown eyes like May's but fidgety with pain. 'To try to be normal.'

Marnie said, 'Shall we sit down?'

'Of course, sorry.' He stooped to shut the laptop. 'I'll make coffee. Would you like coffee?' He moved in the direction of the kitchen, carrying his hurt as a limp in his left leg.

'Just water would be fine.' Marnie let him go. Noah stayed with her, taking in the small changes since the last time they were here. Each visit a little more dust, another layer of neglect. One of the landscapes was crooked on the wall. It stood out like a handprint.

Sean returned from the kitchen with two glasses of water. 'Here.'

'Thanks.' Marnie sat on the sofa. 'We wanted to give you advance warning about a story that might be in the papers tomorrow, or tonight.' She waited until Sean was seated, his hands propped between his knees. 'You might have heard about the traffic accident last night.'

'York Road was closed.' Sean smelt of stale sweat and cigarettes. No ashtrays in the house. Maybe he smoked in the garden. 'Kat had to find another route to work.'

'One of the drivers saw a girl leaving the scene of the crash. We're looking for her. We'll need to make an appeal to the public if we don't find her soon.'

'You think it's May?' His shoulders creaked as he leaned forward. 'The driver saw May?'

'We showed him a photo. He doesn't think it was her.

We're looking for other witnesses, but we didn't want you to see the news and assume it was May. The press are bound to speculate, since it happened nearby and everyone's looking for May, hoping for news of her.'

'It started out like that,' Sean said. 'But they stopped hoping after the first fortnight. *We* haven't. We can't. But it's too long to ask ordinary people to stay interested in someone else's kid. Kat says that at work they won't look at her any more, as if they've decided it's been so long, May must be . . . dead.' His teeth clenched on the word. 'They'll start up again when it comes to trial. When you find whoever did it.' His face collapsed, then reconfigured, scrabbling after a look that didn't spell despair. 'I don't mean . . . It's *them*, not us. We're still hoping.'

But he wasn't. No glimmer of hope anywhere on his face. As if he knew for certain that his daughter was gone.

'We understand,' Marnie said. 'We've not given up either.'

'You came here to warn us not to hope. When we hear the news about this girl from last night, you don't want us to get our hopes up. That's it, isn't it?'

'I wanted you to know as much as we do at this stage. I'm afraid it's not much. As I say, the driver doesn't think it was May, but we're doing everything we can to make certain.'

Sean jerked his head in a nod. 'I understand. Hope's a horrible thing. I've learned that in the last three months. A horrible, horrible thing. But you can't stop. *We* can't stop. Not until you kill it.'

He pointed a nicotine-stained finger at the street. 'When you knock at that door to tell us you've found her?' His hand shook. 'That she's . . . that you've found her. That's when we'll stop.'

10

Aimee

Ashleigh was in the bathroom, trying to get the candle wax and spit off her face. I could hear her moving around. Happy because the heat was off her, even if his spit wasn't. She'd never liked May, and she hated me.

'I was here three fucking months,' that was her favourite bitch, 'before you two showed up.'

True, but it wasn't my fault he liked me best. It wasn't like I *wanted* him to like me.

Christie had been with him nearly two years, longer than any of us. She'd found Grace about a year ago, and the two of them had found Ashleigh. Always the same story, the same hook.

'I know this guy,' Christie would have said. 'He's got this house. He'll let us stay if we behave ourselves.'

Grace probably said something like, 'Yeah? Behave ourselves on our backs, or behave ourselves on our knees?' Ashleigh, too.

And Christie would've said, 'He's not like that,' and I bet Ashleigh was actually disappointed.

The house was decent. Clean clothes, hot water, food. All of it free, and even if it wasn't, so what? We'd all done worse, out on the streets. Except May, but she had me. We thought we were good, May and me, because we had each other. It wasn't until the house got too small and we moved to the flat that the fairy tale turned to shit. We were a couple of stupid, dreaming kids, but we didn't deserve that. May didn't deserve it.

Here's the dumbest thing. We thought *we* chose *him*, not the other way around. We thought we were so clever tricking him into giving us a roof over our heads, free food, presents. Ashleigh with her tits like heat-seeking missiles. Wild Gracie, always fighting. May who looked like an angel but she wasn't, she wasn't – and now everyone knew it. And me, the victim. His favourite. He liked to sit at the side of my bed and hold a cloth to my head, a glass to my lips. He wouldn't touch, except to take my pulse, and even then it wasn't like you'd think. He wasn't the sick one. It was me. Every day a little weaker, lighter, less like *me*. He was wiping me out with his cold cloths and his hot stare.

So in case you're thinking I was mad to ever come here, it wasn't always like that. Once upon a time it was great. And we *wanted* to be in his good books, that's the thing. It wasn't easy to be in Harm's good books. He wasn't like other men, most men. *Any* men. I wished he was.

I understood men. I knew what they wanted and how to keep them happy, but Harm wasn't like that. Grace thought he was, it's why she had to go. Insulting him by suggesting he wanted us in that way. He doesn't. I don't think he can. He never touched May, but she was pregnant and no one knew how. She wouldn't say, wouldn't breathe a word.

I heard Ashleigh finish in the bathroom and walk back to her room. It was quiet, just London's noise washing at the windows. I was waiting for May to come up. She always came to see me before bed. To talk, to say goodnight. I needed to know she was okay.

This place – I could feel it boiling under me.

I wanted her up here with me, not down there with him. If I'd had the courage I'd've gone to her room, braved the dirty looks from Ashleigh, risked getting caught by Christie, or Harm.

My whole fucking life was if-I-had-the-courage.

I'm pregnant.

I'd been counting the minutes, hours, since she'd said that.

Wanting her up here with me.

Scared that she was down there, with him.

And that he'd turned his back.

11

Noah heard the TV as he was unlocking the front door. Shouting and bullets being fired, guttural screams, wet flesh. Another zombie all-nighter. He dropped his keys into the bowl in the hall and toed off his shoes, going through to the sitting room.

His kid brother Sol was sprawled on the sofa next to Dan, their faces lit red and green by the TV, which was showing a close-up of a machete removing the top of someone's head.

Sol grinned up at Noah. 'Hey, bro.'

'Hey. Sorry I'm late. Did I miss supper?'

'I got your text.' Dan rolled upright, coming around the sofa to kiss him. 'Ordered Chinese. It should be here in twenty minutes.'

On the TV, a man with a face like a chisel was wielding a crossbow at an approaching corpse. Sol slapped his knees. 'You're for it now, dick-brain!'

Dan said innocently, 'It's won a Golden Globe.'

'Twenty minutes until the food gets here?' Noah hooked his thumb through the belt loop on Dan's jeans, steering the pair of them into the hall. 'Help me work up an appetite.'

Dan pushed the sitting room door shut with his foot, leaving Sol with the TV. 'We should warm some plates.'

'Hmm. Warm me first.'

'You don't need it, you're always hot.' Dan tossed Noah's tie over his shoulder, leaning in to tongue at his neck. 'Taste good, too.'

Noah let his hips go loose, relaxing into Dan's grip, his breath hitching. 'Christ. . . You've been watching way too many zombies.'

'You don't like being bitten?'

'Rather be sucked.' Pulling at Dan's blond fringe, wanting the hot blue of his eyes. 'Or kissed.'

Dan pressed him into the wall, kissing until Noah's head started to spin. 'You taste of apples.'

'Hmm. That was lunch.'

'DI Rome doesn't feed you?'

'Not her job. We were busy. Over in Battersea, by the power station.'

Dan rolled his hips against Noah's. 'Love it there. Keep getting invited to go climbing one last time before the rest of the chimneys come down.'

'Your place-hacker friends,' Noah deduced.

'Urban explorers,' Dan corrected. 'Take back the city from the planners . . .'

'. . . get arrested for trespass. Break your neck. Just as well you're too smart to say yes to these adrenalin junkies.'

'It's not just about adrenalin.' Dan propped an elbow next to Noah's head, kissing him between sentences. 'It's reconnecting with what's ours, getting through the fences, under the city's skin.'

'Hmm. Your mates'll get caught sooner or later. More

CCTV cameras in the UK than the rest of Europe put together. They know that, right?'

'They know I'm screwing a detective sergeant. That tends to limit the invites.'

'Whatever works. I'd hate to have to handcuff you to a Heras fence.'

'Not going to happen.' Dan laughed into Noah's neck. 'But I get where they're coming from, don't you? Hardly anyone nowadays has a sense of place. You must see it all the time, kids on the streets with nowhere to go, not giving a shit about private property or Keep Out signs. They've got nowhere, so they make everywhere theirs. Go where they please, do what they want.'

'Your urban explorer friends aren't kids and they aren't poor. Most are in work, and well-off. If they weren't, they wouldn't have the cash to finance the exploring.'

'How'd we get on to this?' Dan kissed him again. 'Oh, right. Battersea Power Station, phallic chimneys, *you* being hot . . .'

Someone was buzzing to be let into the building.

Sol stuck his head around the sitting room door. 'Supper's here.'

'I'll get it.' Dan peeled away. 'You can warm the plates.' He headed out of the flat.

Sol shook his head at Noah, tonguing the inside of his cheek. 'You're not even out of your suit, man. What'd your boss say?'

'She'd say, "Is your kid brother still hanging out at your place, Noah, and did he nick your Oyster card?"'

'Needed stuff from home.' Sol fished in the pockets of his jeans. 'Cheers, yeah?'

'Next time, ask for cash.' Noah pocketed the card. 'I need this.'

'Chill.' Sol went in the direction of the kitchen. 'Beer?'

Dan came back with carrier bags smelling of fried rice. 'Let's eat.'

They were decanting the food on to plates when Noah's phone buzzed. 'Boss?'

'May Beswick.' Marnie stripped the words back to a knife edge. 'We've found her.'

Dead.

Noah could hear it in her voice.

May was dead.

He put down the foil dish of rice, turning away from the table. 'Where?'

'Battersea Power Station. How quickly can you get here?'

12

London leaned in through long windows to look at what was done here. Its shadows stained the floors and walls, and the glass gravel in glazed pots where fat cacti sat. The same shadows stained the girl's feet and legs, lying in the gutter of her stomach like dirty water.

Noah stood in the penthouse flat with the power station's famous chimneys at his back, seeing a dead daughter and sister. A murdered girl.

London looked indifferently on May Beswick. Wiped out her face, pressed her hands to her sides, made it hard to read the black scratch of words across her body. She looked very little, lying on the bed. She was sixteen years old. Naked except for a pair of white cotton knickers and the writing. Her body was covered in writing. Black ink, from the broad nib of a marker pen.

Ugly. Slut. Dog. Bitch. The same words, over and over. Up her legs and down her arms. Across her stomach and chest. Higher, right up to her sternum. *Bitch. Slut. Dog.*

In the open palms of her hands. *Whore.*

The words shouted, filling the room, throbbing in Noah's skull as if someone had turned up the volume in here.

Everything shouted. The colours, the smell, her stillness. The way she lay on the bed with her pale-blonde hair brushed neat on the pillow.

Round cheeks and a wide forehead, but she was no longer the girl in the photograph who'd haunted his sleep for the last twelve weeks. He could hear brush strokes in her hair, the slow settling of the blood at the backs of her legs. He clenched his hands and his jaw, focusing on the crime.

The words were neater on the left side of her body. If she was right-handed, she could have written them herself. It was hard to look at her, but he had to look. That was his job, the only excuse he had for being here, staring at a dead teenage girl. The picture broke up and became just so much static. He heard rather than saw it, a high-pitched scrabble adding to the noise in his head.

'We need Forensics. Fran Lennox . . .' Marnie was speaking into her phone. Her mouth marked a line on her face. 'No, I want Fran. Tell her I asked for her especially. And put Family Liaison on standby.' She was at the foot of the bed. 'This is now a murder investigation.'

Noah could hear the man's hands on May's throat, squeezing. Big hands, their size shouting from the blue spread of bruises. She'd been strangled. Recently, by her colour. He could hear her feet kicking. It didn't happen here.

'Talk to me,' Marnie said. 'Tell me what you're seeing.'

'He didn't do it here. She was dead when he put her here. It's not . . . I don't think it's a sex thing. She's . . . a child. He sees her as a child.'

'He undressed her.'

Noah shook his head in protest. 'She looks like a child.'

'We've been looking for a child. The Beswicks' daughter. *Their* child.'

61

'Loz's sister.' He felt nauseous. 'Her big sister.'

'Why isn't it a sex thing? Tell me what you see.'

'The way he's brushed her hair . . .' Noah had seen women laid out like angels by their killers, or laid out like whores. This wasn't the same. 'He's brushed her hair like a child's.'

'Plenty of people kill children. Too many.'

'Yes. But this doesn't sound . . . doesn't *look* like that. Not to me.' He had to stop looking at the bed, just for a moment.

Hanging above it: a painting of the power station. It had been chilling his peripheral vision since he'd stepped into the room. A cool grey study of scale and slippery depth – the feeling that if you looked too long or hard you'd fall into the canvas and struggle like a fly in a spider's pantry before acid ate you alive. He'd seen paintings like it in exhibitions he'd visited with Dan. Dirt scraped from railway arches and storm drains made the paint fat and irregular, clots of dust and hair growing like cysts under the skin of the canvas. His gut fisted, looking at it.

'How did he get her in here?' Marnie turned from the bed towards the long windows. 'It's secure. Probably more secure than it'll be when they've finished the work. CCTV, alarms, patrols.'

A patrol had called in the crime. A security guard, doing his rounds, had found May's body and called the police, sounding sickened but not panicked.

'Jamie Ledger, ex-soldier,' Marnie said. 'He's seen worse, but not in London. He'd thought this was a quiet job, guarding penthouses. We need to talk to him.'

Noah nodded, but didn't move. He wanted to stay here until the body on the bed was quiet. 'The killer risked getting caught to bring her here.' The chimneys were heavy at his back. Monolithic. Iconic. 'He wanted us to find her like this. And *here* . . . right here.' Her hair brushed neat, hands at her sides. 'It's a ritual, or a confession.' All Noah's training, in psychology and as a detective, said that this was someone who'd do it again. It was a long climb through the building site. CCTV, alarms, patrols. 'He went to trouble to leave her here.'

'It's a message,' Marnie agreed. 'But what? What's he trying to say?'

'He has access to the building, or he knows someone who has. We need the names of everyone who knows the security set-up. He came here *before* he killed her. I think . . . he saw all this, and he wanted her to be part of it.'

'An expensive resting place,' Marnie murmured, 'where she'd be found, and quickly. You're right. Workers, estate agents, prospective buyers – we need a list of everyone who's shown an interest in this flat in the last twelve weeks.'

Noah watched the city's lights flexing in the Thames below. 'I was talking to Dan about this place. He mentioned urban explorers, place-hackers. They love it here.'

'Not everyone will be on a list. All right. But we have to start there.'

Noah nodded, remembering what else Dan had said about the lure of places like this.

It's about getting under the city's skin.

He turned back to the bed. Shouting, still. The words on her body. His head throbbed blackly. 'Do you think she did that? The writing, I mean.'

'Lots of Sharpie pens in her bedroom. Sean said she was always sketching.'

'Battersea Power Station . . . Wasn't this one of the things she sketched?'

Marnie nodded. 'This place meant something to her, too. Not just to her killer.' She joined him at the side of the bed. 'Go on. What else?'

'Twelve weeks and a day.' Noah looked at May's hands, and her feet. 'He had her somewhere clean, decent. Fed her, looked after her. Her nails are trim, legs shaved recently, hair washed . . . He brushed it, after he did this. After he killed her. Could he've done the rest of it post-mortem as well?'

'Not all of it,' Marnie said. 'Look at her skin. No bruises, except the ones on her throat. No cuts, no visible damage. She's not malnourished. She was cared for, or allowed to care for herself. She wouldn't have done that if she was afraid. Not if she thought she was in danger.'

'The writing's ugly. Do you think she was doing it to herself *before* she left home?'

'Perhaps. We asked the Beswicks about self-harm, and they denied it.'

'Is it self-harm?'

'At the very least it's an act of self-reproach. A warning, maybe.' Marnie glanced away, silent for a beat. 'She's still blonde, and she's not skinny. But I think we should ask Joe Eaton about the girl he saw. Specifically about the black scratches.'

Noah looked at the jagged ink on May's body. 'You think it was *writing*, like this?'

'I think . . . Maybe. Yes.'

'They *knew* one another? May and the other girl? Or they knew the killer?'

'I'm not saying that. It could be a coincidence.'

'No such thing,' Noah said automatically.

'He read them.' Marnie's voice was so soft he had to turn his head to hear. 'Damaged girls, running away. He found them, took them in. And he read them. He read their skin.' She looked at Noah. 'We need to find him before he does this again.'

Ritual. Spectacle . . .

Everything signalled the start of a killing spree.

London was full of missing girls.

How many of them had this man found?

13

Aimee

I had her pens. May's. The ones she'd used to write on herself. It was Grace's game, but May kept her company, wanting Grace to feel less of a freak, less alone. I'd hated the writing, all those lies. *Ugly. Bitch. Whore.* 'You aren't any of those things,' I'd told her, but she wouldn't stop.

She was gone.

I couldn't believe it. She didn't even say goodbye. Just another empty place at the table when we sat down to breakfast.

'She went back home.' Harm's face was a full stop. 'It's what she wanted.'

No one asked any questions. Not at breakfast, not of Harm. I couldn't swallow his food, had to keep it in the sides of my mouth until I could spit it down the toilet. It was shock, mostly. I was such a *coward*. How could she've trusted me to keep her safe, let alone the baby?

After breakfast, I went to her room, hoping she'd left a message for me, instructions for how to find her. I couldn't stay there without her. But where would I go? If even *she* didn't want me . . .

'What's up, freak? Missing your little girlfriend? Even now you know she's not a lezzer?' Ashleigh was filling a bin liner with things from May's locker. 'Lezzers don't get pregnant.' She tied a knot in the neck of the bag. 'She liked dick.'

'Can I have that?' I held out my hand.

'Yeah? For what? What've you got to give me, freak?'

'Paracetamol.' I put my hand in my pocket. 'I'll give you two paracetamol.'

I was the only one allowed pills, because I was supposed to be sick all the time.

Ashleigh wanted the pills, but she was greedy. 'What about that locket he gave you?' She twisted the neck of the bin bag round her wrist. 'Two paracetamol and the locket.'

'You can't have the locket. He checks all the stuff he gives me. If it's missing, he'll know you nicked it and you'll get a bollocking. I can say I ate the pills because I felt bad.' I took out the foil strip and pressed two into my hand, holding them out. 'He doesn't check these.'

'Why'd you want her crap anyway?' Ashleigh took the pills, gave me the bag. 'She's a dirty bitch. Shagging around, sneaking out to get some. Lucky cow. Unless it was *him*.' She covered her mouth, pretending to be shocked. Only half pretending. If he heard her talking like that, or if I told him, she'd be sorry. It'd be the candle and face-scrubbing all over again, only worse.

'He's not like that. And May's not like that.'

'Oh fuck *off*. She's pregnant. How'd you think that happened? She was sneaking out to get some. Well, good luck to her. And good riddance.' She turned to the locker where she'd put the tin of Vaseline she'd used to slick her lips, and I thought:

You're next.

Good riddance.

I took the bag upstairs, sitting on my bed to look through the things May had left. A couple of T-shirts, old scrunchies with her hair in them, her pens and her sketchpad. I turned the pages, looking at our faces. The others hadn't wanted to sit for her, so Ashleigh's face was just slices. Christie's hadn't turned out right, like people wearing paper masks with her face photographed on them. The ones of Grace were good. I missed her, mad Gracie. No pictures of Harm in the sketchpad, but plenty of me. He'd made May draw me over and over. Sitting at the dressing table with his gifts. Brushing my hair, fastening the locket round my neck, lying in bed. A lot of me lying in bed: *Aimee, in decline.* She agreed to draw me because it meant we could spend time together. I'd liked watching her work, hair tied back, mouth bitten in concentration, sky and clouds leaning in across her shoulder. All of London was out there. If I stood at the window, I could see Battersea Power Station. Its chimneys were the last thing she drew.

I looked for messages, something written just for me. I couldn't believe she'd gone without saying goodbye. We shared everything. That time Christie gave me a box of sanitary pads – I could still feel the flush of embarrassment, *shame*, creeping all over me. I don't know what I'd have done if May hadn't made a joke out of it: 'Padded cell . . .'

No messages in her sketchpad, nothing I hadn't already seen, except that last picture of the power station. We'd watched the scaffolding go up, workmen moving all over the site in their hard hats. They were turning it into flats and we used to say we'd live there one day, May and me and her little sister. In the biggest flat, with the fuck-me windows, making the whole of London into pictures like the ones she'd drawn. Was it a message, this last picture? Was she waiting for me there? She'd found a way out, like Grace. She'd got away, but she'd left me here. With him . . .

The door handle was turning.

I shoved the sketchpad and everything else under the pillow, lay down and shut my eyes, blood thumping in my throat, sweat running like a rash up my arms and down my legs, its itch in my armpits, on my lips . . .

The air in the room thickened, buckling about me.

He came across to the bed and stood for a long time, looking down.

Seeing what he wanted to see.

His sick little girl.

Aimee, in decline.

14

Outside the penthouse flat, the power station looked derelict. Raw cement, rotten tiles, floors tacky with grease and dust. Wiring in nooses from the ceiling, waiting to be connected, plugged into the rest of the city. Down here, the site smelt like a diseased lung.

Marnie was talking to the security guard, Jamie Ledger. 'You're saying you don't have CCTV footage from last night?'

'I'd be surprised. It's why they have us. And the dogs.' He jerked his head at one of his fellow guards walking the perimeter with an Alsatian on a heavy-duty leash. 'Brain on a chain.'

Ex-soldier, mid forties, tattoos on his fingers. He'd seen some trouble in his time, and this? Was a half-arsed job, nothing like the life-or-death career he'd left behind, recently, judging by the buzz cut.

'How long have you been working here?'

'Three weeks on Tuesday.' Ledger put his hands behind his back.

'Has there been any trouble before now?'

'Dead bodies? No, this is the first.'

'But there's been trouble of another kind?'

'Kids, climbers, a couple of drunks. Nothing like this.' Pale eyes in a dark face. One of the finger tattoos was a hawk. He topped six foot, in good shape, better than the other security guards she'd seen on site. All muscle, his gravel-coloured stare summing her up in a single sweep. He'd known she was in charge before he'd seen her badge. A good soldier, she guessed, wondering at his reason for leaving, seeing the coin-sized scar above his left ear. He'd asked if she minded if he smoked, and she'd said no, because she needed him onside. He rolled each cigarette, smoking it to a shred before flicking it away.

'CCTV isn't working inside the main building? Why not? Plenty of cameras about the place.'

'Cameras need connecting. They want to sell more pods before they start spending more money.' He shrugged. 'That's developers for you. Tighter than a camel's arse in a sandstorm.'

'Is this what you think, or what you know? I could use some hard facts. Such as how many cameras are working here, and which ones. Upstairs in particular.'

'None of the ones upstairs. They don't reckon on anyone making it that far unless they've got a few million to spend.' He ran his tongue along a cigarette paper. 'We're supposed to have the perimeter covered down here.' The edge of his eye on her, checking her out the way he'd check a piece of kit to see whether it was likely to jam on him or kick to the side if fired. Nothing personal in it, certainly nothing sexual. He'd checked Noah in the same way.

Marnie needed someone on site who was watchful. It made a change from the average security outfit. What had he said about the guard with the dog? Brain-on-a-chain.

She filed it for future reference. 'You saw the body, upstairs. But you didn't touch anything.'

'No.' The pale stare ran over her like a searchlight. 'It was obvious what it was.'

'What was it?'

'A killing. Some psycho strangled her. Probably raped her too.' A lick of anger in his voice. 'I'd forgotten what a pit London is.'

'How long since you got back?'

He sandbagged the anger with a smile. 'Couple of years, give or take.'

'Where were you?'

'Afghanistan.' No boast in his voice. Serving her the facts, plainly.

'She weighed eight stone.' Marnie matched the man's unflinching tone. 'Whoever carried her up there was fit and strong.'

'And quiet. It's not easy to be quiet around here.' He stirred a booted foot at the loose topcoat of rubble, raising a noise like heavy rainfall. 'I found her on the first sweep. She could've been there a couple of hours before I got started.'

'No one else did a sweep before you came on shift?'

'Everyone, according to the rota. I asked around while you were up there. The rota was filled in, but I'd be gobsmacked if they actually got off their arses and went up.'

'You're the only one who does that?'

'I like the exercise. Beats sitting listening to them whining and farting.' He perfected the cigarette with his fingertips. 'She was already up there by the time I checked in. I'd have spotted something otherwise.' He looked in the direction of the river. 'I don't miss much. It's how they train you. Ears and eyes open. Some things you forget, but not that. Forgot what I was coming home to, though.' He struck a match and lit the cigarette. 'Afghanistan's got nothing on this place.'

In the penthouse, Fran Lennox stood at the side of the bed. 'Mauve is a rotten colour. Dirty. I'd have gone with white. You can't go wrong with white bedding.'

'They're selling to executives,' Noah said. 'It's all very . . . masculine.'

'I hate these showroom flats.' Fran pulled at the ends of her fingers, loosening latex gloves. She wasn't much bigger than May, slim and blonde, with her hair cropped short, all cheekbones and bright, inquisitive eyes. 'I can't imagine anyone living like this, can you? That headboard's like something from a jumbo jet. And don't get me started on the painting . . .' She shuddered, the blue forensic suit turning her skin the colour of milk.

Was she waiting, as he'd waited, for the noise to die down in here? May had stopped shouting at Noah, but maybe Fran was hearing her. No, she'd seen too many dead bodies for that. She was waiting for Marnie. 'Where's the boss?'

'Talking with the security guard who found the body.'

'How is he?'

'Ex-army. He's okay. As okay as you could be, anyway.'

Fran stepped closer, looking at May. 'Could be worse. At least her parents will recognise her.'

Noah wasn't sure if that was better, or worse. The neat way she'd been laid out was cowardly, insulting. As if the killer had taken her family's forgiveness for granted. He'd tidied away their daughter, made her mute and obedient, doll-like. Turned her into a child again. It was one of the worst murders Noah had seen in a long time.

Fran said, 'She was sixteen, wasn't she?'

'Yes.'

'She doesn't look it. More like thirteen. I don't mean physically. The way she's been left.'

'Yes.' Someone hadn't wanted May to grow up. 'The writing . . . Did she do that to herself?'

'If she's right-handed like ninety per cent of the population, then yes.' Fran tipped her head. 'From the pattern of the words, I'd call that a fair assumption.'

'We're wondering about the missing girl from the crash site, whether what Joe Eaton described as scratches could've been this. Writing.'

'I tested the shirt you found. It wasn't blood. Ethanol and isopropanol. Your basic Sharpie pen ingredients.' Fran nodded at the palms of May's hands. 'Just like this, I imagine.'

'Then . . . they knew each other. Two girls, same age, same writing. One of them got away, the other . . .' Noah shook his head, desperately sad.

'Could be a coincidence.' Fran leaned in, studying the bruises about May's neck. 'Large hands. Not necessarily a man's. And it doesn't look like a sexually motivated murder, but don't hold me to that. You'll want pictures of the writing, to show to Joe Eaton.'

'Two teenage girls in the same part of London, both with writing on their bodies? That's too much of a coincidence. They must've known one another, either as friends or victims.'

'The other girl ditched her clothes and went into hiding, isn't that what you said? Maybe she's mixed up in this, but I wouldn't go calling her a victim just yet . . .' Fran straightened, looking past Noah's shoulder. 'DI Rome, you bring me to all the best places.'

'You can thank me later. Your team's coming up.'

'Good. We'll get to work in that case, leave you to

your security guards and CCTV. The way this place is wired? You'll probably know the identity of the killer before I do.'

'I applaud your optimism,' Marnie said.

'Don't tell me the state-of-the-art security's a sham?'

'Oh, it's real. It's just not been fired up yet.'

'Seriously?' Noah nodded at the alarm console by the door. 'None of this stuff's working?'

'Some of it, on the ground floor. Up here? Nothing, according to Jamie Ledger.'

'Who else knew that, apart from Ledger?'

'The developers, the security guards. We're working on a list.' Marnie looked at the bed, her face changing. 'We should break the news to the Beswicks.'

Dawn was making a push at the horizon, light striping Fran's slim hands as she worked.

'Can't it wait?' Noah said. 'Until the morning? Let them get their sleep.'

'You think they're sleeping? We should tell them. Fran, call me as soon as you're ready.' Marnie's eyes hadn't left the bed. 'They'll want to see her.'

15

In Taybridge Road, the wheelie bins were out, ready for collection. Rain had been falling most of the night, pooling in the gutters and the shallow lids of the bins. It was nearly 5 a.m.

Marnie found a parking space and switched off the engine, watching the rain gather on the windscreen. 'Ready?'

'Yes.' Noah released his seat belt, but didn't move from the passenger seat. 'Actually, no. I'm scared. Of saying the wrong thing and making it worse.'

'You won't.' The car's engine ticked as it cooled. 'You can't. This is as bad as it gets.' That sounded too bleak. She tried again. 'I'd rather have you with me for this than anyone else on the team. Precisely because you feel it so much. The Beswicks know that. They trust you.'

Noah nodded. 'Okay. Let's get it done.' He climbed from the car.

Through the deckled glass of the front door, a light was shining at the back of the house. Someone was up early. Marnie knocked and stepped back, shoulder to shoulder with Noah.

Loz opened the door. She looked at their faces and her stare grew hot. 'No. *No*. Go away.' She blocked their way into the house. 'They're not up yet. They're sleeping. Just . . . go away.'

Marnie said, 'We're very sorry. But we do need to come in. We need to see your mum and dad.'

Loz stood her ground. 'Don't you . . . don't you tell them she's dead.' The cuffs of her school uniform nearly hid the fists she'd made of her hands. 'Don't you *dare*.' She didn't look like her sister. Bony where May had been curvy, dark hair growing like brambles around her thin face. No one would ever brush Loz's hair into a blonde fan on a mauve pillow.

Noah said, 'Loz, let us in. I'm freezing out here.'

Black eyes flicked to his face. 'Are you going to say it, or is she? I suppose she has to say it because she's a *woman* and women understand this shit.' She blinked, looking for a second like her dad. 'If my sister's dead, I'm allowed to swear.'

'You're allowed to swear,' Noah said. 'You can punch me, if it helps. But let us in, okay?'

She stepped behind the door, staying there once Marnie and Noah were inside the house. No sound from upstairs.

Noah closed the front door. 'Can you wake your mum and dad for us?'

'They'll be getting up soon anyway. Mum gets up at six, for work.' No colour in her face. 'You can wait, can't you?'

'Sorry.' Noah's face was wet from the rain. He wanted to put his hand on Loz's shoulder, but she looked like she'd break if he did. She needed her mum and dad.

'I'll go up,' Marnie said gently. 'If that's okay with you.'

'*Fine*. I'll go.' Loz pushed past them, heading up the stairs. Halfway up, she stopped, turning to face them.

77

'You'd better put the kettle on.' Her mouth made a shrewd shape. 'They'll need tea.'

Katrina and Sean Beswick sat on the sofa in their pyjamas. Loz stood in the corner of the sitting room, watching them. Watching Marnie and Noah, too. Five cups of tea sat on the low table where Sean's laptop was propped, its battery light blinking.

'Are you *sure* it's her?' Katrina looked half frozen in white silk pyjamas, exposed collarbones like a coat hanger for the rest of her body. 'Don't we have to identify her?'

'There needs to be a formal identification, yes.' Marnie sat on the edge of an armchair close to the bereaved couple. 'But we're as sure as we can be that it's May. I'm very sorry.'

Noah was standing by the window, not far from Loz. He could smell fabric softener from her uniform. She was holding herself in a tight knot, radiating tension.

'She was in Battersea Power Station? Did she . . .' Sean swallowed. 'Can you tell us if she . . .'

'What Dad's trying to ask,' Loz said, 'is did she top herself?'

Her mother's stare found her across the room. 'Loz, no.' Pleading with the open palms of her hands. The light sat in the creases under her grey eyes. 'Not now.'

'It wasn't suicide,' Marnie said.

'So someone killed her. She was murdered.'

'Please!' Her mum snapped the word.

Rain hit the windows of the house like a handful of gravel.

'What, I'm not allowed to be pissed off that some fuck-tard killed my sister?'

'Sweetheart, come here.' Sean's gaze swam, unseeingly. 'Come here.'

Loz ignored his outstretched hand. She sat on a foot-stool in the corner of the room with her knees pulled up to her chin.

Marnie waited for the worst of the storm to leave Loz's face. 'I'm very sorry, but yes. This is a murder investigation. The girl we found was strangled.'

'The *girl* you found. So you're *not* sure?' Katrina insisted. 'It might *not* be her.'

'Mum, they're telling you May's dead. Someone killed her.' Loz hugged her knees, big eyes burning in her face. 'They need you to make a formal identification, that's how it works, but they've seen her so they know.' She looked at Noah. 'Did *you* see her? It was her, right?'

'Yes. I'm very sorry.'

'One good thing. She must look okay, for them to be so sure. She can't have been burnt or bashed about, or rotting.'

Katrina put up both hands to block out the sight of her daughter.

'Sweetheart,' Sean said weakly, 'you need to stop.' He turned appalled eyes on Marnie. 'When? When did you find her, when did it happen?'

'We found her around seven o'clock last night. We're not sure when it happened, but we think not long before then. We'll be able to give you better answers soon.'

'After the post-mortem.' Loz shut her eyes, rocking on the footstool.

Noah waited for one of her parents to cross the room and hold her. Neither Sean nor Katrina moved from the sofa. It struck him that there was no comfort in this house, with its white walls and empty spaces. Loz hugged herself as if no one else ever did.

'So she was alive yesterday morning or yesterday afternoon. As recently as that?' Sean didn't reach for his wife's hand, sitting apart from her as if he feared contact. 'All this time, she was alive?'

'Yes.' Marnie's phone buzzed and she glanced at it. 'That's my colleague, Fran. She's ready for you to see May. When you're ready.'

'Fran?' Katrina echoed.

'The pathologist.' Loz didn't open her eyes. 'The one who'll do the post-mortem.'

The Beswicks couldn't look at their daughter, or at each other. They searched Marnie's face for some crumb of comfort. 'Alice Gordon could come with us,' Marnie said, 'if you'd like that.'

Alice was their family liaison officer.

'No thanks.' Loz lifted her chin, shoving a stare at Noah. 'If I have to see that cow, I'll puke.'

No reaction from the sofa, her parents blanking her out.

Noah wanted to hug Loz, spikes and all.

'You were treating this as murder from the start. I know. I looked it up on the internet. Police procedure for missing persons. If in doubt, think murder. It saves time later on, if the missing person turns up dead.' Loz propped her chin on her knees. 'You've been thinking she's dead for weeks.'

16

Christie

'Aimee's starting a fever,' Harm said. 'She should stay in bed. You'll want to look in on her.'

He was standing the other side of the kitchen, between Christie and the door. But it wasn't desperate, not yet. He was able to look at her. It was when he avoided her eyes that Christie got scared. He wouldn't look at what he did. What he was. She'd go up to Aimee in a bit. Because he expected it, and because she needed to be sure Aimee was okay. She'd thought she could be sure, but after Grace, and May . . .

Christie couldn't be sure of him. None of them understood this. Ashleigh thought she could seduce him. She wouldn't last much longer. As for Aimee . . .

Aimee never stood a chance. The way she looked, her *weakness*. How she'd survived on the streets, Christie didn't know, except she supposed that Aimee was smart, in her way. She wouldn't be sleeping when Christie checked on her, but she'd got good at pretending. Clever, just not clever enough. Aimee thought that May was out there, alive. She didn't know anything.

None of them knew anything.

Not about Harm. Not about Neve, his sister, who'd gone missing when he was a boy. Living on the streets, they'd thought. Harm had searched for her for years, without knowing what he was searching for. No one was ever the same on the streets. There'd been no way of knowing whether Neve had become a slut like Ashleigh, or wild like Grace, if she was a dreamer like May, or a survivor like Christie.

Christie wasn't clever in her head like Aimee. She was clever with her hands and her feet. She was a worker, too. She cooked and cleaned and shopped and planned. There was nothing she wouldn't do for him, but Harm . . .

Harm didn't want a survivor. Aimee was his favourite because she was *weak*. Victim written right through her. He wanted to protect her the way he couldn't protect his sister. Aimee was his new Neve, only this time he'd keep her safe.

It was all about Neve.

He'd told Christie how his parents had knelt all those years ago, praying with their faces and the backs of their heads, with the soles of their feet – hers so full of creases you could count her age there, older every day as she knelt with her fists full of bedsheets and her head filled with Neve, the whole house packed with fear for her. Stories about where she'd gone, who she'd become – a prostitute or a drug addict, a free spirit or someone's slave – anything to stop them thinking she was dead. So many versions of Neve. No wonder he couldn't stop searching, finding her in the faces of other lost girls. It was their secret, Christie's and Harm's. He trusted her. She was different to the others. She mattered. All she'd ever wanted was to matter.

Ashleigh thought she was special, with her shiny smile and her chest pressing against her shirt, as if that was why he'd bought it, to see her body changing. She didn't understand what would happen when she got too big for the clothes he'd given her. She thought it was power, the push of her, that she could grow up and he'd love her for it. She was wrong, so wrong. That wasn't the way to make him love her. He couldn't even look at her now.

Like Grace, like May.

Christie didn't want to think about May. A baby, she'd said. She was having a baby. Whose? It'd been *safe* in here. They hadn't had to worry about that, not any of them. Harm had seen the way men looked at them on the streets, using them up with their eyes, and he'd *saved* them from that. May had put herself in danger, and Aimee too. All of them in danger because she couldn't be glad of what she had. Creeping out for sex, reeking of her weakness, bringing it back here. Her *baby*, a rotten red coil in her belly. Aimee had thought May was her friend, but what kind of friend infected your safe place with her sickness?

Christie had seen birth – a kind of birth. She knew its mess. It wouldn't happen here. Harm wouldn't let it. A baby, but May wouldn't say whose. No matter how hard Christie asked her.

Ashleigh thought she knew. Stinking of hormones, looking at Aimee like *she* was the one ruining it here when the whole point of everything was Aimee. It was all for Aimee.

Harm would have to show Ashleigh. He'd have to.

Or Christie would.

He was standing at the sink, washing plates, shoulders smooth with muscle, the light putting his shadow around the room. She watched him for some sign of weakness. A way in. Sometimes she thought she saw bruises in the open collar of his shirt where the skin was grained like wood, like he was carved from it. Blond wood, with whorls for eyes and a knot for his mouth. You'd need an axe to make an impression, and even then you'd struggle. But . . .

People hugged trees, didn't they?

His neck shifted with shadow, filling and emptying the hollow at the collar of his shirt. She'd ironed that shirt. And his trousers. He liked to look smart, a hangover from his old life. He couldn't let it go, that other life. It ran alongside him like a dog. None of them understood. They didn't hear him tick. They listened to his rules, and followed his instructions. Ate his food, wore his clothes. But they didn't know what he *was*, not the way Christie knew.

Rain wetted the window above his head, bumping and creeping across the glass in broken stripes. So long since she'd felt it on her face. Two years since she'd sat on that pavement, moving her feet out of the way of the crowds. *Plink-plink* in the torn can she'd put out, weighted with a stone. Rust on her fingers, like blood. An ache between her legs, and her insides scraped raw. Everything tasting of metal and meat. Harm had saved her. His neck was knotted, smooth. She wanted to rub her cheek there.

Aimee was learning. Sick again, in her bed. Best place for her. A quick learner, Aimee.

Christie wondered which one of them would be next. The next Grace. The next May.

Ashleigh, she thought.

Ashleigh was next.

17

Pinned on the incident room whiteboard: May's photograph, before and after. Missing, with a smile on her face. Found, with bruises about her neck.

'This writing . . .' Ron peered at the photos. 'Why would anyone do that to themselves? Are we sure it wasn't done by whoever killed her?'

'Fran thinks not,' Noah said. 'There's none on her back, and it's much clearer on her left side. She was right-handed.'

'Did her mum and dad see the writing when they ID'd her?'

'It was covered by her clothes, so no.'

Sean and Katrina had acknowledged the dead girl as their daughter not in words but with sounds: a wrenched wail from Katrina; raw sobbing from Sean.

'Did Loz know about the writing? My sisters always knew my secrets.' Debbie swung away, to answer the station's phone.

'How's the house-to-house going?' Noah asked Ron. 'Any sign of Traffic's missing girl on the Garrett estate?'

'Put it this way, I've had more doors slammed in my face than you've had dirty martinis.'

'I hate martinis.'

'All right. So I've had more doors slammed in my face than you've had blow jobs, Detective Sergeant Pin-Up.'

'How is Mrs Tarvin?'

'Same as always. Last line of defence against the crap raining down on that dump.'

'She'll be keeping an eye out for our girl, I imagine.'

'Bound to be. We should be paying her a wage . . . What?' Ron had seen the look on Debbie's face when she put the phone down. 'Not more bad bloody news.'

She gave an unhappy nod. 'That was St Thomas's. Logan Marsh died yesterday.'

More bereaved parents. Noah's teeth ached. 'When yesterday?'

'They didn't give an exact time, just apologised for not informing us sooner, blamed it on an admin error.'

'Crap.' Ron clasped his hands on top of his head, turning away. He turned back almost immediately. 'We'd better show that writing to Joe Eaton before Traffic decide to arrest him.'

Noah agreed, taking out his phone. 'I'll let the boss know.'

At Battersea Power Station, the wind whipped in from the water, clattering the crime-scene tape at Marnie's back. Fran's team was clearing up. They'd made the showroom secure, collected all the evidence they could.

Marnie had the mortuary's chill in her bones, still feeling the blank terror in Loz's stare, the rage the girl was radiating to keep sympathy at bay. There was too much about Loz that Marnie recognised. She wanted to call Ed, just to hear his voice, but there wasn't time. She was afraid to let the trail go cold. May had been dead less than twelve hours. They had to capitalise on that, get statements from everyone who'd been on site yesterday. Nineteen people, including Jamie Ledger.

Ledger was clocking off. One of the other guards called, 'See you, Ledge,' and the nickname made her wonder whether he'd told the truth about how little he liked the rest of the security detail.

'You need a signed statement,' he said, before she could open her mouth. 'Where're you doing them? Here, or at the station?'

'Here. Your boss has opened the sales office for us.' Plenty of desks between the glossy displays in the room reeking of new carpet, expensive printing.

Ledger shoved his arms into a waxed jacket. 'I'll see you over there.'

'Not me. My team. I'm needed elsewhere.'

'How's the family? She had a kid sister, didn't she? May Beswick. I recognised her from the papers.' His face shadowed. 'I just wondered how she was doing.'

'I'm sorry, I can't talk about it.'

'Right.' He straightened up. 'Tough job, telling the family. I've had to do that myself. I wasn't being nosy, or morbid.'

Marnie nodded, waiting until he'd crossed the site into the sales office before she took out her phone to call Noah.

'Logan Marsh died,' he told her. 'I'm headed over to Joe Eaton's, thought we'd better see whether the scratches on our missing girl could've been writing, like May's.'

'Welland will want all hands here. Unless or until we're sure of a link between the two girls.'

'Eaton might be able to give us that link.'

'It's not a priority. I'm sorry about Logan, but we need the house-to-house team at the power station. We should shorten the perimeter, and keep it tight. I want you back here.'

'I'm on my way,' Noah promised.

Marnie ended the call and turned to face the wind, letting its teeth bite her cheek. The rain had eased off, but it would be back, its blunt pressure pushing behind the clouds. She watched the water fold and unfold like a fist, thinking of Logan Marsh in the mortuary, his parents' pain. Wondering why May had run, where she'd ended up. Well fed, her nails trimmed short. Someone had looked after her. The same someone who'd killed her? Had she felt safe in the weeks before she died? Happy, even?

The phone's casing was blood-warm in Marnie's hand, her fingers tracing Ed's number on the keypad. She'd run, fourteen years ago. Safe at home, but not happy. Running wild when she was thirteen, staying out late, coming home drunk. Testing the boundaries of her parents' care and patience until she finally worked up the courage to cut the ties and go for good. May hadn't been wild, not in the same way. She'd come home drunk a couple of times, smelling of cigarettes, but it'd been enough to make her parents wonder if she'd run away rather than been snatched. Loz had accused the police of deciding from the outset that her sister was dead. She was half right. They'd wasted a lot of time wondering whether May was on the streets, asking questions of anyone who might've seen her sleeping rough. The wrong questions, as it turned out. May had been hiding, or hidden. At home, she didn't wash or eat properly. Neglecting herself, resisting her parents' efforts to put her back on track. Katrina had tried to interest her in clothes, a beauty routine. Spa sessions, retail therapy. Sean took up cooking, hoping to tempt his daughter's palate back to life, allowing her a glass of wine with meals. Nothing worked. May drifted away. Retreating further and further, until one day she was gone. Then displayed like a child on that bed. Who had taken such good care of her in the last three months of her life? Who hadn't wanted her to grow up?

Marnie's phone rang: Fran Lennox. She sought the shelter of a wall, needing to hear the nuances in Fran's voice. 'What've you got for me?'

'Blood tests. High levels of hCG. Human chorionic gonadotropin.'

Rain stung Marnie's skin. 'She was pregnant? How pregnant?'

'Seven, eight weeks. No more than that.'

Noah was coming across the site, his head down, long legs dodging puddles.

'We were wrong,' Marnie said into the phone. 'We thought this wasn't sexual. That the killer saw her as a child. But if she was pregnant, we were wrong.'

'Or she was with someone else when she first went missing. A boyfriend, perhaps. No ligature marks, or trauma. No evidence of restraint. If we're talking about a sexual predator, the evidence doesn't stack up, not yet. I'll know more after the full post-mortem.'

Noah had joined Marnie, sheltering from the rain.

'What else was in her blood?' Marnie asked Fran.

'No drugs, no alcohol. The only thing throwing a spike is sodium. She wasn't far off being hypernatremic. That's salt poisoning, or dehydration. Not enough to interfere with the pregnancy at eight weeks, but not healthy either. If she was being sick regularly, that might account for it. Her parents said nothing about eating disorders?'

'Nothing. They were sure they'd have known, but they didn't know about the writing.'

'Ask her sister about the writing,' Fran said, 'and the eating. Siblings usually know a lot more than parents, and from what I saw of the sister, she's a sharp cookie.'

'Yes. Call me when you have anything more.'

'You'll be the first to know,' Fran promised. She rang off.

Noah rubbed rain from his face. 'What's happened?'

'May was pregnant. Seven or eight weeks.'

'Oh God.' He looked away, pain pulling at his face. 'So he raped her then he killed her? Do you think he *knew* she was pregnant when he killed her?'

'The father and the killer might not be the same person.'

'Do her parents know?' Noah covered his mouth with the span of his hand.

'I've only just found out. They didn't think May was in a relationship of any kind. Well, perhaps she wasn't.' Marnie straightened, pocketing her phone. 'Right now we need to concentrate on how the killer got her here. Fran's worked the immediate area. We need a team pushing back to the perimeter.' She showed Noah on the map. 'The only ways in and out are here, and here.' She pointed to the Kirtling Street entrance Noah had just used, and a second entry point to the east. 'He could've brought her by river, but for now let's assume he came by road. Colin's chasing down all the available CCTV. Let's walk the perimeter, get our bearings.'

In Kirtling Street, the sun was in Noah's eyes and mouth, tasting sour and yellow.

Marnie glanced at him. 'Are you all right?'

'Headache. It'll pass. So we need to speak with the Beswicks again.'

'Yes, we do. I'm thinking the news of the pregnancy can wait until we have the full post-mortem report from

Fran, but I want to ask them again about the possibility of a boyfriend. And the writing. Fran's sure May did it herself. I'd like to rule that in, or out.'

'Debbie thinks Loz might know. Sisters share secrets, she says.'

'Fran said the same . . . Do you think Loz will talk to you?'

'Depends how angry she is.' Noah had lied about the headache. It was a migraine, making his eyes blaze in their sockets. He'd taken pills, but if it didn't clear soon, he'd be no use to Marnie or anyone else. 'When they find out she was pregnant . . .'

'They'll assume she was raped. That's why we need the full results from Fran. If we're going to give them news like that, I want it to be in context.'

They stood in the shadow of the power station's smoke-stacks, smelling the river and the building works, seeing London changing shape around them.

'There are seventeen girls of May's age reported as missing in London right now,' Noah said. 'I checked the system first thing this morning. Four of them went missing in the last six months.'

'You and I both think there's a chance this killer will do it again. We have to be prepared for that. We need to build a profile, which is why we have to ask the Beswicks about the writing, so that we know exactly what we're dealing with.'

'A monster.' Noah shut his eyes. 'Whichever way we look at it, whether or not he held her prisoner and raped her before he killed her – we're dealing with a monster.'

'We are,' Marnie agreed. 'So let's find out as much about him as we can.'

Noah's phone played *The Sweeney*'s theme tune. 'DS Jake.'

'First CCTV sighting.' It was Colin Pitcher at the station. 'Two nights ago, 11.52 p.m. on Battersea Park Road.'

Noah switched to speaker so Marnie could listen in. 'What are you seeing?'

'May and another girl. About the same age. Skinny, wild hair. Could be the girl Joe Eaton identified from the crash.'

'Just the two girls?'

'Yes. They look scared. At least, May looks scared. The other girl's got her back to the camera. Body language says a stand-off, or a fight.'

'Which way were they headed?'

'North, towards the power station. I'm checking the rest of the CCTV on that route, but it's going to take a while. Not everyone's handing it over quickly, no matter how nicely I ask.'

'Send what you've got to my phone.'

'Doing it now.' Colin rang off.

They headed back to Marnie's car. 'Joe Eaton's girl?' she said. 'Do we need to revert to your original plan and pay him a call?'

'A girl couldn't have killed May Beswick, could she? And carried her all the way up to that penthouse? It's not possible.' Noah waited for the file to load to his phone. 'But she and May were headed north. Towards the power station.'

'Towards the Garrett, too. That's north of Battersea Park Road.'

In the car, they studied the film.

CCTV footage, washed-out, making ghosts of the two girls.

May's face was an oval, overexposed under a street light. The other girl kept her back to the camera. She was May's height but skinnier, in black sweatpants and a hoody. The hood was down, showing a tangle of hair, darker than May's, and brighter.

'This was the night before she died,' Noah said. 'She's less than a mile from her parents' house. Why didn't she go home? Why didn't she run? Like this other girl, if it *is* Traffic's girl.'

'Bare feet.' Marnie put her thumb on the screen.

Under the cuffs of the sweatpants, the girl's toes were white and bony.

'It's her,' Marnie said. 'Let's see if Joe Eaton agrees.'

18

Joe Eaton answered the door in his pyjamas. 'I heard the news. Gina Marsh called. I'd given her my number at the hospital.' His face was pillow-scarred, left eye still bloodied. 'Logan died. I said how sorry I was. It's devastating. He was only just eighteen . . .'

'Can we come in?' Marnie was aware of Noah shivering at her side.

'Of course, sorry.' Joe held the door wide. 'The kids are with Carrie. I'm meant to be catching some rest. Didn't think I'd sleep, but I did.' He pointed them towards the sitting room.

Toys, everywhere. A duvet on the sofa, a laptop on a low table. The neck brace from the hospital was in an armchair by the gutted fireplace. The Beswicks had filled their fireplace with bottles of wine. This one was filled with DVDs for the children. Sorcha, and Liam.

'Carrie is their aunt?' Marnie said.

'Ruth's sister. They love her to bits. It's not easy getting them to do what they don't want to. It's just for today, they'll be back tonight. Ruth's improving.' He grimaced with relief, and guilt. 'They think she's going to be okay.

I just wish . . . Logan had his whole life ahead of him. Do you want something to drink? I could use a coffee.'

'Thanks, but we don't have a lot of time. We wanted to ask a couple more questions about the girl from the crash. DS Jake?'

'We have a CCTV sighting.' Noah held his phone where Joe could watch the clip. 'We think this might be the girl you saw?'

Joe leaned close, frowning at the phone. 'She's wearing different clothes, but the build's the same. Has she got bare feet? Yes, it could be her. The other girl – it's May Beswick? I heard on the news that you'd found a body at Battersea Power Station.'

Marnie nodded at Noah, who moved his thumb across the screen, holding the phone up again.

'The scratches you saw on the girl who caused the crash. Could they have been this?'

Joe leaned in again. 'This is . . . writing? You think what I saw was writing?'

'We wondered,' Marnie said. 'You'll understand that we're investigating May's death and what we're showing you is confidential, and sensitive.'

'Of course. Her poor parents. *Christ* . . . Gina's coping better than I would, but maybe it hasn't hit them yet. May was younger than Logan, wasn't she? Still at school.'

'She was sixteen.'

'It could've been this.' Joe peered at the phone, blinking shut his left eye. 'Writing. On that girl. It could've been. But what does that mean? Was she involved in May's death?'

'We don't have any reason to suspect that.'

'But that's May with her, isn't it? That's May Beswick.'

'You've had some good news?' Marnie said. 'About Ruth?'

'The surgery went well. She's responding, that's what they've said. I can see her later, before I collect the kids.' He looked wary, rubbing the palms of his hands on his pyjamas. 'You'll want to question her about the crash, about this girl. I don't know when she'll be ready for that.'

Marnie glanced at Noah. 'We'll be in touch, Mr Eaton. Thanks again.'

In the street, she asked, 'How bad is it?'

Noah put the flat of his hand on the car. He didn't answer right away.

'Migraine?'

He thinned his mouth. 'Sorry.'

'I'll take you home.'

'I can get a cab.'

'It's not far. I'll take you. Get in.'

Noah didn't argue. He climbed into the car vigilantly, as if every bit of him hurt. Fastened his seat belt and shut his eyes. His face was pinched with pain. Marnie started the engine and pulled into traffic as smoothly as she could. She'd known that Noah suffered from migraines, but she hadn't witnessed an attack up close before. He looked like someone had hit him on the back of the head with a blunt weapon. They were headed the right way for the traffic; it took less than twenty minutes to reach Noah's flat. She double-parked and cut the engine, switching on the hazard lights before getting out and opening the passenger door for Noah. She waited while he climbed out, standing back to give him space but staying close enough to catch him if he fell.

'Thanks.' He leaned against the car for a second before straightening. 'Sorry.'

'Don't be.' She glanced across at the house, remembering

how many stairs had to be climbed to reach his flat. 'Is there someone home to give you a hand?'

'Sol . . . But I'll be okay.'

The blare of a car horn made him wince. A white Kia Sportage was waiting for Marnie to move out of its way. She ignored it, concentrating on Noah. 'Come on.'

They crossed to his flat, waiting while he searched his pockets for his keys. The Kia Sportage hit its horn again. Noah found the keys and handed them to Marnie. It was an effort for him to stay upright. She unlocked the door and got him as far as the stairs, sitting him down.

Outside, the Sportage was blaring incessantly. Marnie said, 'Hold on.'

She walked out into the road, to where the Kia was waiting. The driver had a shirt as loud as his horn, suit jacket slung from the hook behind his seat. She motioned for him to wind down his window.

'You can't just stop in the middle of the road, you dozy bitch—'

Marnie shut him up with her badge. 'Find another way round.' She put the badge away. 'And stop playing with your horn.'

She went back to Noah, who was standing and had mustered a smile. 'I've got it from here. You need to be working the case. Give me a couple of hours and I'll be back on my feet.'

It was a long speech, and he looked less ghastly than he had in the car.

Marnie nodded. 'Take care. Call me when you can, but not before.'

Noah climbed the stairs to the flat with his hands on the walls either side of him. Blind, because the left side of his head was a sliding mess of colour, everything red and green like Sol's favourite TV show. The pain was twin hammers in his head, one for each temple. At least he hadn't thrown up in the car. He reached the flat and felt with his fingers for the lock – a snagging sensation like teeth. Fitted the key. Pushed at the door. One foot in front of the other.

Make it to the bed and lie down.

Lie down.

He closed the door, checking it was locked, waiting for the throb of nausea to subside. The migraine had repainted the hallway, set it at an angle hard to negotiate even with his hands holding on to the walls. Like crawling up a tunnel that got narrower the further he went.

' . . . fuck with me, you little fucker!' A stranger's voice.

Noah stood listening. Hard to hear past the thundering in his head and he needed – *God* – he needed to lie down. The stranger's voice came again, too low to hear but raging, anger like a solid object pushing at the wall between him and the sitting room.

'Sol?' His voice came out frayed.

Seven steps from the hall to the sitting room. He took five before his brother came out into the hall. 'Shit. *Shit*. Come here, man.'

Noah held him off with a look. 'Who's in there?'

'No one. A mate.' Sol shook his head. 'You look dead, bro. What's up?'

'Migraine. Who is he?'

'No one. I told you. Come on.' Sol took his arm, steering him away from the sitting room, towards the bedroom. 'Shit, man. Haven't seen you like this in *years*.'

'He was swearing at you.' Noah lay on the bed, blocking the light with his arm while Sol drew the curtains. 'Your mate. Called you a little fucker.'

'Banter.'

Noah kept the crook of his elbow across his eyes. The migraine was an iron spike through his left temple. 'Get rid of him.'

'Yeah.' Sol covered Noah with the side of the duvet he wasn't lying on. 'You gonna puke?'

'Not if I can help it.'

Sol said something like, 'Hang on.' Noah couldn't hear past the thundering in his skull. He badly wanted to pass out. It wasn't nearly dark enough in the room. May Beswick . . .

He should be looking for May Beswick. No, for her killer. That was what he should be doing. Not lying here praying to pass out. He was meant to be looking for a killer.

'Bucket.' Sol put a hand on Noah's elbow, an awkward, brotherly pressure. 'In case you puke.'

It'd been years, but Sol hadn't forgotten what to do when Noah was like this. Pure chance he was here to close curtains and fetch buckets, and who the hell was in the flat, calling him a fucker, threatening him? No good . . .

Noah had to sleep. He had to be unconscious. It was the only cure he knew, when the pain got this bad. 'Tramadol,' he begged his brother. 'Bathroom cabinet.'

Sol said, 'I'm on it.'

19

From the bedroom window in Taybridge Road, Marnie watched the vertical climb of the city, its high-rises topping out the trees in Battersea Park, dwarfing the sprawl of the Garrett estate.

Engineered exclusion: the higher the city climbed, the fewer people had access to it. It wasn't just the penthouses at the power station that cost millions. The cloud-kissing office space was reserved for the elite. For the view from the Shard you needed a pricey ticket and a security scan. More and more of London was being fenced off for fewer and fewer of its citizens, the private stamping ground of the super-rich, or corporations. Good news in this particular case; she was looking for someone who had access to the showroom flats at Battersea Power Station, and the list wouldn't be long – she'd have it in her hands by the end of the day – but she mistrusted the illusion of control. She didn't control the crime scene any more than she controlled the city. No one did. Unless it was the killer, with his rhetoric of terror. What had Noah called it? *A normal reaction to social living.* Marnie turned from the window to look at May's bed.

Clean sheets, a faint scent of fabric softener. Katrina had made the bed on the morning May went missing, before she discovered her daughter wasn't coming home. She'd put clean underwear in the drawers of the dressing table where May's hairbrush was gathering dust. Even before the discovery of May's body, this room had looked odd to Marnie. Everything neat and untouched under a sticky topcoat of dust. Books, CDs, toys – nothing had been moved recently, picked up and put down, used. May had been gone less than twenty-four hours when Marnie first came here, but the room had looked unlived in. 'She didn't spend a lot of time in here,' Sean had said. 'Preferred the kitchen or the sitting room, sometimes Loz's room.' The posters on the walls belonged to a much younger girl. 'She put those up years ago,' he said. 'Never took them down.'

May hadn't lived in this room for a long time, not in the way most teenagers lived. Messily, chaotically, joyfully, grumpily. Impossible to imagine her lying on the bed listening to music or chatting on the phone to her friends. No ghost of her was in the room, then or now. Where had she gone to do her living? To the place where she was killed? CCTV put her less than a mile from here on the night before she died. So close to safety, but she chose to stay away. Assuming she'd had a choice.

'She hated it in here.'

Marnie turned to see Loz standing in the doorway to her sister's room. In the school uniform that swamped her, black hair brambly, eyes big with unshed tears.

'I love my room, love to be sent to it. *Go to your room, Laura!* as if it's not the best place in the house anyway. But May hated it. She liked the garden, digging, planting stuff. She'd come into my room sometimes. I liked it when she did that, but I could never get her to stay. She

101

was always moving around. Like . . . a kite.' Her voice caught.

'Where's your dad? Your mum went for a lie-down, I think.'

'They both did.' Loz put her eyes around the room. 'I suppose this's how it'll stay now. That's what parents of dead kids do, isn't it? Keep their rooms exactly as they were. Except there's no point with May's. Not like she was ever *here*. Not really. Not in ages.'

Marnie recognised the spikes Loz was putting out to keep the world at bay, each one as sharp and shiny as a needle. It was frightening how much of herself she saw in Loz's anger, and her grief. She'd wanted to leave this task to Noah, believing him better equipped to communicate with Loz. She hadn't wanted to be the one asking the questions or seeing at close quarters this girl's pain. It was never easy being face to face with a grieving relative, but Marnie made the effort because it was important. This was different, not any less important just . . .

Harder. Because Loz reminded her so much of the girl she'd been.

'Who's looking after you? Is there someone here apart from your mum and dad?'

'Just them.' Her face was small inside the storm cloud of hair. 'Where's Noah?'

'He got sick. I took him home.'

'Sick from seeing May?'

'No, he had a migraine. He gets them sometimes.'

'Mum felt sick after the mortuary. I told her it was probably adrenalin.' Loz put her thumb between her teeth. 'Do you think she knew who did it?'

'Your mum?'

'May. Most people are killed by someone they know.' Those fierce eyes, demanding the facts more plainly than

102

Marnie had served them to her parents. 'D'you think May knew her killer?'

'What happened with Alice Gordon? You fell out.'

'She was a liar. She said May was coming back, that everything would be all right. We'd be a *family* again, as if that was ever true to begin with. She wasn't even a *good* liar. Did you have to put up with that when your parents were killed?'

The sudden switch of focus made Marnie blink.

'They were murdered,' Loz said. 'I read about it online. Your stepbrother did it when he was fourteen. Stabbed them to death. May wasn't stabbed, was she? She was strangled.'

'Loz . . . It's not appropriate for me to be talking to you about this. Not without an adult present.'

'You're an adult.'

'I'm a detective.'

'Same difference. It would only be a problem if you were trying to get evidence out of me, which you're not. I'm just talking. I'm always talking. I open my mouth and stuff falls out. Until I put my foot in there and stop it, that's what Dad says.'

Her dad had a point.

'Are you part of the Forgiveness Project?' Loz said next. 'It's a prison project to help victims come to terms with what's happened, by forgiving the people who hurt them. Will we have to forgive whoever killed May? Because I won't. Even if Mum and Dad join in, I'm not forgiving them, ever. May wouldn't want me to.' Her stare shone with tears. 'Did you have to forgive Stephen Keele? I googled you after you came here that first time. Actually I googled Noah, but I couldn't find anything so I googled you and I found loads. From five years ago. He's nineteen now.' She bit her lips together until they turned white.

'Have you forgiven him? Did they make you do that? I mean, did you *have* to, because you work for the police? Or as therapy? I bet you had a lot of therapy. You'll be telling us about that next, I suppose. Bereavement counselling, coming to terms with our loss. Or will you wait until we've buried her? If they bury her. Probably it'll be a cremation.' She wiped at her eyes, looking angrily at her wet hand. 'We'll have to wait anyway, won't we? For you to finish the post-mortem, and even then you'll keep her body for evidence. For when you find the killer, which could take ages. You could have her for months and months. Mum and Dad don't get that she belongs to you now, to the police. And then to the courts. She's evidence. She's yours.' She gulped a breath, rubbing her hands on the front of her jumper. 'It's not your fault. No one's saying that. But it's *someone's* fault. The killer's, for starters. I won't ever forgive whoever did it. Just so you know, if you start any of that forgiveness shit around me? I won't join in, not even to please Mum and Dad. I can't do much to help. I can't do *anything*. But I can hate whoever did it.' She had started to shake. 'I can do that.'

Marnie had stayed silent while the girl burned through her questions. Now she said, 'That's allowed. You're allowed to hate whoever did this.'

'Do you hate him? Stephen Keele. Even after five years?'

'I don't know. You're right, they wanted me to take part in the Forgiveness Project. I signed on because it was expected of me. But I didn't believe in it, not then.'

'It's *stupid*. Weak.'

'It can feel that way. But it can wear you down, always being angry.'

'I'd rather be worn down than *accepting*.' Loz shoved her hair back from her face. 'I hate people who do that, who *carry on*. As if none of this,' pushing her hands at her dead sister's room, 'ever existed. I won't do that. Ever.'

She turned her black stare on Marnie again. 'Everyone says *I'm* the strong one. May was the dreamer, always tuning out or joining in. No questions, no trouble to anyone. Well I hope she was trouble to *him*. The killer. I hope she fought back. Even though she never did when she was alive. Not like me, the *awkward* one. The troublemaker. Well, fine. *Fine*. I wish I could make trouble for whoever did this. Strangled her and whatever else he did. When will you know what he did? When's the postmortem finished?'

'Soon.' Marnie felt battered by the girl's unhappiness, her need for answers. Her throat ached with not answering. And with empathy.

'Will you tell me?' Loz demanded. '*They* won't. Or I'll get some safe version. But I want to *know*. I need to know what happened to her. Will you tell me? Promise me you'll tell me.'

'I can't do that. I'm sorry. I won't make a promise I can't keep.'

'They told *you* everything. You didn't have to imagine worse than what actually happened.'

'I was twenty-eight.' And there was no *worse* than what happened.

'You were looking for something.' Loz bit her lip at her sister's room. 'What?'

'The Sharpie pens.' An answer, of sorts.

Loz's stare jerked to Marnie. 'The pens.' Scuffing her toes at the floor. 'You saw, then.'

'I saw the writing. Did you? Before. When May was living here.'

'She showed me. She wanted me to write something once.'

Marnie thought of the words she'd read on May's body. Ugly, insulting words. A solitary act, she'd thought. Facing a mirror or locked in the bathroom. She hadn't imagined an accomplice when May wrote those warnings on her body. 'What did you write?'

'I didn't write *anything*. I wasn't going to put stuff like that on my sister. It was all lies, and *shit*. It was shit. I *hated* it.' Blinking back tears. 'I hated what she wrote.'

'Of course. I'm sorry. But she asked you to write something?'

Loz gave a reluctant nod, not wanting to betray her sister's secrets. 'She called it a game.'

'How long had she been playing it?'

'I don't know. A long time.'

'Did she play it with anyone else?'

Loz hesitated again. 'Sometimes. I don't know for sure, she never said, but I think so.'

'School friends?'

'No.' Loz flashed a look of scorn. 'That place throws a fit if you don't have the right hair extensions. She didn't have any real friends there.'

'Where were her real friends?'

'Loz . . .' Sean Beswick stood at the other end of the corridor, his face haggard, staring at his daughter. 'What are you doing?'

Loz slid her eyes at Marnie with a tiny shrug. 'Asking questions, being difficult, you know me. But you needn't worry. DI Rome's far too professional to talk to me without an appropriate adult present.' She pushed away from the wall. 'I'll make tea. That'd be helpful, wouldn't it?'

Her dad watched her go down the stairs. Marnie read fear in his face, as if he was scared of the questions Loz had been asking. Or scared of her grief.

Why was it so hard for the Beswicks to hug their younger

daughter? Were they afraid of losing her too? The trou-blemaker. How many awkward questions had Loz asked her parents before Marnie arrived? No answers to some of those questions, not yet, maybe not ever. How exactly May had died, what had happened to her in the twelve weeks after she went missing. Why she was killed, and by whom. Marnie wanted the answers as badly as Loz did.

Sean said, 'Sorry. I had to stay with Kat. She's in a bad way.'

'Of course. I understand.'

'You had questions. Do you need both of us? Kat could really use some sleep.'

'I wanted to ask about May's friends, anyone she might've been in touch with during the three months she was missing.'

'You spoke with her friends.' Sean rubbed at his eyes with the heel of his hand. 'Didn't you? We gave you all the names we knew, weeks ago.'

'We spoke with her friends at school, but was there anyone else, someone we might've missed? A boyfriend, perhaps.'

Sean had seen his daughter in the morgue, her clipped nails, clean hair. Hadn't he wondered where she'd been, to be so well looked after? No, of course he hadn't. He'd seen his daughter dead, strangled. There was no 'well looked after' in that. Marnie couldn't stop thinking like a detective, but nor could she expect a grieving parent to think like one.

'A boyfriend? No. I'm sure there wasn't.' A tension in his face, like a barrier to her question. 'If she'd been seeing *anyone*, even someone we hated her seeing, we'd have told you. We'd have given you that name first, probably.' He dropped his hand to his side. 'Why? Do you think she knew whoever killed her?'

'She was missing for twelve weeks. We need to establish whether she was with the same person all that time, or somewhere else. Perhaps somewhere safe, until recently.'

'She was safe *here*.' He punched the wall. '*We* had her safe. Until he took her.'

Marnie waited a moment out of respect for his pain. 'May was an artist. You showed us her sketchbooks. Some of her pictures . . .'

'Battersea Power Station.' He nodded. 'She was obsessed with the place, did an art project recording its history, the way it's changing. When you told us where she was found, I thought we should've looked there sooner. She was always hanging around the place.'

'We searched the area twelve weeks ago,' Marnie reminded him. 'The house-to-house team was very thorough. Did May ever visit anyone on the Garrett estate? A girl, perhaps?'

'No.' Another emphatic answer. 'None of her friends lived over there. Some of the kids at the school for sure, but none of her friends. We told the girls to steer clear of the place. Why are you asking? Did she . . . Do you know who did this? Have you found someone . . .?'

'Not yet, but we have a recent CCTV sighting of May and another girl—'

'Recent? You mean she was *here*, out on the streets? Why didn't she come *home*?'

'We don't know. I'm sorry.'

'What girl?' He dropped his voice, hearing Loz on the stairs. 'Do you have a name?'

'Not yet. She has dyed red hair. Very red, and lots of it. She's slim, about May's height and age. Do you remember seeing May with a girl who answers that description?'

Sean shook his head, eyes straining at her face. 'She lives on the Garrett?'

Loz was carrying two mugs of tea. She held one out for her father, the other for Marnie. 'The Garrett's full of losers. Druggies and cutters, all the worst kids in the school. The police came and gave us a talk because some boys brought knives into school and said they got them from the Garrett. You can get anything over there. Glue, booze, fireworks.'

'Okay, Loz. That's enough.'

'I was just explaining to DI Rome why we wouldn't go there. No *nice girls* on the Garrett.' She looked directly at Marnie, her big eyes unblinking. 'You'd only go there if you were into self-harming or some shit like that.'

'That's *enough*.'

'Go to my room? Fine by me.' She walked to the room, closing the door behind her with a click.

Her unhappiness stayed in the corridor after she'd gone, making the air parched and spiky, lodging its ache in Marnie's chest.

Tim Welland was frowning at the incident room's white-board, a mug of tea in his right paw. He acknowledged Marnie's return with a nod at May's photo. 'How're her parents holding up?'

'Barely.' Marnie removed her coat, going to her office.

Welland followed her. 'I saw the CCTV footage. Is that Traffic's girl from the crash?'

'Joe Eaton thinks so, and he's our only eyewitness at the moment. We should get the crash site footage soon. Nothing from Battersea worth watching.' Her wrists ached from gripping the steering wheel too tightly. 'I'd like to go back to the Garrett to look for this missing girl.'

'You think she might be next?' Welland sucked tea

from his mug. 'Or you think she's part of it? She and May didn't look too friendly from what I saw on the CCTV.'

'No,' Marnie agreed. 'But *she* didn't carry May up to that flat.'

'She could've held the doors open for whoever did. Easier with two.'

'I'm not ruling it out. I just don't think it adds up, yet. The night of the crash she was in shock, half dressed. She could've been hit by Eaton's car. She was lucky she wasn't.'

'Luckier than Logan Marsh. Or May Beswick.' Welland walked to the window, looking down. 'If she had a narrow escape, why not come to us? Why change her clothes and run?' He turned to study Marnie, his heavy brow lowered. 'Give me reasons. Beyond the fact that you know what it feels like to be a teenage runaway.'

'She changed her clothes on the Garrett, so either she lives there or she has friends there. Neither of which disqualifies her from seeking police protection if she's in trouble, but it makes it less likely, don't you think? When was the last time anyone on that estate looked to us for help? Apart from Mrs Tarvin, and she's not exactly our number one fan.'

'That's who she reminds me of . . . Kathy Bates in *Misery*.' He lifted his mug in a toast. 'Sorry, you were saying? Something about this being more than empathy on your part.'

'Do we need to have a chat, sir? Only I'm picking up a vibe.' She moved her hand, gesturing at the distance between them. 'It's a long time since I was a teenage runaway.'

'Nineteen years. Not that long, in the scheme of things.' He watched her across the lip of the mug, his left eye

110

still shadowed by the cancer that had threatened his sight three years ago.

His illness had dragged Marnie out of the pit of her grief. The thought of losing him made her throat hot even now. She wanted to make him smile. 'This isn't empathy. I've no idea what was in May's head when she left home, but I think she *did* leave. I don't believe she was snatched. I'm not even sure she was with the killer until recently.'

'So who got her pregnant? Nothing about a boyfriend in any of the statements twelve weeks ago.' He set his empty mug on the desk. 'I can't think of many sixteen-year-olds with the wit to keep quiet about their sex life. Most of them are splashing relationship updates all over the internet.'

'Not May, or not according to her family. Her sister said something interesting just now: none of May's real friends was at school. Perhaps we've been speaking to the wrong people and she had a life we've not uncovered yet. Not online. A *real* life, somewhere she went twelve weeks ago. Somewhere she met Traffic's girl.'

'On the Garrett? That's not an escape route, it's a dead end. And she had a good life. Her parents were well-off, decent people. No evidence of abuse or neglect.'

'No,' Marnie agreed.

'But you think she ran off. Because she got pregnant?'

'The conception was more recent, so no. I think she left because she couldn't live there, for whatever reason. I think she was terribly unhappy.'

'So this was . . . teenage angst?'

'At that age? Unhappiness can feel like the end of the world. And the Beswicks are . . . box-tickers. I've nothing against them. I feel sorry for them. But in twelve weeks, I haven't seen either one of them hug their daughter. Not even in the last forty-eight hours.'

'Laura Beswick is how old? Thirteen?'

'Young enough to be hugged after her sister's been killed.'

Welland digested this in silence. 'How's DS Jake?'

'On the mend, I hope.'

'You and I know what this looks like. The start of a spree, maybe a serial offender.' He avoided saying *serial killer*, but he grimaced. 'Your boy's good, but he's young. If you want someone with more years on him, or someone senior . . .'

'I don't, thanks. Noah saw what it was straight away. One look at the crime scene and he was working the case. He knows what we're in for. I need his brain and I value his instincts.'

'All right, Boy Wonder stays. Just make sure you've got what you need to keep on top of this. I'd prefer no more corpses in high-profile places, don't want some tourist stumbling on a dead girl in the London Eye, or anywhere else for that matter.'

'I'd like Traffic's cooperation. Are they thinking of going after Joe Eaton?'

'I'll find out. Tell me what the CCTV chucks up, and when and how you want the press briefed.' His face knuckled with distaste. 'The Battersea developer's bitching like a low-grade secretary with my hand up his skirt, so I'll deal with that, too.'

He retrieved his empty mug from Marnie's desk. 'This? Runneth over.'

Ron was scowling at the whiteboard when Marnie rejoined the team. 'Can you believe the bloody shambles over at Battersea? The millions they've sunk into those flats, and they can't connect the ruddy cameras. Talk about getting your priorities straight.'

'Do we have all the statements from the on-site security?'

'For what they're worth. The only one with his eyes open was the ex-squaddie, Ledger. I wouldn't trust the rest of them to see shit if it was sitting on their top lip.'

'What about the list of people with access to the site in the last twelve weeks?'

'We're still pulling it together. So far we've got contractors, developers, estate agents. The estate agents need to give us the lists of people who've been for viewings. You can imagine how they're falling over themselves to do that. Then there's a media party they threw on site six weeks ago. Press, photographers – anyone they hoped would spin a good story and help them shift a few flats. We're waiting on the invite list.'

'Let's start ticking names off the list we do have. How's house-to-house going?'

'The usual, "strangers in white vans". We've got white vans coming out of our arses round there. I'm heading back in a bit. We're getting a picture of Traffic's girl to show around, right?' When Marnie nodded, he said, 'How'd you get on with the parents?'

'Sean Beswick's convinced May never went near the Garrett, but Loz suggested it was worth following up. If Traffic's girl is living there, I want her found. She's our best lead to what happened to May in the hours before she was killed.'

'You think May might've been on the Garrett? She'd be in Emma's book, wouldn't she? Not much gets past our Emma.' Ron sounded proud of the pensioner.

'We know May was obsessed with Battersea Power Station. She drew these.' Marnie handed him the sketchpad she'd borrowed from Sean. 'Make copies for the board. We need to concentrate on the site where she was found and the place where Traffic's girl was last seen.

So the power station, and the Garrett. And let's take another look at May's movements in the last twelve weeks. I want a sense of where she was living. Was she on her own, or with friends? I don't think she was on the streets. She was healthier than she looked in her last family photo. I want to know who was looking after her, and where.'

Like Welland, Ron said, 'Her parents are decent people. We didn't find anything to say otherwise, and we dug deep. Kids run off for all sorts of reasons. Look at Clancy Brand, six months ago. His parents had more money than most, spent it all on alarm systems. Bet *their* cameras were connected. Pair of security nuts. But he still scarpered.'

The Brands had been paranoid about danger, obsessed with what was lurking outside their front door. Hiding from living, and trying to force their teenage son to do the same. Clancy had ended up running away at the age of fourteen – headlong into danger, but preferable, he'd said, to being at home. Some parents bred fear in their kids just by trying too hard to keep them safe. Marnie didn't believe the Beswicks fell into that category, but her conversation with Loz had forced her to rethink what she thought she knew about the family.

'Leave the Garrett until the morning,' she told Ron. 'I want the team fresh and on their toes for the interviews with whoever's been at the power station. OCU's organising extra manpower, but I want you heading up the Garrett team. You know the territory.'

As if the estate was a war zone.

It *was* a war zone.

'Enemy lines,' Ron said, reading her mind. 'I'll draw up a battle plan.'

20

Aimee

May came home. I heard her voice. I was out of bed, half dressed, not caring about his rules or anything else except May.

She'd come back. She was here. I *heard* her.

I was on the stairs in his white nightie with the light making me see-through, nothing between me and his stare, when I stopped.

It couldn't be May. How could it be? She wasn't coming back. They mustn't see me like that. *He* mustn't see me. Tonight at supper . . .

He turned his back on all of us.

Washing at the sink, but his back was turned too long and he kept washing and washing, his shoulders working until I thought he must be crying. He didn't say a word all through supper, didn't tell me to eat up or to drink my water, didn't look at any of us.

Something had happened. It happened days ago, after Gracie left, like she'd taken a bit of him with her when she ran, the bit making him work properly, keeping him from being just broken.

Everything must always, *always* be the same. But it wasn't. It was different. He was different. It was all candle-and-scrubbed-face now. No hugs, no *good girl.*

Christie was trying to act normal, but her eyes were all over the place. 'Ashleigh, you can take first turn in the bathroom.'

He didn't move, didn't speak. He smelt sharp, like firewood.

The candles put a deep, deep shadow up his back.

Christie licked her fingers and pinched at the flames until all the candles were out, just four grey threads of smoke twisting up from the table.

Much later, I thought I heard May's voice. But I was wrong. I'd got her sketchpad in bed with me, hidden under the covers. The room stank of sickness. *I* stank. I needed to wash, and change the sheets, but I didn't have the energy. It was easier to stay where he wanted me, curled in bed. Just like when I was little and Mum kept me home from school, saying I was sick. She was a worrier, my mum. That was why I thought I knew what I was up against with Harm, because I recognised the symptoms, the checking and double-checking, the routines. I thought he was like my mum and that he'd look after me the way she did, until she couldn't any more.

Catastrophising, that's what they call it. A social worker explained it to me, after they took mum to the hospital. It's when you let negative thoughts get out of control and worry yourself to death over things you can't do anything about. You put all these measures in place to try and keep safe but they don't work because your brain just comes up with worse and worse stuff to worry about. They think there's a paranoid gene now. If there is, maybe they'll find a cure. But it'd be too late for Harm. It was too late for my mum, and he was worse than she ever was.

At least May wasn't eating his freeze-dried crap any longer or listening to his lectures about the dangers out there. *He* was the danger. Just him. May was okay now. I made myself repeat that – she was okay. Hard to believe we were ever stupid enough to feel safe here. Except he was different, said we mattered, *I* mattered. You won't understand what that means unless you've lived on the streets. It's not just being hungry or cold or afraid of getting beaten up, or worse. It's the way it *empties* you. I could stand to be hungry and cold, I could even stand to be raped, although it only happened once. What I couldn't stand was not being *me* any more.

Homeless is just another way of saying *empty*.

That night Harm found me . . .

All right, so I thought he wanted sex. I went with him thinking that was what he wanted. I wasn't stupid. Men didn't pick homeless kids off the street without a reason, but I thought it was fair enough given what he was offering. A bed for the night, decent food, a place to get dry. It'd been raining for days and I was sick with a cold, coughing my guts up; I didn't need to fake it at the beginning.

I undressed and showered, because I stank. It was good to get clean. Then I climbed into bed and waited for him. A clean bed, smooth sheets. As long as he didn't hurt me, it'd be worth it. I wasn't a child; I knew what I was doing, and I thought he couldn't be that bad because the room was warm and the house felt safe. Just an ordinary house, but Christie kept it nice. I didn't meet her or the others that first night. He took me to a room at the back and it didn't have a lock so he couldn't keep me there if he turned out to be a pervert. It felt okay. After I'd been in the bed for a bit, I rolled on to my stomach because I thought he might prefer finding me like that, but he never came. I fell asleep waiting for him. Next morning, I put on my old clothes and went downstairs. He was cooking pancakes for breakfast. The smell made my mouth water.

'I left clean clothes out. Why don't you get changed and I'll wash those old things.' He served the pancakes on to two plates. 'After breakfast,' he said, smiling at me.

The pancakes were amazing.

Afterwards, I went upstairs and changed into the clothes he'd left out: black school uniform skirt and a white shirt – and I know what you're thinking, but it wasn't like that. The skirt was long and he'd put tights out, proper thick tights, not kinky. The clothes were a better fit than my baggy jumper and jeans. When I looked in the mirror, I saw a flat-chested schoolgirl.

The uniform was embarrassing, but I got used to it. It didn't mean what I'd thought it meant. Nothing did, with Harm. For weeks I was expecting him to touch me, especially because he was always sending me to bed. My cough cleared up after a few days in the warm, eating good food. But he didn't want me to get well. He wanted to look after me. Just like my mum did, before she got too sick. I used to be good at faking it with her. It was harder with him.

Six of us in that house. It must've belonged to his parents, because I kept finding baby photos. A girl, and a boy who looked like him. Christie, Grace, Ashleigh, May and me – all in that house until he said it was getting too small, too hard to keep safe. He hated the garden even after May tried to bring it back to life. Too easy to break into, he said. That was when he found us the new place, with my own room, the split-level flat.

I hated being in bed there. Ashleigh bitched about it. I got her into trouble by saying she wanted me doing chores like the rest of them. That pissed him off. But I was going mad up there, like that crazy woman in the attic except I wasn't a woman, I was his sick little girl.

Solitary confinement causes hallucinations. Did you know that? People go mad in prison. I was staring at the ceiling with its damp patch like a map, trying to imagine open sky, birds, trees, an outside world. May and the baby . . .

Sometimes I couldn't breathe. It was like something was squatting on my chest. A child or a dwarf, heavy and hot. I could hear its blood beating and feel the weight of it pressing me down. Its breath was disgusting, like something greasy died in its mouth.

Whole days lying like that, and he was glad I was too sick to get up. He didn't care if I was suffocating, if some fucking *thing* was on my chest, holding me there until I wanted to write all over myself, the way Grace did, and May. Except I'd write the truth. About what he was doing to us in that prison we were stupid enough to call home.

Real pain and imagined pain feel the same. They trigger the same part of the brain, the social worker told me. Towards the end, Mum didn't know which threats were real and which weren't. Both kinds felt exactly the same, her brain freezing, then flooding with adrenalin, making her run, making her jump. We're the sum of our fears, the social worker said. That's what I'd write. I'd get the wire out of May's sketchpad and scratch words all over myself, *Harm did this*, and *fuck him* . . .

For making Grace run, and May run. For taking away my best friend, the only thing that made this place bearable. Just me now. Me and the thing squatting on my chest with its breath in my face so I couldn't get up from that bed even if I wanted to, so it was less and less like faking and more and more like the real thing.

It was what he wanted.

Me in that bed. Face up or face down, it didn't matter. Except I suppose in the end he'd lay me face up, with my hair brushed neat against the pillow. I didn't think he'd bury me. I didn't think he'd want to do that. He'd keep me there until I started to smell so bad, someone would call the council to take me out, a foul thing in a black bag, and no one would know what to do with me. No one would know who I was or where I'd come from. Not unless they dug really deep, all the way back to that subway, the tunnels where we sheltered from the rain, where I was sitting with soaking feet, coughing my lungs up. Until he came.

May was okay. She *was*.

I heard them downstairs, Ashleigh and Christie, moving slowly so as not to disturb him.

Could I trust Christie? No, I couldn't trust any of them. He'd made me into a monster, their bogeyman, his precious little girl. No wonder Ashleigh hated me.

The wire wouldn't come out of the sketchpad, not easily, but I was working at it. I thought if I warmed the metal with my fingers and my breath, I could make it come.

It wasn't much of a weapon, but it was all I had.

I wasn't going to make it easy for him. No point with May gone.

I'd kept the peace for her sake, but I was on my own now.

Me and him, that was what it'd come down to.

It was always going to come down to that.

Me, and him.

21

Noah woke to a dark room. His temples throbbed but the migraine had retreated, leaving a soft wash of endorphins in its wake. He lay blinking at the pillow, light-headed with relief.

'You're awake?' Dan was at the side of the bed.

'Mmm.' He moved on to his back, nursing the blissed-out feeling. 'What time is it?'

'Nearly seven.' Dan found his hand and held it. 'How're you feeling?'

'Better.'

Dan's thumb traced his knuckles. 'Sure?'

'Yes. Come here.' He pulled Dan down into a kiss, making it hard enough to persuade the pair of them that he was fine. 'Where's Sol?'

'He went out when I got back, said you needed to sleep it off. He'd been keeping an eye on you. He's a good brother.'

Noah didn't argue. He swung his legs over the side of the bed, waiting to see if the pain would catch up with him before he attempted to stand. Sometimes the migraines hung around for days, but this one was gone.

He let out the breath he'd been holding and smiled at Dan. 'I'm fine. Really. I couldn't fake it if I wasn't.'

Dan said simply, 'I know.' Then, 'Convince me again?'

Noah leaned the pair of them into the wall for a long minute, convincing Dan with his hands and his mouth, before saying, 'I need to eat.'

'I noticed.'

'Come on.' Noah made a fist of their hands, moving in the direction of the kitchen.

When he passed the sitting room, he stopped, remembering the raised voices. Someone in the flat with Sol . . . A mate, his brother had said, but he hadn't sounded friendly. Calling Sol a little fucker, threatening him . . .

The room was empty, just the shape of Sol's head in the sofa cushions. No mess, or nothing that wasn't explained by his brother's relaxed attitude as a house guest. 'Where'd Sol go, did he say?'

Dan shook his head. 'Just that he wouldn't be late.'

They went through to the kitchen. Dan opened the fridge, started taking out eggs, ham.

'Was he on his own when you got home? No one here with him?'

'Just you,' Dan smiled across his shoulder, 'passed out on the bed.'

Sol had got rid of whoever it was before Dan came home. Noah wished he could remember exactly what he'd heard. If Sol was in trouble, and if he'd brought that trouble back here . . .

Noah wanted to know.

Dan was breaking eggs in a bowl, making omelettes. 'You want cheese in this?'

'Yes please.' He dug out his phone. 'I should call in, let them know I'm okay.' He walked into the hall, where the signal was stronger. He dialled Sol's number first, getting voicemail. 'Hey, it's me. Thanks for earlier. Let me know you're okay.' He hung up, and dialled Marnie's number.

She answered on the second ring. 'How are you?'

'I'm great. Slept it off. Any news?'

'Nothing that can't wait until the morning. Get some rest. Fran will have the PM results for us tomorrow. I'll call you if there's anything to report. Otherwise I'll see you first thing.' She rang off.

Noah pocketed the phone and returned to the kitchen. 'That smells good.' His body was craving a hit of fat. He poured orange juice for himself and a beer for Dan, setting two places at the table.

'I heard the news.' Dan was finishing the first omelette under the grill. 'About the body at Battersea. Is that your case?'

'Yes.'

'No wonder you had a migraine.' Dan's blue eyes were a shade darker than usual and there was a thread of worry in his voice, but he didn't ask any more questions. 'Sit down, I've got this.'

Noah's phone purred in his pocket.

A text from Sol: *Cool*, and a smiley face.

Sol code for *Leave me alone*.

Noah returned the phone to his pocket, and concentrated on the food.

A basket of petunias hung over the door to number 14, a shiny car in the driveway. Wheelie bins stood sentry up the street, as they had in Taybridge Road. But this was the other side of London, a different house. Marnie hadn't lived here since she was eighteen. Thirties, detached, big kitchen at the back and a downstairs bathroom where her dad would get clean after washing the car, a brown Vauxhall, his pride and joy. The car in the driveway was an Audi now, but the basket of petunias was the same, red and purple, turning to black under the street lights.

Marnie rested her wrists on the steering wheel, looking through the windscreen at the house her parents had left to her. Everything had been left to her. They'd insisted that Stephen was a permanent fixture in the family – they'd fostered him for six years – yet he wasn't mentioned in their wills. A silent, skinny eight-year-old, the first years of his life a living hell – that was as much as she knew when they began fostering him. No details were given, and she hadn't wanted any. He'd kept her parents occupied, deflecting their attention from her. She was glad, busy with her new life, her career. She'd got away. A teenage runaway, Welland had called her, seeing some likeness to May Beswick, but Marnie had never been mute in this house. She'd been a scourge, making the whole place rock around her. A wild child, running on anger. The memory made her cringe against the steering wheel.

Do you hate him? Stephen Keele. Even after five years?

May had never fought back at home. Loz was the angry one. Like Marnie. Like Stephen, except he'd buried his anger too deep for Children's Services to see. He'd lived quietly in this house, spying on her when he was twelve and she was twice his age, watching her undress in the guest bedroom, reading her skin's secrets, the tattoos she'd kept hidden from everyone. She'd been good at keeping secrets. The drinking when she was fourteen, the affair when she was sixteen . . .

Some houses soaked up secrets.

Was it like that at Taybridge Road? May and Loz and Sean and Katrina all living under the same roof but knowing so little about each other's lives, each other's pain?

The steering wheel pressed into her chest as she leaned to look up at the bedroom, her room until she'd moved out. Empty for three years, then Stephen's for the next six, before he took a knife to her parents one morning when Marnie was miles away, at work, being a detective.

Have you forgiven him? Loz hadn't waited for an answer.

Above the hanging basket, the bedroom window was curtained, quiet.

What was it like for Stephen living in her room? Why didn't he paint the walls, put her belongings into the attic, move the furniture around? Because he knew he wouldn't be staying? Or because he liked the room full of her things? He'd said he'd killed them for *her.* His latest assault, a new bid for her attention, or something more?

What had he found, or thought he'd found, in her room? What clues did she leave to make him think she was unhappy here? Dust in her hairbrush, like the one in May's room? Untouched books? A room that hadn't been lived in, not properly. A room she'd run from again and again, unable to stand the feel of its walls around her.

He's such a little boy, Marn, and he's had such a hell of a life. We'd like to make it up to him.

What had they done to deserve what he did? What had they done to deserve her anger, her restlessness, her running away?

She sat back in the car, shutting her eyes.

It was late. She should be home with Ed, not parked here looking at a house she'd not visited in five years, arranging the tenancy from a distance because she wasn't ready to sell, still hoping for evidence she'd missed, clues to why he'd done it. She closed her hand around the house keys. The leather fob was soft, polished by skin, by her father's fingers. The keys bit their teeth into her palm. It was her house. She could serve notice on the tenants and go inside, search for the clues she'd missed. The clues they'd all missed. If Stephen was a strange boy, no one had noticed it. Not her parents, or their neighbours. He hadn't run from this house even once. He'd helped her dad to wash his Vauxhall, played on the swing in the garden, gone to school every day. His social worker couldn't explain it, and nor could the prison psychiatrist. Her parents had never said a word against him to anyone. Mrs Poole, the neighbour, had seen Marnie storming out and sneaking home, but she never saw Stephen put a foot wrong. Not until that morning when the screams brought her out of her house and into the street.

None of the neighbours had noticed anything amiss on Taybridge Road before May went missing. 'A happy family,' they'd all agreed. But it wasn't true.

Was it true for anyone, anywhere?

Marnie started the engine, checking the car's mirrors before pulling away from the kerb.

A CCTV camera had been bracketed to the wall of number 8. Home security. It hadn't been there five years ago. The murders had made people nervous, given this nice neighbourhood a bad reputation. She wondered what reputation Taybridge Road would get when the news broke that May had been murdered, whether the penthouses at Battersea would ever be sold, and to whom. Who would want to live in a place where a body had been found?

She drove back up the road, respecting the speed limit, past the detached houses with their yellow-lit windows and locked doors.

Was May's killer in a house like this?

He was out there somewhere. She'd delayed going home in the hope of news, some glimmer of the trail that had felt warm in the early hours but was increasingly chilly.

This man knew how to hide. You didn't display a body the way he'd displayed May unless you had a good hiding place and a fully functioning survival instinct.

Clean crime scenes filled her with dread. Clean killers were the hardest to catch. It was possible that May wasn't his first. It looked certain that she wouldn't be his last.

Marnie turned left, past streets and streets of houses with the same face, home to Ed.

Ed was lying on the sofa in an old T-shirt and the bottom half of a pair of pyjamas. Headphones on, laptop open, watching an episode of *Seinfeld*. Odd socks on his feet, bed-head brown hair, his fringe in his eyes. Marnie sat on the arm of the sofa and leaned down to kiss him.

'Have you eaten?' He pulled the headphones off.

She could smell bacon. 'Have you?'

'I had breakfast.'

'Breakfast was hours ago.'

'I ate it for supper.' Ed stretched, putting the laptop aside. 'I had a craving. I'll make you some.'

'In a bit, maybe.' She kissed him again, keeping her hands in his hair. He tasted of brown sauce, the same colour as his eyes. 'You have some bad habits, Belloc.'

'Mmm.' He smiled against her mouth. 'You're the best of them.'

She moved her hands to his hips, liking the narrow feel of him, the way they fitted together. After a while, they went into the tiny kitchen at the back of the flat.

'I heard the news about Battersea,' Ed said. 'Is it that poor girl?'

'May Beswick, yes. We'll be confirming it in the morning.'

'Murder?' Ed cracked an egg over the pan.

'Yes.'

He shook his head, saying nothing more.

Marnie found a bottle of Guinness in the fridge and shared it between two glasses. 'Very clean,' she said. 'Very nasty, but very clean.' She knew Ed would understand what that meant.

'How are her parents coping?' he asked.

'Not well. Her sister Loz is very angry. I'm worried there's no one taking care of her.'

'Family Liaison?'

'Not a good match. Loz is tough. It's going to be hard to help her. She needs someone who won't deal in platitudes. She's thirteen, but in some ways she's much older than May was.' Marnie watched Ed turn the bacon in the pan. 'May was pregnant. Just a few weeks.'

He looked across at her. 'The killer?'

'We don't know. That would be the obvious conclusion, but the way he left her . . . It didn't look like a sex crime. Not to me, or to Noah.'

Ed served the food on to a plate and sat with her while she ate. Marnie hadn't known how hungry she was. When she'd finished, they returned to the sofa with what was left of the Guinness.

'Loz asked me about Stephen,' she told Ed. 'She'd googled me, wanted to know if I was taking part in the Forgiveness Project.'

'What did you tell her?'

'That I didn't believe in it when I signed up. She can't imagine ever forgiving the person who killed her sister. I said I understood but that anger can be exhausting. Stupid of me. It's too soon for her to be hearing stuff like that. She *should* be angry.'

128

Ed put his hand on her waist, his fingers finding the bare skin at her hip. It reminded her of what else Loz had said. 'May wrote on herself with Sharpie pens. She was covered in writing. We think the girl from the traffic accident was the same. They knew each other. We can't find the other girl, but we think she might be on the Garrett estate.'

'That's a hard place to search,' Ed said.

'Yes . . . I used to write on myself, before I saved up the money for the tattoos.' She'd never told anyone this before. 'I know what it's like to keep those sorts of secrets. And the ritual, the urge. It helped me to cope, strength-ened my resolve to escape. It was like a first draft of my rebellion. Not that it was ever much of a rebellion.' She was exhausted. Emptying herself of words, letting Ed take custody of these new confidences. 'May wrote "whore" in her hands, in the palms of her hands. And other insults, all over her body. She was very unhappy. But why would she write that word? If the killer got her pregnant, it wasn't likely to have been consensual.'

'What words did you write?' Ed asked her.

'Oh, nothing like that. Pretentious nonsense, like the tattoos.'

Ed stroked his thumb over the words inked across her hip: *Places of exile.*

'Seventeen teenage girls are reported as missing in London right now. Even if we narrow it down to the ones who went missing recently, that's four lost girls. And this man. He's not going to stop.'

'Very nasty, and very clean.'

'Exactly. He looks after them, to begin with. May wasn't malnourished, no signs of restraint. She wasn't living on the streets. If she was with the killer all that time, then he took good care of her. That's why I don't think he'll stop.'

'How did he find her if she wasn't on the streets? Do you think she was snatched?'

'I'm worried she might have found *him* rather than the other way around.'

'Social networking?'

'She didn't use a computer or a phone. Not like other teenagers, anyway. We checked the laptops in the house – nothing. She liked sketching Battersea Power Station. Perhaps that's where he saw her. If she was lonely, he might've been able to use that, flatter her, make her feel special . . .' She was thinking of a party sixteen years ago, a stranger offering her a light, his mouth crooked around a cigarette, his eyes a hot band of blue. Adam Fletcher. Her first big mistake.

'Loz suggested we look on the Garrett. Where we're looking for the other girl.'

'I know a couple of the families there.' Ed scrubbed a hand at his scalp. 'From what they tell me, they're living under siege.' He worried about the families he was helping; not in his nature to switch off when he left work. Time to change the subject.

Marnie reached for the Guinness. 'Stephen's being moved to an adult prison.'

'When?'

'In a few months. He'll be twenty, and things have been tricky at Sommerville lately. They must have moved his name up the list.'

'Which prison, do you know?'

Marnie told him. 'Can you think of one with a worse reputation? I can't.'

Self-harm, suicide, violence. Stephen's new home ticked every box, and unlike Sommerville, it was in Greater London. No excuse not to visit, if she intended keeping the promises she'd made to the Forgiveness Project.

Ed was silent, his hand still on her hip, fingers smoothing her skin.

'I said I'd go and see him before he's moved. Paul Bruton thinks I might give him a pep talk, help him to focus on his rehabilitation.'

'Isn't that Bruton's job?'

Marnie held his hand to her hip. 'Stephen knows about this. The tattoos.' Ed's fingers were on the words, *Places of exile*. 'He told me that's the reason he did it, the reason he killed them.'

'What . . .?'

'I should have told you sooner. He must have watched me at the house, years ago. Saw the tattoos but never mentioned them. Then the last time I visited, he said that's why he killed them. "I did it for you."'

'What bullshit.' Ed's eyes were bright with anger. 'That bastard.'

'I know it's bullshit. It's okay.' She smiled, holding his hand steady. 'I know he's lying. I even know *why* he's lying. To mess with me. It's what he does, all he has. At least . . . We talked about care packages. Someone's sending him food, books. He claims he doesn't know who it is. His parents, probably. But he's not interested in playing games with them. It's my attention he wants.'

'He should've been moved to an adult prison years ago.'

'I don't want him moved.'

'What?' Ed stared at her.

'Part of me wants it, of course. Part of me's glad he's finally going to be punished properly. But it's a part of me I'm not proud of. Just as I'm not proud of the way I behaved when I was May's age and going off the rails, chasing trouble, putting my parents through hell. *That* girl cheered when she heard the news of Stephen's move, but I don't like her very much. I'm trying not to be her any longer.' She waited, but Ed didn't speak, staying close, hearing her out. 'Do I want my parents' murderer to be punished? Yes. But do I want him in a place where he's likely to learn worse ways to hurt other people? No. And that's if he survives. There's a good chance he won't, and if he dies before I've come to terms with what he did, I'm not ready to cope with that. I want him alive and safe, and *growing up*. I'm managing to do that, and I want the same for him. I want him to regret what he did. Even if he can't explain it, I want him to be *sorry*.'

Six months ago, a bereaved mother had told Marnie that remorse was a weapon: 'If there was someone you wanted to punish, someone who'd hurt you personally, that would be the way to do it. Make them feel remorse. Inflict it on them in whatever way you can. There's no pain like it.'

Remorse as punishment. Was she hoping to *hurt* Stephen by forcing him to face up to what he'd done? She didn't want to believe it, but it had the hard ring of truth.

'You're remarkable,' Ed was saying. 'Did you know that?'

She shook her head. '*Remarkable* would've moved on by now. Or opened up to you much sooner than I'm managing.'

'Take me with you?' He curled his hand around hers. 'Next time you go to see him. Not into the detention unit. I'll wait outside. You needn't talk afterwards, just let me be with you.'

'Of course.'

'I know someone at the prison he's being moved to. This man's been in isolation for eight weeks, from choice.'

132

'How is he?'

'Paranoid. Hostile. That's what isolation does. Makes you afraid of everything.' Ed shook his head. 'You're anticipating danger the whole time and you're scared, so you start behaving aggressively, which makes people avoid you. The stuff of vicious circles.'

Marnie was intimately acquainted with the damage fear did, how it stopped you in your tracks, eroded your identity. According to plenty of profilers, killers were afraid – of seeing what they couldn't have, and of always being alone. They felt threatened, especially by those they selected as victims. 'Fear gets a foothold,' Marnie's therapist said in the months after her parents' deaths, 'and we close all the doors. Living is hard. Living with fear is even harder. To get past that place you have to fight, and it might be the toughest thing you ever have to do.'

How many girls were fighting right now? How many were living in fear, perhaps even with May's killer? And was *he* afraid, too? Feeling threatened, isolated—

Her phone rang and she reached for it.

Tim Welland said, 'Sorry to spoil your evening, but since Traffic have stuck a road cone up mine, I thought I'd pass the pain along. They're treating Logan Marsh's death as manslaughter. Joe Eaton is waking up to a whole new headache tomorrow.'

'Have they arrested him?' Marnie uncurled from the sofa, putting her feet on the floor.

'They're interviewing the bereaved parents. Sergeant Kenickie, d'you know him? One-man circle-jerk, cracks walnuts with his bare face . . . He's taken a dislike to your eyewitness, for reasons best known to himself. I thought you'd want to know he's on the warpath.'

'Thanks for the warning. How are Logan's mum and dad?'

'Much like the Beswicks, I imagine. With divorce thrown in, and no surviving sibling.'

'I should give them my condolences . . .'

A nod in Welland's voice. 'Kenickie would approve. He's rattling a sabre for your missing girl. Expect interference if you find her.'

'I'll take all the interference on offer,' Marnie said, 'if we can find her alive.'

22

Christie

Harm was washing at the sink, the light sharp on his shoulders where the muscles moved like music, up and down, up and down. Scooping water from the basin on to his face. The light catching the water, making it shine, polishing his neck and hands.

The water in the sink ran brown, but his neck was silver-white. Christie wanted to kiss it. She wanted to rest her face between the blades of his back and whisper what she knew.

Ashleigh.

Ashleigh was gone.

No more slick smiles across the supper table, or clumsy fumbling with her eyes. She was never any good. He'd thought he could help her like the others, but he couldn't. She was rotten when she came here, when Christie brought her back.

'Let me help,' she whispered.

He didn't hear, still turning his hands under the water. Christie knew what he was thinking. So many girls living on the streets, needing help. Lost girls, like his sister, Neve. Sometimes he could save them, set them straight. When they listened, if they wanted to be saved.

Ashleigh had only wanted one thing, the usual thing.

The one thing he wouldn't give them.

But here was Harm with the light like an axe on his back, shining, shining.

Not knowing, not yet, what she'd done.

23

Noah reached the station just after 7 a.m.

Marnie was in the incident room, tacking photos to a clean whiteboard. Girls' faces, smiling, posing for the camera. One was blowing a kiss, another so heavily made-up it was hard to see how young she was underneath. Noah counted seventeen photos. Marnie had highlighted four, next to the evidence board from Battersea. She'd added new sketches by May, of the power station.

'You're early. Is that coffee?'

'Yes.' He'd bought two flat whites on the off-chance he wouldn't be the only one wanting to get started this early. 'These are the girls who've gone missing in London recently?'

'None of them looks like Traffic's girl, but at least three went missing in circumstances similar to May's. Normal family life, no inciting incident, nothing taken from the house. The fourth is the right time and place but the investigating officer thought she was a classic runaway. Trouble at school, tension at home, new stepfather . . . If we counted every teenager who ran away from home or care, we'd need evidence boards from here to Rockall. Runaways typically come back. Missing means taken.

SARAH HILARY

These girls? Are missing.' Marnie sipped at the coffee. 'I'm filling in time until we can get started on the house-to-house, or until Fran calls. All this could be nothing. Coincidence.'

Noah stepped up to the board to study the girls' faces, and to memorise their names.

Sika Khair wore a mask of make-up, false eyelashes, a piercing through her bottom lip, black and gold tiger stripes in her hair. Sixteen years old. The girl blowing a kiss to the camera was Ashleigh Jewell. Hair scraped into a high ponytail, the kind worn by the girls on the Garrett. Lots of lip gloss, a vest top showcasing spray-tanned cleavage, distinctive crook in her nose, heavy ear lobes pierced in three places, studded and hooped in gold. Fifteen, missing for nearly four months. The other two girls had the same spray tans, vest tops, heavy lips and lids, skin-lifting ponytails.

'Why do they do that?' Noah wondered. 'Dress so alike? We see it all the time where we live. The girls look the same even when they're out of uniform. Boys too, as if there's a factory somewhere cloning them . . . Must make it hard if you don't fit the mould. That's a lot of pressure, conformity.' He thought of his own teenage years, choosing to come out when his mates were joining gangs. Hard to swim against the tide, to keep your identity when everyone around you was acquiring camouflage of one kind or another. He thanked God for Dan, the safe place they'd found, their happiness. 'Which is the girl with the stepfather?'

'Sika Khair.' Marnie perched on the edge of the nearest desk in jeans and a grey crewneck, her hips as narrow as a boy's. She looked at the faces on the board and she must have been thinking the same grateful thought about safe places, because she asked, 'How's Dan?'

'Good, thanks. How's Ed?'

She nodded. 'We should get together some time. The four of us.'

It was a big deal. She ring-fenced her privacy. Noah said, 'I'd like that.'

'I don't mean a dinner party.' She arched an eyebrow, smiling with one side of her mouth. 'I wouldn't subject you to that. Maybe a drink somewhere.'

'Great.' Noah smiled back. 'I know a couple of places. Not a club crawl,' he added, in case she was imagining that.

'What makes you think we wouldn't be up for a club crawl, Detective?' She was deadpan, but he knew her well enough to recognise the laughter behind her eyes.

'In that case we'll plan a night of it. Does Ed like tequila?'

'He spent a year in Mexico. I'd call it a safe bet.' Marnie nodded at the board, refocusing the pair of them. 'Fran thinks May was dehydrated. The full autopsy should give us a better idea.'

'So maybe she wasn't as well cared for as we'd thought? Street kids get dehydrated. Did the security at Battersea not throw up anything?'

'Nothing on the front-of-site CCTV or the riverside. We're getting plans through this morning to see how else he might've got her in there.'

'These sketches of May's are good.' He followed the pencil lines, remembering what Dan had taught him about art. 'She loved the power station, but it scared her too.'

'Show me?' Marnie moved to stand at his shoulder.

Noah traced the lines with his thumb. 'It's the places she's put the shadows. Intimidating, don't you think?' The chimneys, grotesquely tall, looked almost human.

'She was somewhere with a view into the site,' Marnie said. 'When she drew these.'

'Inside the Garrett, in one of the south-facing flats? The floor above Mrs Tarvin's would have a view like this. Do you think he was holding her on the estate?'

'I doubt it. Too many people around. How would he get her there without being seen? The residents might not like the police, but they wouldn't hide a child killer. No, I think he'd want somewhere private. Maybe Colin can work up a structural plan of the area, possible hiding places with a view of the chimneys.' She made a note and stuck it on the corner of Colin's monitor. 'I've told Ron to head up the team on the Garrett. I need you to work on a profile of our killer, see whether it matches anyone with access to the site in the last twelve weeks.'

'What's happening with Traffic's girl? Do they know she's connected to May?'

'Not yet, or not officially. Welland's going to break the news just before the press briefing.' Marnie's phone rang. 'Fran. Are you ready for us?'

'And waiting.'

The mortuary cafeteria was doing a brisk trade in bacon sarnies. Marnie and Noah joined Fran at a table with a view of Westminster's rush-hour traffic.

'So . . . May was pregnant, as you know. Seven or eight weeks at the outside. No evidence that the sex was anything other than consensual. No lesions or bruising, nothing nasty. Nothing recent, either. No semen in or on the body. No DNA that wasn't hers.' Fran crunched a piece of toast. 'I got the writing off with baby oil. No needle marks, bruises, abrasions. No defensive wounds, nothing to suggest she put up a fight. But nothing to say she was unconscious when he strangled her. Most fit young people would fight back.'

'When *he* strangled her,' Noah said. 'You're sure it was a man?'

'Based on the bruising, the width of the palms, yes.'

'Have you narrowed down the time of death?'

'No more than six hours before she was found, no less than two. That puts it between about one and five p.m. You found her just after seven, so it was close.'

'He drove a dead body through rush-hour traffic, and got her into that site before it was dark.' Noah was making notes on his phone. 'That was risky.'

'And he's careful. He wore latex gloves, kept everything clean. Stomach contents is interesting. Lentils and smoked fish. Not what I'd have picked for a last lunch. The fish was full of salt. Highly preserved, in other words. She'd been eating too much salt for some time, judging by the state of her kidneys.'

'Hypernatremia.'

Fran nodded. 'Generally caused by a deficit of free water in the body, only rarely by excessive sodium intake. My first thought, seeing the bloods, was an eating disorder, but she wasn't malnourished and her protein intake was high. No evidence that she was sweating excessively, or being denied water. Skin condition was good. She'd been eating too much salt. If the rest of her diet was like the fish, then maybe dry-salting, brine-curing – whatever our ancestors relied on before we invented fridges.'

'What would the symptoms be?' Marnie asked.

'Thirst, mainly. Possibly vomiting or diarrhoea. No evidence she was suffering from either of those. Twitching, tremors. Confusion's common with elderly sufferers. Worst-case? Seizures. Coma. May's wasn't a worst-case, but it was severe. I'd have wanted her IV'd if she'd been found alive.'

'High protein intake,' Noah said. 'But wasn't she a vegetarian?'

'According to her parents.' Marnie nodded. 'For six months or more. Sean thought it accounted for her lack of appetite.'

'Well she ate a lot of meat in the last twelve weeks,' Fran said. 'Salt-cured, possibly. But red meat. No other way to account for the protein levels. Quinoa's good, but it's not that good.'

'Talk us through the strangulation. You said she didn't put up a fight?'

'My best guess? She was lying on her back. He was over her, probably kneeling either side of her torso. If he was a big man, and she was sleeping when he got into that position, it would've been hard for her to put up a fight.' Fran sipped at her tea. 'He was quick. Didn't drag it out, didn't play with her. He just wanted her dead. I'm going out on a limb and saying this isn't a sexual psychopath. He wasn't taking pleasure in what he did, or not in the sadistic sense.'

'He left her on display,' Marnie said. 'Naked, more or less. That suggests contempt.'

'Perhaps he wanted us to see the writing. She'd been keeping it a secret, hadn't she? From her parents, friends. It was the first thing we saw when we looked at her. Not her body, not even the marks he left on it, but her writing. Not what *he* did to her, but what she did to herself.'

'Do you think he'll want to do it again?' Marnie asked. 'Even if he took no pleasure in it. The ritual, the way he laid her out. The *spectacle*. That made us think he'd do it again.'

'I can't argue with that.' Fran finished her tea, glancing at her watch. 'Over to you.'

Back at the station Noah said, 'Learned helplessness. I'm wondering if that's what happened to May, why she didn't put up a fight, ate his food, all that long-life crap, meat when she's a vegetarian. Learned helplessness means complete passivity, your victims emotionally and physically unable to disobey, or to take the initiative.'

'Stockholm syndrome with a topspin.' Marnie suppressed a shudder. 'Here was me hoping she was somewhere safe until he found her.'

'The boyfriend theory? It could still be true. If Fran's right and the killer's not a sexual psychopath, then perhaps he's not the one who got her pregnant.'

'But he's the one who found her. And maybe not just her . . . Yes, DC Tanner?'

Debbie was waiting outside Marnie's office. 'Ruth Eaton's being discharged this morning. Joe called to let us know. She says she saw our missing girl and she can give us a description.'

'Good. Get her help with the e-fit. This girl was one of the last people to see May alive. We need to find her as a priority, whether or not she's at risk.'

'Will do, boss. Oh, and Calum Marsh is downstairs asking to see you. I didn't make any promises, knowing how busy you are.'

'I'll see him. Thanks.'

On their way downstairs, Marnie told Noah, 'Sergeant Kenickie, Serious Collision Investigation Unit, has been stirring things with the Marshes. Expect an angry father seeking justice for his son.'

'Then this is damage limitation, or public relations?'

'So cynical . . .'

Calum Marsh was sitting in a plastic chair under a poster warning visitors of the penalties for violent or threatening behaviour. In an open-collared shirt and dark trousers, elbows on his knees, hands hanging, head down. He looked beaten, defeated.

'Mr Marsh. I was so sorry to hear about Logan.'

Calum got to his feet, shaking Marnie's outstretched hand. He was wearing the laced shoes he'd struggled with at the hospital. No neck brace or sling, but fatigue had set new shadows everywhere on his face. 'Thanks. I'm not here to give you a hard time.' He nodded at Noah. 'I know you're flat-out busy, but I wanted to know if you'd found her, the girl from the crash. Is she okay?'

Sergeant Kenickie might have done his best to stir up a sense of injustice in Logan's parents, but he'd failed, at least in the case of Calum. Nothing but bleak concern in his face as he searched Marnie's for news of the missing girl. 'Logan volunteered at homeless shelters, made friends with kids who were living rough. If this girl was like that, he'd want to know she was safe.' He rubbed at his collarbone, blinking sleep-starved eyes. 'She can't have meant to cause the crash. From what Joe said, she was desperate . . . I've been trying to remember details about how it happened, anything that might help you.' He looked ready to fall down. 'I want to help.'

'Let's find a quiet room,' Marnie said. 'And would you like a cup of tea, or coffee?'

'You're busy,' Calum repeated, but he followed them to the interview room. 'I don't mean to take up your time. I can't do anything for Gina, not with the divorce . . . I'm a fifth wheel.' He tried to smile, but his mouth wouldn't cooperate. 'Can't stand being useless.'

Behind the pain in his eyes was blame, and guilt. Had Gina accused him, maybe just by her silence? Noah hoped not. It was easy to see how heavily blame would sit on this man's shoulders.

'We're talking with Ruth Eaton this morning,' he told Calum, 'hoping for a better description of the girl.'

'Ruth's okay. That's good.' He put his fingers to his

eyes as if he was afraid of finding tears, but it was only pain spilling over. 'Their kids'll be glad to get their mum back.'

The room smelt of sweat and carpeting. They sat at the metal table.

'I know Sergeant Kenickie's been in touch,' Marnie said. 'I'm sure he'll keep you informed of progress with the investigation.'

'Kenickie,' Calum repeated. His jaw moved. 'Yes, I met him. He's got it in for Joe, expected me to feel the same, but Joe wasn't driving *my* car. I should've reacted faster.'

'From what Joe said, there was no time for that.'

'Ruth saw the girl, that's what I don't understand. They both saw her, but I didn't. How could I have missed her? She must've been directly in my headlights. If Joe swerved into us, then she must've been right *there*.' He jabbed a thumb at the table. 'I should've let Logan drive. He had his provisional licence and he was doing *great*. Nothing fazed him. He was all grown up, didn't need my help with anything, not any more. If I'd let him drive . . .' He shut his eyes for a second before blinking them back open. 'He'd want to know the girl's okay. It cut him up to think that kids like that were out there. I know Kenickie thinks it's *her* fault for walking out into the road, but Logan wouldn't agree.'

'How's his mum doing?' Noah asked.

'She's got her parents round. Logan's gran and grandad. Mine died a couple of years back; he only had Gina's mum and dad.'

'Do *you* have someone?' Noah hoped the man wasn't on his own. 'Brothers, sisters?'

Calum shook his head, as if he didn't matter. 'This girl . . . If she's homeless, on the streets, Logan would want to help. He wasn't volunteering for his CV or because his mates were doing it. He *cared*. The kids he met . . . They were like him, that's what he always said, just that he was lucky enough to have a roof over his head. "Dad, can you imagine living like that? Being scared and on your own, no one to look out for you?" It cut him up. That's what I keep thinking about. How much he *cared*. He'd hate this girl to be lost, no one taking care of her. Her family wondering where she is, missing her, praying for news . . .' He hugged himself the way Loz had done, rocking slightly in the seat, blinking at nothing. 'I hope Ruth gives you something. I wish *I* could. Wish there was some way I could help, but I didn't see her. Didn't see anyone, just Joe's car coming right at us, and . . . Logan, hitting the windscreen.'

'Poor bloke,' Noah said, as they climbed the stairs back to the main office. 'How long d'you think he'll keep blaming himself?'

'Until he's able to forgive himself, or until his wife does.' Marnie wore the thread of a frown at the bridge of her nose. 'Or until Kenickie backs off. He's gearing up for a manslaughter conviction. If he keeps on at Gina and Calum about the need for someone to pay the price for Logan's death—'

Her phone thwapped. 'DC Tanner, we're on our way back up . . .' Her eyes sharpened as she listened, and she switched to speakerphone. 'Again, please.'

'We've got another one.' Debbie's voice was stressed by static. 'Another body.'

'Where?'

'On the Garrett.'

Marnie and Noah turned back down the stairs, towards the car park. 'Who's on the scene?'

146

'DS Carling and the house-to-house lot. Ron's sealing it off.'

'Another girl?'

'Yes, but he says it's not like May. This one's been dumped.'

'Dumped where? Who found her?'

'Kids. He says kids.' Debbie sucked a breath. 'Not drugs, it's not an overdose. They've had their share of those on the Garrett, but this girl was killed. Strangled, he thinks. Like May, but not clean. He strangled her and then he dumped her.'

'Is it Traffic's girl?' Noah asked.

'Ron doesn't think so. She's too big, and there's no writing as far as he can tell. He's sealed off the scene and he's waiting for Forensics, and you.'

'Tell him we're on our way.'

24

May Beswick's murder had been loud, her body shouting at Noah from the bed in Battersea. This new murder was noiseless, shoved against a brick wall still bleeding with recent rain. A tall girl, bigger than May, but the killer had turned her into a smudge, as if a dirty thumb had been rubbed against a hard surface unthinkingly to remove a stain.

Marnie crouched, gesturing for Noah to join her. He saw the distinctive crook in the dead girl's nose. The fleshy lobes of her ears were pierced in three places.

Marnie said, 'It's Ashleigh Jewell. Yes?'

'Yes . . .'

The girl from the whiteboard at the station, the one blowing a kiss at the camera. Her face was closed, lips swollen shut by blood, blackish, a match for the marks around her neck.

The scratch of litter across tarmac made Noah turn his head.

Ron Carling caught his eye and glanced away, as if the crime scene shamed him.

'Do you think it's the same killer?' Marnie asked.

Noah looked. 'Yes.'

'Tell me why.' Her voice was freighted by calm, holding him here, making him respect the crime scene despite its smell, its meanness, its futility.

'The bruises. The pattern is the same. Big hands.'

'What else? Is anything else the same?'

At first glance this killing had nothing in common with May's. Ashleigh Jewell was fully clothed. No writing in the palms of her hands or on the visible part of her sternum. Her hair had not been brushed. She'd been dumped in the corner where the flats met – a litter trap reserved for communal rubbish – her body at a right angle, brick wall at her back, her face half buried in chip papers and an empty pizza box, her hands lying loose, no sign that she'd been tied. Wearing what looked like a school uniform, white shirt and black skirt, opaque tights, trainers on her feet. No watch or rings, no jewellery. Her hair was loose, its ends matted by the shallow tide of rubbish. No make-up or nail polish, although Noah could see the speckle of old polish at the base of two of her nails, a gritty line of silver close to her cuticles.

'She's clean.' He looked across at Marnie. 'She's *too* clean. And she smells the same as May. Underneath, I mean. Soap and water. She smells of Pears soap.' His nose pinched shut, protesting the memory. 'The uniform is . . . wrong. As if someone dressed her to look like a child. She didn't look like this in the photograph you put on the board.'

'No, she didn't.' Marnie straightened and stepped back from the body.

Noah moved with her, working the perimeter for evidence that needed tagging. A breeze sucked at their crime-scene suits, and at the polythene tent erected too late for the handful of residents who'd gathered to see what was happening. A bad vibe from the crowd, too much static making Noah's scalp prickle. He sensed a fight coming.

Marnie glanced in the direction of the rubberneckers before crouching back by the side of the dead girl. 'Go and see what's happening. I'll finish up here.'

Noah moved outside the cordon, ducking under the tape to where Ron was holding a trio of teenage girls at bay, his hands raised against their questions.

'The fuck's going on?' one of them demanded. Dressed for school, but not like Ashleigh Jewell. This girl wore skin-tight trousers and a black sweatshirt with the neck ripped out, a white vest top underneath. Black-spoked eyes, blusher slashed on her cheeks, hair gelled back into a ponytail that looked like a whip. Everything about her was hard and tight, from her laced ankle boots to her lips. 'The fuck's going on?' Pointing her chin at Ron.

'Back off. Now. This is a crime scene.'

'Yeah? Sat on someone, did you?' Throwing a laugh in the direction of her friends.

'Back off, Abi. I won't tell you again.'

'I saw you with the old cow again.' She was Abi Gull, the fire-starter who was terrorising Emma Tarvin. 'Eating her fucking biscuits like a *pig*.'

Ron said, 'Go to school. Or nick off, it's all the same to me. But this is a crime scene and you need to stay clear of it.'

'I've a right to know. I gotta live here. You get to piss off home when you're done wringing us out.' Craning her neck and catching Noah's eye. 'What?' Tightening her stare. 'Saw *you*, too. With that old bitch. Like she's your gran, sucking up.'

'Aw, Abi.' One of her friends, same uniform, but baby-faced. 'He's *peng*.'

'So? He's still a pig.'

'You would, though, wouldn't you? *I* would.'

Laughter from the other two girls, but Abi just stared at Noah. 'Someone died. You're wearing the white suit. Who's dead?'

Ron put his hands up again, palms out towards the girls. 'Clear out, now.'

'I fucking *live* here. I've a right to know whether one of my mates is dead.'

'We don't know, all right? Who she is or how she died. Let us do our job, make this place safe.'

'You wouldn't know *safe* if it sucked your dick.' Stretching the stare to Noah. 'Fucking feds, you're all the same. Even the black ones are dirty white.'

She turned on her heel and walked away, flanked by her friends.

Noah recognised the shape they made. Arrowhead formation, Abi a stride ahead of the other two, all three swaggering. They might not be the only gang on the Garrett, but they owned it. The other two girls kept turning their heads, scoping for enemies. Noah had grown up watching kids like this. Avoiding kids like this.

'That was Abi Gull,' Ron said. 'In case you were in any doubt.'

'I wasn't.' Noah unzipped the forensic suit and pulled it off.

'No wonder Emma's living like a whipped dog with that little bitch working her patch.'

'She's thirteen, is that right? She looks older.'

'They all do. This dump adds ten years to everyone who sets foot in it.' Ron squinted across Noah's shoulder and raised a fist in greeting. 'Kenickie, you old bastard.'

A middle-aged, middleweight man came across the tarmac towards them, his stare flat and sand-coloured, a shade darker than his thinning hair. Acne scars as deep as fire damage marked his face. He nodded towards the tent, juggling the keys to his BMW in one hand, seat-belt creases in the front of his shiny suit. 'This our girl?'

'We don't think so,' Noah said.

'Where's your ball-grinder of a boss?' Kenickie showed his teeth, humourless. Smoker's teeth, shrunken gums. 'Only I don't fancy chatting to the monkey.' He looked at Ron. 'Logan Marsh died, remember?'

Ron nodded. 'We're pretty sure this isn't her.'

'She was seen here.' Kenickie swivelled his neck, scanning the estate. 'Right?'

'Looks like it.'

'But you lost her.' Bringing his stare back to Ron. 'Got your best people on it, have you?'

'We're looking. Joe Eaton's wife's helping with the e-fit—'

'Eaton's a mess. Admits he was drinking even if he scraped the breath test.' Eyeing Noah. 'I thought you lot were up to your ankles in dead body over at Battersea.'

'And now this.' Ron nodded. 'Never rains but it shits.'

'Pervert.' Kenickie had his eyes fixed on Noah. 'Over at Battersea. Heard it was a sex killer.'

Ron ran a finger under his shirt collar. 'Too soon to say.' He glanced at Noah, then away.

'I'd like to run house-to-house here.' Kenickie bounced on his heels, car keys jangling in his fist. 'For our girl.'

'Best leave us to ask the questions. Now that we're talking two murders.'

'Three if you count Logan. I know his mum does. She's in bits, and his dad's not much better. Pure chance he was on that road that night. They need answers which make sense. Something better than a silly cow out for a stroll and a tosspot full of carbonara and Chablis.'

'We're working on it.' Ron rubbed at his face. 'Trust me, you wouldn't want the gig. We'll be at this all day and night.'

Kenickie bared his bad teeth again. 'Just as well you've got a stroke of midnight on your side.'

A stroke of midnight. Noah hadn't heard that insult in a while, but apparently Kenickie was old-school.

'All right, mate.' Ron's hands came up, the way they had when Abi Gull was baiting him. 'Leave it alone.'

'Good luck with your pervert.' Swinging on his heel, away from them. 'Laters.'

Ron let out a breath through his teeth. 'Kenny never was a morning person.' He shot a look at Noah, on the brink of an apology.

'Cheer up.' Noah clapped a hand to his shoulder. 'I've had cocktails with worse names.'

Ron squinted at him.

'Midnight Pervert. Half price at happy hour . . .'

They turned their heads as Marnie came out of the tent, peeling off the forensic suit. 'DS Carling, I need you to make a start on the house-to-house. Who saw what, and when.' She tidied her red curls from her face, nodding at Noah. 'We need to confirm the identity of the dead girl and contact her family . . . Was that Traffic's radio interference I was hearing?'

Ron nodded. 'They still think the missing girl is theirs. Logan's mum's in pieces.'

'A lot of mothers are in pieces. May Beswick's, and now this new girl's. Show the e-fit during the house-to-house, but in connection to May. The RTC can wait.'

'That's what I told Kenickie.'

Marnie nodded towards the knot of onlookers. 'Are those our arsonists?'

Abi Gull and her gang had retreated to the shelter of

a doorway, but they were watching, arms across their chests, chins pointed towards the tent.

'I told them to stay away.' Ron scowled. 'They should be in school.'

'Did they see the body?'

'I don't think so,' Noah said. 'They knew someone had died, because of the suits and the tent. But I don't think they saw anything.'

'Ashleigh went missing in Dartford about four months ago. If anyone on the estate saw her before today, we need to know.'

'You're thinking they're connected,' Ron said. 'May and this girl, maybe even Traffic's?'

'Too soon to say. No definitive similarities between May's killing and this one, but let's keep an open mind. Without encouraging too much speculation from the public, or the press.'

Several onlookers were holding phones, filming the scene.

'We'll be on YouTube before we know it,' Ron grumbled.

'Let's hope some of them had their eyes open last night, or early this morning.'

Fran Lennox was making her way towards them, blonde hair spiked with gel, wearing grey jeans and a leather jacket, looking like a pixie dressed as a punk. Abi and her friends watched narrowly, as if they were seeing a rival, not a pathologist. 'Another fine mess for me?' Fran asked.

'Dead girl. DS Jake and I are seeing a link to May Beswick, but you might want to put us straight on that score.' Marnie nodded at Noah. 'I've got this. You get back to the station and see what you can find out about Ashleigh Jewell's last known whereabouts, and her next of kin.'

25

Fran knelt at the dead girl's side, studying her swollen face before touching gloved fingers tenderly to the bruises.

Marnie stayed back, not speaking, watching Fran work. Her presence made the scene feel less like an annihilation. She was taking the temperature of the crime, finding its pulse, feeling for its edges. Until now, Marnie had wanted to cover the dead girl, hide her from prying eyes. She'd seen the way Ron had looked at the body, embarrassed and angry. A teenage girl dumped like garbage, appallingly vulnerable. With Fran kneeling beside her, she looked safe.

'She's been dead less than twelve hours, possibly as few as six. Time of death? Let's say between nine p.m. and one a.m. Strangled, like May. Same pattern of bruises, same size too. You might be right about it being the same killer.' Fran raised her head and scoped the immediate area. 'Not much of a tableau here. No writing, either. Unless it's well hidden, under her clothes.'

'Not a tableau, but a message, maybe. Just as there was in the penthouse.'

'May as an angel, this poor girl as trash?'

'If it's the same killer.'

'She's May's age. Or thereabouts.'

'We think she's Ashleigh Jewell. Fifteen. Went missing from Dartford four months ago.'

Fran was holding one of the dead girl's hands, studying the nail beds. 'Another one he looked after, if this is the same killer. She was in good shape until yesterday.'

'He finds them, takes them in, feeds them. Then he kills them. Why? Why take good care of someone you're going to discard like this?'

'Maybe they disappoint him.' Fran was feeling the girl's abdomen. 'No obvious sign that she's pregnant, but I'll let you know if that's another similarity with May.'

'They disappoint him,' Marnie repeated. 'Or he finds someone else. Someone new.'

'You said this girl was missing for nearly four months. That puts her in the same time period as May. He's not taking them one at a time.' Fran straightened. 'Assuming it's the same killer.'

'Too much speculation.' Marnie nodded. 'Let me know how you get on with the results, anything connecting this killing to May's, or anything ruling out a connection.'

'Security's been tightened at the power station, I take it?'

'No chance of anyone leaving a second body in the same place. That might have necessitated leaving Ashleigh out here.'

'Riskier, in some ways.' Fran looked around. 'No privacy. More chance of being seen, and of the body being found quickly.'

'Perhaps that's what he wanted.'

'Not the first death on this estate this year, unless I'm wrong.'

'Not even the first murder. A fatal stabbing back in

January, and a drug overdose not long after that.'

'I remember the overdose,' Fran said. 'Young boy, ten or eleven. Horrible waste of a life.'

They exited the tent. Most of the crowd had dispersed, but Abi Gull was keeping vigil with one of her friends. The third girl was gone. Abi had one foot wedged behind her on the wall, paint-stripper stare aimed at the crime scene. The sort of girl who didn't miss a trick. Marnie wondered how much she'd seen of what had happened here between 9 p.m. and 1 a.m., whether she could be coaxed into sharing whatever knowledge was sealed behind her tight lips.

'She looks friendly,' Fran murmured. 'If looks could kill, I'd be doing your post-mortem next.'

'She's in good company. I doubt there's anyone here who sees us in a good light, and that includes the pensioner being terrorised by our friendly neighbourhood arsonist over there. A deficit of trust all round. And much too much paranoia.'

'I remember hearing a pregnant mother on the news,' Fran said, 'from an estate like this. It might even have been this one. Saying how she despaired of having another daughter, knowing what was in store for her. Sons are no better, I imagine. Drugs, violence, aimless crime. No future, as the tabloid headlines would have it. But in some ways the girls have it worst. They learn to lie and accuse and seduce. No tricks they don't know and won't use – that was the gist of the mother's story. You see girls like that one,' looking towards Abi, 'and you know she's right. How old would you say she is? The same age as our victim?'

'Younger,' Marnie said. 'She's only thirteen.'

The same age as Loz. Abi's hardness didn't look like an act, but Marnie was wary of buying it wholesale.

157

On a place like the Garrett, everyone assumed a disguise. Survival camouflage, adapt or die. Those photos on the whiteboard . . . Ashleigh blowing a kiss for the camera. May, sweetly demure. Had the killer seen through the disguises? Or was it the disguise that attracted him? Lost girls, their identities already corroded. Easy to dominate, easy to control. Was that how he chose them, *why* he chose them? Girls like that would always want a place to hide, and there were so many different ways to do that. By staying behind bolted doors like Emma Tarvin, or strutting with a gang like Abi Gull. Easy to imagine that Abi wasn't scared of anything, but Marnie had worn the same disguise when she was thirteen, reinventing herself, refusing to examine too closely the girl she was becoming. Hiding from everyone, even herself.

Abi Gull didn't move from the wall where she was propped, watching Marnie's approach through slitted eyes. Her mate stayed nearby, trying to match Abi's disdain but failing, her mouth a nervous pout when Marnie produced her badge.

'Detective Inspector,' Abi read. 'You're the boss, then. Seen you on the seventh floor.'

'You've got sharp eyes. Did you see anything this morning, or last night?'

'What, like a murderer?' Contempt sing-songing her voice. 'Like a dead body?'

'Exactly like that.' Marnie put the badge away.

'Just you lot putting up that marquee like it's party time over there. Who was she anyway?'

'We don't know yet.'

'I heard she was naked,' Abi's friend said.

Abi shot her a look of undiluted contempt. 'Shut up.'

158

'You're Abigail Gull.' Marnie nodded at the other girl. 'Are you Natalie Filton?'

'Yeah.' Colouring. 'And?'

'Where did you hear she was naked?'

'Nowhere.' Dropping her eyes to the tarmac. 'I made it up.'

'Yeah, you did.' Abi looked at Marnie. 'Was it drugs?' A new edge in her voice. Was Abi dealing, or taking drugs herself?

Marnie shook her head. 'We don't think it was drugs.'

'So she was killed.'

'Yes.' The straight answers made an impression; Marnie saw the girl sizing her up properly. 'If you've seen any strangers, it would be useful to know.'

'Everyone round here's a stranger.' Abi flicked a finger at her ponytail. 'No one gives a shit about anyone else. Not even your mates.'

Natalie bit her lip, but didn't speak.

'Seriously. I could drop dead of an overdose and not one of them would bat an eyelid. That cow on the seventh floor would throw a party in your marquee. Tea and biscuits, bitch.'

'Mrs Tarvin keeps an eye on what happens here. She told us she'd seen a girl two nights ago. A stranger. Red hair, wearing a white shirt. Did you see her?'

They shook their heads, no hint of deception in either girl's face. Abi said, 'If you're taking witness statements from that cow, you're desperate.'

'I'll take a statement from anyone with anything to tell me.' Marnie handed the girls her card. 'Keep in touch. And stay safe.'

At the station, Noah handed Marnie the paperwork he'd uncovered. 'Ashleigh was in the care of Children's Services when she ran. Her mother and stepfather weren't able to cope with her at home. She was getting into trouble at school, and with the police. With everyone, as far as I can tell.'

'So they put her into care?'

'It was what Ashleigh wanted, according to Children's Services. They'd tried curfews, cautions; nothing worked. She ran away from home more than once. The last time she said if they made her go back, she'd burn the place down.' Noah rubbed the bridge of his nose. 'She accused her stepfather of abuse, but there was no evidence to support it, no charges brought. Her mother sided with the stepfather, said Ashleigh was out of control, acting up. Her mum was seven months pregnant at the time, felt she couldn't cope with Ashleigh and the new baby. Everyone seems to have breathed a sigh of relief when she was taken into care.'

'Until she ran away. How did her parents react when that happened?'

'They made an appeal for Ashleigh to get in touch, but the baby was born prematurely and he takes up a lot of their time. They were in the hospital with him most of the first month when Ashleigh was missing. He's been in and out for operations ever since. Ashleigh's the least of their worries, that's the impression I was given by Children's Services.'

'When she went missing – that was the first time she'd run away since going into care?'

'Yes, but she didn't hang around. Two months after they took her in, she was gone. No clue as to where, no text messages to friends, no contact with anyone in the family or at school. Her social worker said that was unusual. Ashleigh was always texting someone or other.'

'But they're sure she ran, no reason to suspect she was snatched?'

'She took her make-up and clothes. A suitcase job, not a stroll out.' Noah pointed to the relevant page in the paperwork. 'Police questioned the stepdad and mum. Interviews at the school, at the care home. All procedures followed to the letter. A couple of CCTV sightings, then nothing. No more text messages, her phone out of service. Just like May Beswick.'

Not quite like May, whose photogenic blondeness had made her headline news. Marnie couldn't remember a single press story about Ashleigh's disappearance.

'What about her biological father?'

'He was never married to her mum. Army man, posted overseas a lot. Ashleigh had no contact with him. The stepdad came on the scene when she was twelve. They never hit it off, although it looks like he tried to make it work. All the reports say he's a decent guy doing his best. Children's Services found no risk of harm in the home other than the pressure Ashleigh's behaviour was putting on her mum at a vulnerable time in her pregnancy.'

'Where were the CCTV sightings after she went missing from the care home?'

'Liverpool Street station. Then Camden. Once they knew she was in London, Misper got pessimistic about the chances of finding her. She looked like a classic case, probably on the streets, one of tens of thousands of kids who run away from home every year . . . What did Fran say?'

'Superficial similarities to May. The bruises, mostly. She'll be in touch as soon as she knows more.' Her phone buzzed: Sean Beswick.

'Mr Beswick. How are you?'

161

'We didn't know.' May's father sounded shattered. 'We *didn't*. Everything we told you was the truth – what we thought was the truth.'

'What's happened?' Marnie reached for her coat. 'Mr Beswick?'

'Drawings, we found more drawings. I can't . . . Not over the phone. Can you come round? It's not . . . We know you have to see these, but they're not right. It's not right. I'm sorry. We didn't know, we really didn't. Loz says . . . but *we* didn't. Me and Kat. We didn't know.'

Marnie nodded at Noah. 'We're on our way.'

26

The house in Taybridge Road was overexposed, a blaze of light from every window.

Marnie remembered burning electricity like this at her parents' house, wanting to bleach the smell and stains left by Stephen. She climbed from the car with Noah, checking her phone for messages from Fran. Nothing yet.

Sean answered the door, his face crooked with grief and this fresh worry. 'Thanks for getting here so quickly.' Glancing across his shoulder at the stairs. 'Come in.'

When they were standing in the hall, Marnie saw Loz sitting at the head of the stairs in her school uniform, elbows on her knees. 'Hello.'

Loz looked through her, at Noah.

'She should be in school,' Sean said, 'but we didn't want to take her in, not today.'

Noah and Marnie followed him through to the kitchen, where Katrina was sitting, gripping a mug of tea between her hands. Like Sean's, her face was redrawn with worry, the morning's make-up in lines under her eyes. Dressed for work in a red jacket over a black dress, statement necklace, bracelets, heels. Lipstick on the mug, a scum of tannin on the surface of the cold tea. Her hands looked raw, a gold watch hanging at her left wrist. 'You'd better sit down.'

On the table was a heavy wire-bound sketchpad with a yellow and black tiger on the cover. May's parents looked at it fearfully. Marnie pulled out a chair and sat, Noah taking the seat at her side. She drew the pad towards them and opened it, turning the pages.

Thick paper, chalk-white, smudged with grey. May had used charcoals and pencils, filling the pad with sketches. Anatomical at first glance, but they weren't just that. Graphic, certainly. Close-ups of mouths, breasts, male and female genitalia. Sex acts, almost too intimate to look at. May hadn't meant these to be seen by just anyone, certainly not by her parents or the police.

'Where did you find this?'

The silence in the kitchen was underscored by the sound of cracking from the freezer, ice breaking somewhere inside.

Marnie raised her gaze from the sketchpad to see Katrina covering her eyes with her hand. Sean shook his head, numbly. 'Loz found it, in her room. Hidden, in her room.'

'*I* didn't hide it.' Loz was in the doorway, scuffing her toes at the kitchen floor. 'May did. But she never told me.' Her voice was tight with tears.

'Where in your room did she hide it?' Noah asked.

'Behind my plushies, on the top shelf.'

'Toys she collected,' her dad said, 'when she was a kid.' As if she was an adult now.

'You say you didn't know May had hidden it, but had you seen it before?'

Loz shook her head, biting at her lower lip where the skin was chapped and sore.

Under Marnie's fingers, the thick wire of the sketchpad

was furred by torn paper, discarded pages. 'Are you sure?' she asked, as gently as she could.

'Duh. I'd remember seeing *that*.' Keeping her eyes away from the table where the sketchpad was sitting open. She sounded, for the first time, like a child.

Noah turned another page. More of the same. And something new.

A tunnel, lit by rectangular boxes mounted along both walls. A subway? Bodies sleeping on the floor, faces turned to the wall, graffiti over their heads: *Fearz* in chroma yellow; *Rents* in neon pink. At the edge of the page, May had sketched a face inside a hoody, all eyes and mouth.

'Is this a real place?' Noah looked at May's parents. 'Do you recognise it?'

They shook their heads.

'It could be anywhere, couldn't it? Not somewhere we'd want the girls to go, obviously. We warned them about taking subways, and that's . . . She's drawn that after dark. She can't have been in a place like that after dark.' Sean kept his eyes away from the sketchpad. 'But perhaps she was. We couldn't believe the rest of it. *Can't* believe it. She didn't even have a boyfriend.'

'We've had the first results from the post-mortem.' Marnie waited, to give them the chance to say that Loz shouldn't hear this. They didn't speak, staring mutely at her. 'May was seven weeks pregnant when she died.'

It visibly rocked Sean. Katrina dropped her hands to the table, studying her bracelets as if they were handcuffs. Her throat convulsed, soundlessly.

'She was . . . raped?' Fury under the shock in Sean's voice. 'He raped her?'

'We don't know the identity of the father. There was no evidence of assault.'

'No *evidence*? You've just told us she was pregnant! What more evidence do you need?'

'The father may not be the killer.' Marnie put her hand on the sketchpad. 'I know you've said May didn't have a boyfriend, but in the light of these . . .'

'She was an *artist*. Just because she could draw, you're calling her a whore?'

'No. Absolutely not.' He'd chosen the same word May had written in the palms of her hands. 'I'm just asking if it's possible she was seeing someone you didn't know about.'

Katrina twisted her wedding ring on her finger. 'It's possible.' She looked at Marnie, then at her husband. Finally, blindly, at Loz. 'It must be.'

Sean shook his head, white-lipped.

'We knew something was wrong,' Katrina said. 'We just didn't know what. She'd stopped talking to us. It was like having a ghost in the house. We thought . . . She was growing up. Of course she was growing up, but we thought . . . Friends. Outside interests, maybe a little teenage rebellion. *Yes*, it could've been that.' Sean had made a sound of protest. 'They grow up so suddenly. I don't mean physically. Just . . . one day they're *there* and the next they're not. We lost her. Somehow.' She turned her hands up empty on the table. 'We lost hold of her.' She covered her eyes again.

'And you can't think of anyone she might have been seeing? None of these faces is familiar?' Marnie kept her hand on the pad. 'Or anywhere she might have gone. To this subway, perhaps?'

They shook their heads.

'Loz . . . do you know where this might be? Do you recognise it?'

'No.' Loz didn't look at the sketch.

'And you don't recognise any of the people?'

Loz shook her head fiercely, still biting her lips. The face at the edge of the page was young. Fifteen, maybe sixteen. It was hard to look away from the stare. May had captured all the arrogance of a teenage runaway, a poster child for Shelter. In the larger sketch: ragged grass at the mouth of the subway, graffiti tags. 'Did May talk about meeting homeless people in a place like this?'

'She never talked to me about stuff like that.'

'Why do you think she hid this in your room?' Noah asked. 'Rather than her room?'

'You didn't search my room when she went missing. I guess that's why.'

'That would mean she planned to leave.'

'She didn't.' Katrina took her hands away from her face. 'If she planned it, why didn't she take more things? A bag, clothes – *anything*. It wasn't planned, it can't have been.'

Before Marnie could respond, Noah said, 'Look at this.'

He'd turned to a new page in the pad.

Another face, in close-up.

Female, pouting.

Distinctive crook in her nose.

Gold hoops through the fleshy lobes of her ears.

Ashleigh Jewell.

27

Aimee

My fingers burned from working at the wire. I'd got it half free from the sketchpad, but it was taking too long. I had to work under the covers, in the bed.

Funny to think I'd been good at this shit once. Sneaking around, watching out for myself. Now I was no use to anyone. Harm didn't want me to be good at anything except being sick. Just like my mum when I was little. Home sick home.

Christie was keeping an eye on me. Coming right up to the bed. I heard her breathing, watching me pretending to sleep. Just as I was starting to think she knew I was awake, she'd go away. But she waited longer and longer. I'd thought it was only him I had to worry about. Now it was her too, and she'd come from the streets so she knew all the tricks. Harm was never on the streets, not living on the streets. He'd grown up in a nice house with a nice family, not that it meant anything. It hadn't meant anything to May. She'd been safe, she'd said, at home with her family. She'd loved her little sister. She just couldn't live there. Sometimes you just can't.

The wire bruised my fingers. I sucked them to get the feeling back.

I'd decided to try and take a knife, at supper.

It was just the three of us now. Me and them.

Ashleigh was gone.

I hadn't thought I'd miss her, but I did. Missed the camouflage, the way she'd drawn Harm's stare from me. I missed her tits. I'd been in awe of her tits. They'd been a big fuck-off to that make-believe crap, the game we were playing. Dressing like schoolgirls, swallowing his shit. Her tits had been a flag for the real world, whatever was going on out there, away from him.

I couldn't steal a knife. He was too careful in the kitchen. May tried to steal food when she first had cravings, but he'd got it all locked down. He watched us, or Christie did.

More and more, it was Christie who watched. Harm went out, sometimes for hours, but she never left. I heard her creaking on the stairs and it used to be okay, but then she'd started coming inside my room. Right up to the bed. Her eyes on me, watching me pretending to sleep.

That's what I'd go for, with the wire – her eyes.

Stop her spying for him, seeing something she shouldn't. He didn't look, not properly, but she did. She knew something wasn't right with me. I could hear it in her breathing. She *saw* me. She was stronger, too. Bigger, taller, her hands like fucking trowels, but I'd have her.

I'd fucking *have* her.

I used to live on the streets, in the tunnels.

May knew . . .

That was where she'd found us, living like rats when

the rain came, pretending it wasn't a pit, pretending we were streetwise, free spirits, sharing stories about the fuckers we'd escaped from. Dancing in the rain, I remembered that. Dancing in the *fucking* rain.

Ashleigh had a story about her stepdad. Some shit about him watching when she got undressed. We all had a story like that, and she was lying, I could tell. She *wanted* him to watch, that was my guess. All she had were her tits and arse. If no one was looking at those, no one was seeing her, and we all wanted to be seen. We thought it'd be impossible to be ignored when we were sitting right *there* under your feet every day. But you managed it somehow, managed to make us invisible. Ashleigh couldn't stand being invisible. She'd be out there right now, showing her tits to someone, getting noticed. Good luck to her. We were all just trying to stay alive. If she needed to get groped to feel that way, then good luck to her. I hoped she was getting groped right now.

May needed looking after with the baby coming, so I got that, too. Why she had to go back home to her little sister, who'd be an auntie soon. I didn't blame her for running. I'd have done the same if I wasn't being watched so well. By her now, as well as him.

The wire stabbed my finger, scratching blood from under a nail.

I sucked it, tasting salt.

I was thirsty, all the time. It was the food, everything salted, dried, preserved. Maybe that was what he was doing, preserving me from the inside out like an Egyptian mummy. He'd pull my brains through my nose and put my kidneys into jars. I'd have skin like leather and huge hollow eyes. He'd love me like that.

Footsteps on the stairs.

My heart skittered.

I curled on my side with the wire under me, tucking my hands away.

Shallow breaths, shallow, don't give the game away.

Cold air snaked into the room.

Was it him, or her?

I was sleeping, look. I was sleeping.

My mouth open on the pillow, breathing through my mouth.

Asleep. Don't wake me.

His shadow over me, like a stone. Or hers, was it hers?

Silence packed like soil, green and black behind my eyes, flecked with white like spit. Shallow breaths through my mouth, damp on the pillow. I was sick, sleeping. Let me sleep.

I didn't want to wake. I didn't.

Eyes on my skin, on my throat, like fingers pressing, squeezing. I couldn't breathe. It was only eyes. His or hers. Watching me sleep. But it felt like fingers, hands on my throat.

I couldn't breathe, couldn't breathe, couldn't breathe.

Panic hitched air into my chest, making me jump. I turned it into a snore, frowning in my sleep, not waking. My whole body prickled with fright, every hair spiking into my skin. But I didn't wake, didn't open my eyes, didn't move past that first kick of panic.

I was good at this, still good.

His good little girl. And hers.

The stone shifted over me, moving back from the bed, retreating to the door.

I felt the long pull of the shadow as it drained like water from the room, leaving me damp and twitching in the bed.

28

'So our dead girls knew each other.' Welland studied the whiteboard as if its content was a personal affront. 'Any idea where they met?'

'We're looking for the subway in the sketch,' Noah told him. 'It's our best lead.'

'A drawing? Who's to say she didn't pull it out of thin air?'

'She drew the power station, and other landmarks.' How had she felt about the bland landscapes on her parents' walls when she was producing sketches as rawly intimate as these? 'We think the subway exists. We're looking at places close to her house and school.'

'That's all we've got to go on?'

'And the graffiti. Taggers are territorial. If we can identify the tags, we might be able to work out the location of the subway. Transport Police have a database, so we're starting there.'

Welland eyed the tags in May's sketch: *Fearz*; *Rents*. 'That'll give us where the girls met but not how they ended up dead within forty-eight hours of each other.'

He pulled on his upper lip. 'Ashleigh's parents haven't got any ideas? Or the care home she ran from?'

'Kent Police broke the news to the parents and the care home. They showed them May's photo, but no one remembers seeing her with Ashleigh at any point before she ran. They must've met after she got to London. My guess is they met in the subway. What May was doing there, I don't know. Sketching, maybe. I think that's where the killer found them.'

'What about the third girl, Traffic's missing one?'

'We've got a better e-fit, thanks to Ruth Eaton. The house-to-house team's showing it around the Garrett. A lot of frightened people there after we found Ashleigh's body this morning.'

From the whiteboard, Ashleigh blew a kiss, eyes flirting, shoulders cocked. Trying to attract attention. Not like May, or not like they'd imagined May. The sketchpad changed a lot of things.

Welland kneaded the skin under his eyes. 'Where's DI Rome?'

'With Fran Lennox for the post-mortem results. One thing: Ashleigh wasn't pregnant. Fran's ruled out any recent sexual activity. No evidence of abuse or assault.'

'So he just strangled and dumped her. What a gentleman.' Welland peered at the sketches copied from May's pad. 'The Beswick girl was a dark horse. Taking an A level in pornography, was she?'

'It's not pornography,' Noah said mildly. 'It's life studies.'

'And now she's dead. Whose *life* was she studying?' Tapping his thumb to the most graphic of the images. 'Our killer's? What does the sister have to say? These were found in her room.'

'Loz didn't know about the drawings. She's upset by

them, but not in the same way as her parents. May was keeping secrets from her. It's made her feel even more isolated.'

Back at the Beswicks' house, Loz had told Noah she was being threatened with a therapist. 'I don't need shrinking,' she'd said. 'My world's small enough already.'

Noah had said, 'It might help. To talk. To realise you're not alone with this thing.'

Loz had looked straight at him. 'You do realise that sounds like bullshit?'

Welland was growling at the sketches. 'Pity she didn't draw more faces. I don't fancy having to ID our killer from his private parts.' He clicked his tongue. 'Keep me posted, Detective.'

'Ashleigh Jewell was hypernatremic,' Marnie told Noah forty minutes later. 'Fran's confirmed it. What's more, her stomach contents was a match for May's. Salted fish and lentils. They were in the same place eating the same meal just before they died.'

'He had sex with May, but not with Ashleigh.'

'Someone had sex with May,' Marnie corrected. 'We don't know it was the killer.'

'He puts May on the bed, brushes her hair, lays her out. Ashleigh he dumps with the trash.'

'The bruises are a match in terms of size and pattern. Latex gloves again, traces of talc. No other DNA evidence. He may have dumped her, but he was careful not to leave any clues. As careful as he was with May.' Marnie rubbed at her left wrist. 'If it's the same killer, he held both girls for weeks. Fed them, clothed them, at least in Ashleigh's case. The underwear was from Marks and Spencer, like the school uniform, even though Ashleigh wasn't attending school. He bought them clothes, then he killed them both within the space of forty-eight hours. Why? What happened to make him do that?'

'Even if May's pregnancy was the reason he killed her, that doesn't explain Ashleigh. We were looking for May; her face was in the papers, on the news. Ashleigh's wasn't. If he's worried about being caught, then dumping her in the vicinity of what's already a crime scene looks desperate.' Noah shook his head. 'Or he *wants* us to know what he's doing, wants our attention on him.'

Marnie didn't dispute this. 'Ashleigh's parents are coming to identify the body. Once that's done, we'll release her photo and name. Until then, May is the only official victim.'

'What will you tell the press this morning?'

'To report it responsibly.' She tidied her hair from her face. 'We're putting out an alert to the homeless charities, letting them know we'll have more feet on the ground over the coming weeks. If he's targeting runaway girls, we need to be watching the places of greatest risk. Any joy locating the subway in May's sketches?'

'Not yet, but Dan knows someone who's cataloguing London's street art. If we hit a dead end with the BTP's Graffiti Unit, then I'm hoping he'll recognise the tags.'

'You said Dan might know other ways into Battersea Power Station? None of the developer's people is giving us anything useful on that score.'

'I'll ask him. At least we have the lists of everyone with access to the site in the last twelve weeks. I put copies on your desk; anything jumping out at you?'

'The media party seems to have been a free-for-all. Anyone with more than five hundred Twitter followers got the champagne treatment.' Her eyes were stormy, the frown stitched deep at the bridge of her nose. Frustrated, like Noah. 'I'm following up on a couple of things.'

'Something we've not talked about since Taybridge Road . . .' He stopped.

But Marnie kept step with him, not missing a beat: 'Sean Beswick accused me of calling his daughter a whore.'

'So it wasn't just me. That was . . . weird. Using that word. May was sixteen. He might not like the idea of her having sex, but at that age? It's hardly unusual.'

'We looked at the parents when she first went missing. Nothing lit up.' Marnie picked a thread from the sleeve of her jacket with the tips of her fingers. 'Did we miss something? Control, or abuse? It would give us a reason for May leaving home. It would explain the sketches, and the lack of contact. Katrina wasn't surprised to hear that May was pregnant.'

She drew an unhappy breath. 'They don't look at each other, or comfort each other. Have you seen either of them hug Loz, or just hold her hand? I haven't. That could be grief, or it could be worse. And if May knew Ashleigh, then it's possible Sean knew her too.' She met Noah's stare head-on. 'A statistician would remind us of the probability that May knew her killer.'

They were quiet, thinking the same horrendous thought, and it was their *job*, Noah knew it was their job to think thoughts like this. Look at the facts coldly, even savagely. Take apart Taybridge Road a brick at a time, nothing at face value, no benefit of the doubt for anyone. It was their job to suspect Sean and Katrina, even Loz. Measure each human being in that house against the stone fact of May's death. Laid out like a child with the same word written on her hands . . .

Whore. The word her father used when he was white with anger at the suggestion that his daughter was having consensual sex, almost as if he preferred to think she was raped . . .

No. That was unfair. He was angry because his daughter was dead, and appalled that she might have been raped before she died. If that was an act, then Sean Beswick was one of the best actors Noah had seen. Self-deluded, self-assured and—

'Loz. Do we need to get her out of there?'

'On what grounds? Because he used the word *whore* instead of another word? Because there's so much pain in that house no one can get past it to comfort anyone else?' Marnie shook her head. 'We follow it up, because it's giving us both a bad feeling. We go back through the statements from the house, look at it all again. Double-check Sean's alibi for the day she went missing, and the day she died. But we remember *they* brought the sketchpad to *us*. We don't stop looking for someone else, and that includes our missing girl.'

'I don't *want* it to be him,' Noah began.

'Neither do I. But let's put it in the mix.' She checked her watch. 'I need to get to the press briefing. Keep in touch.'

29

Marnie recognised a handful of the journalists who turned up for the press briefing, but there was one face missing from the crowd. She'd expected Adam Fletcher to make an appearance. His name was on the Battersea media party list, and it wasn't like Adam to miss the chance to spin a story from a tragedy, especially when he could boast of having been in what was now the crime scene.

Six weeks ago, Adam had been drinking champagne and eating expensive canapés in the flat where May's body was found. The developers did their best to woo the press. In Adam's case, they failed. He wrote about the price of the penthouses, inviting comparison between the development and its surrounding area, name-dropping the Garrett estate, quoting statistics on homelessness in south London. The paper ran a photo of a homeless boy, his face not unlike the one in May's sketchpad, Battersea's famous chimneys in the background. Marnie looked for Adam's byline on the press stories about May's murder, but so far he was keeping quiet. Digging for something better than dry facts, looking for an angle. Adam had always been great at working the angles.

Easy enough to find his address. Had he not lived so close to the station, she'd have left it to someone else to cross him off the list of people with access to the crime scene. As it was, she walked the short distance to a narrow block of flats, pressing the intercom and standing where the CCTV could show her face to whoever was watching. The door buzzed open and she found her way to his front door, knocking twice before he answered.

Bare feet, stained chinos, white T-shirt. 'Detective Inspector.' He leaned his long body into the door frame. 'Is this an arrest?'

'Should it be?'

'I thought you were hunting a murderer, not paying house calls to old flames.'

'Can I come in?'

'Without a warrant?' Adam propped his elbow on the wall by his head. 'Doubt it.'

'I wanted a chat. About the party at Battersea, six weeks ago. Your name's on a list. I'd like to check it off.'

'You couldn't have phoned?' He hadn't slept in days, judging by his eyes, more grey than blue. And he'd lost weight; his leanness had a hungry edge.

'I tried.' He hadn't slept, but he'd washed. Smelt of shower gel, not cigarettes. Had he kicked his old habit? 'You've changed your number.'

'Dodging nuisance calls. You know how it is.' A seasoning of hostility in his stare, as if he was remembering the circumstances of their last conversation – Marnie's speech about moving on, leaving the past behind. 'What d'you want to know about the party?'

'Whether anything stood out, or anyone. Someone showing too much interest in the place, for instance. Or asking a lot of questions about security.'

Adam's gaze narrowed. 'You can't figure out how he got her up there.'

'It's not immediately obvious. Anyone spring to mind?'

'Maybe.' He shifted his position in the doorway. She saw bruises on his bare feet. 'Hard to say, off the top of my head.'

'You're not working on a story about May Beswick's murder?'

'I didn't say that.' Adam shrugged. 'If it bleeds, it leads.'

Six months ago, he'd shouldered his way into her investigation with information, he'd said, to help her find the killer of two young boys. His fingers had been burned by that encounter, or his pride had. Now, he was giving her nothing. But anything out of the ordinary at the media party and he'd have spotted it – the next best thing to having had a detective at that party.

'I'm trying to find a murderer,' she said. 'If you can help with that . . .'

'A murderer, or a serial killer?' Propping his head on his hand. Bruises on his fingers, too. 'You found another body this morning. On the Garrett estate. Another dead girl.'

'Where did you hear that?'

'Twitter. You take a good photo, Detective Inspector. You and DS Jake.'

'Who beat you up?' Marnie nodded at his feet and fingers.

'Flatpack furniture.' He didn't even blink. 'I was building a bookcase.'

'Can I see?'

'Without a warrant?' Crooking his mouth at her, but it wasn't a smile. He wanted her gone.

He'd lost his daughter, a coach crash when Tia was fourteen. Everything led from that – his restless curiosity and sense of injustice – as if his past was a corpse inadequately weighted below the water of his present life, always on the rise.

'You're getting domesticated,' Marnie said. 'That's new.'

'Everything's new,' Adam said. 'Except you.'

Walking back to the station, it occurred to Marnie that Adam could find out who was sending care packages to Stephen Keele. It was possible he already knew. Six months ago, he'd told her he was trying to solve the puzzle of why Stephen had killed her parents. Without her permission, without asking whether she wanted his help. She'd made it clear how little she liked his interference, but perhaps she should make use of his talents. Adam was good at what he did. He might be able to find the answers that were eluding her. He was smart and resourceful. She'd discovered that when she was sixteen. Adam was one of the reasons she'd run away from home. He'd told her once she wasn't a bad daughter, but she hadn't believed him.

Her phone thwapped. 'Noah. What have you got?'

'A lead on the subway, I hope. Dan says he knows the tagger Rents. He's based in Stockwell. I'm going to send him the sketch, see if he can give us a location for the subway. And Dan's put me in touch with one of his urban explorer friends who might know other ways into Battersea.'

'Good. I'm going to check in with Ron to see how the house-to-house is going. Then I'm meeting Ashleigh's parents at the mortuary.' She paused. 'Anything on the alibis?'

'Sean was home alone both afternoons. The day May went missing, and the day she died. Loz got back from school around four o'clock. Unless she's covering for him, he was in the house. Her mum got home later, around the time Jamie Ledger found May's body. I'm checking both cars, Sean's and Katrina's, in case they were near the power station that afternoon. If anything turns up, you'll be the first to know . . . Did the press behave themselves?'

'More or less. Once we tell them about Ashleigh, that might change.' Adam wouldn't be the only one to see a link between the killings of two teenage girls within the same square mile. 'If the killer *is* panicking, we need to contain the story. Find Traffic's girl and identify the subway in May's sketch – see whether anyone else went missing from the same place in the last four months.'

'You think he's holding more girls,' Noah said bleakly. She knew he was seeing the faces from the whiteboard. Sika Khair and Kim Nguyen, sixteen. Sasha Ronson, fourteen.

'Keep in touch,' Marnie told him. She ended the call, ringing Ron's number. 'Anything?'

'Apart from earache? Not yet.' He sounded strung out. 'It's getting edgy here, boss. Some shit-stirrers are suggesting a racial motive, stressing that our victim was a white girl, which isn't making it any easier.'

'Tell DC Tanner to get in touch with the Community Safety Unit and ask them to be on site with you. I'll do the same. Keep me posted.'

30

'Abandoned places are best,' Dan's friend told Noah. 'The ones everyone ignores. Sometimes it's about spectacle, sure, like those students putting Santa hats on the spires at King's College, or getting a car on to the roof of the Senate House. Sticking two fingers up because why not? But a lot of us just like the quiet places, seeing a different side of the city, you know?'

Noah handed him a cup of coffee from the stall across the street. 'Dan told me about King's College. I hadn't heard about the car on the Senate House.'

'They had to cut it into pieces to take it down. So, yeah. Spectacle. But most of us are happier staying out of the papers. It's about passing under the radar, not lighting the system.' Riff was in his thirties. Booted and suited, with a middle-management haircut, gold wedding ring, square-toed shoes. A surveyor by day. By night, an urban explorer. 'I'm telling you this in the past tense, yeah?' He worked the plastic lid from the coffee. 'I gave it all up months ago.'

'Why did you?' Noah asked.

'Aged out.' Riff shrugged. 'Like Dan.' The skin around

his eyes was tanned and lined. Old scars on his hands, knots in his wrists from climbing. 'What you've got to understand is that most of us had decent jobs, nice homes, money coming in. Finest edgework I ever saw – bravest – came from a call-centre worker. Said his job drove him insane because it was so safe and inconspicuous.'

'Edgework. Because it's about finding the edge of the city? What about the security? How did you get inside so many places?'

'The more sophisticated the security, the more places you can breach it. We didn't even have to be clever a lot of the time. We wore hi-vis and hard hats; that got us into a ton of places in broad daylight. Sometimes we ninjaed the scaffolding. Otherwise, it's about finding the cracks in surveillance, vanishing points. Access points.'

'Vanishing points,' Noah repeated. Was that what the killer had done? Found the vanishing points at Battersea Power Station and on the Garrett? Harder, surely, with a dead body in tow.

Riff drank more coffee, watching him. 'So how's Danny boy?'

'He's good.' Noah smiled. 'We're good.'

'Still climbing?'

'On holidays, sometimes. Mostly he's working in galleries, and on installations. Like the one at the power station a while back.'

'Not the rotten apples?' Riff grinned when Noah looked blank. 'They filled a cage with like a hundred thousand apples and let them rot. Whole place stank of cider for *months*.'

'Before Dan's time, I think.' A trio of kids mooched towards the bus stop on the other side of the street. In uniform, like Abi Gull and her friends, but no more in school than Abi had been earlier in the day. They glanced towards Noah and Riff, then blanked them, busy with their phones. 'If I was looking for a hiding place, where would I start? Construction sites?'

'Maybe. But too much of London's been rinsed now.'

'By rinsed, you mean hacked. Explored.'

'Yeah. Sometimes you think you've found a place, that you're the first ones there. Then you see the markers – someone else beat you to it.'

'Markers like tags? Graffiti?'

Riff nodded. 'But honestly? You're asking the wrong person. I'm aged out. When you can't find the edge any more, or not without taking massive risks, it's time to call it a day.'

'I thought it was all about the danger.' Noah smiled. 'Dan still says he despises safety.'

'It's about connecting. Belonging. To the real city, and to your team, your tribe.'

'What was your best time? Dan said you had a soft spot for Battersea. I know he does.'

'For sure.' Riff shut his eyes, tipping the coffee cup to drain its last mouthful. 'Can't stand what they've done to her. Those wankers' mansions.'

'I saw the show flat. On top of the old boiler house.'

'Fucking waste. She was a princess. You should've been there when the Millennium fireworks were kicking off, should've felt her chimneys shake. Best buzz of my life.'

'How'd you get in? Dan said the security was always pretty tight.'

Riff shot him a glance, then grinned. 'I've got a photo of Danny with one of the chimneys. He fucking loved the princess.'

'He told me.' Noah smiled. He waited, not pushing.

'They got paranoid about security. Searchlights, dogs. It got a *lot* harder once they decided they could make money out of her. Soon as we heard about the penthouses, we knew we wouldn't get to see her the same again, maybe ever. That got a few of us wanting a last trip. Goodbyes, you know?'

'Did you get to say goodbye?'

Riff shook his head, still smiling. 'That'd be illegal.'

'Okay, sure. But say someone wanted to make one last trip. With security the way it is right now. It's illegal, but would it be impossible?'

'Nothing's impossible . . . The show flat's on top of the old boiler house. That's where you found her, the girl that was murdered? He took her up there to kill her?' Riff looked ill. 'Freak.'

'He didn't kill her there. I can't give you details, but he wanted her found in the power station.'

'That's sick. If you're thinking he was an explorer . . . None of us would've done a thing like that. It's the opposite of what we're about.'

'We don't think he's an explorer. But we can't figure out how he got her into the power station. Past the security. The guards and the dogs.'

'There's more than one way in.'

'He didn't come by river.'

Riff was quiet for a moment, then he said, 'The guards with dogs. You've checked those out, right? I've paid a few bribes in my time.'

'We're checking everyone with access to the site in the last four months.' Noah made a mental note to revisit the security lists. 'You mentioned taggers. We're looking for a street artist called Rents.'

Riff shook his head. 'Don't know him.'

It was a long shot, but Noah took out his phone, scrolling to May's subway sketch. 'And you don't recognise this place?'

'Sorry.' Shaking his head again.

'If you think of anything, can you give me a call? Via Dan, if you prefer.'

Riff nodded. 'Good luck.'

Dan called as Noah was making his way back to the station.

'Hey,' Noah said. 'Any luck getting hold of Rents?'

'He's not called back yet . . . Have you seen Sol?'

'Not since the migraine. Why?'

'He was coming home when I was leaving for work, looking like someone beat him up. He wouldn't talk about it, told me not to get you involved. I didn't make any promises.'

Noah picked up his pace. 'Badly beaten?'

'Not that I could see. A bloody nose, bruises. He'd brought himself home, so he can't have been that bad, but I thought you'd want to know.'

'Yes. I'll give him a call.'

'He wasn't answering the phone to me,' Dan said. 'I tried his number just now, and then the flat. If he's there, he isn't picking up.'

'Okay. I'll see if I can get hold of him. Thanks.'

Noah rang Sol's number and listened to the voicemail message. Hung up and tried the landline, getting the answerphone. Whatever he was up to, Sol didn't want to talk. *Shit*.

Noah felt a familiar pinch of panic. Worrying about Sol had been a part of growing up. He'd trained himself out of it more or less, but the voice he'd heard in the flat two days ago, Sol's visitor making threats . . .

Life had been full of people like that back when Sol ran with the crowd on the council estate, getting into every kind of trouble. Knives, pills, even an amateur

187

protection racket. Lately, there'd been signs he was straightening himself out, but that could be wishful thinking on Noah's part. Or Sol could be finding it hard to shake off the trouble. If he'd been running with the wrong crowd, there'd be no easy exit. Same for the gangs on the Garrett: Abi and her schoolmates setting fires, terrorising old ladies. Once you started down that road, it was impossible to stop without losing face or losing friends. All those hard stares on the estate this morning . . .

Abi and her friends, who were little more than kids.

Even a dead girl hadn't moved them, beyond curiosity and a certain morbid hostility.

Any one of them could be next. Did they know that?

Was that why they refused to look scared? Refused to stay indoors?

Standing out in the open, in their school uniforms, pretending to be grown-up.

Daring anyone – even a killer – to take them on.

31

'She was always such a stranger. Even when she was tiny. I never really . . . *recognised* her. I blamed myself, thought I was going mad, post-natal depression maybe, because, "Who *is* this child? Where did she *come* from?" She wasn't like me or my sisters or anyone we knew. Maybe she was like her dad. I didn't really know him, not the way you're supposed to know the person you have a child with. And he was off as soon as she was born. I was stuck at home with this stranger, and she . . . never liked me, cried whenever I went near her, hated being held or cuddled. She hated *me* . . . We were such strangers.' Helen Collier stopped speaking at last, standing dry-eyed by her daughter's body. Bewildered. As if Ashleigh had done another inexplicable thing by dying. 'I tried to love her, but she made it impossible. She wouldn't even let me *like* her, or look after her. Wouldn't let me teach her how to lace her shoes when she was little, or how to put on make-up. Everything I did, everything I *tried* to do, she pushed me away.'

Ashleigh's stepfather put his arm around his wife's shoulders. A nice-looking man, fair-haired, his face lined by hope and worry. Helen was a big woman with a once-pretty face, wearing a dark dress sagged and faded at the waist; Marnie could see her holding a child in her lap. Not Ashleigh, but her son Jolyon, the sick little boy who'd been in and out of hospital since Ashleigh ran away.

'Do you have any idea where she might have been living in the last two months?'

'None.' Robin Collier shook his head.

'Could she have been with other girls, runaways?'

'She didn't like other people.' Helen blinked at her daughter's body. 'Especially not other girls.'

'Did she have a boyfriend?'

'Not while she was living at home. She knew some boys, but she didn't like them, that's what she always said.' Her face worked. 'She wasn't raped. He didn't do that to her, at least.'

Marnie waited a moment. 'The care home said she used her mobile phone a lot before she went missing. Sending texts or chatting to people.'

'No one we knew. She never called us, never took our calls.'

'She hadn't been in touch since before Jolyon was born,' Robin said.

'How is he?'

'Better, just for the moment. We're counting our blessings, a day at a time.' He hugged his wife closer. 'I wish we could've helped Ashleigh, but Helen's right. She wouldn't let us. As far as we knew, she wouldn't let anyone help her.'

'Has her biological father been in touch?'

Helen shook her head. 'I don't even know how to get hold of him. We lost contact years ago.'

'Someone else Ashleigh didn't want to know.' Robin looked sad. 'I suppose she felt rejected by him, but it was more than that. She was fiercely independent, as Helen says. Hated being a child, wanted to grow up and get away. We just couldn't . . . connect to her.'

Marnie was quiet for a moment, waiting for one of the Colliers to say something more, but they just stood looking at the stranger who'd died after running from their home.

Eventually Helen said, 'Can we go? It's her, we can confirm it's her. That's all you needed, isn't it?' She glanced at her wristwatch. 'We promised my mum we'd be back for Jolyon's bed time.'

At the entrance to the mortuary, Marnie shook their hands. 'Thank you again, and I'm sorry.'

'For our loss,' Helen said mechanically. 'I don't mean . . . It's horrible, of course it is. I wish she wasn't dead. I wish she could've been happy.' She wiped at her dry eyes. 'I hope you catch whoever did it. Ashleigh didn't deserve this.'

'One thing.' Robin frowned. 'She was a clever kid, street-smart. She didn't trust anyone, let alone strangers. Whoever did this, you're looking for someone very clever or very fast. I can't believe she'd be taken in by just anyone. She was such a cynical kid, the last person in the world I'd have expected to find like this. But she *was* just a kid. She didn't act like it, but she was.' His eyes clouded and he put an arm around his wife again. 'Poor kid.'

'Thank you,' Helen said to Marnie. 'For making her look so nice. I was scared to see her. I'd thought she'd look much worse. Her skin was always so . . . *fiery.* She used too much make-up, which made it worse. In there, she looked like a little girl again.' Her mouth made the messy shape of a smile. 'Thank you for that.'

Marnie nodded, but she thought, *That wasn't us.*
It was the killer.

'So Ashleigh was no May Beswick.' Ron was studying the new sketches on the whiteboard, the ones Welland had called pornographic. 'Not that May was such a nice girl as it turns out.'

'Because she had talent?' Noah said.

'It's not *how* she drew, it's *what* she drew. I wouldn't want my kids turning out pictures like that. Bet her mum and dad had a fit when they found these.'

'Her sister found them,' Noah said shortly. He had his hands in his pockets, shoulders up.

Marnie watched him, wondering what had happened to put him on edge. Or was he thinking about the Beswicks still, as she was? About grief and guilt, and the places in between.

'Ashleigh had street smarts,' she told the team. 'May knew which places to avoid after dark. Neither girl was the kind to be taken in by strangers. So how did they end up with our killer? Fran's found no evidence of restraint on either girl. All the signs say they went with him. Lived with him, ate his food, slept under his roof. Why? How did he seduce them?'

'You think he's good-looking?' Ron sniffed. 'Rich, maybe. If he had a flashy car . . .'

'What was it about these girls that attracted *him*?' Noah said. 'They had nothing in common. Different upbringings, different personalities, physically different.'

'They hung out in the same subway. Maybe it's as simple as that. He saw them together so he took them together. And because there were two of them, they felt safe going with him . . . We need to find the subway. If it even exists.'

'It exists. Rents is a street artist from Stockwell. He's used that tag all over south London. He'll know where the subway is. We just need to find him.'

'How's that going?' Marnie asked Noah.

'Dan gave me a phone number. I've left a couple of messages. He hasn't called back yet. BTP's Graffiti Unit has him on a list, no name or address. He's tagged a few of their trains in the last year. They've failed to catch him, seemed to think we'd fail too. I said we'd keep them posted.'

Marnie looked at Colin. 'How soon until we finish with the lists of people with access to the power station?'

'We've eliminated thirteen so far, wrong profile or with an alibi for the day May was killed. A couple look interesting, so we're following up. One's on the security crew, a shift worker like Jamie Ledger. Served time for an assault in Lithuania. He wasn't working that day, but we're looking at anyone who could've been bribed to turn a blind eye to security shortfalls.'

'Put him on the board.' Marnie handed him the pen.

Colin wrote, *Romek Malis*.

'What kind of assault in Lithuania?'

'Domestic. We're getting details.'

'No sign of restraint on either girl.' Noah moved closer to the photographs of Ashleigh and May. 'So this was . . . what? Capture bonding?'

'Speak English,' Ron said. He was tired. They all were.

'Two bright girls went willingly with a maniac who ended up strangling them. He didn't tie them up, they didn't fight back. Why? They trusted him. Maybe they even liked him. Or they were scared of him, they knew they had to do as he said to survive. They went along with whatever he wanted. That's capture bonding. Living in fear – actually *within* it – can feel safe. In that state, you reinvent what feels rational and irrational. Even if these girls are completely dominated by the source of their fear, the chances are they *feel* safe. Fearless, even. He didn't snatch them, they *chose* to go with him. They're in a different reality. It's only when they step back across the line that it hits them. Maybe that's why Traffic's girl was so disorientated. She'd been surviving by submission.'

'Ashleigh didn't sound the submissive type,' Marnie said. 'Her stepdad thinks we should be looking for someone clever and fast. Three missing girls in three days, two of them dead. He's certainly moving fast. So let's up our game. Find the subway in May's sketch, and our e-fit girl.'

She nodded at Noah. 'DS Jake?'

Noah followed Marnie out to the station car park. The rain had cleared, sunshine lying like litter on the tarmac. 'Something's bothering you.' Marnie unlocked the car. 'What is it?'

'Sol's in trouble.' Noah climbed in. 'Dan says he had a bloody nose when he got home this morning. I'll talk to him tonight.' He fastened his seat belt. 'Where're we headed?'

'Back to Battersea.' Marnie fired the engine. 'I want another look at the crime scene. And a chat with Romek Malis. What's new on the Beswicks?'

'Katrina's car was on York Road half an hour before May's body was found.' A muscle stressed in his cheek. 'It's her route home, the same route every day. It could be nothing.'

Or it could be Sean Beswick's hands around his daughter's neck, his wife helping to clear up the mess. Marnie didn't want those images in her head any more than Noah did. She drove in silence until they hit a snarl of traffic. 'Sean nearly said something when he called to tell us about the sketches. He said, "We didn't know, we really didn't. Loz says . . . but *we* didn't. Me and Kat." I want to know what Loz said. I think she knew about the sketches. Maybe she hid the pad in her room to help May, or when May went missing, because she didn't want us to find it.'

'She wants to find May's killer. She wouldn't hold back anything that'd help us do that.'

'Not intentionally, but it's possible she doesn't understand the significance of the sketches.'

Their fear for Loz was like a solid object in the car – a body on the back seat.

After a moment Noah said, 'I can't imagine them together. May and Ashleigh. Something doesn't fit. But we know they were in the same place, from the food they ate as much as from May's sketches. Salted fish and lentils, survival food. Highly preserved, Fran said. Maybe he's got them holed up off the grid. Somewhere ultra-safe. No access to shops, no need to leave the house. The uniform's weird. Ashleigh wasn't attending school, so why was she dressed like that? We're dealing with a control freak.'

'Who attracts out-of-control girls. Something in our killer appealed to Ashleigh Jewell, and to May Beswick. To the missing girl, too. Maybe other girls . . .'

'Maybe not just girls,' Noah said. 'Plenty of homeless teenage boys out there. We're assuming he hasn't taken any of them, but if there's no sexual element to what he's doing, if it's just about control, he could've taken boys too.'

They'd reached the power station. Marnie showed her badge at the barrier, and parked up. When they climbed from the car, the river's smell came up to meet them, the tide on the turn.

'Ashleigh was left less than a mile from here.' Marnie

checked her phone. 'I'm betting we find that subway within the same square mile.'

Noah tipped his head to look at the chimneys, feeling all of London packed into this square mile. Forget an off-grid prison where this man was keeping the girls. He was *here*. 'He's close. Can't you feel him?'

'The subway is close,' Marnie said. 'It must be. We know May wasn't away from home for any length of time in the weeks before she disappeared. She was sketching at the subway on her way to and from school. That's a narrow radius.'

'I wonder what it's like in that house for Loz. Even if our bad feeling's wrong, Sean and Katrina are very . . . polite, professional. To us. I wonder what they're like as parents.'

Marnie didn't answer, going ahead of Noah into the heart of the site. She'd asked the same question about her own parents in the weeks after Stephen destroyed her family, wondering whether as foster-parents they'd been different, more patient perhaps. Less quick, surely, to see their faults magnified in him, since there was no blood between them. And Stephen – when had he first known he was going to kill them? Or hadn't he known until the moment when it was happening, unfurling in him like an alien rush of hormones, of hate?

Battersea was full of shadows and the charred smell of cut stone, hot metal. The workmen were drilling to the left, the judder of it coming through the walls, getting into her bones. Noah looked up at the remaining chimneys. 'You know they tried to demolish these once before? From the inside. They stripped out the lining, then they noticed the chimneys were spreading. The lining, all that poisonous black rot inside, was holding them together. It's how they'd stayed standing so long.'

'You said May loved this place but it scared her.'

He nodded. 'It was in her sketches.'

'If our killer saw the sketches, that could explain why he left her here. We've been assuming he's obsessed with this place, but May was obsessed too. Perhaps he left her here because of the way *she* felt about the power station, not the way *he* did.'

'Afraid?'

'And in love. She loved it here, but it scared her.'

Like living, Marnie thought, *like life for a teenage girl.*

'You have to make friends with fear.' Noah stared up into the sightless eye of a CCTV camera. 'That's what my dad always said.'

'In relation to what?'

'Life in general. Growing up on an estate like the Garrett, staying on the straight and narrow. It was a good speech. About accepting our limitations, respecting our fault lines. Making peace with who we are, and who we're not. I suppose it was a speech about identity.'

Had his brother Sol valued that speech? Two boys growing up on the same estate but going in different directions, Noah finding the police while Sol went the other way. Families were hard work. The killer had capitalised on that, picking off the ones who couldn't live at home, making them into different people, into children. Unrecognisable, in Ashleigh's case, to her own parents.

The penthouse was sealed off, forensic tags on the floor and bed.

'Are you police?' A woman in a tight blue suit had followed them. Late thirties, whip-thin, with a wide face, tired make-up, scuffed shoes, high heels frayed by the site's gravel. 'Is there any news?'

Marnie showed her badge. 'And you are . . .?'

'Toni Shepherd, senior marketing manager. Have there

been any developments?' Eyes busy on the bed, where the covers held track marks from the removal of May's body. 'Anything positive?'

'We'd like to speak with your security team. Not everyone was on shift when we conducted the first interviews. Romek Malis, is he working today?'

'You'd need to check with the site manager.' Moving her feet away from a forensic tag, calf muscles clenching. 'I was hoping you'd be able to tell me when we can let the cleaners in here to spruce the place up for viewings. We've got a backlog building up.'

Spruce the place up.

'These are people who've booked a viewing since the body was found?'

'I know what you're thinking, but they're not ghouls.' She slapped out a smile. 'We run very thorough checks before we let people in here.'

'What sort of checks?' Noah asked. 'To see if they can afford the prices you're charging? Or to be sure they're not ghouls? How *do* you check for that?'

Toni switched her stare to him, smiling reflexively the way women always did when they saw Noah. 'The former, as a matter of course. It doesn't rule out any other motive, but I doubt anyone in the business of buying a flat like this one would waste their time or ours wanting to see a crime scene. There are plenty of cheaper places they could visit if that was their real interest.'

Marnie's phone rang and she turned away to take the call. 'DI Rome.'

'Are you at Battersea?' It was Colin Pitcher. 'Ron said you wanted to speak with Romek Malis.'

'We're on site, yes. What've you got?'

'I was speaking with someone from the media party, Marc Amos, events manager for a local charity. He was offered a guided tour by one of the security crew, behind-the-scenes stuff. He turned it down because the man wanted money and Amos didn't have enough cash on him. But he was tempted, out of curiosity. The man said he could show him what corners were being cut, implied there were a lot of dodgy dealings on site. Amos says he's surprised none of the journalists took the man up on his offer. Everyone was sick of the silver lining, looking for the cloud.'

'Did the man have a name?' Marnie walked away from Toni Shepherd, who was trying hard to hear what was being said over the phone. 'Was it Romek Malis?'

'No name, but Amos gave me a description. Thirties, tough-looking, shaved head. Tattoos on his fingers. One of the tattoos was a bird of some kind.'

'A hawk.' Marnie turned to catch Noah's eye. 'It was Jamie Ledger.'

'Ledger's on my list,' Colin said. 'We took a statement at the scene. Do you want his address and contact number?'

'Text it to me. I'm going to see if he's working today. Thanks, I'll call you back.'

'Developments?' Toni said, her eyes working hard at Marnie's face.

'Please stay outside this room, and keep it locked. DS Jake?'

In the security cabin, two men were drinking tea from a Thermos. Both looked bored when Marnie showed her badge. Neither was Jamie Ledger or Romek Malis.

'Romek's on nights. Haven't seen Ledge in a couple of days.'

The other man agreed. 'Skipped a shift yesterday. Not like Ledge, but it got me a bit of overtime, so . . .' He shrugged.

'Can I see the rota?'

'Help yourself.' He nodded at a clipboard of pages, tea-stained.

Signatures, scribbled. Times in and out, illegible in places. 'J. Ledger' was printed on the list for yesterday's shifts, no times or signatures. Earlier in the week, he'd signed in and out for a number of shifts, including the one during which May's body was discovered.

'Is there an electronic version of this?' Marnie asked.

'Ask Aaron, he's in charge.'

'Where can we find him?'

'Riverside,' a jerk of the head, 'taking deliveries.'

'Ledger is down for a shift this afternoon. What time would you expect him?'

'Any time now. He eats lunch here, uses the bog before he gets started.'

Something in the man's voice made Marnie ask, 'That's unusual?'

'He scrubs up here, carries his stuff around in bags like his missus kicked him out.'

'Did she?'

A shrug. 'He doesn't talk about it. Doesn't talk about much. That's Ledge.'

The foreman, Aaron Buxton, had a similar story. And a gripe. 'He dumped us in it when he didn't show up. We've tightened security just like we promised. We need him here.'

A barge was unloading breeze blocks from the river. Buxton's broad face was shiny with sweat under a hard hat. He wore a business suit with steel-toed boots. Short, stocky build but his hands were thin, almost womanly.

'Did he call in sick?' Noah asked.

'No, not a dicky-bird. Walked off site just after you

finished questioning him and he's not been back. I was going to report it if he didn't show up today, but he still might.'

'Do you have a contact number?'

'In the files, sure.'

'Did you call him when he failed to turn up to work yesterday?'

'Personally? No. I've got my hands full. But the agency will've chased him for sure.'

'We'll need a contact at the agency.'

Buxton took out his phone and thumbed through a list for the name and number. 'Anything else I can help you with?' He eyed the barge, shifting his weight between his feet, looking harassed. The whites of his eyes were lemon-tinged, like a drinker's. 'Only we're behind schedule.'

'We'll wait,' Marnie said, 'to see if Ledger clocks on. I'd like a contact number for another of the security crew. Romek Malis.'

'The agency . . .' Buxton looked distracted. 'They'll have details. At least Malis is reliable. He's on nights, hasn't missed a shift yet.' He slipped his phone back into his pocket. 'Neither had Ledger, until now.' Eyeing Marnie and Noah as if they were to blame for his diminishing workforce. 'A thing like this makes people twitchy. I didn't think Ledger was like that, what with being in the army. He must've seen worse, stands to reason. And he needed the work more than most. Just as well the agency's got plenty of names on its books. I liked Ledger, but we can't hold jobs open for long. We need reliable people, like Malis.'

'Why did Ledger need this work more than most?'

'He was in a hostel, trying to get back on his feet. This job was good for him, that's what he said. But we can't hold jobs for people who don't show when they're expected. Especially not now, with security the way it is and running behind schedule.' He nodded towards the barge. 'Sorry, but I'm needed. Stuff to sign. Call me later, if you need to.' He reeled off a number, which Noah logged in his phone. 'Let's hope Ledge shows up for his shift.'

Marnie and Noah waited another twenty minutes, until it was evident Ledger wasn't going to clock on. They'd put a call through to the agency and were expecting a message back from the woman who'd chased Ledger when he failed to show up on site yesterday. The phone number he'd given in his police interview wasn't working.

'He's gone. Don't you think?' Noah turned up the collar of his coat against the wind pushing in from the water. 'He found the body. He was told to stay in touch. But he's gone.'

'Let's wait in the car.' Marnie walked away.

Noah followed. 'You spoke with him on the night. Did you pick up any vibe?'

'Anything to suggest he might run, or have a reason for running?' Her voice was terse. 'No.'

She was blaming herself, Noah thought, but he knew she wouldn't have let Ledger go if there was even the smallest suspicion that he was their killer.

Her phone rang as they reached the car. 'DI Rome. Yes, that's right . . . I see. Can you tell me which number you tried to reach him on?' She unlocked the car and got in. 'Thank you, and the address you have? No, go ahead. Stockwell. Yes, I've got it. No, he didn't turn up for work. Yes, I'm sure Mr Buxton will. Thank you.'

She ended the call, and started the engine. 'They haven't been able to get in touch with him. They have the same number he gave us. Same address, too. Paradise House in Stockwell.'

'A hostel?' Noah asked.

'Let's find out.'

32

Paradise House was a converted paper mill with narrow windows repeated at intervals, too many for much privacy inside and each one caked with the city's dirt. Not a place Marnie would have wanted to call home.

Noah must have felt the same, saying, 'Christ,' as they climbed from the car.

Marnie buzzed to be let into the hostel, showing her badge to a CCTV camera in case it wasn't as dead as it looked. After eight seconds, the door opened and they went inside.

Mould, was the first impression. Creeping green and black patches on the ceiling, and on the carpet tiles. Spores in the air. Her lungs didn't like it. Somewhere underneath the damp was the dry scent of papyrus from when the building housed paper instead of people.

A door banged at the end of the corridor and a woman strode out. Blonde hair swept into a French pleat, navy suit, heels. She flashed a smile at Marnie and Noah but didn't stop, leaving the building by the front door, disappearing up the street. At first glance Marnie had mistaken her for a member of staff, but she was a resident. Her smile was the giveaway: a chipped front tooth and too much breath freshener. How many more of the residents could pass for professional people? Jamie Ledger had fooled Marnie during their conversation on the day of May's murder. Smoking coolly, scoping her out like a piece of kit. No clue that he was homeless. No chipped teeth or bad breath.

'Can I help you?' A man in his fifties came down the corridor towards them, his face schooled to an expression somewhere south of helpful. Short and round-hipped, with dishwater-blond hair, fleshy cheeks and lips. In a green body-warmer over a red shirt, bleached jeans, hi-top trainers. His lanyard ID said simply, *Staff*.

Marnie showed her badge, introduced Noah and asked if there was somewhere they could talk in private. The man's expression didn't alter. 'Which one is it, Arkinstall?' He walked them to an office. 'He hasn't been here in two nights. We reported it to his probation officer.'

'Did you?' Marnie waited to see what else he'd say.

The office was small, smelling as bad as the rest of the place, a black fan of damp on its ceiling. Filing cabinets locked with a vertical bolt, a desk with a computer and a wire tray for post, orange plastic chairs with scuffed seats, moth-eaten carpet the colour of bile. The man sat behind the desk, pointing Marnie and Noah at the other chairs. 'Residents are issued with a tenure agreement and a set of house rules. The rules are there for a reason, not for our amusement.'

'Which rule did Arkinstall break?'

'No smoking except in their own bedrooms.' He pointed a finger to where a laminated copy of the house rules was pinned next to a poster for an addiction support group.

Had he laminated the rules himself? A labour of love, perhaps.

'How many bedrooms do you have here?' Noah asked.

'Thirteen for men. Seven for women.' A first flicker of

emotion curdled his face. Distaste, or just inconvenience? 'Segregated, of course.'

'I imagine that makes it tricky.'

'Arkinstall didn't think so. That's why you're here, isn't it?'

Marnie said, 'I'm sorry, we didn't catch your name. Mr . . .?'

'Welch.'

'We were hoping to speak with one of your residents. Jamie Ledger.'

His eyes widened. 'Ledger? That's why you're here?'

'That surprises you?'

'If he's in trouble. I didn't think he was the sort.'

'You saw a lot of him? Enough to form a good opinion?'

Welch scratched at his cheek. 'He was quiet, followed the rules. We didn't see a lot of him, but that's a good sign, generally speaking.'

'Is he here now?'

'Might be. We don't ask residents to sign in and out, unless they're on probation.' No curiosity in his face. No questions, not wanting to know why the police wanted to see Ledger.

Marnie said, 'How many staff do you have here?'

'A minimum of two, plus a night security officer.'

'Could you show us to Mr Ledger's room? We'd like to speak with him.'

Welch gathered up a set of keys on a numbered ring and led the way down the corridor, where the mould was having a field day. Marnie saw Noah's face pinch shut, his profile narrowing. 'You have a problem with damp,' she told Welch.

He didn't argue, just quoted from the rulebook again: 'This is only ever meant as a temporary step on the way back. The aim is always independent living.' As if the mould was doing the residents a favour by giving them an incentive to step up, get out.

Ledger's room was locked.

Welch knocked, waited, knocked again. Then called, 'I'm coming in.' He unlocked the door, pushed it wide with his arm at full stretch, keeping his feet firmly in the corridor. Another house rule? Protecting Ledger's privacy, or anticipating trouble?

The room was empty. Thin curtains pulled shut, a small table and a single bed made with military neatness. No wardrobe, not even a locker. Holes in the skirting board had been filled with plaster and bits of raw wood. The light bulb hanging from the ceiling was red. No lamp-shade, just a cobwebbed black cord. Imagine lying on the bed – a sagging divan, stained up its sides – trying to read, with the room lit red and the damp curling the paper away from the walls. Marnie couldn't have done it. She thought of the efficient way in which Ledger had rolled his cigarettes, smoking each one to a shred of paper. Standing with his shoulders back, sweeping her with his stare, all watchful attention. Precise, orderly. No doubt he'd slept in worse places than this, but from choice?

I'd forgotten what a pit London is.

What had it done to his dignity to call this place home? To check in and out with the addicts and ex-offenders? Just another face for people like Welch to blank, stripped of his identity, all notion of comradeship obliterated by a tenure agreement dictating when he could and couldn't lie under a red bulb breathing in mould spores. No control over any of it, after his life had been all about control, routine, orders. Just Welch's house rules, no smoking except in your own room.

Ledger hadn't smoked in here. No trace of tobacco, no shreds of paper. Nothing.

Marnie hadn't expected to find him here, but she'd hoped for some clue as to where he might have gone. She was out of luck. 'Was he friendly with any of the other residents? Someone who might know where we can find him?'

'I've never seen him talking with anyone. Mind you, he isn't here much of the time. Comes and goes, keeps himself to himself, knows better than to get comfy here.' Welch's tone said he wished more residents shared Ledger's attitude. 'He spoke with the volunteers sometimes.'

'Do you have many volunteers?' Noah asked.

'Quite a few. I can get you a list if you need one.'

'Thanks. And we'll need to see the contact details you have. Ledger's next of kin and so on.'

Welch nodded. Even now he had no questions, his face the same empty mask he'd worn when they'd arrived. Perhaps it was a necessity. His camouflage against intimacy, or pity, or aggression – any of the things that might make his job more difficult, more human.

'He isn't here much of the time,' Marnie said. 'What did you mean by that?'

'Just what I said. He's here enough to justify the room, but he doesn't *live* here.'

'So where is he living?'

'No idea.' Welch looked surprised by the question, but uninterested in its answer. 'Just glad he's got the good sense not to try and put down roots here. That's the thin end of a fat wedge.'

And a short route to aspergillosis.

'One last question,' Marnie said, 'for now. Is there anywhere else on the premises where residents can leave their belongings? Lockers, or a safe?'

'This is it.' Welch indicated the stripped-down room. 'If it's not in here, he took it with him.'

33

Aimee

See that row of windows to the right of the power station, the place with the flat roof? That's a hostel. I spent a couple of nights there, before I met May. The whole place stank of damp and I stayed up all night with my bed jammed against the door in case someone decided they liked the look of me. You can laugh, but plenty of people liked the look of me, before Harm.

In the new place, it was a long way down. Too far to jump even if he hadn't fixed the windows. Too far for anyone to see me waving or shouting for help. If I was getting out of there – and I was getting out – I had to go through them.

Harm, and Christie.

The wire was taking too long. I needed a broken glass or a knife. I'd had a knife on the streets after I was raped, but it was risky carrying a knife. If you were robbed, there was a good chance they'd stab you, and hostels made you empty your pockets in case you were a druggie or a psycho. I got rid of the knife before I met May.

It was my fault she'd been there, in Harm's safe place.

As soon as I saw her in the subway, hiding from the rain, I wanted her with me. I'm not being romantic; this isn't a love story and I wasn't a *lezzer* like Ashleigh thought. I wasn't anything. But I'd loved May as soon as I saw her. Wanted her with me in the house, and then in that place where it was too high to jump and too far to wave. Only one way out – through them.

It was my fault May was there, but it was their fault she was gone.

Harm and Christie.

It could've been good, *should've* been good. Better than that fucking dump with the mould on the walls where I was scared of getting raped again, where I had to stay awake all night.

We'd sit up there, May and me, for hours. I'd brush her hair with his silver brush and she'd tell me about her little sister and—

Fuck, I loved her. So much it hurt. I wanted to be out there. Even if it was cold and wet and I ended up getting knifed, it'd be worth it to see her again. Even if she didn't want me, if she was back home with her sister waiting for the baby to come, I'd see her and it'd be worth it.

So I was getting out, if I had to kill the pair of them to do it.

No more *if I had the courage*, no more *Aimee in decline*. I was growing a pair and getting out.

Let them try and stop me, just let them fucking try.

I'd have them. You watch.

I'd fucking have them.

34

'Paradise House is a hostel,' Marnie told Tim Welland. 'Run by staff and volunteers. They take homeless people with particular problems, usually drug- or drink-related. They also take ex-army personnel who are struggling for one reason or another.'

'James Ledger was struggling,' Welland surmised. 'With what, exactly?'

'PTSD. Panic attacks, night terrors. His neighbours complained to the council about the noise. He'd wake screaming around three a.m., putting his fist through walls. His wife asked him to leave because she was scared they'd lose the house. He wouldn't take any of the help on offer, insisted others needed it more than he did. Refused medication because it made him catatonic, and how could he take care of his wife if he was like that?'

Marnie smoothed her thumb over Ledger's picture, pinned to the whiteboard. 'He does a good impersonation of a functioning human being, but according to his wife and doctor he's anything but. Paranoid delusions, violent outbursts, controlling behaviour. The works.'

Susie Ledger was listed at Paradise House as Jamie's

next of kin. She'd answered Marnie's questions quietly, sounding exhausted. Asked if her husband was okay, if he was coping, if he was safe. Marnie hadn't been able to answer her questions.

Welland was studying Ledger's face. 'You think he's our killer?'

'He fits the profile. He's been living in this part of London for the last two years, since he was discharged from the army. He's plausible, someone girls might trust, with access to the site where May was found. *He* found her, and he's missing. The hostel says he's not been back since the morning of the police interviews, walked off site after we moved in. No one's seen him since.'

'What about this offer of his to show journalists around the place?' Welland stroked his cheek. 'That was risky, if he was planning on leaving a body up there. Why draw attention to himself?'

In the photograph, Ledger was smiling but his eyes were serious.

Marnie had liked him. It hurt to think she'd got it wrong.

'Everything this killer does is risky,' she told Welland. 'Ledger thrived on risk when he was in Afghanistan. Nothing fazed him apart from complacency. Civilian complacency. He thinks most of us live like zombies, that we need waking up to what's happening in the world.'

'This is coming from his wife?' Welland lowered his brow. 'She hasn't heard from him?'

'Not in nearly three months.'

'What about their friends?'

'He doesn't have any in London. The hostel said he had no visitors, no messages left for him.'

'So he's homeless, a loner, ex-military. Dangerous,

paranoid and violent.' Welland gave a slow nod. 'What else, or is that enough?'

'He's been working on new-build sites for some months, so we're looking into those. He spoke with Marc Amos at the media party. It's possible he approached several journalists too. Maybe one of them took up his offer of an inside story. We're following that up. He has a phone that he's either switched off or thrown away. We're tracing it. DS Carling's showing his picture around the Garrett to see if anyone's spotted him recently.'

'It's time to tell the press about Ashleigh Jewell.' Welland put his hands together, measuring their long palms. 'I'm thinking we release Ledger's photo at the same time. Person of interest.'

It would look like progress on their part. Two dead girls and a man who was missing. The public would assume Ledger was the killer, whether or not the press pointed them in that direction.

Marnie didn't like it, and said so.

Welland shrugged his big shoulders. 'We need some forward momentum.'

'And if it comes back to bite us?'

'You can say you told me so.'

By 9 p.m., Ashleigh's face was on television, her death linked to May's, the two girls looking as different in life as they had in death.

Marnie watched the news at Ed's flat, feeling thinned out, her body lighter than it should be. Her head fizzed emptily, not quite a headache. Ed was next to her on the sofa, ballast for the night. She knew she needed to sleep. When she shut her eyes, she saw the girls' faces, so unalike. And the other faces, the missing girls from the whiteboard. Sasha and Kim and Sika. Traffic's girl too,

213

for whom they had no name. Some homogeny haunted her, a tyranny of sameness behind those too-bright smiles, make-up like warpaint, empty eyes, hair extensions, painted nails, fake tans. So little space to be different, to be yourself. Had life been like that when she was fifteen, sixteen? She remembered carrying the weight of her difference – red hair, pale skin, spikiness. Whole weeks when she'd radiated hostility towards everyone, giving out a lighthouse signal that was part warning, part SOS. She'd wanted rescue, safety. Someone to take her away from everything, including herself. Had it been like that for May and Ashleigh, and the other girls? Had they learnt the same hard lesson she'd learned? That no matter how loud you shout, sometimes you're left alone. Sometimes, no one comes.

Dan intercepted Noah as he got home, to say Sol was cooking in the kitchen. 'He's making reggae nachos. You should see him go.'

'He's feeling better.' This was Sol in penance mode, hoping to avoid unwelcome questions. The food smelt great. 'When's it ready?'

'Not for ages.' Dan's eyes gleamed. 'Fancy a shower?'

Later, the three of them sat around the table eating. Sol had made rice with the nachos, and black-eyed peas. Noah resisted a reference to his brother's own black eye, fading to green.

Sol was on top form, cracking jokes, refilling their drinks. He could've dodged a bullet, never mind an awkward question. Noah was glad of the distraction. He'd made a promise to himself when he started doing this job that he'd switch off when he got home. It wasn't easy, especially since he'd started working with DI Rome on cases like this one. Six months ago, it had been dead brothers, young boys left to die in an underground bunker. This new case wasn't any easier, but he was glad he hadn't grown a thick skin like Kenickie, dismissing murder as if it was just another statistic. Where was Kenickie's girl, missing since the night of the crash? And where was Jamie Ledger, who might be their killer? Noah had lost half a day to the migraine. The loss nagged at him.

After supper, he told Dan he was going for a run.

'Do you want company?'

Noah shook his head. 'I'm going to take a long route, try and figure something out. I'll be a couple of hours.'

He caught a bus to Chelsea Embankment, needing to get the power station in his sights as soon as possible, wanting to understand its lure for Ledger or whoever had put May's body there. Until recently it had dominated the cityscape, but all that was changing. From across the river, he could see straight through the main turbine hall, gutted by the developers, full of empty windows. From this angle, by a trick of the light, it still had all its chimneys. When he got closer, the missing chimney was obvious, a chunk of London's history gone. Its new frailty, the way it was being swallowed by glass penthouses, made him think of Emma Tarvin outflanked by the girls on the Garrett. Old London eaten up by savage ambition, and boredom. He started a slow run, pacing himself, his focus on the site's changing shape as the river curved and dipped.

He ran between plane trees, their branches growing horizontally towards the water, coming out into a dazzle of sunset. Past stone steps that fell away with wear, dropping to mudflats and pebbled shoreline. Alongside odd buildings like old teeth that had survived the ravages of the planners, grass growing in hollows where iron railings had been ripped out.

215

Everywhere he felt the tug of the Thames.

Crossing Chelsea Bridge, he lost sight of the power station between the new-builds, catching glimpses through the ranks and ranks of glass apartments. He'd grown up not far from here. Once upon a time he'd known this part of London like the palm of his hand, its alleys and arteries, the white smokestacks a useful landmark when he was a kid navigating his way around his city. Tough luck for anyone trying to use them as a compass now. London was losing its identity. Like the girls the killer had found. An exercise in control and sanitisation, all the character torn out.

When he reached the Garrett, he stopped running.

The dark was moving in, shouldering out what was left of the day, the four tower blocks pocked with light. He didn't need to look far for the kid. The lookout. Circling on his bike, the beanie hat making a round bullet of his head. Noah knew better than to approach him. He sat on one of the concrete troughs, propping his elbows on his knees, hanging his hands and head while he got his breath back. He'd sprinted the last leg, spurred on by this sudden idea of seeing the kid.

He'd not told Marnie, or anyone, but . . .

He had been the lookout once.

Years ago, when he was just a kid.

On an estate like this. Circling, pretending to be bored when actually he was thrumming with watchfulness. Not on a bike. Noah had done his circling on foot. Chosen for the task because he could sprint, and because he didn't look like the rest of them, with their hair shaved full of chevrons, their gold-chained swagger. Because he looked like a nice kid. Decent.

Six flats got cleaned out that afternoon when Noah was the lookout.

Afterwards, he'd pretended to himself that he was tricked into the role; he'd misunderstood what the gang leader wanted, was just looking out for his kid brother. Sol had been in and out of the flats so fast. The gang picked him because he was small and because he had a nice-looking big brother who would swear he was elsewhere.

Memory made Noah's skin burn.

He linked his hands at the back of his neck, holding his head down, eyes fixed on the tarmac under his feet. He'd lied for Sol on and off for years. Not to the police – no one had connected Noah or Sol to the robberies that afternoon – but he'd lied to their parents and at school, to his friends. He was lying to Dan right now, by letting Sol doss down at their place without full knowledge of what he might've done and where he might've been, who he was bringing back to the flat.

When was he going to stop lying, dodging the truth? Face up to the fact that Sol was still the narrow-shouldered boy who'd squeezed through windows a decade and a half ago, grinning at Noah when it was done, 'I was fast, yeah?', inviting his big brother's approval, wanting it even. But not *needing* it, not enough for Noah's disapproval to mean anything. When had he stopped trying to persuade Sol on to a better path, or had he even started? When he'd joined the police, Sol hadn't spoken to him for a couple of years, more disgusted than he'd been when Noah came out. He'd got over it – Noah's career choice and his sexuality – but he'd dug deeper into the gang, especially in those early days, protective of his status as a hard man, law-breaker. Noah had learnt to stop asking awkward questions, to accept his brother's life choices as Sol had accepted his, but who was he helping, really? If Sol was bringing strangers into their flat, getting beaten up. Where did it end?

The kid on the bike was still circling.

Noah unlocked his hands and lifted his head, reaching into the pocket of his sweatpants for a packet of gum. He unwrapped a strip and folded it on to his tongue, tossing the foil paper into the concrete trough.

When he looked up, he caught the kid unawares, making eye contact before he could look away. How old was he? Ten?

The kid scowled, stood up on the bike's pedals, shoving closer to Noah because backing away would betray weakness, and he'd learnt never to show weakness. Now he'd been spotted, he made a point of studying Noah, black eyes going from his running shoes to his face, sizing him up. No way he didn't recognise Noah out of the suit. He was a sharp kid, all eyes and skinny legs working the pedals, keeping the bike steady even though it was barely moving now. Scruffy jeans, but a good brand, and his trainers were top-end. Logoed sweatshirt. Under the beanie, his face was soft, but his jaw was starting to square off and his cheekbones would stand out soon. Sooty eyelashes that he probably cursed in the mirror but which the gang loved because he was baby-faced. In a year's time he'd be squeezing through windows and they'd have a new lookout, this boy's brother maybe.

Noah offered the pack of gum, not speaking.

'Pervert.' The kid had heard Sergeant Kenickie working his verbal magic.

Noah kept his arm outstretched, the gum on offer. Tempting to talk, try out the old gang-speak, see if it still had currency. Or to drop some of the slang Sol had picked up. But he kept quiet, judging it the better tactic with this kid.

'I ain't after your gum.' But he edged closer, holding the bike dead steady, feet arched on the pedals. Curiosity getting the better of him. It was a dull job being the lookout.

He used two fingers to twitch a strip of gum from the packet. Unwrapped it with his teeth, spat the wrapper into the concrete trough. Chewed. He kept his eyes on Noah, but his neck swivelled loosely, giving him the perimeter. If anyone came out of the flats, he'd be off, caught dead before he was caught talking to a copper. 'Seen you with the sket.'

Did he mean Ashleigh Jewell, or Abi Gull?

Not Abi. She had too much power here. Probably this kid was her lookout, but either way he wouldn't disrespect her. Noah shook his head, looking away from the kid, bracing his elbows on his knees as if he'd be leaving as soon as he had the energy.

'What? You don't talk to no blacks?'

'I don't talk to kids. It's against the rules. You're what – ten?'

'Fuck you. I'm eleven.' The sting in his voice said he was counting the months. 'Pervert.'

'Right.' Noah got to his feet, moving off.

The kid followed him as easily as if Noah had put him on a leash. '*Pervert.*' He was going to keep repeating that word until he got a reaction, or just because it was his protection, a short cut to his social worker if Noah decided to get nasty. 'You think I don't know nothing? I know stuff. I know more stuff than you, pervert.'

'Great. Have a nice night.'

'You think I don't know shit?' Standing up on the pedals, keeping the bike at Noah's side. 'I see everything goes down here. *Everything.*'

'I believe you.' Noah crouched to re-lace his running shoes, taking his time over it. 'Too bad I'm not allowed to interview you.'

'I seen that sket and all the others. For *years* I seen them. Ones with the hair. Ones with the *writing*.'

Noah stayed down, trying to keep the tension out of his body. The kid was only talking because Noah wasn't reacting. If he saw his words making a difference he'd shut up, or get lost.

The ones with the writing . . .

Did he mean May Beswick? Or Traffic's girl?

Noah was fast on his feet, but he doubted he could keep pace with a bike, not when this kid knew the estate like the back of his hand. If he scared him away, he might stay away.

'Like I said, too bad. My job'd be a lot easier if I was allowed to talk to ten-year-olds.' He straightened, dusting his knees like he was brushing off the kid's affronted expression.

'Fuck you, pervert. I know stuff'd solve your case *bang*. Stuff you don't know *shit* about. I know *Christie*. You ain't got the first *clue* what you're looking for.'

Noah didn't look at him, glancing at his watch, injecting an extra dose of boredom into his voice. 'Christie who?'

'Christie *Faulk*, bitch. I know Christie Faulk.' He ran his tongue across his top lip, looking nervous despite Noah's lack of interest. But he wouldn't back down now, too afraid of showing fear.

Noah felt sorry for him. But he wasn't about to back down either. His tactics might be underhand, but they were working. 'We're not looking for Christie Faulk.'

'Yeah? You should be. She's the one brought that sket here.'

'What sket?'

'The *dead* sket. The one with the crap trainers and the nose like someone smashed it.'

Ashleigh Jewell.

'So – what? Christie Faulk brought her here. That's what you're saying?'

'I *see* shit.' Standing tall on the pedals, jaw squared, black eyes fixed on Noah's face. Behind him, the whole estate stood in silence, its lit windows like eyes. 'I see more shit than *you* do. Any of you. Nothing starts round here that I don't see.'

35

Christie

The kitchen reeked of wax. Fourteen candles burning but they didn't make it brighter, just dragged in more of the darkness. Greedily, the way his pain pulled at her, at everything. There was no end to it, his pain. No end to him.

Christie tried to sit still. She tried to be that for him, a quiet place where he could rest. She searched for the right words but could only find, 'The house was better. It's too high here, they get giddy. It's the view.'

'What view?' Harm demanded. 'I put up blinds, didn't I? What view?'

The view in their heads, she thought. She couldn't explain. She listened hard for the sound of Aimee overhead, but there was nothing, as if they were floating in space. 'The house was better.'

'The house was no good.' He shoved it aside with his hand. 'Too full.'

'We could go back. Fewer of us now.'

'Full of *them*.' His eyes shifted, snarling with pain. 'Full of *her*.'

'Neve.' She said his sister's name as softly as she could, but she hated Neve. Like she'd hated May, and Ashleigh. Like she hated Aimee.

Harm leaned towards her, his shoulders stacked hot with shadows. 'What did you do?'

'What did you do?' she echoed. Asked.

They eyed one another across the candles' fire and smoke.

'I gave them a home,' Harm said. 'I took them in.'

'You took them in,' Christie agreed.

'I took *you* in.'

She smiled at him with the whole of herself, everything he'd saved, everything he'd made.

'What did you do,' he insisted, 'to Ashleigh?'

'She's back out there.' Christie used the words he'd used to explain May. 'It's what she wanted.'

He covered his mouth with his hands.

'For you. I did it for you.'

He covered his eyes.

'There's Aimee,' she said. 'It's better like this, just the three of us. We're a proper family. We need you,' she said. 'You're in control.'

He needed to be needed. She understood.

'You saved them, gave them your protection. If they'd followed your rules, they'd be safe. *You're* in charge here. They should've respected that, respected *you*. Living under your roof, owing everything to you.' Her eyes stung from the smoke. She licked her fingers and snuffed the nearest candle, pinching it dead. A drop of wax caught her thumb, shrinking to a scab. She picked it off and laid it on the table, a tiny upturned shell with her thumbprint trapped inside. 'We owe you everything.'

'Aimee . . .' He sighed her name.

'She owes you. We all do.' She snuffed another candle.

223

'You're the man of the house and this is our home. None of us had a home until you found us. You lost Neve, but you found us.'

'Neve's dead.' A crack in his voice, like a boy's. 'I loved her and she's dead.'

Christie reached for his hand. 'Neve's lost, not dead.'

'She's *dead*. You don't know how we had to keep . . . pretending.' He pulled away. '*I* had to keep pretending. Hoping like they did, playing their game to keep her alive, when I *knew*. Do you have any idea how . . . *heavy* that was? Praying with them, pretending she wasn't dead?'

The candles curled away from him, shivering towards Christie.

'I was dead,' she said, 'until you found me. Living with that woman like an animal, and then on the streets . . .' She tasted the twist of her mouth, sharp. 'They didn't deserve you, Grace and May and Ashleigh. You gave them *everything* . . .'

'Did you see her?' Harm demanded. 'The words she wrote. Did you see?'

'May?' Shouting all over herself, screaming those pictures in her sketchpads. Grace was noisier on the surface, but May did the most damage. Getting pregnant, ruining everything. 'I saw.'

'I wanted *them* to see. The pain she was in. How she felt, what she was going through. I know how much it hurts to keep those kinds of secrets.' Looking at her at last. 'Do you?'

'Of course.' Christie frowned. 'You know I do.'

'And you know *why* I left her where I did.'

'The power station.' She was tired of talking about May. What was the point? May was dead and gone, finished with. 'Because she loved it there, and because you wanted everyone to see her secrets. To understand

224

how much she was hurting and how hard you tried to help. You wanted them to hear how loudly she'd been shouting for help.'

'I *did* help.' He straightened, rocking the room. 'You said I helped you all. I loved May.'

Christie didn't speak. The wax scab was a dull pink spot on the table.

'I loved Ashleigh.' The shape of his skull was on the floor, the walls. 'Did you?'

'I did it for you.' Her thumb throbbed softly, new and bare where she'd peeled the wax away. 'Everything is for you.'

'And Grace.' Harm leaned in, his face bruised yellow by the light. 'What did you do to Grace?'

The watch ticked at his wrist. He'd taken her hands once, pulled her up from the pavement out of the rain. His hands had been empty, warm. She'd never be able to repay that.

'You looked for her,' she said. 'After she'd gone. But you couldn't have brought her back.'

Ungrateful Grace, who'd never had to live like an animal.

'You can't control them,' she told Harm. 'That's what makes them run. That and the view up here. They can see too far, it makes them giddy. You couldn't ever have succeeded with May, or with Ashleigh. Not because of you, because of *them*. Aimee's different. Maybe she's like Neve. Now it's just the three of us, it'll be good again. It *will* . . .'

'What did you do to Grace?' he repeated. 'Where is she?'

'She didn't want to be here. She didn't deserve you. When there are places out there that will kill you, that killed *me*.' She clenched her hands on the table. 'Places

225

that scrape you out.' She set her teeth. Met his eye. 'Grace got what she deserved.'

He stood, so tall she was dizzy looking up at him. 'Where is she?'

'Gone,' Christie said. 'She's . . . gone.'

36

'Is this Detective Inspector Marnie Rome?'

'Yes, it is. Who's this?'

'You've got a call from Sommerville Detention Centre. Will you take it?'

Marnie shut the door to her office. It was early, but her team was hard at work. 'Yes.'

Silence. A click, then another. Silence. Had she been cut off? 'Hello?'

'Hello.' Stephen Keele.

A decade since she'd heard his voice over the phone, but she knew it straight away. She listened to the silence, until he said, 'Are you busy? I expect you're busy.'

'What did you want?'

'May Beswick,' he said. 'And Ashleigh Jewell.'

The connection was poor, stressing the sibilants in each girl's name. If they'd been face to face, she wouldn't have heard sibilants in Stephen's voice. He spoke too carefully for that. She pushed her free hand at her desk, watching her knuckles turn white. 'What about them?'

'I've been following it on the news.' A beat. She heard him transferring the phone to his other hand. 'You should speak with one of the girls here. Jodie Izard. She says she knows the girl you're looking for. The girl with the red hair from the photofit.'

Marnie pictured him in his grey sweats, the phone pressed to his ear under his black curls, slim body slack against the wall. Happy to have her attention. She kept her silence, her only defence.

'She's called Grace,' Stephen said. 'The girl in the photofit. Grace Bradley. She was living on the streets about a year ago. That's how Jodie met her.'

'All right. Thank you.' Using the voice she'd use to any other potential witness. Polite, non-committal. 'I'll have someone come and take a statement from Jodie.'

'*You* should come,' Stephen said. 'She's a liar. Not the world's greatest liar, but a good one. She pretended she knew May Beswick, too. And Ashleigh Jewell. She's lying about that, but she's telling the truth about Grace. And there's something else . . .' He stopped.

Her turn. He wanted her to dance with him. He'd missed this. Her attention. That was what he really wanted. Not to help to find a killer, or a lost girl. To have Marnie to himself again, with her questions and her pain. The Forgiveness Project was his idea of the perfect joke . . .

Knock knock, who's there?

Control freak. Now you say control freak who?

'I'll send someone,' Marnie said. 'To take a statement from Jodie Izard.'

'There's something else. Someone you should be looking for.' He waited. 'They kidnapped Grace Bradley. Which probably means they kidnapped May, too. And Ashleigh. Jodie saw them take Grace. She described them to me.'

Silence. Marnie's hand ached. She lifted it away from the table, studying the marks on her knuckles, watching the blood return to her fingers in red bruises under the skin.

'I know what the killer looks like,' Stephen said. 'And they're going to do it again.'

He hung up so suddenly, she flinched from the pulse of static in her ear.

She waited to see if the detention centre was still on the line, but the call reverted to a dial tone. She replaced the receiver, keeping her hand on it as her mind came upright, working through the possibilities.

Stephen wanted her attention, and this was a great way to get it. They let the kids watch TV at Sommerville. He'd seen the news about May and Ashleigh, heard her name given out as the investigating officer. Clever of him not to mention Jamie Ledger. That would've been clumsy. This way she might come to Sommerville to question Jodie Izard, maybe even to see him while she was there. He wanted her attention, the same as always. Her fear was he'd wanted it five years ago. That this whole bloody mess had been about getting her attention.

She picked up a pen and wrote, 'Grace Bradley.'

If he was after her attention . . . She'd only ever been interested in her work, and he'd made himself that by killing her parents. Forcing her to spend time with him, bringing her close and keeping her there. What were the chances he knew someone or something connected to this new case? Minimal, although she couldn't discount the fact that he was in a mixed-sex juvenile detention unit. Some of those inmates had spent time on the streets. Most of them had been in care, like Stephen, and Ashleigh. Sixty-one per cent of the girls in places like Sommerville had been in the care system; another of Welland's favourite statistics. Marnie couldn't afford to make the assumption, however reasonable, that Stephen was lying about this.

She walked the short distance from her office to the whiteboard.

'Traffic's girl might be Grace Bradley.' She wrote the name on the board.

'Did you find a new witness?' Debbie asked.

'Possibly. Possibly just a time-waster, but let's see.' She put the pen down, turned to face the team. 'What else is new this morning?'

'Ron's back on the Garrett,' Colin said. 'No one recognises Ledger, yet. We're still trying to talk to people who may've seen Ashleigh or Traffic's girl. Lots of doors not being answered, but Ron says they're making progress, ticking residents off the list. Over seven hundred flats, that's around two thousand residents to speak with. People saw the news last night, which might help.'

Or it might not, Marnie thought.

'What's the mood like this morning? On the Garrett.'

'Community Safety's over there again. Ron says it's very edgy still.'

'Keep me posted.' She glanced up as Noah came into the room, seeing news in his face. 'Yes?'

'The subway. We've found it.'

'Where?' She reached for her coat.

'Stockwell. Less than half a mile from Paradise House.'

'Forensics will want to get over there,' Colin said. 'If it's where he found May and Ashleigh.'

'Let's take a look first.' Marnie nodded at Noah. 'Good work.'

In the car, she said, 'Was it the Transport Police or Dan's friend who called you?'

'Rents, the graffiti tagger.' Noah fastened his seat belt. 'He's not a friend of Dan's, or anyone's as far as I can tell. Dan had to convince him it wouldn't get back to the BTP. Rents says he's not been to the subway in months but it was always full of kids, boys as well as girls.

230

Teenagers, but wet behind the ears. Not real street kids.'

Easy pickings, in other words, and less than half a mile from where Ledger had been living for the last three months.

The traffic was on their side. Noah was tense, his profile exaggerated by stress. If she listened hard, Marnie could hear him thrumming. 'Did you talk with Sol?'

He shook his head. 'But it's cool, I think.'

Not Sol. He was stressing about something else.

'You'd better tell me,' she said lightly. 'Even if you think I won't like it.'

Noah threw her a quick look. She smiled. 'Come on, we've been working together how long now? I can tell when something's eating you.'

He put his shoulders down. Returned her smile, briefly. 'Okay, but you really might not like it. I . . . spoke with the kid on the Garrett last night. The one on the bike, the lookout.'

Marnie switched lanes behind a taxi. 'Go on.'

'I went for a run. Wanted to see the power station, just the lie of the land. I didn't head out there to talk to anyone. I know that could mess up the investigation. And he's just a kid, which could get us into trouble, but . . . He was on his own, and I knew how to talk to him. I knew he'd seen stuff, because that's the job of the lookout.' He stopped, watching for Marnie's reaction. 'Sorry.'

Her mind leapfrogged its first thought – Welland telling her in a few choice words what he thought of her boy wonder breaking the easiest-kept rule in the book, 'Keep all big sticks away from buckets of shit' – and landed on its second. 'What did he give you?'

'A name. Christie Faulk. She used to live on the Garrett. He saw her with Ashleigh Jewell.'

'On the night in question?'

Noah shook his head. 'I thought that's what he meant, but he says he's not seen Christie in months. It was back before Christmas when he saw her with Ashleigh.'

'What's his name? Your witness.'

'I didn't ask him for a name. He wouldn't have talked to me if it was on the record. I know that means it's useless as evidence. It's why I didn't call you last night. I didn't know whether you'd want me putting Christie's name on the board, given how I got it.'

Marnie thought of the name she'd added to the board this morning: Grace Bradley. The source for that was hardly more reliable than Noah's nameless boy. 'How sure are you that it's a lead?'

'Pretty sure. I know kids like that, grew up with them. This kid's not lying.'

'You'd better follow it up. Get DC Tanner to search the system for Christie Faulk.'

Noah took out his phone and made the call. When he hung up, he changed the subject. 'Dan's curating a new show. Prisoner art. It made me think of May's sketches, all those vertical lines. And on the Garrett. Emma Tarvin living like a prisoner. Even Abi and her friends are trapped there. The kid last night's the same. Everyone's terrified. It wasn't that bad when I was growing up. I mean, it wasn't *good*. There were a lot of problems, but there wasn't this paranoia. We knew who was on our side and who wasn't. Then you've got people like Toni Shepherd making a living out of it. All those promises of security, privacy, *apartness* . . . The artwork in the flat where we found May, the landscape over the bed? That was designed to make you want to pay extra for the locks on the doors and the CCTV cameras. "Look how scary London is", that's what they're saying, what they're selling. "Look how scary it is *out there*. Wouldn't you like to be safe in here instead?"'

Panic rooms. Safe houses. Gated communities. A whole industry had grown up around people's fear of invasion, or attack. Easy to turn up the volume on paranoia.

'As if the world wasn't frightening enough,' Noah said, 'without inventing things to be afraid of.'

In Stockwell, the subway shone with recent rain. Its shape was instantly recognisable from May's sketches, the entrance with grass growing at either side, orange light from boxes mounted on the walls. The graffiti was just as May had drawn it, contrasting shades of neon. *Fearz* and *Rents*. The rest was recent litter, and kids sitting in a short group against one wall. Two on a tartan picnic blanket. The other, a teenage boy, on a Waitrose carrier bag. Not homeless, just truant. They'd been drinking Becks, empty bottles at their feet, and was that a Kettle Chips bag?

'Hello. I'm Detective Inspector Rome. This is Detective Sergeant Jake. What're your names?'

The boy on the carrier bag squirmed to face her. A nice face, round like a child's. 'I'm Joel.'

'Hello, Joel.' Marnie nodded, looking at the other two. A boy and a girl, both dressed in skinny black jeans and hoodies, Dr Martens.

The girl's boots were floral-patterned. Uggs for hipsters. 'Daisy,' she said.

The boy said, 'Corin.'

All three were moon-pale. Truants with liberal parents who'd paid for the expensive boots and jeans by working long hours, too long to spend time wondering what their kids got up to after school, or before it. May's friends had been kids like these. Neglected, but not in the usual way.

'Have you been coming here for a while?' Marnie asked.

'Not really,' Joel said. 'It was raining and we didn't want to get wet, that's all.'

The kids looked spooked. By Marnie and Noah? She smiled, to show them it was okay. 'We're looking for a couple of people who might have been here recently.' She nodded at Noah.

He took out his phone, showing them the pictures of Jamie Ledger and Traffic's girl.

The kids shook their heads. Corin said, 'Is he the killer?'

They knew about the killer, but they chose to hang out here after school instead of going home.

Daisy said wistfully, 'I like her hair.'

Marnie wondered about the face in May's sketchpad, the poster child for Shelter. None of these three had that androgynous face with its arrogance and vulnerability. What had happened to that child?

'Did any of you know May Beswick?'

They shuffled a look between them before Joel said, 'Not really. Just on the news, you know. We heard about her on the news.'

'She didn't hang out here?'

'Not when we were here.' Another quick look at the other two. 'We've not been coming here that long. Only in the last couple of weeks, and just when it's raining.'

It had rained, on and off, for most of the month.

'I'd like hair like that,' Daisy said.

Marnie imagined the girl's mother paying for an expensive colour job, the way she'd paid for the floral-patterned boots, taking the guilt trip gladly because it was a short cut to her daughter's diminishing affection. Daisy's mouth was turned down in a pout.

'Did you know her, Corin?' Noah said. 'May Beswick.'

The boy shot a scared look at Joel, shutting his mouth

so hard the shape of his teeth showed through his lips. He shook his head.

Noah said, 'You looked as if you knew her, when DI Rome mentioned her name.'

Corin shrugged, linking his elbows around his knees.

Daisy belched. 'Pardon me.' She giggled, pointing at the empty Becks bottles. 'Blame that.'

'How old are you, Daisy?' Marnie smiled at the girl. 'Sixteen?'

'Seventeen.' Defensively.

'May was sixteen. In the sixth form at Robert Fiedler, studying art and design.' She kept her eyes on the girl's face, knowing that Noah was watching Corin. 'Are you in the sixth form, Joel?'

The boy shifted on his carrier bag. 'Yes.'

'Which school?'

'Same. Robert Fiedler.'

'But you didn't know May Beswick.'

'It's a big school, loads of us go there.'

'If you didn't know her,' Noah asked Corin, 'why are you so upset?'

'Because she *died*.' He kicked at an empty bottle. 'What're you – a freak? Jesus.'

Noah took out his notebook. A prop, but it worked. All three of them stiffened in response.

Marnie said, 'I think we'd better take your full names and addresses.'

'She came here.' Daisy wound a finger into her hair, ignoring the filthy looks the two boys gave her. 'We didn't really know her, but she came here sometimes. To draw stuff.' She pulled at her hair, glaring at Corin and Joel. 'I am *not* getting another fucking lecture off my dad, all right?'

'So you've been coming here for three months or more. When was the last time you saw May?'

'Back before Christmas,' Joel said.

'Ages before that,' Daisy corrected him. 'That's when I got these,' sticking out her feet. 'She never got to see them.'

'Bonfire Night,' Corin said, biting at his thumbnail. 'She was drawing the fireworks over Battersea Power Station. She loved it there.'

May had gone missing on 31 December. Why did she stop coming to the subway two months before then? Or had these kids stopped coming when the weather was cold, deciding they could stand to be in their warm houses after all?

'Did she come here with anyone else?' Marnie asked. 'Or was she by herself?'

'By herself.'

'You didn't come forward when she went missing,' Noah said. 'Why not?'

'We hadn't seen her in ages, didn't see what use it'd be telling you that. They asked us questions at school, but we didn't know anything useful.'

'And you didn't want your dad giving you a lecture,' Noah said, 'about hanging out here.'

Daisy looked up at him for a long moment before she nodded.

'Who else hung out here at that time? Just the four of you?'

'Different people,' Corin said, 'come and go. It's not like we're a *gang*.'

Noah showed his phone again. 'How about her? Did she come and go?'

'That's Ashleigh Jewell,' Daisy said naïvely. 'We never saw her.'

'But you know who she is.'

'Saw her on the news. Like that skinhead you showed

us. Your Tumblr must be *so* depressing, photos of dead girls and killers . . .'

'Who else came and went around the same time May was here?'

'Sasha,' Joel said. 'Eric. A whole bunch of us. But people move on, if they can. Better than being stuck in this wasteland.'

'Sasha Ronson?' Noah asked.

Joel shrugged. 'Just Sasha. She never said her surname.'

'Have you seen her recently?'

'No. She cleared off before May did.'

'What about Eric?' Marnie said. 'Do you have a surname for him?'

Joel shook his head. 'He was kind of a psycho, never talked much. Haven't seen him in ages anyway. Guess he got away.'

'These people who move on,' Marnie asked, 'are they all your age?'

'I suppose so . . .' Joel looked distant.

Corin got to his feet suddenly, kicking his corner of the tartan blanket out of the way. 'I'm going home. Are you coming, Dee?'

Daisy rolled sideways to her knees. Climbed to her feet, dragging the blanket with her. She wrapped it around her left arm, waiting while Joel got up from the floor. He tidied the empty bottles into the carrier bag, making a show of being civic-minded.

'We'll take those.' Marnie held out her hand. 'And we'll need your names and addresses. In case we want to contact you.'

She didn't want to lose sight of these kids. Noah took their details. He and Marnie stood back, waiting to see which of the kids would lead the walk out. In the end, they fell into step, moving like the gang Corin said they

237

weren't, hiding under their hoods when they hit daylight.

'What do you think?' Marnie glanced around the subway's low tide of litter. 'Is it worth getting Forensics out here?'

'They could have been lying about how recently they saw May.' Noah held the back of his neck in the crook of his hand. 'I don't think they recognised Ledger, from my phone or the news last night. But May was here, more than once.' He eyed the cracked tiles where old rain had collected like dark brown soup. 'She sketched here, with Ashleigh.'

Marnie nodded. 'Let's seal it off. I'll call Forensics.' She tied a knot in the neck of the carrier bag and put it down on the tiled floor with the rest of the litter. 'Fran will want to know we've found this place. She might even be able to rush the results for us.'

Noah didn't question the decision, looking relieved to be doing something, even if it was only unwinding tape to keep any more kids from finding their way in here next time it rained.

After she'd put the call in to Fran, Marnie rang Debbie at the station. 'We need a uniform.' She gave the location of the subway. 'We've taped it, and Forensics are on their way, but we need to keep it sealed off until they're finished. Anything on Grace Bradley?'

She wanted Debbie to say no, but . . .

'There's a Grace Irene Bradley in the Missing Persons database. She went missing from care a year ago, when she was fourteen. I'm trying to get hold of a decent photo. The one they have could be anyone. It *could* be Traffic's girl.'

'Where was she in care?'

'Wolverhampton. No connection that I could see to Ashleigh or May.'

238

'Send me whatever you've got. How about the other girl, Christie Faulk?'

'She's next on my list. Ron's going to call you. The Garrett's getting to him.'

'Keep digging. I want everything you can find on Grace and Christie.'

Marnie ended the call, looking at Noah. 'Uniform's on the way. We've got a possible lead on Traffic's girl. Grace Bradley went missing from care in Wolverhampton a year ago. DC Tanner's double-checking and sending through the Misper record.'

'That's good, isn't it?' Noah saw her frowning. 'If we've got a name for her? That's good.'

'Let's see what comes through.' Marnie wiped her thumb at the screen of her phone, waiting for it to deliver the message from Debbie, or the call from Ron.

Debbie's text came first.

The photo of Grace Bradley was poor quality, black and white, her face in shadow. Marnie searched for a resemblance to the e-fit, the barefoot girl in the CCTV footage. 'Is it her?'

Noah bent his head close to look. 'Maybe. Yes.' He pointed at the girl's jawline, strong, with a forward slant. 'I think it's her.'

Marnie was silent long enough for him to ask, 'Where did the lead come from?'

'Stephen Keele. He called this morning from Sommerville. One of the girls there, Jodie Izard, was living on the streets with Grace. He says. Jodie recognised her from the e-fit on the news last night. She's also claiming to know Ashleigh and May.'

Noah's face thinned, frowning. 'What else?'

'According to Stephen? Grace was kidnapped, and Jodie can describe who took her. Our killer, perhaps. If Grace is Traffic's girl, then we should interview Jodie and get the full story.'

'I could go.' Noah waited, wearing a neutral expression. 'If you prefer.'

'I'll go,' Marnie said. 'I want you here, looking for Grace. And Christie Faulk.'

37

Marnie left as soon as the PCSO arrived to guard the subway. She took the car, leaving Noah to catch the tube back to the station. He briefed the PCSO, warning him to keep everyone out of the subway until Forensics had finished. 'Look out for kids, especially. They like to hang out here.'

The PCSO peered into the tunnel and pulled a face. 'Rather them than me.'

That had been Noah's thought, seeing Corin and the others sitting inside the subway, albeit on a picnic blanket with pricey beer and crisps to keep them happy. He knew what his dad would say, 'Kids like that don't know they're born,' but it shouldn't have spelt death for May and Ashleigh. He headed back towards the tube station, counting his blessings. His mum and dad, Sol. Dan. He was lucky not to know what it was like to live in a family that had ceased to function. Look at Marnie. Her foster-brother had destroyed her parents, changed her life.

This offer of help from Stephen – Noah didn't trust it. He doubted Marnie did. She'd gone to Sommerville because Jodie Izard was a potential witness who had to be interviewed, but was Stephen following *every* case where Marnie was SIO? Was this the first time he'd offered his help? What was he playing at?

As he passed through the ticket barriers, his phone played Marnie's tune.

'I'm stuck on the M25.' Her voice was clipped. 'How quickly can you get to the Garrett?'

'Twenty minutes, tops.' Noah headed back into the Underground, fishing with his free hand for his Oyster card. 'What's happened?'

'Assault and arson. Emma Tarvin's been taken to hospital.'

'Abi Gull?'

'That's what it looks like. DS Carling's on site, so check in with him. I'll join you when I can, as soon as I've taken the statement from Jodie Izard. Call me when you're on the estate and let me know how bad it is. I need to keep Welland one step ahead of the press.'

At the Garrett, Community Safety officers were unloading riot gear from the back of a van. One of them, armed with a loudspeaker, was trying to clear the crowd for the fire crew.

Smoke uncurled like a fist from the sixth floor. Noah felt its sting in his eyes even from a distance. He started towards the tower block, showing his badge to anyone who got in his way, looking for the boy on the bike, but he was either not here or well hidden.

Ron was at the main entrance, talking on his phone. 'He's here now. Yeah . . . will do. Thanks, boss.' He ended the call. 'Well, this's gone tits up.' Flecks of soot under his eyes, blood on his hands. 'Emma's. She's a right mess. Vicious little cows.'

'They took her to hospital?' Noah asked.

'And Abi Gull's in the back of the custody van.'

They stood aside for the fire crew going into the building.

'Where's the fire? Not in her flat?' Noah was picturing net curtains ablaze, Emma down on the floor, trying to stay under the smoke as Abi and her friends put their boots into her.

Ron shook his head. 'Little buggers lit it on the floor below, must've known she'd come out for a nosy. They were waiting for her.'

'They smoked her out.'

'That's exactly what they did.' Ron looked sick with disgust. 'You know what Abi said when I arrested her? "It was worth it." At least now we get to lock her up.'

'Were her friends involved? How many arrests did you make?'

'Just the one, for now. I'm betting Natalie Filton was part of it, but she'd cleared off by the time we got here. Abi was having too much fun to stop until we made her.'

'How badly is she hurt? Emma, I mean.'

'The paramedics got here quickly, and she's a tough old bird. I'm hoping she'll be okay. I don't want to miss the look on her face when we tell her Abi's going down for this, at last.'

Perhaps Emma would say the same thing Abi had said: *It was worth it.*

The fire crew were coming back down the stairs. Noah asked, 'How bad is it up there?'

'It's out,' the crew manager said. 'Arson again. Someone said you got them this time?'

'In the custody van.' Ron nodded. 'How bad's the damage?'

'To the flats? Not bad. Mainly along the deck access. Like every other time. You'd think they'd get bored of it, wouldn't you?'

'Not this one,' Ron said. 'But we've got her now. No way she's walking away from this.'

'Is it safe to go up?' Noah wanted to see the damage for himself.

The man nodded. 'As long as you stay wide of the investigation crew.'

Noah thanked him and left Ron at the main entrance.

He climbed with the aftermath of the fire black on his tongue and his head stuffed with the image of Emma fighting her way through thick smoke to where the girls were lying in wait.

On the sixth floor, there wasn't much to see.

A shallow slick of water from the hoses, pieces of burnt cloth and paper floating on its surface. Brown stains reaching up the walls. The estate was already absorbing the mess. Arson left a scar, but this one was hidden by all the others, just an extra layer to the Garrett's natural camouflage.

Noah kept going to the seventh floor, counting the time it would have taken Emma to reach the spot where the girls attacked her. Less than a minute, even allowing for the fact that she'd have moved more slowly than he did. No time at all.

Emma's flat, when he reached it, looked the same.

He curled his hand and blocked the light to look through the wide window into the sitting room. Net curtains filtered the view to sepia, as if he was peering into an old postcard. He could see the notebooks on the low table where Emma kept her one-woman neighbourhood watch.

From inside the flat, he could hear . . .

Knocking?

The fridge, or the boiler, perhaps. He listened to its irregular beat before trying the handle of the door, expecting to find it locked.

The door was on the latch, but awkwardly, as if it'd been closed in a hurry. It almost clicked shut, but he sensed the delicate pressure of the latch and eased it open.

Stepped into the hallway to the smell of burnt milk and smoke. 'Hello?'

The knocking was louder now. Not a fridge or a boiler, more like . . .

Feet, or fists.

Noah's scalp tightened. He followed the sound to the bedroom at the back of the flat.

'Hello? Police. I'm Detective Sergeant Jake.'

The bed had a floral duvet cover, matching pillows. Curtains were drawn at the window, their thin cotton pulling flower-shaped shadows into the room.

The knocking was coming from a cupboard built into the back wall. The cupboard doors were fastened with a length of yellow nylon washing line, wound around the handles and knotted off. A good knot, naval.

Noah struggled with it.

'Hang on. Police.'

The knocking didn't stop, but nor did it get louder or more urgent, not even when he repeated his rank and name in a bid to reassure whoever was shut inside.

The bedroom smelt of talcum powder, a pink scratch at the back of his throat. He struggled with the nylon knot, thinking of Emma Tarvin's big hands. His fingers were sweating with the effort.

'It's okay, I'm police, hold on . . .'

He got it undone at last, dragged the line through the handles, threw it behind him to the floor . . .

She fell out at his feet, sucking for breath.

Yellow rope at her wrists and ankles, elastic bandage gagging her mouth.

Skinny, half dressed, her bound hands holding on to his feet, pulling at him as she lifted her head and tried to focus on his face. He crouched to her level.

Sharp bones, and a wild scream in her eyes.

Red hair, white skin written on in black pen, blue bruises . . .

Traffic's girl.

The girl they'd been looking for since the night of the crash, the one Kenickie wanted to arrest for the manslaughter of Logan Marsh.

The girl whose name had come from Marnie's foster-brother, Stephen.

Grace Bradley.

38

Sommerville hadn't changed. The same stew of light from fittings filled with dust and dead insects. Same acoustics, making Marnie's footfall punchy. Same wait for Paul Bruton to authorise her access to the centre, even after she'd called ahead to say she needed to see Jodie Izard as a matter of urgency.

Only one thing had changed. She might have come and gone without noticing if she hadn't been made to wait for Jodie to be brought to the visitor room.

At the end of the corridor, a glass door looked into the main body of the detention centre. Marnie had been through the door more than once. She had no intention of going through it today. She intended to take a statement from Jodie and get back to London as quickly as she could. Noah would be on the Garrett estate by now. She was expecting his report.

As she waited for Bruton, she saw a man standing the other side of the fireproofed glass. Her height, perhaps a shade taller, in jeans and a grey sweatshirt. Broad-shouldered, his hair buzz-cut to a dark shadow on his scalp. Standing very still, watching her.

It was only by the stillness that she recognised him. Stephen Keele.

Marnie tensed in alarm, her skin pricking everywhere, the way it did when she caught sight of a stranger as she walked home alone late at night – a cold punch of fear through her veins.

She knew him, but she didn't.

A grown man, a new stranger.

Stephen Keele.

Acid burned the back of her throat, blood beating in her ears. He was strong, she could see it in his shoulders. He could take her. His shadow reared up the wall.

They stared at one another across the empty length of the corridor.

He was nineteen years old. He'd been a boy the last time she saw him, still skinny, with black curls and a red mouth.

She hardly recognised the man behind the glass.

How had he changed so much in six months? She didn't need to ask *why* he'd changed. He was being moved to an adult prison – working out, getting strong. Ten years ago, she'd been able to lift him on to a swing in her parents' garden. Now he looked dangerous, immovable. It wasn't just his new bulk and the buzz cut. It was the dip of his head, his warrior stance.

The pulse of his hostility reached her from thirty feet away, and she had to struggle to control her fight-or-flight response, the skin at the back of her neck and knees flushing damply. Like a flush of shame, except she wasn't the one who should be ashamed. She'd done nothing but grieve the loss of her parents and ask questions, holding out for answers past the point when it became obvious he wouldn't or couldn't give her any. A lick of anger in the back of her throat, salty like tears . . .

He'd lost his disguise. No – he'd stripped it away. The last signs marking him out as a child. His curls, his narrowness, the limpid way he'd used his stare to pull her back into that past where she'd made promises to her parents to take care of her new brother. A boy they'd rescued from a broken family, wanting to make him whole again. Six years they spent trying to love him. There wasn't any trace of that boy in the man standing on the other side of the glass. Gone . . .

He's gone.

Good.

I can hate him now.

The ferocity of it shook her. For a second she was in free fall, euphoric, her head light and empty. She was dimly aware of moving in his direction, towards the glass door.

'DI Rome?'

Time slowed. She felt it unravelling, each strand separate and static.

She stopped, three feet from Stephen.

He hadn't moved from his side of the glass.

Light stripped the blood from under his skin, rendering his face in black and white. She was close enough to see the details in his irises.

'DI Rome?' Paul Bruton was standing in the doorway to the visitor room.

Marnie could see him without looking, without breaking eye contact with Stephen. Her hands hurt. She'd clenched them into fists.

She stepped back. Relaxed her hands. Turned to face Bruton.

'Jodie's ready for you.' Bruton was looking past her at the glass door, but he was too far away to see what Marnie had seen in Stephen's eyes.

Under the hostility, the freshly forged aggression, was a smile.

Stephen was smiling.

Glad to have her here, but more than that.

Glad to have her hating him.

And fearing him, at last.

39

Marnie wasn't the only one afraid of Stephen Keele.

Hunched over in her chair in the visitor room, Jodie Izard was chewing her cuticles in concentration. When the door opened, she flinched upright.

Paul Bruton said, 'This is Detective Inspector Rome. She needs to ask you some questions, Jodie. If you like, I can stay with you.'

'You're all right.' She slid her stare past Bruton's shoulder to Marnie. Her ash-blonde hair was chopped to shoulder length, its roots burned by too much peroxide. She wore a black nylon skater's skirt over thick black leggings, Adidas trainers. A clingy white yoga top head-lined the fake tan streaked across her shoulders and the visible portion of her chest. Her face was an oval, ghosted over with cheap make-up, a halo of lipgloss around her mouth, a partially healed piercing in one thin nostril. Her eyes were pretty. Sea green, scared.

She waited until Bruton had left the room before saying, 'You're his sister.' Her voice was low, with a Somerset burr. 'You're the one he . . .' She put her tongue between her teeth and bit it.

The one he . . . What? What had Stephen told this girl he'd done to Marnie?

'I'm here to ask you about Grace Bradley.' She made her smile encouraging but not gullible. Stephen had said Jodie was a good liar, and he would know. 'What can you tell me about Grace?'

'Knew her on the streets, didn't I?' She couldn't stop staring. 'In Gloucester, a year ago, bit longer maybe. It was cold, I remember that. Hard as a cat's head, Grace. Broke all the rules, did whatever she liked, but she hated the cold. Got an offer, so she cleared off. I should've been so lucky.' She rattled the information out, wanting to move on to other things. 'He killed your mum and dad. Said he stabbed them—'

'Where did Grace go? You said she got an offer. What kind of offer? Who made it?'

'I suppose she thought it was safe. You get into all sorts of shit when you're sleeping rough. Spat on, pissed on. People think you're a piece of meat. Sex. That's if you're lucky.' She leaned forward under the ceiling strip of light, her pretty eyes glinting, catlike. 'He says it's what you wanted. That you and him—'

'Grace got an offer of sex, is that what you're saying?'

Marnie didn't want to hear whatever lies Stephen had told this girl, and possibly the rest of Sommerville too. All the time she'd been coming here, those strange looks from the kids when she walked in and out. She'd thought they stared because she was a detective, their eyes itching at her skin. It fell into place now. Under the lip of the table, she clenched her hands, concentrating on the blunt pressure of her nails in her palms. 'Who made an offer to Grace? And what was it?'

'Not sex,' Jodie said, tonguing her cheek. 'We're not all perverts.'

Above them, the light snarled as if a wasp had flown into the fluorescent tube.

'Then what? Where did Grace go?'

'Somewhere safe.' A shrug. 'It's what we all want, isn't it? Somewhere safe.'

'Where did Grace go that was safe?'

'Off the streets. Someplace warm. It's not like we can all go *home*.' She said the word like an obscenity, still digging at Marnie's face with her eyes. 'Grace couldn't. Her stepmum wanted to change her name, said *Grace* was old-fashioned and she should be *Ray* or some shit like that. Threw out all her stuff, clothes and toys. Wanted her in a bridesmaid's dress, made her grow her hair so she'd look nice at her dad's wedding, made Gracie call her *Mum* like that wasn't weird, like it didn't fuck with her head. Gracie said she wiped her out. That was her *home* and she wiped her out.'

'Who made Grace an offer, and where did she go? Somewhere in Gloucester?'

'Doubt it. Never saw her again.' She touched the scabbed piercing in her nose. 'Good luck to whoever took her, though. Probably bashed his head in and nicked his wallet. She's fucking mental.'

'Did you see who took her?'

'Maybe.'

For the first time, her stare slid away from Marnie. She was lying. Just as Stephen had said she would. Unless . . . Had he *told* her to lie? To keep Marnie here?

'If you saw who took her, I need to know. Two girls are dead. Girls like Grace who couldn't live at home, but who weren't safe on the streets. Not lucky enough to get convicted for shoplifting and end up in here where it's warm. They're dead. If you have information to help us find whoever did that, then you need to give it to me right now. Forget whatever game you're playing for Stephen Keele, or anyone else. Tell me.'

The girl's eyes had snapped to attention at the speech. She glanced towards the door as if she'd remembered where she was. Fear found its way back on to her face. 'I wouldn't disrespect you, yeah? You're his sister.' Not afraid of the police, or Marnie. Afraid of Stephen.

'Tell me,' Marnie repeated. 'What you know about who took Grace.'

'I didn't get a proper look, but it could've been him. Yeah. The one off the telly, the one you're looking for. It could've been him.'

Marnie didn't say Ledger's name, waiting to see whether Jodie would. If she'd seen Ledger in the flesh, then his name would have registered when she heard it on the news. Even if she hadn't known it a year ago, the name would have registered. Jodie said nothing, looking at Marnie with her pretty eyes, anxious to please because she wouldn't disrespect Stephen Keele's sister. If that was her motivation, then Marnie could use it.

'Let's talk about Stephen. He told you what to say to me, didn't he? Gave you orders, instructions. And you didn't want to upset him, so you went along with it.'

'I never.' The girl sucked her mouth small. 'I *saw* Grace. Right? I knew her.'

'But you didn't see who took her. You didn't see Jamie Ledger – or anyone – take her off the streets. Did you?'

Jodie hesitated, weighing up her options, torn between two brands of fear.

'If you lie to the police,' Marnie told her, 'that's a criminal offence. It will add time to your sentence, and it will piss me off. You don't want to do that. Why would you?'

'You're not in here.' Through her teeth. '*He* is.'

'Not for much longer. He's being moved to an adult prison. You'll have perjured yourself for no good reason. Did you see who took Grace Bradley?'

Jodie shook her head. But she said, 'You should've kept him out of here. You *could've*. Kept him out, given evidence—'

'What evidence?' Marnie demanded.

'You could've told them why he did it.'

'*I* could have told them?' She was incredulous. 'You think *I* know that?'

As if all this time she'd had the answers she was seeking tucked up her sleeve like a magician's trick. Exactly what lies had Stephen told this girl? The same ones he'd told Marnie?

'He did it for you,' Jodie said. 'Because of what you had, the two of you.'

The same lie, again.

Marnie was sick of hearing it.

Anger spiked through her, the way it used to when she was fifteen, a bright, hot spike.

'Because of what we had? We had *nothing*.'

Jodie shook her head. 'You could've told them, but you didn't. That's why he's pissed off with you.' She sucked a breath. 'That's why he's going to finish you.'

40

The street boomed bright and empty, steel-coloured, on the brink of rain. Christie stood blinking, unsteady on her feet. Outside was always a shock. In jeans and a coat, but she felt naked. Just for a second she wished it was two years ago. Back when she was invisible.

Harm was at his window, watching her go. She felt his stare dimming as she reached the turning in the road. He'd forgiven her, he said, for Grace and Ashleigh.

But, 'Bring me a new girl,' between his teeth.

She crossed between parked cars, hiding her hands up her sleeves. Too far for him to be watching now, but she felt the tug of the thread connecting them as if she'd stitched it herself – pierced her skin with a needle, sewn the other end to the blades of his back or the lids of his eyes. Keeping watch on her even as she ducked into the tube station.

Packed with people, their smell swallowing her up. She worked numbers into the ticket machine with her fingers jumping, stashed the credit card back in her pocket, headed for the barriers.

One stop, a lot of stairs.

Up into the blue light of a shop selling coffee and pastries. Its smell made her stomach clench. So long since she ate good food. *Bad* food. She ate properly now. Coffee dehydrated you, and cake was just empty calories slowing you down, making you sick. Her reflection in the shop's window was hungry, hollow-eyed. She forced her face to smile. *Hot chocolate*. Her tongue touched her lips, tasting it sweet and fatty in her mouth, and just for a second she wanted to run. Snip the thread. Get free, get *away*. Too late, it was too late now.

She swung away from the shop, in the direction of the tunnels.

The subway sat with its mouth open, turned towards the road. Its roof dripped as she ducked inside, out of the rain.

Suddenly, it wasn't London. The noise she'd carried with her was gone, and so was the metal-meat smell of the Underground. Orange light in rectangles from boxes fixed to the walls, but the light rolled away, back into the tunnel's throat. Dark, and dry. She remembered this. How weird it felt to be warm when there was no door and the rain could blow inside. Pipes under the floor ran all the way back to the power station. Harm had taught her that. Miles and miles of pipes taking excess steam to the council estate across the river.

Four kids on the floor, faces inside hoodies, empty bottles at their feet. Sitting like cave-dwellers, hands hanging, heads down. If Christie did this right, there'd be three kids tomorrow.

'I'm looking for Neve.'

Two of the faces turned towards her, slackly. She ignored the flare of contempt from under her ribs and made a judgement based on instinct. The girl with the big eyes, she was the one. The one Harm would choose. Just a kid, lost-looking.

'Neve,' Christie repeated. 'Any of you seen her?'

'No.' One of the boys, speaking for the group. Tough, or pretending to be. If he was tough, he wouldn't be running in here at the first sign of rain.

'Shit.' She leaned into the wall, then slid until she was sitting on the floor of the subway. '*Shit*.'

The boy stared and moved his mouth. 'What?'

'I think she's dead.' Christie put her head back against the wall, under the sign that said *Fearz*. 'Neve. I think she's dead.'

'Who is she?' The girl with the big eyes had spikes in her voice.

'My sister.' Christie wiped her face with the cuff of her shirt. 'She's my sister.' It was near enough to the truth. Harm's sister, the one he'd given up for dead. 'Been everywhere, all across London. Everywhere she used to go.' She kicked at the scarred tilework. 'Fuck. *Fuck*.'

'We haven't seen her,' the boy said. 'Sorry.'

'Forget it. She's gone. Just can't stop looking, you know?'

Silence. The seep of heat under her legs. Miles of pipe packed with steam from the long-dead chimneys of the power station. Like the core of the earth coming up.

'D'you think she was killed?' Big Eyes looked twelve, maybe thirteen. Wild hair like black brambles. Clothes too big for her, just like her eyes. Spikes in her voice and in her stare.

'I don't know,' Christie said. 'Maybe. It happens.'

'It's happened recently,' Big Eyes said. 'More than once.'

The boy nodded, looking important. 'The police were round here earlier. We had to wait until they'd cleared off. They're looking for a killer.'

'Yeah, I heard about that.'

'D'you think it happened to your sister?'

'Don't know.' She shut her eyes. 'Stupid thing is, I've a place to stay now, somewhere safe. That's all she wanted, and if she'd just waited, two or three weeks . . .' She broke off, shaking her head.

'Where?' Big Eyes asked.

'What?' Rolling her neck tiredly, as if she didn't care about the question or its answer.

'Where're you staying? Somewhere safe, you said.'

Big Eyes was quick, not another Aimee. Harm wouldn't see that, not right away. He'd see her face looking lost in its tangle of hair, and how she hugged herself. He'd like her, until it was too late. He'd choose her. Until it was too late.

'Yeah. I got lucky. Too late for Neve . . .'

'A squat?' The boy had a home to go to. Only someone with a home would say, *A squat?* like it was somewhere cool he'd read about in a book or on a website.

Christie opened her eyes but turned her head away. 'Not a squat.'

Big Eyes was watching her. She had a hot stare, like Harm's. It made Christie angry. 'Look, piss off, okay? There's no room, anyway. No room for anyone else. We're full.'

'How long's she been missing?' Big Eyes asked. 'Neve.'

'Weeks. Months.' That was not good. She should know exactly how long. She should be counting every hour. 'Thirteen weeks and four days.'

Big Eyes nodded, dropping her stare. 'Sorry,' she said, losing some of the spikes.

'That's okay.' A breath. 'I'm Christie, by the way.'

'Hi,' the kids said, one after another. The boy said, 'I'm Joel,' and one of the others gave his name too. Big Eyes didn't say hers. On her guard.

Christie didn't look like one of them any longer. Was that it? She'd lost her disguise. With Grace and the others, it'd been easy. Tell them about the house – somewhere warm, with free food, beds – and they followed like mice to a trail of crumbs. Big Eyes was suspicious of her, the way Christie had been suspicious of the rich creep in his plastic cape. Had she become someone like that, to be feared? Or like the religious couple telling her to be ready for what was coming when they had *no idea* what that was. Harm had saved her from the pervert, the threats and promises. She owed him. Even if she didn't, she couldn't go back empty-handed. But she could take someone he wasn't expecting, someone to remind him why he needed *her*. Christie. He wouldn't know what to do with Big Eyes, not without her help.

'Did you know them?' she asked the kids. 'The girls who got killed.'

Joel shot a look at Big Eyes, but she shook her head. 'We heard about them, on the news.'

'Have you got somewhere to go?' Christie asked, grudgingly. 'Safer than this, I mean.'

Joel said, 'Depends what you mean by *safe*,' as if he had a story he could tell.

Christie could guess the story. Abuse. Boys like Joel always thought abuse made them special. Boys like Joel didn't know they were born. He had a watch on his wrist that another kid would've killed for. And still might. She could see him dead. A look of surprise on his face that said, *I didn't deserve this*, but he did. For sitting drinking beer from glass bottles, telling sob stories to his friends, every one of whom had a home to go to. Playing at being lost. Like the rain was a stream they could paddle their soft feet in before going back to their warm beds.

Big Eyes was different. She looked lost, but it could

be a disguise or a trick of the light. Christie wouldn't know for certain, not until she took the girl home to Harm.

'What about you?' The tunnel took her words, made them hard.

Softly, Harm always said. *Softly, softly.*

'What about me?' Big Eyes was staring at Christie, soaking her up with her stare. *Seeing* her. The way Harm had seen her two years ago, the way no one else ever saw her. Christie wanted to scream. She wanted to put her feet into these kids until her shoes were sticky.

Bring me another girl.

'Have you got somewhere safe to go?' she asked softly.

Big Eyes said, 'No.' It was a lie, but Big Eyes was good. She didn't care whether Christie believed her or not. She wasn't like Joel or the others; this wasn't a game for her. She was here because she'd run out of whatever else was on offer. Tears and shame and all the rest of it. Nothing left of her. She'd reached the end.

Christie pictured a house for Big Eyes, like the one she'd run from years ago. A nice house on a nice street. Curtains at the windows, pale carpets. Take your shoes off at the door, a rule of the house. Wooden floors downstairs so that echoes chased you and you held your breath when you crept to the kitchen at night to drink milk from the carton in the white hum of the refrigerator. Nice people sleeping in the bedroom upstairs. A man and a woman, him with brown hair and eyes, her highlights expensively done every six weeks, body tight as a twang, no comfort in her anywhere. The milk tastes blue and fatty and it's forbidden like this, straight from the carton. Through the kitchen window, the cat's eyes watch you. It's shut out at night. You should be shut out too. Lists pinned to the fridge door, things to do and buy, goals for the week. The fridge's cold breath makes the lists move, but they're pinned with magnets, don't fall. You gulp at the milk so it spills, staining the neck of your T-shirt. You'll smell bad in the morning. You tip your head and drink, seeing yourself in the copper belly of the pendant lamp, the greedy way you're sucking at the carton's cardboard lip, your body squat, features spread fat across your face. You give Ugly a bad name.

This is the house Christie pictured for Big Eyes.

Nothing wanting, everything provided and paid for. She had no complaints, only that she couldn't eat, couldn't breathe, couldn't live.

It was the same for Big Eyes.

She'd reached the end of being her.

Ready to be wiped out, like Ashleigh and May.

Big Eyes wanted to die.

Christie could help with that.

41

'Grace must have been in here the whole time,' Noah told Marnie. 'When we were talking with Emma about the crash, when she was telling us about the arson. She was in here the whole time.' The cupboard was fetid with the girl's fear. 'We found a note in her pocket with this address on it, and Emma's name. Someone told her it was a safe place to stay . . . The paramedics said she hadn't eaten in three days, maybe longer. Sedated. Hypernatremic. Twitching, just like Fran said, but that could've been shock.' He turned to look at Emma Tarvin's bedroom. 'I can't believe it. Can you?'

He couldn't believe a seventy-six-year-old woman had taken a fifteen-year-old girl prisoner. Starved her. Tied her up and beaten her. Or maybe it was Emma's arrogance he couldn't believe, drinking tea and fielding questions with their missing girl locked in the next room. Inviting their attention by reporting Abi time and again, her opinion of the police so low she couldn't imagine being caught.

A glass on the bedside table was filled with dead water where the old woman put her teeth at night. Marnie could picture the teeth inside the glass, water magnifying their grin.

'And *why*?' Noah said. 'Why did she do it?'

'I don't know,' Marnie said. 'But I'm wondering if Abi Gull does.'

'Yeah,' Abi said. 'I know what that cow is. Like *you* finally give a shit.'

'What is she?' Marnie asked.

'An evil bitch.' Balling her fists in the high pockets of her hoody. 'An evil *murdering* bitch.'

'Who did she murder?'

Abi stared at the wall. She wasn't going to speak his name, not in here. But Marnie had done her research after Ron called in the fire, or rather she'd asked Colin to do the research while she was driving back from Sommerville. Thanks to Colin, she knew exactly what Abi was hiding.

'It was worth it, that's what you told DS Carling. Worth being caught. Worth being arrested.'

This was personal between Abi and Emma. Fire was personal, and so was violence of the kind Marnie had seen in Emma Tarvin's eyes, and was seeing now in Abi's.

'Your brother Clarke died of a drug overdose in January.'

'So?' The same edge had been in Abi's voice when she'd asked whether Ashleigh Jewell had died of an overdose. 'What's that supposed to mean?'

Marnie had suspected Abi of being a dealer. But that was before Colin told her about the girl's brother. 'Clarke was ten when he died. How long had he been an addict?'

'He wasn't an *addict*.' Kicking the leg of the table. 'Bitch.'

'Where did he get the drugs that killed him?'

Silence. You didn't speak to the police; that rule was written all over this girl's face.

'Come on. It's obvious. He got the drugs from Emma Tarvin.'

'Prove that, can you?' Abi was scared of Emma. Not as terrified as Grace had been, but Emma hadn't locked Abi in a cupboard and beaten her with a walking stick.

'You've been watching her,' Marnie said. 'Did you see Grace Bradley go into her flat on Tuesday night? The night of the crash.'

'Seen a lot of kids going into her flat.'

'You knew we were looking for a girl with red hair. DS Carling showed you a photo.'

Abi shook her head, reluctantly, as if it pained her to tell the truth. 'I never seen her.'

'How often does Mrs Tarvin leave her flat?'

'Not often enough, or I'd have done her before now, wouldn't I?'

'We found prescription drugs in her flat. Painkillers. Antidepressants. Too many for one person, but she has prescriptions. So we have proof of hoarding, but that's not proof of dealing.'

'In other words, there's fuck-all you can do. Like there was fuck-all you did about Clarke.' Abi leaned forward, stabbing at the table with her finger. 'I *told* the police it was that bitch, said I seen kids going into her flat and coming out off their tits on whatever she'd sold them. How'd you think she afforded that big telly? She's got them doing her shopping, running errands, anything she likes. She's got a *lookout*, for fuck's sake. That's how she gets to stay in her flat being waited on hand and foot. She loves us lot grovelling because she hates our guts, wishes we were dead like Clarke. Sweets, that's what she calls them. It's not like coke, not like heroin. She'll give *sweets* to anyone thick enough to go up there and beg her for it. Little kids, she doesn't care how young.'

'What's her lookout's name?' Noah asked.

'Linton Mays.' Curling her lip. 'He was mates with Clarke until shit started going down. Now he works for that bitch. Telling her who's new, who wants to score. Making sure you lot don't get in the way of her fucking deals.'

'Eleven years old. Wears a beanie, rides a girl's bike. That's Linton Mays?'

She nodded. Blinked. 'He was a nice kid, before she got her claws into him.'

'Do you know a girl called Christie Faulk? Linton says she used to come on the Garrett.'

'*Her.*' Abi folded her arms, hard as nails again. 'Yeah. Why?'

'Have you seen her recently?' Noah asked.

'Not since the abortion.'

'Christie had an abortion?'

'She's whoring for that old bitch, so yeah. She gets an abortion because she's told to. Then Tarvin chucks her out anyway. That's the kind of cow I'm talking about. She lets you stay, pretends she likes you, and maybe you fall for it, because she's old, like *your nan* old. Gets you hooked on her shit until you're paying for it any way you can. Nicking stuff, whoring. Christie moves in, and it's like the sun shines out of *Emma*, yeah? Cooking, cleaning, shopping. She'd have shaved her head for that bitch. But Tarvin chucks her out as soon as she sees which way it's headed.'

'Which way was it headed?' Marnie asked.

Abi screwed a finger to the side of her head. 'She's going nuts. Trying to be what *Emma* wants. Dressing like a slut, going with anyone, even old blokes, the ones no one else'd touch. Tarvin liked whoring her to the weird ones. Found her on the streets, so yeah. Probably she

266

was scared she'd end up back out there. Always trying to fit in, trying to please everyone. Stupid cow.'

'Emma found Christie on the streets?'

'Begging, that's what she said. Silly cow probably thought she was being saved. She was so *grateful*, it made me puke. So loyal. Nothing's too much trouble as long as *Emma*'s saying she counts for something. Like giving blow jobs gets you a case review.'

Noah tried to imagine the girl Abi was describing. Desperate to please, frantic for a foothold in what must have looked at first sight like a normal life. A woman old enough to be her grandmother, who needed help with shopping and cleaning. Someone Christie could help, a place where she felt wanted, valued. What had it done to her to be thrown out by her protector?

'When was the last time you saw Christie?' Marnie asked Abi.

'Back before Christmas. Way back.'

'Linton says he saw her with Ashleigh Jewell.'

'Yeah? I never, but it figures. Probably pimping for that old bitch. She told me if I was ever in trouble I could go to *Emma* for help. Told loads of girls the same shit. Seriously, she was *mental*. If you're looking for her, you'd better have a fucking straitjacket.'

'Did you ever see her with this man?' Noah showed Ledger's photo on his phone.

'Saw her with loads of men.' Abi didn't look at the photo. 'It's not the men you want to worry about. It's *her*. Tarvin. And it's the kids. It's *us*. What're you doing about us?'

Her eyes burned in her face. 'I seen eight-year-olds up there. *Little* kids. She doesn't give a fuck, makes you beg her, "Please, Mrs Tarvin. Thank you, Mrs Tarvin." She's a psycho. *Evil*. So, yeah.' She threw herself back in the seat. 'I kicked the shit out of her, and you know what? I wish I done a proper job, not stopped until I'd put her *in the ground*. Before another one of *us* ends up there.'

Tears heated her stare suddenly, and she was a thirteen-year-old girl grieving for her dead brother, grieving and scared. 'None of us is safe with her up there. None of us.'

Back in the incident room, Noah updated the whiteboard with Grace Bradley's details, and the rest of the information gleaned from Abi Gull. 'The hospital says we can't interview Emma until a doctor's seen her. Grace is a different problem. We can see her, but she's not talking. To anyone.'

'We need that to change if we're going to find Christie Faulk.' Marnie broke the seal on a bottle of water. 'What about Jamie Ledger?'

'Plenty of phone calls in response to the news last night. Colin's working through them. And we're checking the sites where Ledger was working before Battersea, in case he made any friends or found any boltholes.'

'Call the hospital again. Tell them we're bringing in a victim support officer to see Grace. Explain what's at stake.' Marnie drank a mouthful of water. 'And find out when we can talk to Emma. It's possible she spoke with Grace before she started beating her, or while she was beating her.' She fastened the cap back on the bottle. 'Since we'll be charging her with assault and unlawful imprisonment, I imagine she'll want to cooperate.'

'You don't think there's a chance she was involved in anything worse?' Noah was thinking of Emma's hands, knuckled with rings. 'May, or Ashleigh? Grace was with May the night she found her way on to the Garrett, and if the girls knew Christie Faulk . . .'

'You heard what Abi said. If Emma had been outside her flat in the last fortnight, Abi would have put her in hospital before now. Let's ask Emma about Grace, and Christie. But our killer's still out there. Maybe he's connected to Christie, but it's too soon to make that assumption.'

'If Christie put the note in Grace's pocket, she's dangerous. Or disturbed, like Abi said. Who'd direct a frightened girl to Emma's door?'

Marnie nodded. 'Let's see if Emma knows the answer to that.'

42

'I hope you've got her locked up.' Emma showed her arms, livid with bruises. 'See what she did to me? Bloody animal.' Propped in the hospital bed in a private room, her legs covered by a waffled blanket, the thin skin of her scalp broken in places by Abi's boots.

'We need to talk about Grace Bradley, the girl you assaulted in your flat. What happened there?'

'Oh, *her*!' Contemptuous. 'Ask her yourself. I gave her a place to stay, didn't I? How was I to know what kind of girl she was?'

Noah saw her scanning Marnie's face for weakness, some sign that DI Rome wasn't prepared to wait all night for an answer to her question. When she didn't find what she wanted, Emma's mouth crabbed.

'She asked for my help and I gave it to her. Next thing I know she's stealing pills from my cabinet, getting drugged up, trying to push me around. I get enough of that from the animals who did this. So I shut her in the cupboard to calm her down. She was doing damage to herself as well as me and my property. I took the necessary precautions, that's all.'

'It was a necessary precaution to beat her with a walking stick?'

'Who's saying I did that? Her? She's a liar. She was high as a kite, walking into things left, right and centre. If I'd known she was a pillhead, I'd never have taken her in.'

'You knew we were looking for her. Why didn't you call us?'

'And have you ignore me, the same as always?' She clutched at the blanket. 'I thought I'd cope with this one on my own, thanks very much.'

'Grace had a piece of paper in her pocket,' Marnie said, 'with your name and address on it. Did you know her before you locked her in your cupboard?'

'Never seen her in my life.' Sucking at her false teeth. Roll-calling her frailties.

'Then how did she know your name and address?'

'No idea. Maybe she was coming to rob me, or start a fire. Maybe Gull knows her.'

'We asked. She doesn't.' Marnie put the evidence bag where Emma could read the scrap of paper found in Grace's pocket. 'Do you recognise the handwriting?'

'It's not Gull's.' Her eyes shivered. 'I've seen enough of her hate mail.'

'Someone directed Grace to your flat. Who would do that?'

'I've no idea, love. Just as well *I'm* not the detective. Like I said, she came knocking and I let her in. Tried to help. Got pushed about for my trouble.'

Marnie rested her eyes away from the woman, as if she was sick of looking at her, and sick of listening to her lies. 'We have your walking stick, and photographs of the bruises on Grace. It won't be hard to prove what happened. And you might want to think about what it will be like going back to the Garrett once word gets around about what you did to a frightened fifteen-year-old.' A beat. 'Not to mention the other children, the ones you've been dealing drugs to. Abigail Gull is making a full statement in defence of her actions. But perhaps I'm underestimating the tolerance of your neighbours. Perhaps you'll be given the benefit of the doubt.'

Emma Tarvin gathered her spit and hawked it at Marnie's feet. It landed hard, the colour and size of an old ten-pence piece, on the floor of her hospital room.

'Trying to scare *me*, lady? I've seen the way people get treated on the Garrett. Not just by that lot of bloody savages, either. The police and the papers, everyone. The youngsters are the worst. Scum. No respect for anyone or anything. Never mind my mum worked in the factories through the war, stuffing bombs to keep this country safe. I wish I'd kept some of the bloody things to blow up those little cows. Teach them a lesson, the only kind they'd learn from.'

Marnie heard her out. When Emma stopped speaking, she said, 'Grace Bradley was locked in a cupboard, by you. She was starved and beaten and scared to death. By you.'

'They deserve to be scared. The whole lot of them. Think I'm just going to sit there in my slippers while they set fire to my flat again? Think that's all I'm fit for?' Her eyes fixed on Marnie, wrathfully. 'I played by your rules for years, and look where it got me. Filling in forms, getting talked down to by Victim Support. About time some of us remembered who we are. Better than those bastards running round like they own that place, skipping school, spreading their legs for anyone who throws a second glance.' She shook with contempt. 'Nasty little whores. They're filth. They should be locked up.'

Marnie put a freezer bag of pills on the table at the side of the bed. 'And these?'

'What about them?' Running her stare up and down Marnie. 'You look like you could use a few. Not exactly full of the joys of spring, are you, love?'

'You were selling pills to the children on the estate. Abi's brother Clarke died of an overdose after taking them. No wonder she decided you were public enemy number one.'

'That slut doesn't need any excuse for what she does. She loves it. Lighting fires, throwing stones. It's in her blood. Know what else I've seen her do? Hike up her skirt and take a piss on the pavement.' She sat back, out of breath. 'She's an animal, like the rest of them. Animals.'

'You don't deny selling these pills?' Noah hadn't thought it would be so easy to get a confession from her. 'Dealing drugs to children?'

'Seeing as how you've got a fridge full of evidence, handsome? No, I don't.'

'And you're not sorry? You're not ashamed?'

'Ashamed?' She drew herself up against the pillows. 'I'm *proud*. I'm making something of myself. Isn't that what we're meant to do? I'm not the one with the habit. Oh, I *could* be. Plenty of my friends get hooked on the rubbish they dole out to keep us from moaning too loudly about our dicky bladders and arthritis and God knows what else besides. They'd love me stuffed to the gills with that poison. Shut me up nicely, wouldn't it? Seeing as we're all living longer, it'd be nice if we could be kept quiet.' She spat again, but weakly, the spittle landing on the front of her cardigan. 'So I'll take the pills, thank you very much, whatever's going. And I'll sell to them that can't get through a day without a little snort, a little sniff.' Her eyes brightened, red-rimmed with age. 'I'll tell you what, love. Never been treated so well in my life as I am by the pillheads. Bowing and scraping, calling me *Mrs* Tarvin. Shaking in their shoes because they need something to stop them feeling so cold and empty when they don't know what it is to be cold and empty. It's what they *deserve*. Not one of them is any better than they should be.'

Not just a financial convenience, in other words. This was revenge, and wickedness. Abi had been right. The money was a bonus, but it wasn't the main reason this woman was exploiting the weakness of the kids living on the estate. She took pleasure in it.

'You should be glad I'm not a burden on the state. Got more than enough for what I need. Her two doors down? Starves herself week after week to pay for insurance for the next time she's robbed. *Starves*. Because she knows she's going to lose it all again and it's the only way she'll be covered. That's if she's not ripped off by the insurers. Not one of us isn't scared of what's coming through our doors or windows next. All I'm doing is taking charge of the situation. Who else is going to do that? Not you lot. Too busy covering your own arses to care about mine.' She sat back, looking pleased with the frown on Noah's face. 'I expect you'll be investigated. They'll want to know why you couldn't find that girl when she was right under your noses. You were in and out of my flat all last week. You and that fat fool who eats my biscuits.'

Ron had liked Emma for her courage. She'd held him in nothing but contempt.

'Yes, it hadn't occurred to us that you'd drugged and beaten a child before locking her in your cupboard.' Marnie got to her feet. 'But we have the measure of you now, so that's progress.'

Emma looked up at her in surprise. 'You're going, are

you? Call that an interview? I've been asked more probing questions in the Co-op.'

Under the sneer, she looked scared. What would a jury make of her? Right at this minute, she looked like a vulnerable old woman. Would they be able to see past that?

'Did you speak to Grace at all?' Marnie paused in the doorway to the room. 'When she first arrived, perhaps. When you offered her a place to stay. Why did you do that, incidentally?'

'The goodness of my heart not good enough for you, Detective Inspector?'

Marnie ignored this. 'I imagine you saw a new victim, someone to sell drugs to, someone to prostitute. That's what your notebooks are for, isn't it? Lists of children you can exploit. A new girl, looking desperate, must have made your night.'

'She had her tits out, didn't need my help with that. Did I talk to her? No. She wasn't interested in talking, just wanted food and a place to stay. Thought she'd landed on her feet, finding me.'

'And then you gagged her,' Noah said. 'So there was no talking after that.'

'I like a quiet house.' Fussing at the blanket, making it neat. 'We weren't all raised in the ghetto.'

'Christie Faulk,' Marnie said. 'Was she another girl who thought she'd landed on her feet?'

That penetrated Emma's defences. Her mouth cracked open in surprise, her eyes slitting. 'Who?'

'Christie Faulk. She lived with you for a while a couple of years ago. Until she got pregnant and you threw her out. I imagine prostituting a pregnant teenager would tax even your ingenuity.'

Emma wetted her lips. 'I don't know what you're on about, love.'

'Was it Christie who wrote the note we found in Grace's pocket? A place of refuge, but a last resort. I can't imagine Christie has many happy memories of her time spent under your roof.'

'I don't know any Christie.' But she looked frightened for the first time.

Prostitution, abortion – the pills were bad enough. She might live down a drugs offence, but not a charge under the Sexual Offences Act, not on the Garrett estate.

Marnie said, 'DC Tanner will conduct a full interview. She'll also make a formal arrest for the drugs and soliciting, assault and imprisonment, and for the false statements you gave to the police.'

'Passing the buck? You'll never get ahead with that attitude. You want to make your mark, leave some evidence that you were here. That's what I'm doing, love.' She leaned forward again, her anger soaking up the light. 'Leaving my *mark*.'

43

Ron was waiting with Debbie in the hospital corridor, looking miserable, as beaten down as the rest of them by the revelations about Emma Tarvin. One look at Noah's face told him she'd confessed, and was unrepentant. 'Jesus.' He turned away.

Marnie asked, 'How's Grace?'

'In shock,' Debbie said. 'They've got her on fluids. It looks like she was given a lot of diazepam and tramadol. She's very hazy. Not much better than she was when Noah found her.'

'She was traumatised before this happened,' Marnie reminded them. 'When she walked out in front of Joe Eaton's car, she was in shock.'

As if her words had summoned him, Traffic's Sergeant Kenickie came through the double doors towards them, hands bunched in his pockets. 'G. I. Bradley. Which room's she in?'

Marnie nodded at Debbie and Ron to go into Mrs Tarvin's room. 'Grace Bradley is off limits,' she told Kenickie. 'Not my rule, the doctor's. If you don't like it, take it up with him.'

To Noah, she said, 'We need to get back to the station.'

'I've an arrest to make.' Kenickie ignored Noah, concentrating on Marnie. 'Gina Marsh deserves that much, unless you're ring-fencing the victims in this mess.'

'There are more than enough victims to go around.' Marnie glanced at her watch. 'We're looking for a murderer, or possibly two. Unless you're able to take one of those off our hands, I suggest you do your posturing somewhere else.'

'I can take one off your hands right now. Even if we have to call it manslaughter. Your girlie killed Logan Marsh.' Kenickie rattled the keys in his pocket. 'When were you planning on telling us you'd found her?'

'It wasn't high on my list,' Marnie admitted.

She started walking away. Noah followed.

Kenickie raised his voice after them. 'Didn't know the positive discrimination ran to suspects as well as staff. If she was a bloke, or if Logan was a girl, you'd be all over this.'

Marnie didn't reply, but her profile was ferocious. Noah lengthened his stride to keep up with her. 'I wonder if Gina Marsh appreciates his crusading.'

'I doubt it. I imagine she's too busy grieving for her son.'

Outside, it was raining fretfully.

As Marnie unlocked the car, her phone rang. 'DI Rome . . . Mr Beswick, hello . . . No, I was on my way back to the station.' She stopped, her hand on the car door. 'Tell me again.'

Her face changed as she listened, its lines in sharp relief. 'I'm on my way.'

She shut the phone, looking across the car at Noah. 'Loz is missing.'

'*Loz* . . .' Noah's throat clenched. 'When?'

'Before school. She insisted on walking in, but didn't turn up for registration. The school quizzed her friends, one of whom said Loz had drawings her sister did. Of a subway. Loz had told this friend that she was going to find whoever took May. The friend thought she was joking.'

'We sealed it off. The subway—'

'Forensics worked fast, because we asked them to.' Marnie shook her head. 'The tape came down hours ago, while we were in Emma's flat.'

'Shit.' Noah's eyes stung. 'Joel and the others – were they lying?'

'Let's find out.' Marnie thumbed her phone, held it to her ear. 'Joel, this is DI Rome. Where are you? I see. Stay there, please. We need to talk.'

In Starbucks, Daisy was nursing a gingerbread latte. Joel and Corin were watching the door. They looked scared to death when Marnie and Noah came through it.

'Loz Beswick is missing,' Marnie told them. 'We think you might have been the last people to see her. In the subway, not that long ago.'

Noah saw lies crowding in the boys' eyes. He cut them short. 'We know she was headed to the subway. She's *missing*. Give us the truth, now.'

'We didn't know who she was,' Corin said. 'Not until she told us.'

'What did she tell you?'

'That she'd found May's sketchpad. She'd worked out where the subway was, said she wanted to see it for herself. We let her hang out with us. She was pretty sad.'

'Why didn't you call us?' Noah demanded. 'You had our number. You knew we were looking for a killer. Loz is thirteen years old. She's counting on us to find whoever killed May.'

That surprised a laugh from Daisy.

Joel and Corin moved back in their seats, away from her.

Daisy stirred with a wooden stick at her drink.

'Why is that funny?' Marnie asked.

'Because she's not counting on anyone,' Daisy said. 'She's looking for him herself.'

'She told you that?'

'Yeah. But it's okay. She's not really *missing*, just hanging out for a bit.' She licked aerated cream from the wooden stick. 'It's like . . . we've all done it. I can see why her mum and dad are having a fit, but seriously? It's not a big deal.'

May had been murdered. Loz was missing. *Not a big deal*.

'Where is she hanging out?'

Daisy shrugged. So did Joel and Corin. As if they were unable to imagine any fate for Loz less comfortable than theirs, sitting in Starbucks sipping overpriced syruped milk.

'She's okay,' Daisy insisted. 'Just hanging out.'

'Where?' Marnie repeated.

'Somewhere safe,' Joel said. 'You don't need to freak out.'

Corin nodded, but his eyes were unhappy. Regardless, he repeated the lie picked for them by Daisy. 'She's safe. She must be. I mean, who goes looking for a killer? She was kidding. Right?'

44

'How are her mum and dad bearing up?' Welland asked Marnie. 'They know the drill, at least.'

'I'm not sure that makes it any easier.'

'They let her walk to school on her own?'

'She's been doing that for years. Both Sean and Katrina felt they had to give her some space, and they trusted her to stay safe.'

'Do *we* trust *them*?' Using his gruffest tone. If they'd missed a trick . . .

'We looked at them when May first went missing. And DS Jake's been taking another close look in the last twenty-four hours, after the sketchpad showed up.' Marnie paused. 'If you'd seen them just now . . . They're out of their minds with worry. Neither car's been out of Taybridge Road since yesterday. Neighbours saw Loz in her school uniform walking with her usual bag at the usual time. We could waste time quizzing the Beswicks further, but I'd rather spend it looking at the subway. There's CCTV all around there. We're checking the routes from Taybridge Road and the school, in case she doubled back.' If they'd only kept the police tape up longer; if she hadn't asked

Forensics to work so fast; if she'd been able to win Loz's trust . . .

Welland knuckled the base of his neck. 'We're tracing her phone?'

'She's not used it since last night. We're hoping she has it with her. It's our best lead right now. And we're checking her computer. May didn't use one, but Sean says Loz lives on the internet. So far all we've found is photos of road signs and role-play accounts.'

'What's a role-play account?'

'Pretending to be someone she isn't. Nothing sinister, just playing at being characters from her favourite books and TV shows. Escapism. Nothing that looks as if it will turn into a lead.'

Welland frowned at Marnie's report. 'Tell me about this woman, Christie Faulk.'

'In her early twenties. According to Jodie Izard, a year ago she had dark hair and brown eyes. That was over in Lewisham, where she took Grace. Our three from the subway say the woman Loz went with was blonde, brown-eyed. We're assuming it's the same woman.'

'Early twenties, but we think she's our killer? Or just his recruitment agent?'

'We don't know.' Either way, Loz had gone with her, willingly. How much pain must she've been in, to take a risk of that magnitude? 'We need to find Christie, obviously.'

'Any connection between Faulk and Ledger?' Welland asked next.

Marnie shook her head. 'But we don't have a formal ID for Christie yet. No ID and no photo. We're hoping Grace can help. I'm going over to the hospital to speak with her.'

'She's in the same place as Kathy Bates?' He meant Emma Tarvin.

'On separate floors, but yes.'

Welland tugged at his lip. 'I had Traffic back on the phone, bitching about that.'

'I hope you bitched back. Kenickie is a nasty piece of work.'

'He's off my Christmas card list. What else from the subway? I gather Forensics got quite the haul. Condoms, shitty toilet paper, the works.'

'Fran's looking for DNA to match to Missing Persons. Joel and the others mentioned a boy called Eric, and Sasha. We showed them a picture of Sasha Ronson, but it's not the same girl.'

'Even so,' Welland said, 'lots of missing girls in the vicinity of this madman's hunting ground. If he's got more, do we have any good reason to hope he's keeping them alive?'

'Whoever killed May and Ashleigh made their deaths public. There's no reason to think they wouldn't have done the same with any other girls they killed.'

'Unless the others were killed first. Botched jobs, say. It might've taken a while to work up to the public displays. Isn't that the usual pattern with these lunatics?'

Marnie didn't want to think of any other girl as this killer's botched job.

'Displaying them in public places could be a comment on the way we're ignoring their pain,' Welland said. 'Isn't that how Ledger's wife said he felt about civilian life – that we needed waking up to what was going on around us?' He kneaded the skin under his eyes with the ends of his fingers, looking more cynical and weary than usual. 'Demonstrating he has the freedom of the city, comes and goes as he pleases, doing what he likes. No boundaries, just plenty of risk-taking.'

Marnie didn't comment. He could be right, that was

the miserable fact of the matter. Welland could have put his finger on exactly what was happening.

He leaned towards her. 'Are we giving Laura Beswick's photo to the press?'

'Not yet. It could spook our killer. That might be why Ashleigh was dumped so soon after May.'

'But he's still taking girls. What's he up to? Playing Manson families, some sort of cult? He's not raping them, or not yet. Which makes sense if the killer's a woman. This Christie Faulk.'

He hadn't made up his mind, Marnie realised. Not about Jamie Ledger, or Christie Faulk.

She got to her feet. 'I'll let you know what Grace has to say. Otherwise, all hands are on the search for Loz. If you can get us *more* hands . . .'

Welland nodded. 'Leave it with me.'

Jodie Izard had described Grace Bradley as a born survivor, hard as a cat's head.

The girl in the hospital bed was wretchedly thin and bruised, her hands knuckled at her sides, the bump of bone showing in her wrists. They hadn't tried to remove the writing from her skin, its black scrawl smudged in places by the abrasions from Emma Tarvin's walking stick.

Marnie could read a handful of the words.

Liar. Animal. Dead.

Fran had used baby oil to clean the writing from May. Marnie wanted to do the same for Grace. She sat at the side of the bed. 'Grace, I'm Detective Inspector Rome. I need your help.'

No response, not even a flicker in the grey eyes, too big for her face. Like Loz's eyes.

'I need your help finding the place where you and May were staying. Can you remember?'

Grace shut her eyes. She turned her fists until her arms were lying in plain view along either side of her body. *Liar. Animal. Dead.* Words, but not the ones Marnie needed from her.

'I need to find Christie Faulk. I think you know her. She's taken May's sister. You knew May. You were with her, and Ashleigh. That's right, isn't it? Only now Christie's taken May's sister Loz. Loz is thirteen years old. We're very worried about her. I think you know where Christie's taken her. It's the place you were running from when Emma took you in.' Marnie didn't mention the car crash, or the cupboard, or the beatings. 'Help me to find Loz, please. She's angry and scared. She wants to find whoever killed her sister. We think she went with Christie believing Christie would take her to May's killer—'

The sound coming out of Grace was raw and low-pitched. She rolled her head against the pillows weakly.

'You didn't know May was dead,' Marnie realised. 'I'm sorry, I thought you knew. I thought that's why you ran from that house, because you saw how dangerous it was.'

She waited, to see if Grace's distress would get worse. But there wasn't any time. There wasn't any time to wait.

'Grace, tell me where Christie has taken Loz. Somewhere safe,' she said. 'I know there's food, and shelter. I know she looks after you, to start with.'

'Y-you don't.' A whisper, broken. 'You d-don't know.'

'*Tell me.*'

Grace rolled her head again. Refusing to answer Marnie's question, or unable to? Not crying, or not with her eyes. No tears came from under her shut lids, but her chest rose and fell beneath the blanket.

'It's all right.' Marnie reached for her hand and held it. 'It will be all right. You're safe now. You can help me. I need your help. You can help to save Loz and whoever else is still inside the place Christie lied about. Because it's not safe. It's very, very dangerous. We need to get Loz and the others away from there, just like you got away. Tell me where she took you. Help me.'

Grace stopped shaking her head. Her chest hiccuped before it went still. Too still.

Marnie was about to check her pulse when the girl pulled her hand away, lifting her arm and putting it across her eyes, her wrist bent at an odd angle, unnatural.

Light lay along her forearm, highlighting the words written there.

Liar. Animal. Dead.

Marnie saw Grace and May sitting together cross-legged on a stranger's floor, writing on their skin with black marker pens, picking their words like weapons.

But there was something else on Grace's skin.

A word Marnie had missed, until now.

Just above her left wrist.

In spiky letters, smaller than the rest:

Killer.

45

Christie

'This is home,' Christie told Big Eyes. 'What d'you think?'
She shed her coat, transferring the keys to her jeans
pocket.

Big Eyes took a hard look around the kitchen.
Cupboards, table, knife rack. 'Nice.'

'Want to see the bedrooms?'

'I'll have to share, right?'

'Not necessarily. Depends on who's staying the night.
We come and go, pretty much.'

'Do I get a key?' Big Eyes said. 'If I can come and go,
I'll need a key.'

'Sure.' Christie nodded. She opened a drawer next to
the stove 'Help yourself.'

The drawer was full of door keys on plastic key rings.
Big Eyes picked a green one.

'We'll be eating soon. There's plenty of food here. Do
you cook?'

'A bit. Not really. But I can help out. I guess that's
what everyone does, right?' Big Eyes tucked the key into

her pocket, still looking around the kitchen. Every second sweep her eyes went to the door. She'd not bothered looking at the windows. Too high up. Only one way in and out.

Christie moved past her to shut the drawer. She'd found the keys in a junk shop, a job lot. Not one of them opened the doors here. But they looked good, all jumbled in the drawer.

Help yourself, come and go . . .

Harm's idea, to make the girls feel safe. None of them had tried the keys on their first day, not even in their first week. Later, when it was too late, they cried when they found the keys didn't work. Or like Grace, they fought.

Standing in the kitchen, Big Eyes looked old. She wasn't. She was younger than any of the others, but she looked ancient. Fear snaked into Christie's throat. What had she done?

She picked up a glass. 'Water's here.' She walked to where the barrels were stacked, showing the girl how to work the tap that Harm had fitted.

'What's wrong with the sink?' Big Eyes said.

'They haven't connected the water. This's a new-build. No water, no gas. No electricity except what Harm's fixed up for us.'

'Who's Harm?'

'A mate.' Christie shot her a look. 'Don't freak. It's not like that.'

Her face flickered, on the blink. 'Like what?'

'Whatever you're imagining.' Christie sucked a breath, drinking from the glass until the snake stopped moving in her mouth. 'I was the same when I first came here. It looks weird, because we're not used to anyone else giving a shit about us.' She shrugged. 'Some people do, that's all.'

'Like Harm.' Big Eyes put her hands in her pockets, shoulders up, trying to look tough.

'Yes.' Christie watched her across the smooth lip of the glass. 'Just like Harm.' She paused, then added, 'You'll have to give us a name.'

'Laura.' It might've been her real name, or a lie.

All the girls lied, sooner or later. Even May, who'd been the only one Christie had trusted with a real key, certain she'd come back that night after helping Grace to get away. But it was Christie who'd scared Grace into going to Emma Tarvin's, knowing the old woman would keep her quiet, and teach her a lesson she wouldn't forget. May had come back alone, or so Christie had thought. She hadn't known about the lie in May's belly, and the way it would ruin everything.

'Come on.' She walked Laura to the room May had shared with Ashleigh. 'This's yours. I'll fix you up with some bedding.'

'Thanks.' Her eyes were on the mezzanine floor. 'What's up there?'

'Another bedroom.'

'Is that where you sleep?'

'No. My room's at the back.'

'Who sleeps upstairs?'

'Aimee, for now.' Christie shrugged. 'I'll introduce you later. She'll be sleeping now.'

'Why? Is she a baby?' Laura looked as if the idea of a baby frightened her.

'No. She's had the flu so she needs a lot of rest. I'll take her some food in a bit.'

'Okay. I'll help if you like. I'm good at looking after people. My mum drinks, it's why my dad left. I looked after my little brother until they took us into care.'

Christie was used to listening to the girls' stories, setting her face to *sympathy*. It helped that she was afraid of Laura. She didn't know why, only that the girl looked ancient, a spell-breaker, like she'd been alive for ever. Harm had wanted a girl and Christie had brought him one. Let him deal with it. 'What happened to your brother?'

Laura walked to the window with its tinted glass and its view of the chimneys at Battersea. She said in a stiff voice, 'He died. It's why I ran away, so I didn't end up the same.'

Christie nodded. 'I get it.'

'Do you?'

'I told you about Neve.'

Laura turned so the light was behind her, blanking her eyes. 'How did you find this place?'

'Harm found it. He was working here when the new flats were going up. They never finished building, permissions expired, they ran out of money.' Christie recited the story with a shrug. 'He says sooner or later someone will come and kick us out, but it hasn't happened yet.'

'So we're squatters?'

'More or less. It's safe, that's the main thing.' Could this girl hear the hard hammering of the lie in Christie's throat? 'So . . . are you staying?'

Laura had her hands in her pockets. Christie saw her curl a fist around the key she'd taken from the drawer. The key that didn't fit any of the locks in here.

She nodded. 'For a bit, thanks. If you're sure it's okay.'

'It's great,' Christie said. 'Good to have you with us.'

46

'We have a problem with Grace Bradley.'

Marnie stood beside the girl's photo on the whiteboard, addressing the team. 'She's clearly very distressed by whatever happened to her and whatever she witnessed before *and* after she found her way on to the Garrett. A trauma specialist is trying to piece together what she knows and how it might help us find Loz.'

'So it's not true that she confessed.' Ron folded his arms.

'There was no confession.' Marnie looked at each member of her team in turn. 'Some of you, I know, have seen the photographs of the writing on Grace. All of you, I'm sure, have heard the rumour going around that someone, maybe Grace herself, wrote the word "Killer" on her left arm.' She paused, needing their attention focused on what mattered. 'There are a lot of words on her arms, and on her legs, and elsewhere on her body. One of those words is "Killer", another is "Dead". I don't believe her to be a killer, and thanks to DS Jake's sharp ears, she's not dead. To be clear, we have *no reason* at this time to believe Grace was responsible for the death of May Beswick, and certainly not of Ashleigh Jewell, since at that time she was locked in Emma Tarvin's flat. We need to find out where she was before that happened, where she ran *from* on the night of the crash. She was coming from the west, according to both Joe and Ruth Eaton. She was on foot and she'd covered some ground.' Grace's feet were bruised and swollen, raw with walking. 'We're looking for anything we can find on Christine or Christie Faulk. She was seen with Loz eight hours ago. We're putting together an e-fit so we'll have a face to show to people soon. And we're still looking for Jamie Ledger. DS Jake, you have an update on that?'

'Ledger has worked on a series of new-build sites across London in the last thirteen months,' Noah said. 'We're checking the ones to the west of Battersea Power Station and the Garrett. We know Grace was picked up by Christie over in Lewisham, so we've favoured sites in that direction. DC Pitcher's drawn up a map. It's on the board. Take a look.'

'Loz hasn't used her phone since texting last night,' Debbie said. 'Mum and Dad have tried texting and calling but the phone's switched off and may've been dumped. We're trying to trace it.'

'We're thinking somewhere large enough to hold more than one girl at a time and where they'd feel safe.' Colin removed his glasses, polishing them. 'At least to begin with. May and Ashleigh were clean and well fed. We're not looking at a warehouse or a derelict site. This is somewhere with running water, meals. A home. We're assuming that's where Christie's taken Loz.'

'Our witnesses from the Stockwell subway didn't get a scary vibe from Christie.' Noah nodded at the missing faces pinned to the whiteboard. 'She isn't forcing these girls to go with her, but she's clever. Manipulative. She wanted to take Loz and she knew how to make it happen.

Joel and the others thought she'd be safe – didn't see Christie as any kind of a threat. Loz isn't naïve, but she is desperate. To find her sister's killer.' He paused. 'I can believe she went with Christie hoping Christie would lead her to the killer. But I can't believe she went thinking Christie *was* the killer.'

'She could've got that wrong,' Debbie said. 'She's thirteen, and not thinking straight.'

'Bradley won't give us anything?' Ron demanded. 'An address, a general location?'

'She's in shock,' Marnie said. 'Give her time.'

'We don't *have* time. Loz's been gone five hours. With some nutter who's either killing girls or handing them over to some other nutter who is. Her parents must be out of their minds.'

Marnie didn't argue. Sean and Katrina Beswick were stunned, still trying to process the fact that Loz had gone in search of May's killer. 'Why?' Katrina kept asking. 'Why would she do that? Does she *hate* us?' As if Loz was a mystery to her, the way Ashleigh had been to her mother.

'What about the other teenagers Joel told us about? Eric – any matches in Misper for him?'

'Just one.' Debbie handed Marnie a print-off. 'Eric James Mackay. Fifteen years old, missing from care since 2012. Criminal record, so don't be taken in by the sweet face.' The photo showed a dark-haired boy with high cheekbones and a shy smile; one of those almost-familiar faces that so many missing children seemed to share. 'This was taken when he was twelve.'

'What were the charges?'

'Kick and run. Malicious damage. Nothing major, but he could've been in worse trouble since.'

'No recent sightings,' Noah said. 'Not much to go on, and the photo's out of date if he's fifteen now. Joel called him a psycho. You can bet he doesn't look like that any longer.'

Marnie studied the photograph, wondering what Eric Mackay looked like now. Had he, like Stephen, shed his angelic disguise, become a shaven-headed thug?

'Send a copy of this to my phone.' She handed the photograph back to Debbie. 'And to DS Jake's. We should show it to Joel and the others, see if they can identify him as the boy they knew. Christie is using this subway to collect kids. May and Ashleigh, now Loz. We should trace anyone who used it as a place to hang out, anyone who might know Christie and where she's taking these children. Our priority is finding Loz. Commander Welland is pulling in help with house-to-house and CCTV checks. We're on this until we find her. DS Jake?'

Noah followed Marnie into her office. She sat behind the desk, connecting her phone to its charger. He took the seat opposite, waiting to hear what she was thinking.

'We need to be careful with Grace,' she said. 'Kenickie's double-parked outside her hospital room wanting to make an arrest. DS Carling's somewhat sympathetic to his cause.'

'Ron's upset about Emma,' Noah said. 'He can't believe he misread her so badly.'

'It'll be worse when he sees the statement I took from Jodie Izard. She makes Grace sound like the sort of girl who'd get a kick out of causing a traffic accident, even a fatal one.' Marnie pushed her hair from her face, and reached for her phone when it rang. 'DI Rome.' Her face tensed as she listened. 'You realise this is a murder investigation? Good. Do that.' She got to her feet, motioning for Noah to do the same. To the caller, she said, 'I'll see you at the station.'

She hung up and reached for her coat. 'That was Adam Fletcher.'

'The journalist?' Noah remembered Fletcher from their investigation six months ago. His name had been on the media party list from Battersea. 'What's he got?'

Marnie was at the door. 'Jamie Ledger.' She pocketed her phone. 'Or so he says.'

Adam Fletcher looked as if he hadn't slept in a week, blue circles under his eyes, blue stubble on his chin. In chinos and a white T-shirt, boat shoes on his bare feet. Not enough clothes for the weather; he shivered as he jerked his head at Noah, before focusing on Marnie.

'You're looking for Ledger,' he said, 'but he's not your killer.'

'Where is he? You said you had a good idea.'

'He took me to this place in Mitcham six weeks ago.' Fletcher gave Noah the address. 'Used to be a family planning clinic about a hundred years ago, bought by an American who's waiting for permission to convert it into a glass box. Right now it's boarded up, aluminium sheeting, the works. But Ledger knew a way in. Had a camping stove, bottled water, a sleeping bag. Said he wasn't living there, just a place he could crash, off radar.'

'And you were interested why?' Marnie asked.

'For the irony.' Adam shrugged his shoulders. 'Family planning clinic bought by a Texan developer with links to pro-life campaigners? I know an editor who'd love that story.'

'You met Ledger at the Battersea media party, is that right?'

Adam nodded. 'Said he had a story about the developers taking backhanders. I wasn't convinced he had anything worth paying for, not at Battersea, but he said he knew other places with dodgy developers on board. So I gave him fifty quid and he took me to Mitcham.'

'When were you last in touch with him?'

'Two, three weeks ago?' Adam shook his head. 'Long before you started finding bodies.'

'You said he's not the killer.' Noah was searching his phone for details of the derelict clinic in Mitcham. He glanced up, wanting to see the man's response. 'What makes you so sure?'

'I've met killers,' Adam said inflexibly. 'He's not crazy enough.'

'He's breaking the law,' Marnie said. 'Trespassing. Squatting. And he's been missing since we started a double murder investigation.'

'Whoever put May Beswick up there wants to be seen. Ledger doesn't want that.'

'He had access to the penthouse,' Noah said. 'He was working there the night May died.'

'Yeah, I bet you're kicking yourselves that you didn't arrest him when you had the chance.' Adam shoved his hands into his pockets, goose bumps on his arms. 'Look, am I making a statement or what? Only I'm freezing my bollocks off out here.'

'You're making a statement,' Marnie said shortly. 'What number do you have for Ledger?'

Adam thumbed through his phone, showed Noah the screen. 'He's not answering.'

Noah put the number into his phone and dialled it.

'You've been calling him,' Marnie said.

'Since you found May. Knew he wasn't the killer. Wanted to see if he had anything, though.'

'Did he?'

'God knows. Like I said, he isn't answering. Didn't think it was a big deal until I saw his mugshot in the paper this morning.'

'It was on the TV news last night.'

'Didn't catch it. Are we done?'

Marnie looked at Noah, who shook his head. Ledger's number had rung several times before it went to a generic voicemail. 'Anything else we should know about this place in Mitcham?' he asked Adam. 'Such as how to get inside, and whether he has weapons of any kind in there.'

'No weapons that I could see. We used a fire escape at the back of the place next door. Two floors up, you can cross into the clinic. It's a bit dodgy, but at least you won't be doing it after dark.'

'That's how you got the bruises,' Marnie said. 'On your hands and feet.'

'He warned me to wear gloves.' Adam crooked his mouth. 'I thought he was worried about fingerprints, but he meant climbing. You'll want good shoes, too.'

Like Dan's Red Chili climbing shoes from his days with the place-hackers. Ledger wasn't a place-hacker. Just someone who liked, or needed, to go off radar. Riff had said security guards sometimes took bribes to turn a blind eye. Had Ledger done that? Or something worse?

'Forget the shoes,' Adam said. 'You'll be going through the front door, I guess.'

Marnie nodded. 'They'll take a full statement inside.'

She watched him go into the station. When he was out of earshot, she said, 'The girls weren't held in a derelict building.'

'We didn't think so,' Noah agreed. 'And Mitcham's outside the radius we drew for places where Ledger was working, but it's not far out. We should get it checked. He could have moved once he realised we were on to him.'

'All right, let's organise it.' Marnie nodded. 'I'll check in with the hospital and see how Grace is doing. Keep in touch.'

47

Aimee

I was dreaming, which was never good, but this was worse because it was about May.

She was standing in the doorway to the bathroom, on the white tiles with the light making her hair shine. Smiling at me the way she always did, because she always knew. The only one I couldn't hide from. None of the others saw me. Not Ashleigh, or Grace. They only saw Harm's good girl, his sick girl.

May was standing on the white tiles with her bare feet like mine only smaller, pinker. Her hair was loose and the light was making her nightdress see-through. I could see her stomach and her breasts, everything. She was beautiful. I wanted to touch her.

I knew what Ashleigh would say, her and the others.

They'd call me a lezzer, a freak. But May knew. She saw me.

Under the clothes he made us wear, the skirts and tights. Under his uniform. Like dolls, but I was a Russian doll, hiding inside another that was hiding inside another that was . . .

I held out my hand to May and she took it, pulling it to the front of her nightdress.

Cool cotton under my hand, hot skin under that.

I was touching her.

She was saying my name, asking me to tell her what I was hiding, who was inside.

I shouldn't have done it, I know.

I shouldn't have done any of it.

But I did.

48

The derelict clinic in Mitcham was brown inside, sticky floors, walls stained by smoke. On the second floor the roof let in the rain, broken tiles and plaster littering the floor.

Camping stove, sleeping bag, bottled water. Just as Adam Fletcher had said.

Pigeon droppings rotted the floor, an acid taste on Noah's tongue. He stood at the side of Ledger's makeshift bed, trying to measure this half-life. Not even half a life; less than that.

Ledger had been in Afghanistan, returning shell-shocked, struggling to adjust to civilian life. Perhaps this was preferable to living in a house, faking a degree of normality. Preferable to the mould at Paradise House. He'd been alone here. The neatness of the stove, the sleeping bag – he'd been on his own. Off radar. The aluminium windows sucked up the sound of traffic and people and planes, as if six radios were playing simultaneously at a distance. Life's soundtrack happening outside, elsewhere. How often had Ledger woken on this floor, shouting from nightmares? Maybe it was better to have them here, away from people.

Noah turned a slow circle under the sagging ceiling.

Light through the brickwork picked out the dimpled plastic of the water bottles, the metal zip of the sleeping bag. Otherwise, it was dark despite the sunshine outside. Cold, too. Beneath the rotting plaster and pigeons he could smell tobacco. He crouched on his heels, moving a gloved hand under the edge of the sleeping bag, keeping the beam of his torch on the same spot.

Tucked underneath the nylon bag – a battered yellow and green tin.

Noah opened it, shining the torch inside.

Shredded tobacco and cigarette papers.

In the pinched red shred of the tobacco, he could see the precise shape of Ledger's thumb and forefinger.

'Nothing in Mitcham,' Noah told Marnie when he was back in the fresh air. 'He was here, on his own, but not in a while. There's a good layer of dust on the stove, and the sleeping bag's growing mould. It's a dump, beats Paradise House even. I wouldn't want my worst enemy living like this.'

He looked up at the building, its boarded windows scrawled by graffiti. 'How's Grace?'

'The doctor's with her. Fluids helped to calm her down, but I'm not sure we'll get much sense out of her in the next few hours.'

Noah heard the frustration in her voice. 'No sightings of Loz and Christie?'

'None. Colin's looked at every route away from the subway on foot or by car. If she was in a car, I think we'd have something by now. The CCTV on the roads is good. Much patchier if they were on foot. I'm thinking Christie knew which route to take to avoid the cameras.'

'Makes sense. She's been taking kids for months now.'

Noah started walking in the direction of the tramlink. 'I'm headed back to the station, unless you want me somewhere else.'

'I'll see you there.'

'It's me,' Marnie said.

'Hey.' Ed was at work, office white noise in the background. 'You okay?'

'Loz Beswick's missing. We think she's with the killer.'

'*Shit*. How . . .?'

Marnie touched her hand to the ignition key, but didn't start the car. She was waiting for news from the doctor who was with Grace. The car was quiet, and it was private. 'Loz knew where May went when she wasn't at home. It was all in her sketchpad, hidden in Loz's room. A pedestrian subway in Stockwell. Loz was there this morning; now she's gone. A young woman took her. Three kids saw Loz leave with her. They didn't think it was anything to be worried about.'

Joel and Corin and Daisy, sucking on her gingerbread latte, knowing a killer was at large but unable to link that fact to their lives, or to Loz's life. Believing themselves immune.

'We found the girl from the Traffic accident,' she continued. 'Grace Bradley. She's in hospital but she'll be okay, at least I hope so. She knows where this woman takes the girls but she can't help us, not yet. A trauma specialist is with her, but it's taking too long. We need to find Loz quickly. He's killed two girls already.'

'He?'

'I don't think the woman taking them is the killer. But I may be wrong.' Marnie shut her eyes for a second against the craze of light coming from the hospital's windows. 'I went to Sommerville this morning.' Dancing to Stephen's tune, and she'd broken her promise to take Ed with her the next time she went there. 'It was connected to the case; one of the girls said she recognised Grace from the news last night.' She reached her free hand to the steering wheel, picking at a patch of fraying plastic. 'I saw Stephen. Not to speak to, but he was there. He's . . . changed.'

'How?' Ed asked.

'He's working out. Getting strong. Maybe he's scared about the move to adult prison.'

'Did he look scared?'

Smiling at her through the fireproofed glass, buzz cut showing the bones of his head. 'No.'

'But you're okay,' Ed said.

'I should have spent more time with Loz. Asked better questions, helped her to trust me. She knew where May was going but she didn't tell us. Any of us. She's cut off from her parents and I knew that, but I thought she'd talk to me or Noah if she had any sort of evidence. She didn't trust us to find May's killer. She went looking for him, on her own. Ed, she's thirteen.'

'It wasn't because she didn't trust you. At that age? It's just really hard to talk.'

Marnie knew he was right, but she also knew that Loz would have talked to Ed. Everyone talked to Ed. It was his superpower.

'This sketchpad we found in Loz's room. Life studies, X-rated. I think Loz knew it was there, maybe she even hid it herself.' Remembering the wire under her fingers, furred by paper torn from the pad. Had Loz torn pages out before she'd let her parents see it? If so, why? And which pages? 'She was protecting May, and she was scared. Ashamed, too. The whole house is ashamed . . .' She dropped her hand from the steering wheel. 'I'm not making much sense, sorry. I'm tired.'

'Where are you?' Ed asked.

'St Thomas's, waiting to speak with Grace's doctor. I'm all right. Better for being able to talk to you. Just wishing I'd done a decent job of talking to Loz when I had the chance. That shouldn't have been impossible. I saw how it was for her in that house. I saw how lonely she was. And she asked me about the Forgiveness Project, about Stephen. I should've been able to make a connection – get her to talk, or to trust me.'

'Don't beat yourself up,' Ed warned. 'You need to stay on top of this.'

'I know.' She straightened and checked the mirror, wiping the self-loathing from her face. 'The doctor should be finished with Grace soon. Then I have to try and find a way to get her to talk to me.'

'Can I help?' Ed offered.

Victim Support.

It was his job. His superpower. And Grace was afraid of Marnie, didn't want to talk to the police.

'I can be there in half an hour,' Ed said. 'If you need me.'

She closed her eyes in relief. 'Please.'

49

Christie sorted the dirty clothes into piles. Counted the water barrels in the kitchen. Checked the food levels and corrected the chart to show what was running low. They needed more fish, more grains, more powdered milk. She sorted the rubbish into black bags to put with the bins on the next street, where the houses were full of people. Counted batteries, and gas canisters for the stove. Her period was due, so she made a note to buy pads. Aimee was a late developer; she'd only had two periods in ten months but she wasn't well, didn't eat properly. Christie hadn't told Harm about the bright red blood she'd seen in Aimee's pads, too bright to be normal. Maybe Aimee really was sick and not just pretending, to keep Harm happy.

A sound from the stairs, the mezzanine floor.

Christie stood and listened, tensing until her neck cramped.

Laura, exploring. Nosy. Dangerous. What would Harm make of her? Christie sucked a finger into her mouth, trying to put a name to the shaking under her skin. Not fear, or not just that. She'd done what he'd asked, brought him his new girl. Old girl. Ancient.

What'd she done?

She put down the shopping list and walked to the barrel, holding a glass under its tap until the glass was full and the barrel belched. She carried the glass from the kitchen, moving slowly so she could listen for Laura. She knew every creak in this place and every groan, heard the emptiness of Laura's room as she stood with the glass in her fist. Upstairs . . .

Laura had gone upstairs.

Christie stood listening with her chest and the ends of her fingers, wet on the glass. A bubble burst in the water, its pressure pricking her thumb. If she looked down, she'd see her face lying in the glass, mouth squirming into a smile.

Laura was walking across the floor of Aimee's room, towards the bed.

Another two steps and she'd be there, right at the side of the bed where Aimee was sleeping, or pretending to sleep. Christie knew all her tricks. She *knew*.

Another step, one more.

Why had she stopped? Because she was scared?

Christie lifted the glass to her lips.

The water tasted blue and dead.

She stood and listened to the silence spreading and spreading overhead.

50

'You didn't witness May's murder. You didn't know she was dead until DI Rome told you. She was alive when you left, but you left in a hurry, in shock. What was happening in that place? What did you see to make you run?'

Grace's eyes moved around the room, fretting at the distance from her bed to the door. She wanted to run again. Half dressed, half starved, covered in bruises. She didn't feel safe here.

'What's happening in that place?' Ed asked again. 'Tell me one thing. Anything.'

He was sitting at the side of Grace's bed, in a soft blue shirt and twill jeans, his fringe in his eyes, his elbows on his knees. All his attention on her. The easiest person in the world to confide in.

'No . . . no water.' Grace's voice was thirsty, small. 'In the taps.'

Ed filled the plastic tumbler from the jug on the bedside table, holding it for her to drink a little. 'No water in the taps. That's odd. What else is unusual about that place?'

'No lights. No . . . heat.'

SARAH HILARY

'It's an old house?'

'Not . . . a house.'

'A flat? Or something else?'

Grace lifted a hand above her head, wincing. 'High.'

'A high-rise? An old high-rise.'

'New.' She was whispering. 'All new.'

'A new-build.'

She nodded, shifting in the narrow bed, looking in surprise at the bruises on her arms. 'What happened to me?' Her eyes scared to Ed's face. 'I don't remember.'

'It's okay. You were dehydrated, that's making it hard to remember, but it'll get better. You're in hospital, being looked after.' The doctor was pleased with Grace's response to the fluids, predicting a complete physical recovery, but the trauma specialist had warned them to be careful with the questions they asked. 'Tell me about the flat. It's a new-build but it's not finished. No water, no light or heat. What're the rooms like?'

'Nice.' She shut her eyes. 'They're . . . nice.' She squeezed her eyes tighter shut. 'I want to go home. When can I go home?'

'Where's home?'

'I told you. High. New.' She wanted to go back to the place she'd run from.

Her hands were folded meekly. Where was Jodie's survivor, hard as a cat's head? Marnie needed that girl, that Grace.

'Did you have a nice view?' she asked. 'From your window?'

'Just . . . chimneys.'

'These chimneys?' Marnie held up her phone. 'Grace? Are these the chimneys you could see from your window?'

The girl blinked at the screen: May's sketch of Battersea Power Station. 'Yes.'

'Did you have to share your room? With May, or one of the others?'

'Not . . . not always.'

'So it's a big place. How many rooms, can you remember?'

'Four.'

'Four bedrooms?'

'And the one upstairs.' Grace turned her head away. 'The loft room. Five, with the loft.'

A big flat, lots of rooms and a loft. Marnie could picture the place, mezzanine bedroom ticking the trend for loft living. How many unfinished new-build flats with loft space were inside their radius around Battersea? Her thumbs pricked. She texted the new information to Colin and Noah, keeping it brief, concise.

'Tell me about the loft room,' Ed said. 'Who sleeps up there?'

Grace's gaze fixed on Ed. He didn't make her nervous, the way Marnie did. 'Aimee.'

Another girl. How many more?

'How old is Aimee?'

'Sixteen? I don't know.'

'Aimee sleeps in the loft room?'

'He . . . keeps her up there.' Biting her tongue, turning her head away.

He. Who?

Marnie held her breath, willing Ed to get a name from the girl.

Grace dropped her eyes, moving her thumbs across the words written on her wrists. 'She's special, doesn't do anything with the rest of us.' She pressed her nail into the writing. 'Except May.'

Ed led her through the safe questions, earning her trust. 'What did Aimee do with May?'

309

'Talked.' Grace shrugged her thin shoulders. 'I don't know. They were up there all the time. Ashleigh bullied them about it.'

'How did she bully them?'

'Always on at Aimee, hated her being the special one.' She pushed her hair out of her eyes. 'If I was Aimee, I'd have shut her up.'

Marnie got a flash of Ashleigh lying in the Garrett's litter, her lips swollen shut.

'Who's in there right now?' Ed kept very still at Grace's side. 'Can you tell me their names?'

'May and Ashleigh and Aimee.' Without drawing breath. 'All of us.'

Marnie waited for her to remember that May was dead. Grace didn't correct the list of names, but she added to it: 'All of us, and Christie and Harm.'

'Harm.' Ed glanced at Marnie, careful to keep the concern out of his voice.

Marnie was texting Noah the names. 'Who's Harm?' she asked.

Grace shrank into the pillows, her lips tightening, not speaking. Marnie glanced at the name she'd blind-texted to Noah. 'Is Harm a man?'

'I want to go home.'

'Home to . . . Harm? Who is he? Is he a friend of Christie's?'

Grace retreated further, lifting her arm in the same gesture as before, twisting her wrist until Marnie was reading the word Ron had mistaken for a confession: *Killer*.

Harm was the killer?

'Tell me about the writing.' Ed gathered the girl's attention back to him, gently. 'The words you and May wrote on yourselves. Who started it?'

'Me.' Her fingers twitched. 'Long ago, when I was little.'

'May copied you?'

'To keep me company, to make me less lonely.' Her face shrank. 'May was *kind*.'

'How did you choose the words to write?'

'They chose them.'

'Who's they?'

'Everyone else. *Everyone*.'

'They're wrong, though. You're not a killer. You're not dead.'

'You . . . don't know.'

'Who have you killed?' Ed asked lightly.

'Me.' Her fingers curled inwards. '*Me*. I want to go home. When can I go home?'

'Okay. Tell me more about home. Is it near here? How long would it take you to get home?'

'I . . . don't know. *She* took me. It was dark.'

'Christie?'

Squeezing shut her eyes. 'Yes.'

'But you can see the power station from there. It's high up, a new building. A tower block?'

'Secret,' Grace said. 'It's only safe because it's a secret. You have to keep it safe.'

'Did you feel safe there?'

'Better than before. He was better. Let us be *us*. Loved us.' Grief tugged at her face. 'I was *good* there. I've never been good before.'

'But you had to leave. Why? What happened?'

A sob. 'I just wanted him to like me more.' She touched the words on her wrists. 'Too many of us. He couldn't see me. *Me*. I wanted to be better, for him to like me better.'

'What happens,' Ed said, 'if he doesn't like you?'

'He doesn't . . . hug you. Doesn't look at you. You're

311

nothing again.' Hurting her wrists with her nails. 'I didn't want to be nothing again.'

Marnie saw the girl's pain reflected in Ed's face. He waited a moment before saying, 'Tell me more about the place where he lives. I know it's a secret, but can you help me picture it better?' He waited. 'No water in the taps. You must've been thirsty. And how did you keep clean?'

'Bottles. Lots of bottles . . . He takes care of us. He takes *good* care. When can I go?' A stubborn score in her voice, but she was breaking down into sobs. 'You don't *know*. Let me go home.'

'It's okay, it is.' Ed put a hand on her wrist, covering the word written there, easing her fingers free of her skin. 'Is Harm in the flat now? With the other girls? With Christie?'

'Not always. Comes and goes.'

'Like Christie.' A nod. 'Was it Christie who gave you the note with Mrs Tarvin's address? We found it in your pocket. Did Christie write it?'

Grace nodded. 'Said it was *safe*. Said she would . . . *help*.'

Christie had sent a traumatised girl to Emma Tarvin for help. Knowing what the woman was capable of. Why? To punish Grace? Or intending Tarvin to keep her quiet?

'Christie took May's sister,' Marnie said. 'Just this morning. Loz is thirteen. She must be very scared. Has Christie taken her to the flat? To Harm?'

'Yes. *Yes.*'

'You need to tell me where the flat is. Help me to find Loz and the others. Please, Grace.'

The girl was shaking with tears. Marnie knew she should stop, call a nurse, leave Grace alone. But Loz was alone, with a killer. She thumbed through the photos on her phone until she found Jamie Ledger. 'Is this Harm? Please look, it's so important.'

Grace curled her free hand and beat weakly at the bed. 'Let me go . . . home.'

'I can't do that. I can look after you, I can make sure you're safe, but I can't take you back to that place. I won't. You know it's dangerous, that's why you ran. Harm and Christie tricked you into thinking it was safe, but you know that's not true. Loz is *thirteen*, she's May's little sister.'

How could she reach this girl – make Grace trust her enough to help?

'You were with May the night you left.' Ed held Grace's hand. 'The night of the crash. You got away, but May didn't. She went home, just like you want to go home now, and she was killed for it. You're the lucky one, Grace. The one who got away. The only one who can help us save Loz.'

Grace twisted her head on the pillow. Ed reached up and freed the hair clinging to her face, smoothing each strand between his fingers. 'It's okay. You're safe now. You can help us.'

Marnie could hear the ticking of her watch, time slipping away, maybe Loz's life slipping away.

'You're safe now,' Ed repeated.

Grace sat upright in the bed, thin arms reaching for a hug.

Ed held her, stroking her hair, letting her weep.

After a minute, the girl went quiet, leaning into him. 'Show me?' she whispered.

Marnie passed her phone to Ed. He showed Grace the photo of Ledger. She blinked her eyes against the cotton of his shirt. 'N-not him.'

'It's not Harm. Are you sure?'

313

Grace pushed upright, taking the phone from Ed and holding it in both hands. 'Not Harm.' She sniffed, her voice coming back to something like normal. 'It's not him.' Her thumbs moved over the keypad, as if she was remembering how a phone worked. 'Aimee . . .' She'd scrolled to another photo and looked up at Ed. 'This is Aimee.'

'Show me?' Ed moved so Marnie could see the screen too.

Grace turned the phone towards them.

Marnie's throat tightened. She shook her head. 'This isn't—'

'She's changed. But it's Aimee.' She handed the phone back to Ed. 'I can tell by the smile.'

A shy smile. High cheekbones. Grace thought Aimee was sixteen, but the face in the photograph didn't belong to a sixteen-year-old girl.

It belonged to a fifteen-year-old boy, missing from care since 2012.

The boy Joel had described as a psycho.

Eric James Mackay.

51

The room was empty, that was Loz's first thought.

The door was shut but there was no one here, just dust doing that dance it did when you opened a door into an empty room. Round windows at either end like cloudy eyes looking back at her. A dressing table, bed, wardrobe – a stale, mushroomy smell. No one was up here. That woman, Christie, had lied. Maybe this wasn't even the place. The place May went where she died . . .

Then Loz remembered what Christie had said – *She's had the flu so she needs a lot of rest* – and her eyes went to the bed in the far corner.

The bed had a high wooden frame. She couldn't see whether it was empty. To see, she'd have to go all the way into the room, away from the door and the stairs. Risk getting trapped up here. She felt for the key in her pocket, counting its teeth with her thumbnail. Something about the key bothered her, but it made her feel a bit braver. 'Hello?'

Some sound from the floor below made her freeze.

Christie, coming up the stairs?

Loz bit the inside of her cheek so hard it bled into

her mouth. She didn't want to be caught up here by Christie, who was only pretending to be nice and might actually, probably, be insane. She listened, blood banging in her ears, to the unfamiliar sounds of the building. The block was spooky, no one living here except Christie and the others. Loz hated it. She wanted to run. What was she even *doing*? Never mind Christie, *she* was insane.

'Hello.' From the bed.

She jumped so hard she bit her cheek again.

Shitshitshit . . .

Shut up.

You came here to find out, didn't you? To find out who killed her.

'Hi.' She made herself move in the direction of the bed, freezing when the duvet moved and a figure sat up like a doll against the pillows.

Spiky black hair and black eyes. Really pale and pretty, like Haruka Nanase or any of those anime boys with their huge eyes and pointy faces.

But Loz knew this face. She'd seen it before. In May's sketchpad.

It was all in May's sketchpad, like a story for her to follow, only not one she could explain to the police or anyone else. A story just for her, of where May went and who she saw. The story of who killed her. That was how Loz knew . . .

The girl in the bed wasn't real. She didn't exist.

'I'm Aimee.' The voice was like a girl's, just a bit deeper. It was a lie.

You're not Aimee. She doesn't exist.

'I'm Laura.' Now they were both lying. She was never *Laura*. She was only ever Loz.

'You're new.' Aimee sat up higher in the bed, linking

316

her arms around her knees. Most of her was under the duvet, only her skinny neck and shoulders showing. Wearing a white vest top, her arms skinny too. No writing on her.

Loz had expected writing.

She made herself look away from the bed, around the rest of the room. She didn't want Aimee thinking she was afraid. Something silver on the dressing table – a hairbrush. Light bulbs studded round the mirror. School uniform on the wardrobe door. The mushroomy smell made her stomach squeeze up. 'You live here?'

'Yes.' Aimee propped her chin on her knees.

Loz saw her in the mirror. Half of her, one big eye watching without blinking. 'What's in the cupboard?' she asked, to keep speaking. The silence was scary.

'Water tank.'

'There's no water,' Loz said.

The mirror cut her in half. *Aimee.*

'Christie says there's no water in the taps.' Loz turned to look at her. 'It's all in barrels.'

Calling her a liar now, but *Aimee* didn't care.

That eye like a crow's, fixing on her. Daring Loz to call her worse.

'You're sick,' Loz said.

Blinking. Black.

'Christie said you had the flu.'

'I'm sick,' Aimee agreed.

Loz walked to the foot of the bed. Towards the face from her sister's sketchpad. May had drawn this face. The last thing she ever drew. Loz had known it wasn't a girl's face the second she saw it. She knew the way her sister drew, the way her sister *saw*. That was when she'd started to understand what had happened to May. In this place, with this liar. She stopped in the line of light between

317

the windows where the dust was dancing, tickling her cheek. 'How long have you been here?'

'A while. Months.'

'How many months?'

'Three, four months. Something like that.'

May lying frozen in a steel drawer. Her sister. Her kite.

Loz let go of the key in her pocket and put her hands on the wooden frame at the foot of the bed. 'What did you say your name was again?'

'I'm Aimee.'

'No. You're not. Do you want to know how I know?'

Black eyes crawled all over her. 'How?'

'Because she was my sister. May. Because she was my sister and she drew you. I've got pictures of your *face*. Pictures from the subway. She *drew* you. Before she came here to be killed. Was it you? Did you kill her?' She was scared, and angry. The wooden frame hurt her hands enough to bring tears to her eyes. 'She was my *sister* and I will never, *ever* forgive you. So do whatever you do. Kill me, like you killed her. Like you killed Ashleigh Jewell. I know what you did, what you are. You're not *Aimee*. Aimee doesn't exist. You're a liar and a murderer and I hate you. I *hate* you.'

The frame was shaking under her hands, blurring the figure in the bed until she couldn't see anything but its stare, burning her.

'Go ahead. *Do it*. What you did to her, because you've done it anyway. Killed me, made me *nothing*. She was the only one who saw me. The *only* one. You're a pig. You're a sick *pig*. She wasn't . . . She never hurt *anyone*. She was hurting all the time, but she *never* hurt anyone. She was kind and quiet and the *only one* who loved me, who made me easy to love.' Her throat choked with tears. 'There's *nothing* in that house now. Just them hating me because it should've been *me*. Me they had to go and look at in that drawer, to *identify*. I'm rubbish, stupid, ugly. But she . . . she was so kind and quiet and I loved her so much. If you killed her, you . . .'

She only stopped when his hand was over her mouth, grinding her lips against her teeth.

She hadn't even seen him move from the bed, not properly, just as a wet blur.

He hissed hot against her cheek. 'Shut up.'

Loz tried to bite, tried to kick him. He held her hard against the bed with his hand over her mouth until red stars burst in her eyes.

'I'm warning you,' he hissed. 'Shut up!'

She dragged at his hand, but he was strong. Stronger than he'd looked in the bed. His arms weren't skinny at all, hard muscle under his skin. Her eyes rolled up in her head until she was seeing him standing over her.

Black eyes, cheekbones, the curve of his jaw just like May drew it. *Aimee*. How had anyone in this house believed he was a girl?

He bent lower, his hair scratching at her eyelid, at her eye.

She'd stopped struggling, too scared to breathe let alone fight.

He put his mouth close to her throat.

'Better,' he breathed. 'That's better.'

52

'Eric James Mackay. Fifteen years old, missing from a care home in Derby since May 2012. We know he hung out in the subway in Stockwell, but Joel and his friends haven't seen him there since September, a couple of months before May stopped going to the subway. We know she met Eric there. She drew him. Grace has identified the sketch.' Marnie pinned May's picture next to the photo of Eric Mackay. 'None of us recognised him from her sketch, but Grace had the advantage of living with him. He's changed more than we thought.'

They'd been imagining a shaven-headed thug, but Eric Mackay had metamorphosed into an angel-faced androgyne. A better disguise, perhaps, for a street kid. But surely more dangerous.

'Why was he in care?' Ron asked.

'His mum was sick,' Debbie said. 'Munchausen by proxy. She kept him off school, fed him pills, wouldn't let him out of the house. Children's Services got him eventually, but it sounds like he was messed up, spent the first six months at the care home hiding in bed like that's all he knew.'

'He calls himself Aimee Finch now.' Marnie touched May's sketch. 'According to Grace, he's been with Christie and Harm for the last three months. He and May arrived at the same time.'

'The porno pictures,' Ron said. 'Are those Mackay too?'

'We don't know. Perhaps. He and May met in the subway, but we don't know where he was living at the time. It's possible he's part of the recruitment drive, just like Christie.'

'Didn't Joel call him a psycho?' Ron said.

Noah nodded. 'But when we pressed him for more information, he wasn't very helpful. The extent of Eric's psychosis seems to have been jumping from the subway roof on a couple of occasions, and dancing outside when it was raining. A teenager's idea of psycho, in other words. Joel did say that Eric wasn't scared of anything. Went with strangers for sex on more than one occasion.'

'Men, or women?'

'Both. He wasn't picky, that was Joel's phrase.'

'And now he's living in this nuthouse,' Ron said, 'dressed like a girl.'

'Not just *dressed* as a girl,' Marnie corrected. 'Grace was convinced he *was* a girl. She says everyone in the flat was convinced of it, including May and Ashleigh.'

'Are we sure of that?' Noah was studying May's sketch of Eric. 'From this, it looks as if she might've known he was a boy.'

'Grace could be wrong. But she's adamant that Harm doesn't know Aimee is Eric.'

'Which means he's not abusing them,' Debbie said. 'Or he'd have found that out by now.'

'Grace says Harm never touched her. Or any of the others. From the way she described it, that's the creepiest thing about him, the fact that he's not interested in them in that way.'

'She's got a funny definition of creepy.' Ron's low opinion of Grace hadn't improved since the girl had started talking. 'Why'd she run off, if everything's so cosy up there?'

'It isn't cosy, but it is safe. Locks on the doors, blackout blinds, strict rules about quiet. Three months ago, they were squatting in a house in Chiswick. Harm decided it wasn't secure enough; that's when he moved them into this flat.' Marnie glanced at Colin. 'Any luck locating it?'

'We've narrowed the list, but getting information out of developers is like blood from a brick. Hundreds of new-builds across London, private housing, offices, flats. Lots of stalled projects.'

'Why can't she just give us the bloody address?' Ron argued. 'She's talking now.'

'She rarely went outside the building until the night she ran, when it was dark and she was panicking. She's working with DC Waywell to help us pinpoint the location.'

'What about this squat in Chiswick?'

'We're looking for it,' Marnie said. 'Grace doesn't remember the exact address, but she's given us bits and pieces. We want her to concentrate on helping us find the flat.'

'Do we think Loz knew Eric, or Aimee?' Noah was still examining the sketch pinned to the board. 'She must've seen this in May's sketchpad.'

'She'd have told us.' Marnie wanted to believe that. 'If she knew anything she thought would lead us to May in those weeks when she was missing, or to her killer now – she'd have told us.'

'Harm,' Debbie said. 'What do we know about him?'

Marnie nodded at Noah. 'DS Jake?'

'He's roughly the same age as Jamie Ledger, so mid forties.

Perhaps a superficial likeness, but Grace is adamant that Ledger isn't the man she knows as Harm. We'll have a photofit soon. She didn't want to tell us anything, but luckily we had Ed Belloc on our team. From what Grace told Ed, Harm's a loner with some serious survival skills. A control freak. Food, water, affection – all strictly rationed. Lots of rules for the girls to obey, and he dresses them the same, in school uniform. He's obsessed with security. It's why they moved from the squat. The flat's easier to defend. His words.'

'Sounds like an ex-army man to me,' Ron said.

'He's made the building secure, rigged up heating and light, off grid. He's handy, and he's strong. Grace is scared of him, and she doesn't scare easily. She's also inclined to keep his secrets, so we can assume he did a psychological number on her. He doesn't stay in the building the whole time. Grace says he comes and goes. The girls are given keys but the keys don't work in the locks, so presumably that's a trick to make them feel secure. If Harm's going out of the building on a regular basis, it suggests he has a life somewhere else. Maybe even a job.'

'Ledger had a job,' Ron pointed out, 'until recently.'

'We're still looking for Ledger,' Marnie said. 'But the priority is finding this flat. We'll need a team on standby. Hostage negotiators, too. Grace is scared of Christie as well as Harm. She doesn't think Eric's a threat, but that's because she's still thinking of him as Aimee.'

'How does he shave?' Debbie asked. 'He must be doing that every day to pass himself off as a girl. Surely someone noticed something wasn't right.'

'Grace says *Aimee* is left alone most of the time. Harm has her confined to bed, convinced she's sick. Maybe Eric stays under the covers, doesn't let the others see too much of him. That ties to how he grew up, with his mum's mental health problems.'

'What difference does it make whether he's a boy or a girl in there? If Harm isn't abusing them, or trying to abuse them, couldn't he just as easily be Eric?'

'Harm hates teenage boys,' Marnie said. 'It's one of the things he lectured Grace and the others about. Drugs, promiscuity, diseases. So we can imagine how he reacted to the news of May's pregnancy. He saved them from all that, from the perils and pitfalls of living on the streets. At the same time he's dressing them in uniform, keeping them meek. DS Jake's right, we're dealing with an obsessive control freak, probably with a history of trauma.'

'Grace didn't know about the murders,' Ron said. 'May and Ashleigh. So what was she doing with May the night before she got killed?'

'Grace left in a panic after a confrontation with Harm. She wasn't keen to say exactly what happened, but reading between the lines, she made a pass at him in the hope of privileges of some kind. He reacted badly, and she ran. May went after her, wanting to help. May was always trying to help, Grace says. She took a change of clothes and the address Christie had given her for Emma's flat. Supposedly a safe place to stay, although I'd question Christie's motive. Grace tried to talk May into going with her, but May insisted on heading back to Harm and the others.'

'Why? She'd got away. Why go back? If she hadn't done that . . .'

'Grace doesn't know exactly, but she's still talking about that place as "home". She says May insisted on going back home, that she couldn't leave Aimee alone there.'

'She went back and it got her killed,' Ron said. 'How did Grace react to that?'

'She was upset, but not entirely surprised. Especially when I told her May was pregnant. She'd already figured out something was very wrong in there. Harm didn't lose his temper in the usual way. She says he went white hot – froze her out. She ran because she was scared of what would happen if she hung around.' Marnie paused, until the room was quiet. 'We know that two of the girls who went into that flat were killed. By Harm or Christie or Eric, we don't know which.'

'If Harm hates teenage boys,' Debbie said, 'then Eric's in danger too.'

'That's what Grace says,' Marnie agreed. 'Either way, we need to find the flat before anyone else is hurt or killed.'

53

'Sit still and shut up.' He walked to the door and stood listening before coming back to the bed where he'd put her.

Loz hadn't moved, other than to get the key into her fist. There was only one way out of the room. Through the door he'd just checked. No weapons in here, or none that she could see. The key was all she had.

He stood staring down at her, looking like all her favourite anime heroes rolled into one, with his spiky hair and heart-shaped face, in a loose white vest top, dark-blue pyjama bottoms hanging off his hips. 'You're Loz,' he said. 'May's little sister.'

'Shut up.' She shook with hate. 'You don't say her name, you don't get to do that. You—'

'Be quiet. Do you want Christie up here?' He put his hands on the frame at the foot of the bed. He had long fingers, neat nails. His knuckles were white. 'Why are you saying she's dead?'

'Because she *is*. You killed her. You . . . *freak*.'

He stared her down, eyelashes like blades at the bridge of his nose. 'You said your parents had to look at her, identify her.' His voice was rigid, low in his throat. 'Is that true?'

'*Yes.*'

'She's really dead?' The bed frame creaked under his grip, the muscles in his arms standing out in slim lines. His eyelashes shone with tears. 'When?'

'Two days ago.'

'Where?' He bit each word out, but he was crying now.

'Battersea Power Station.'

'How?'

'She was strangled.'

He doubled up as if she'd kicked him in the stomach. The bed scraped at the floor.

Loz looked at the distance to the door. She forced herself to stand up.

He was crying with his whole body, rocking on his heels, his head between his outstretched arms, face hidden. She could make it, if she was quick. Get past him, down the stairs to the kitchen. Christie had locked the door, but Loz had a key. She opened her fist and looked at it, to convince herself. She had a key. *Look* . . .

Its teeth were smooth, too smooth to make a decent weapon. Too smooth for the key to be recently cut. It was an old key, but the locks in here were all new. This key . . .

Wouldn't open the new locks. She'd known there was something wrong with it ever since Christie had invited her to take it from the drawer. It was useless as a weapon, and it was useless as a way out. 'You didn't kill her,' she said to the boy.

He sobbed, shaking his head. 'We . . . we were . . .'

Loz put the key into her pocket, moving closer to the foot of the bed. 'You were what?'

'In love. I *loved* her. She was having our baby.' He lifted his head, red-eyed, wet-faced. 'The police . . . Who found her?'

'A security guard at Battersea. The police haven't given us the post-mortem report yet. But they told us she was pregnant.' Loz looked at him. 'Is that why she was killed?'

He moved his mouth, not speaking.

'Who killed her?' Loz demanded. 'If it wasn't you?'

'I don't know.'

'Whoever it was, did they know she was pregnant?'

'Everyone here knew.' He wiped at his tears with the crook of his elbow. 'She told them. I didn't want her to tell them, but she came out with it in front of everyone. I was scared for her. For all of us. You can't just say a thing like that, not here, not to *him* . . .'

'You didn't know she was dead, but you knew she'd gone.' Loz tasted old blood in her mouth, from where she'd bitten her cheek. 'Why didn't you go after her? Why didn't you *look* after her?'

'I didn't *know*. He said she'd gone back out there. On to the streets, or home. I thought she'd gone home to you. And even if she hadn't, if she was in a hostel . . . I knew they'd give her a place if she told them she was pregnant. She was better off without me.' His shoulders shook, anger cutting across his face suddenly. 'I wasn't brave enough to stand up to him. She was better off out there.'

'Who said she'd gone back out there?'

'Harm. It was Harm.'

They looked at one another. Loz said, 'What's your name?'

'Eric.'

'How come they think you're Aimee?'

'*He* thought it. When he took me home that first time. I didn't know, just thought he wanted . . . sex. And I was desperate. I needed a place to stay.' He flushed, looking feverish. 'When he made me put that on,' pointing to the girl's school uniform on the wardrobe door, 'I thought he was kinky. I thought he *knew* I was a boy, but he didn't. Then I got too scared to tell him after he started with the lectures about staying safe, keeping clean. I thought if he found out, he'd go crazy.'

'So he doesn't know.'

'No one does.'

'But she was pregnant. How do they think *that* happened if they believe you're a girl?' Her stomach churned. 'Do they think *he* did it?'

'No. *No*. He doesn't touch us, any of us. If he'd touched her, I'd have killed him. They thought she was sneaking out. She did go out, with Grace. But she always came back. For *me*. It's my fault.' His face kept breaking, blurring with tears. 'I took her to the house because I fancied her.'

'What house?'

'The place before here. We lived there for a bit. May liked it, she liked the garden. It was a place we could be together and I wanted that, more than anything. But I knew there was something wrong with him and I never warned her, not properly, because I wanted her to stay and there wasn't anywhere else I could be with her. It's my fault she's dead. If I hadn't got her pregnant, if I'd warned her—'

'Why does he want you all here, if he isn't touching you? What're you *for*?'

'We make him feel like a man. He has to *be a man*. It's how his dad treated him, growing up.' He spoke too fast, like he'd been alone for so long he'd forgotten how to talk to people. Loz had to concentrate to keep up. 'It screwed with his head, like my mum screwed with mine.

Only for me, it was the opposite of *be a man*. I just had to stay in bed, being sick for her.'

She didn't understand that, but she wasn't interested in his mum. 'Why does he need so many of you?'

'Safety in numbers, he says. He's obsessed with safety. It's why he moved us up here. The house wasn't safe. His job's fitting alarms, listening to people go on about break-ins and robberies. He thinks he's got it sorted, that he's keeping us safe. That's how it starts. He finds us, or *she* does, brings us back, takes care of us. To start with.' He wiped at his face again. 'It's like he's . . . searching for someone. Or he's guilty about something. I don't know, I can't figure him out. Just that he's not right. I didn't think it was worse than that. I didn't know he was a killer.' Sucking a breath. 'I'd never have let her come here if I'd known that.'

'What about Christie?' Loz needed a chink in the armour of this place. She'd have taken a knife from the rack in the kitchen if Christie hadn't watched her so well. 'Where does she fit in?'

'I suppose she was abused. She doesn't know when to stop, thinks she's in control but she's not, not really. I knew girls like her in care. Usually they'd been abused.'

'You were in care.'

'All of us were. Grace, Ashleigh.'

'May wasn't.'

'No.' His face broke again. 'I can't believe she's dead.'

'Can't you?' Loz looked at him pityingly. Her head was ringing with dizziness. She'd not eaten in hours. 'You've just told me what a psycho he is. And you're up here because you're scared of him. Why's it so hard to believe he killed her? And not just her. Ashleigh's dead, too.'

Eric stared at her. His eyes were weird, flat. Was he on drugs?

'How did you find us?' he said.

'The subway, I told you. May had drawings of you. I knew where she went, but I didn't know about you. Not properly. Not until now.' Loz looked around the room. 'What else about Christie?'

'She's been with Harm a couple of years. His watchdog. I suppose she's in love with him.'

Loz wrinkled her nose. 'Worst advert for love, ever.'

He nearly smiled.

'I didn't just mean *her*.' Loz headed for the door.

'Where're you going?'

She took out her phone. 'No signal in here. Otherwise I'd have called the police already.'

'She let you keep your phone?' His face twitched with panic. 'She never does that.'

'She gave me a key, too.' Loz wanted to see if he knew about the keys. She couldn't be sure he was telling her the truth. About May, or Christie, or any of it.

'The keys don't work.' He dropped his hands to his sides. 'Gracie told me that.'

'Who's Gracie?'

'She lived here too. She was the first to go. The day before May . . . before May went.'

'You mean Gracie's dead as well?'

'I don't know.' He frowned. 'Maybe. If Ashleigh's dead.'

He didn't believe it. Or he didn't care.

'Does Grace have red hair?' Loz asked.

Eric nodded. He was so skinny and pretty. She had to remind herself how strong he'd been when he grabbed her.

'And she writes on herself?'

'Yes.'

'She's not dead. At least I don't think so. She caused a car crash, the night before May was found. The police are looking for her.'

'Do they know you're here?'

Should she lie? Tell him she had backup, that the place was surrounded? That was what they'd do on a TV show, or in a book.

'Maybe. I'm not sure. They'll be looking for me.' She glanced at the window, her eyes stinging suddenly. 'Mum and Dad'll be freaking out.'

'Why did you come?' he demanded. 'You thought I'd killed her, that's what you said. Why did you come here if you thought that?'

'I wanted to know for sure. No one would tell me anything. All I had was this.' She took the page from her pocket, torn from May's sketchpad, carefully so DI Rome and DS Jake wouldn't notice it was missing. Christie's face, like a bad photo, but it was her. May didn't draw faces like bad photos, not unless there was something wrong with the person she was drawing. On the same page, her sketch of the subway, grass growing around the entrance, graffiti on its walls. Loz had torn the page at random, knowing the police would take the sketchpad, but needing this evidence of where May had gone. 'She drew you, too.' She'd left Aimee's face in the sketchpad, for DI Rome, along with all the other sketches of the subway.

Eric stared at the picture of Christie as if he hated her. 'It's not safe here.'

'It's not safe anywhere. That's why you're here, isn't it? Why you haven't tried to leave.'

'I was in trouble with the police. I thought I'd be arrested. May said it wouldn't happen. She said she'd keep me safe, but it wasn't for *her* to do that.' He rubbed weakly at his eyes. 'I should've been the one looking after her, not the other way round.'

'Because you're a boy and she's a girl? That's stupid.'

'I wasn't good enough for her. She deserved someone better.'

'She chose you, didn't she? Over us.' Her nose burned with held-in tears. 'Over me.'

'No.' He shook his head. 'She talked about you all the time. How brave you were. She wished she was more like you, that's what she said. She made me want to meet you. She loved you.'

'Stop it.' Her legs felt funny, rubbery. 'Stop saying shit to make me feel better. Stop lying.'

'I'm not lying.' He came towards her, holding out his hand. 'She told me you'd make the best auntie in the world because you were so brave. Nothing scared you, not really, not for long. If the world gave you shit, you gave it straight back. That's what she said.'

Loz shook her head. Her throat was so swollen and salty she couldn't speak.

'She was brave too.' Eric took her hand and held it. His fingers were cold. 'She stood up to Harm. Not like Grace did, by shouting or fighting. Quietly. She kept me sane. I'd have gone mad without her. I *was* going mad . . . She's the bravest person I ever met.'

Loz blinked. Her shoulders wouldn't stop shaking.

'She'd have fought for us.' Eric put his arms around her. 'If I'd let her. And she loved you. She *loved* you.'

'Then why did she leave me?' Loz sobbed. 'Alone with them? If she loved me, why did she leave me on my own?'

'She was coming back.' He was crying too. 'She *was*. We were going to live together. You and me and her. And the baby. We were going to be together.'

He was making the side of her neck wet.

Loz pulled away. 'I'm going.' She rubbed her face dry, wiping snot from her hands on to her jumper. 'Are you coming with me?'

He stared at her. 'You can't just . . . leave.'

'Why not?'

'She won't let you.'

'Christie? She let me keep my phone.'

'She won't just let you go. Especially not now.'

'What's that supposed to mean?'

'You know about Harm, this place.' He half shut his eyes. 'Dead girls, you said. Murders.'

'So? You're not going to tell her. You're too scared.'

'I don't have to tell her,' Eric said. 'She already knows.'

'What?' Her head throbbed with confusion. 'How?'

'She's been out there the whole time. Listening.'

Loz looked at the closed door, feeling sick. 'She . . .'

'Listens. It's what she does.' He stared at the door like he loathed it. 'It's who she is.'

The handle of the door held the light.

A brass handle, dark brown with a lick of white running through it. No lock. A heavy door, the kind that shut itself with a chain even when you tried to leave it open.

Loz thought of all the rooms she had to get through to get out of here. Then the stairs, flight after flight of stairs before she was safe in the street.

'We need to go. Now, while it's just her. Before Harm gets back.'

'Too late.'

'What?'

'Can't you feel him?' Eric hadn't stopped staring at the door, hating it with his whole face, his body tight as a fist. 'He's back. He got back while we were talking.'

His eyes burned at the door. 'He's here.'

54

'Grace remembers stairs leading up to the rooms where they were being kept. At least a dozen flights of stairs. Inside the building.' DC Terence Waywell pinned five photos to the board. Blocks of flats and offices, each with an address. 'They didn't use the main entrance, she says. There was a second entrance around the back. Like a social housing concession inside a private development.'

'Poor doors,' Debbie said. 'Isn't that what they call them?'

Terence nodded. 'That's the sort of thing we're after. Me and Col have narrowed it down to these five, based on what Grace can remember. Best thing would be to walk the route with her, working backwards from the crash site, but the hospital's saying she isn't fit for that yet. So this's what we've got to work with.'

'Don't any of these places have proper security?' Ron complained.

'Let's find out,' Noah said. 'Call the site managers, or whoever's in charge of each place. We're looking at a relatively small area. We don't want to alert the killer by sending in teams to neighbouring sites. Let's try and narrow it down as quickly as we can.'

'The boss is still with Welland. Guess that means she's having to beg for back-up. You'd think two dead girls would've got us SWAT teams coming out of our arses.'

'We'll only need one SWAT team,' Noah said. 'If we do the next bit right.'

'This witness statement about Grace Bradley.' Welland looked tired, the skin of his face too tight around the eyes. 'I don't like it.'

'You think she can't be trusted?' Marnie asked.

'No. I don't like the source of the statement.' He touched a hand to the paperwork. 'You went to Sommerville for this. Why didn't you send DC Tanner, or Waywell?'

'It was quicker for me to go. They know me there. I was able to get what we needed and get back here, fast.'

'With a young girl missing?'

'We didn't know at the time that Loz was missing. We didn't know Grace was in Emma's cupboard. We needed a witness statement from Jodie Izard and it made sense for me to get it.'

Welland hooded his eyes from her. 'Did you see Stephen Keele when you were there?'

'Not to speak to,' she said truthfully.

'But you saw him.' His expression was unforgiving, censure a distant outpost. It stung her, the way it always did. She wanted Welland's approval, and not just because he was her boss.

'Yes, he was there. Look, Eric Mackay's in the place where the girls are being kept. Christie, Eric and this man Harm. I need a hostage negotiator. I'd like Toby Graves if he's available.'

'Noted. Who do we think is the more dangerous of

the three? The survivalist, Harm? Christie Faulk, who's luring the girls away? Or this boy who's pretending to be something he's not?'

'I don't know. We have to assume all three are dangerous.'

'But only one of them,' Welland pressed the taut skin above his left eye, 'is a killer.'

'Probably, yes.'

'A lot of role-playing going on. A lot of smoke and mirrors. I don't like it.'

He could have been talking about Stephen, about the roles Stephen was playing. Foster-brother, senseless killer, police informant. 'None of us likes it,' Marnie said.

'The press have latched on to the Beswicks. A second daughter missing. It's making them look unlucky, or dodgy. Are you sure we shouldn't be looking in that direction?'

'I'm not ruling anything out. But their house is clean, no clues there. We need to find the place Grace ran from. We're getting close, thanks to DC Waywell and Colin Pitcher.'

'I hope you're right. This is enough of an unholy mess. Would you believe I had the Mayor of London rattling my cage about foreign investment at Battersea? Corpses aren't good for business, I'm told. Especially not young, pretty ones.'

'Toby Graves,' Marnie said. 'And a SWAT team on standby. That's what I need. I want to go in as soon as we have a location.'

DC Waywell unpinned one of the photos from the board. 'This one's out. Stairs aren't finished, according to the developers.'

'The list's coming down, that's good. Keep at it.'

Noah tried to see the evidence afresh, searching for a

clue they'd missed, something to lead them to Loz. Her face looked back at him, big-eyed, accusatory. She hadn't liked having her photo taken. Had she let her sister sketch her? She'd known about May's sketches of the subway, where to search for her sister's killer. Why hadn't she given that lead to the police? Because she didn't trust them to find the murderer, or because she was keeping her sister's secrets?

All teenagers kept secrets, that was part of growing up. Noah looked at the other girls on the board, their faces caught by the camera, slick with smiles but with the same accusation in their eyes. Who had looked out for them? No one. Grace's photo was pinned below Logan Marsh's, next to May's post-mortem results. Pregnant; hypernatremic. Grace, falling from the cupboard at his feet, twitching. Both girls had been taught how to salt fish, how to survive. Taught by a killer. Trained . . .

Noah's hand moved to the photo of Jamie Ledger, hesitating there.

Ron was talking on the phone in a low voice, 'If I can, mate. We're working all hours here. I've got to get on. Yeah, will do.' He hung up, catching Noah's eye. 'Memorial service next week for Logan Marsh; his mum's organising it. Kenickie wanted to know if we'd be going.'

'How is Logan's mum?'

'Bearing up. Kenickie says the dad's staying out of the picture. Guilt, he reckons. Logan's mates are helping out. They've put up a Facebook page about his volunteer work, stuff he did for charity. He was a bit of a local hero. I know we've got other things to think about, but I'm going to try and make it to the service. He was just a kid, like the others.' Ron pinched his nose hard with his fingers. 'Think we'll find her in time? Loz Beswick.'

'Not like this,' Noah said. 'Let's eliminate more of these sites.'

Ron nodded and picked up the phone.

Noah went to his desk, pulling up the profile he'd been working on, for the killer.

White male, mid forties, loner. It read like a textbook entry. Psycho 101. That felt wrong, for starters. The profile matched Jamie Ledger, but Grace insisted he wasn't the man who'd given her a home. *Harm*, with his rules, obsessed with sickness, survival. Three teenage girls and Eric Mackay, pretending to be a fourth. Was it Eric who'd got May pregnant?

Noah's phone buzzed and he took the call. 'DS Jake.'

'It's Riff. Dan's mate? You got a minute? Only I think I might know how your killer got that girl's body into Battersea.'

'How?' Noah reached for a pen and paper.

'Tunnels. Really big fucking tunnels right under the river. Used for siphoning off steam to heat the council estates over in Pimlico, right up until the early eighties. Didn't mention them before because we all thought they'd been sealed off at ground level, but I checked with a couple of contacts, who seem to think there's access to the boiler room. You said the penthouse was above the boiler room? I thought you'd want to know.'

'Access to the boiler room, from underground? From these tunnels?'

'Yeah, who knew?' Riff sounded nostalgic for his old life. 'This's what I meant when I talked about vanishing points – fucking miles of tunnels, and who knew?'

'Who *did* know? Can you give me the names of your friends?'

'Contacts,' Riff corrected. 'Sorry, no. I could give you their online aliases, but I'm not sure how much use those'd be. You should check on site, though. Not much point in them lying about this, and like I said, the tunnels are a matter of public record. Public record says they're sealed off, but since they say that about every place in London that's been rinsed . . .'

'I'll look into it, thanks.'

'Sure.' Riff rang off.

'Something?' Ron asked.

'A way into Battersea Power Station we didn't know about, assuming the source is reliable. I'll call the site manager, Aaron Buxton, but this may need a visit back out there.'

'We don't have time, unless it's going to help us find Loz and these loonies.'

'Maybe it is.' Noah pointed at the map on the board. 'We're talking tunnels. If the killer used them to get into the power station, he or she could be using them right now. It could be why Christie and Loz didn't show up on any of the CCTV footage from Stockwell.'

'Underground . . . *Shit.* You've just doubled our hunting ground.'

Noah nodded. 'We need to check it out.'

55

Christie

'Harm is home.' Christie ignored the thing on the bed. 'He wants to meet you.'

Loz was shaking all over, her face a mess, smeared with tears. Whiter than the bed. *Laura*, she'd said her name was. She'd lied.

'Don't be scared.' Christie could smell her. 'He doesn't like you to be scared.'

To Eric, she said, 'You'd better stay there.'

Disgust on her tongue like a pellet of gum with all the flavour chewed out of it. She wanted to strip the bed. Set fire to it. Bleach out the stains, the lies. Drag that *thing* by its fringe and throw it at the floor, at the walls. But she couldn't. Harm would want to do it. Harm would have to see what he'd shut up in here, what he'd been looking after. He wouldn't believe it from Christie, or anyone else. He'd have to see it with his own eyes, and then . . . he'd want to deal with it.

She waited at the door for Loz. 'He's in the kitchen.'

She pointed for the girl to go ahead of her, down the stairs.

Eric didn't move, half hidden under the covers of the bed.

A patch of sun sat on the carpet at the side of the bed where Christie was supposed to kneel, worrying and praying, where she would never now kneel. Her tongue tasted grey.

'He's waiting,' she told Loz. 'In the kitchen.'

Harm was heating rice, his neck bent over the stove, nursing the thin flame with the curl of his palm. Candlelight licked at his back from the table laid with cutlery, plates. A spicy smell from the stove, red and green. For a second it was the same, just for a second.

'This is Loz.' Christie stood out of the light, letting Harm see the new girl. Using her real name, not the lie she'd told Christie.

Harm was busy with the flame under the food, but he smiled across his shoulder. 'Hello, Loz. Welcome to the family.'

Christie leaned into the smile, jealous of the girl standing at her side, shaking so hard she might fall down, stinking of fear.

The shadow of Harm's hand fell across the table, among the forks and knives. 'I hope you like curry.' The stove puttered, purring when he coaxed it, stirring at the rice in the billy can.

Loz said, 'Yes.' Her voice was dried up, rattling in her throat like a coin in a tin. She was keeping her eyes away from the weapons on the table.

Try it, go on.

Christie thought of the boy upstairs that Harm had protected. Shelter, warmth, food, love – all for that. *Aimee.*

The locks, the lights. Barrels of water, batteries. The thirsty ache in her gut making her feet dance at night, tremors in her thighs and fingers until she wanted to crawl under Harm just to keep still, just to be kept quiet and still by the weight of him.

She'd helped him, after May. When he came home from the power station, bent and weeping under the weight of what he'd done, she'd made a promise that he'd never be alone like that again. She'd taken care of Ashleigh. Got rid of his leavings, the way she'd once cleared the corpse of a mouse from the kitchen floor before her mother could curse the cat for doing what it was normal for a cat to do. It was normal for Harm, too. Christie understood. Death wasn't the worst thing, wasn't even close to the worst thing. He'd said nothing after Ashleigh, not *thank you*, not anything. He'd gone looking for Grace, as if he wanted her back. Christie didn't look for thanks. She'd do it again, whatever he asked, whatever he needed. She owed him and she understood; he could keep his hands off them until he couldn't. She was here to help when he couldn't, but it made her sick to think how much of it was done for Aimee, who didn't even exist.

'Bring us water, would you?' Harm nodded at her.

Christie went to the barrel, working the tap to fill each cup in turn, remembering rain slicking off plastic sheeting, the man with the copper coins, the one Harm had saved her from just like he'd saved her from going back to Emma Tarvin, who sold girls more cheaply than she sold smack, who'd sneered when Christie bled all over her bathroom floor before telling her to get out.

Harm had saved her twice over.

The barrel boomed as the water reached its new level.

Candlelight wavered in the cups as she brought them to the table.

343

'Here.' Harm pulled out a chair for Loz, and she sat.

He looked her over, his expression serious. Her hair was a scrawl around her face, like Grace's but black not red. No make-up, no jewellery, no polish on her nails. No tits, either. There wasn't much to be done to her, not much that needed changing.

Harm's eyes met Christie's over the girl's head. Not seeing, not yet, what she'd done. Just seeing his new girl. The one he'd told her to bring back here.

'Good,' he said. 'It's good to meet you, Loz.'

56

'Yes, there were tunnels under Battersea,' Aaron Buxton said, 'but there's no way into them from the site. Not here and not on the other side of the river. They sealed everything off years ago.'

'The tunnels ran from the power station under the river into Pimlico. Is that right?'

'Yes.' Buxton was working; Noah could hear the site traffic in the background of the call. 'It kept the boiler house from overheating, sent the steam where it could save money. Smart thinking, you might say. But the tunnels have been shut off since the early eighties.'

'I've seen photos online. Recent photos. People are getting into the tunnels.'

'You mean trespassers, hackers, whatever they call themselves. They might be finding a way in, but they're not coming out over here. Not unless they've found a way through ten feet of concrete.'

'You're absolutely certain? We're in the middle of a murder investigation . . .'

'Save yourself some time and take my word for it. I'll take a photo of the concrete if you need convincing. That's not how he got her on site. I wish it was. Then I wouldn't need to be double-checking everyone on the security detail in case one of them's not doing his job properly.'

'Or more than one of them.'

'Thanks,' Buxton said gloomily. 'That's made my morning.'

Noah ended the call, knowing how the man felt. But, 'Good news,' he told Ron. 'The hunting ground just got halved again. We're back where we started.'

'We're owed a break.' Ron rubbed his eyes. 'In the case, I mean. It's an all-nighter for sure.'

Noah worked the crick out of his neck, walking over to the whiteboard.

The killer wasn't underground. He worked in the open. They'd thought that as soon as they saw May's body. This wasn't someone who was hiding, not in any usual sense. He was happy to be found by the right people. By lost girls like Ashleigh, and Loz. Maybe even by the police. He'd made a mistake with Eric Mackay, which meant he was fallible. It also meant he wasn't abusing these girls, not physically. So what was he doing, and why had it ended – twice – in murder?

'Grace calls it home,' Marnie said at his shoulder. 'This place where he's keeping them. She wants to go back there, even now. She's scared of the alternative, but it's more than that. Even knowing what Harm's done, she wants to go back.'

'But she didn't on the night of the crash. Only May went back.'

'For Aimee's sake. That's what Grace said. May couldn't leave Aimee there.' Marnie was looking at the faces on the board. 'She knew, didn't she?'

'That Aimee was Eric? I think so. It's in her sketch . . . I'm wondering if Eric was the father.'

'I'd say there's a good chance of that.' Marnie's blue eyes darkened. 'What's wrong with our killer that he can't see a teenage boy when he's right in front of him? And if May and Eric were having sex, he missed that too.'

'Maybe he's not looking too closely. The uniforms, the rules . . . Maybe they're all the same to him, like dolls. Ultimate objectification.' In which case, he was in for a shock with Loz, who was the least doll-like girl Noah had met. 'That would explain what he did to May after she was dead, the neat way he laid her out, tidied her away.'

'But not Ashleigh.' Marnie's stare worked the board for clues. 'Grace says Ashleigh was a flirt, and we know Harm doesn't like that. He likes good little girls, sexless, no make-up, no jewellery. If he found out May was pregnant, and if Ashleigh was flirting with him . . . They both broke the same rule. By being women instead of girls, instead of children.'

'And Christie? Where does she fit in? She's a woman, by any standards.'

'One woman's allowed, if she's playing mother. From what Grace said, that's the role Christie self-assigned.'

'Some mother. She's hardly keeping these girls safe . . . Do you think Loz is still alive?' He asked the question quietly, then wished he hadn't. Afraid it was stupid, optimistic.

Marnie said, 'I hope so. We have to hope so.'

'I thought we'd found a lead. Tunnels under Battersea. But it's a dead end.'

'So we keep going forward.' Marnie touched a hand to his elbow. 'Take a break if you need to. Call Dan, or Sol. Remind yourself of what's important. I need you on this.' Her phone rang in her office and she went to answer it.

SARAH HILARY

Noah speed-dialled Dan's number, but got voicemail. 'I'll be late, sorry. Love you.'

He tried Sol's number, because Marnie was right, and because the whiteboard was starting to look like a brick wall. 'Hey,' he said when his brother picked up. 'You okay?'

'I'm cool.' A beat. The sound of Sol scuffing a foot at the floor. 'I messed up, but it's sorted.'

'Is it?' Noah walked to the window, needing a change of view. 'I'm not on your case, just worried and wanting to help if I can. If you need my help.'

'Thanks, but it's cool. I was getting free, you know? Just . . . trying to get free.'

'A gang?'

'Yeah.' Sol gave a long sigh. 'But I'm cool. I think . . . it's gonna be okay.'

'Good. Look, I'll be late home. Dan knows. Don't wait up for me. And take care.'

'Yeah. Noah? Thanks.'

'Sure.' He rang off. He was going to have to talk with Sol properly. Bite the bullet and have the conversation neither one of them wanted, about how much trouble he was in and how hard he was trying to get out of it. Sol would never ask for his help, Noah knew that. But if he *needed* it, then Noah was going to have to make the first move.

Loz's face looked at him from the whiteboard, next to her sister's. A missing girl, and a dead one. Why hadn't Loz asked for their help? Why had she given up so quickly? Going to that subway was an act of despair, or worse, of suicide. She hadn't trusted the police to find May's killer. Noah's laptop was open at her Tumblr, photos she'd taken of road signs. Arrows mostly, as if she was making a point, subconsciously perhaps, about her life lacking

348

direction. Or just searching for a way through her grief and loss.

In the days since May's death, she'd researched police procedure and the CPS, statistics on sentencing, the Forgiveness Project, prison overcrowding. She'd found the names of the girls who were missing in London, seen photographs of Ashleigh and the others. Researched the traffic accident, followed the news of Logan's injuries and his death, remembering the questions Marnie and Noah had asked her parents about a red-haired girl who might live on the Garrett estate. Loz had investigated everything she could, and then she'd gone offline, to search for real.

Colin had been through her browser history. No clues there. Just a record of how hard she'd worked to arm herself with knowledge, everything from the evidence needed to secure a murder conviction to the tributes paid on Logan's Facebook page. Noah's eyes snagged on the messages of condolence. Kenickie was right, Logan had been a local hero, running marathons to raise money for charity, building schools overseas, volunteering at home-less shelters and drop-in centres—

He stopped, scrolled back. Double-checked what he was seeing.

Shit.

'DC Tanner, you took a message from Gina Marsh, Logan's mum.' He was on his feet. 'Do you have her number?'

'Somewhere.' Debbie searched her desk. 'Why?' She handed up a sheet of paper.

Noah took it. 'I'll let you know.'

57

'News?' Marnie read Noah's face when he came into her office.

'Something, maybe. Yes.' He brought his shoulders up, making himself narrower. He'd found something but he wasn't sure of it, not yet. 'Logan was working as a volunteer at drop-in centres and homeless shelters. One of them was Paradise House.'

'Ledger's old address.' Marnie nodded for him to sit down. 'I don't remember his name being on the list we were given by Welch.'

'It wasn't, but Logan was eighteen, a part-timer. Maybe Welch only kept a record of the full-time volunteers.'

'So . . . Logan might've known Ledger?'

'I think it's closer to home than that.' He was tense, with doubt or excitement.

'How much closer?'

'I spoke with Gina Marsh. She says the volunteering was Calum's idea.'

'He mentioned it, didn't he, when he came here?'

'Yes, but he didn't tell us *he* was often at homeless shelters. Helping out, fixing stuff. He's an electrician, but he can turn his hand to most things, that's what Gina says.' Noah stopped.

Marnie studied the thinness in his face. 'Go on.'

'I thought . . . an electrician?' He rubbed at his temple. 'His name wasn't on the lists we got from Battersea. But the company that hires him, Resa Electrical? Their name *was* on the list. I'm waiting to hear who they sent on site in the last six weeks.'

The skin tightened at Marnie's wrists. 'And you think . . .'

'The twitching,' Noah said. 'When we interviewed him at the hospital, d'you remember? He was twitching. I thought adrenalin, shock. But it was in his face as well as his feet and hands. Tremors just like the ones Fran described. And Kenickie said it was pure chance he was on that road that night. It wasn't his usual route. What if he was out searching for Grace? Because he knew she'd run from wherever he was keeping her.'

A phone rang somewhere in the station.

Two, three rings before someone answered it.

'Calum Marsh,' Marnie said. 'You think Calum Marsh is Harm.'

Logan's dad. The man who'd sat in this station with his head in his hands. Their killer.

'It makes sense, doesn't it?' Noah was waiting for her to push back, needing her to try and pick his theory apart. 'Even his coming here makes a kind of sense. We knew this was someone who wanted to be seen . . .'

'He had Logan with him that night. Why?'

'Coincidence. Gina says she phoned him at short notice, asked him to collect Logan as a favour because she was held up at work.'

'An eighteen-year-old? Why couldn't Logan take himself home?'

'He'd come off his bike a week earlier, was only just off the crutches. She'd promised to collect him, he had no money for a taxi, so she called Calum. He said he'd do it, no problem.' Noah drew a short breath. 'Gina said they shouldn't have been on that road that night, it wasn't on their way home. They shouldn't have been anywhere near York Road. When she asked him about it, Calum said there were roadworks on their usual route. I checked. There were no roadworks. So why was he there?'

Noah's tension was infectious. Marnie's pulse skipped. 'Where's Calum now?'

'He's been missing since that day he came here. Gina can't get hold of him. She'd assumed he was feeling guilty, couldn't face talking to her. She says he blamed himself for Logan's death. Not Joe Eaton, who swerved into him, not Grace for walking out into the road. He blamed himself.'

'He denied seeing Grace,' Marnie remembered. 'When we spoke with him at the hospital, and here, at the station. He said he never saw a girl walk into the road.'

'That might've been true. He was driving the other way. But if he was out *looking* for her . . . He could have lied to us. He could've been trying to undermine Joe's version of events.' Noah leant forward, his wrists on his knees. 'I called his work, his home. No one's seen him since the accident. Gina spoke with him, just one call, the afternoon Logan died. I checked the time. Logan died on the day we found May's body, at just about the time Fran said she was killed. What if losing Logan pushed him over the edge? Gina said he sounded insane, out of his mind with grief. It's not the first time he's lost someone, either. His parents died two years ago, and there was something about a sister. We thought our killer had been through a trauma of some kind—'

His phone rang.

'DS Jake. Yes. If you could . . .' He listened, his face fierce with focus. 'Got it. Thanks.'

He ended the call and looked at Marnie. 'That was the hospital. I asked them to check the records from the night of the crash. Calum Marsh was hypernatremic.'

'We need to speak with Gina.' Marnie got to her feet. 'Put out an alert for Calum. His SUV was a write-off after the crash, but find out what other vehicles he drives.'

58

Gina Marsh answered the door in a dark suit, no shoes. Her face was puffy with grief and she was holding an iPhone, its screen shattered in one corner. 'I was looking through his phone for photos. I just . . . wanted to see his face.' She held it towards Marnie and Noah. 'It's the girl on the news. The dead girl.'

'May Beswick?' Noah took the phone, tilting the screen until the light stopped running into the cracks across the display.

'The other one. The girl you found on the estate. Ashleigh Jewell. It's her, isn't it?'

'Yes.' In the photo, Ashleigh was grinning, lips pouting. Flirting – with Logan?

'Logan knew her.' Gina shivered, sounding numb. 'He must have known her, to take that. He never mentioned her, but he had so many friends.'

The photo had been taken on 20 October, just before May went missing. Noah scrolled through the other photos taken around the same time. More faces, boys mostly. A couple of selfies, Logan grinning at the camera.

'That's the only one,' Gina said. 'The only one of her.'

She held out her hand for the phone, taking it tenderly when Noah surrendered it, her fingers snagging on the shattered screen.

'Where was the photo taken,' Marnie asked. 'Do you know?'

'On the news they said she'd been living on the streets, so I'm guessing a homeless shelter? Logan was volunteering at shelters . . . You'll want to come in. Come through.'

She led the way to a living room where all the lights were on, taking an armchair and waiting for Marnie and Noah to sit on the sofa. Photos of her son on the walls. None of his dad. They'd have to ask her for a decent photo of Calum.

'Can you remember which homeless shelters Logan was volunteering at?' Noah asked.

'His dad organised all that. Lately it was somewhere in Stockwell, I think.'

'Paradise House?'

'Paradise – yes, that sounds right. Before then he was working with younger people. He was out two or three evenings a week, and at weekends. His dad's idea. Character-building, Cal said. He wanted Logan to be responsible, was always lecturing him about that.' She strained her eyes at the photos on the wall. 'Both of us, in fact. Cal . . . likes to lecture.'

'We'd like to speak with him. Can you think of anywhere he might have gone?'

'I've tried everywhere. I'm organising the funeral and he's . . . *gone*. I don't know where.'

'When was the last time you spoke with him?'

'The afternoon Logan died.' Her face clenched. 'I couldn't get any sense out of him. Going on and on about his mum and dad, that madhouse he grew up in. He

355

hardly mentioned Logan.' She opened her hands, nail marks in her palms. 'You have to understand something about Cal. He's not . . . he's never been *with* us. Me and Logan. Not properly. He was reliable, responsible, all the obvious things. Didn't drink or have affairs, was always here when we needed him. In the house, I mean. But at the same time, he . . . wasn't.' She closed her hands again. 'I think he'd have preferred a daughter, someone to protect, you know? He did all the things a dad's supposed to do, taught Logan to fish and ride a bike. Brought him up to respect girls, and women. Earned a living so I didn't need to work when Logan was small. He wanted me to stay home and be a mum. He was scared Logan would get sick.' She gave a small smile. 'Logan never got sick. He was a happy baby, but Cal couldn't stop worrying. I suppose because of what happened with his sister. It took me ages to see how he was, how little he *cared*. I know that sounds . . . He did everything right, ticked all the boxes, never put a foot wrong, but it was all about *out there*. The dangers out there, all the things wrong with the world . . .' She stopped. 'Sorry. I'm sorry, you have a job to do, better things to worry about than my ex-husband and his hang-ups.'

Right now their job *was* her ex-husband's hang-ups.

'What happened with his sister?' Marnie asked.

'She went missing when she was seventeen. Ran away from home. Cal was a couple of years younger. They never found her.' Something moved behind her eyes and she stiffened fractionally, sitting tighter in the chair. 'Why are you asking all these questions about Cal?'

She knew, Noah thought. Even if she hadn't made the connection between Ashleigh and her son, between the homeless shelters and her husband's strange absence from his family, his missing sister. She knew why they were asking the questions.

'His parents died a couple of years ago,' Marnie said. 'Is that right?'

Gina nodded. 'But he'd not been in touch with them for years. They didn't come to the wedding. I never met them. I suppose with what happened to his sister . . . They lost touch.'

'Where were they living? Where did Calum grow up?'

'They had a house in Chiswick, but that wasn't where he grew up. His dad was in the army, so they were always moving around.'

'Do you have an address in Chiswick?'

'Somewhere.' She glanced around the room, hopelessly. 'There was a solicitor's letter, but Cal probably took it when he moved out.'

'A recent letter?' Noah asked.

'From two years ago, after they died. That's when he got the house.' She stood up, putting her son's phone aside to search the box files on the bookshelves. 'He was going to sell, but it needed clearing and he kept putting it off. It was tough for him, seeing his sister's photos, all those unhappy memories. Then he lost his job, and we were going through a bad patch.'

'How did his parents die?'

'A ferry accident in Italy.' She opened another box file, moving her hands mechanically through the contents. 'They were on holiday, on a cruise.'

'Calum's an electrician, is that right?'

'It was good work, but he lost his job after they died. He . . . It was a difficult time. He should've taken time off to grieve. But Cal needs to be working, always. I told him it was good, me being the breadwinner for a bit. My turn, that's how I saw it. But he hated it. He's

357

one of those men who needs to feel *needed*.'

Calum had said the same thing at the station, *Can't stand being useless*. And about Grace Bradley, *Wondering where she is, missing her, praying for news*. Had he been talking about his own family, the loss of his sister?

'Do you know where Calum's been working recently?' Marnie asked Gina.

'Freelance jobs, nothing permanent.' She stopped searching for the solicitor's letter. 'I can't find it, I'm sorry. He must've taken it with him. It was somewhere in Chiswick. I never saw the house and he didn't talk about it, just said it was full of memories. His sister's things. Not a happy place, he said.'

Grace had called the house a squat. Calum had moved them out, she'd said, because he was worried about security. The half-finished tower block was better, safer.

'He always tells me where he's working.' Gina wiped her hands on her skirt. 'In case I want to get hold of him, like I did when Logan needed a lift that night.' She blinked, moving her eyes as if she expected to weep or break down, but her face stayed stubbornly blank.

'Was he working in any new-build tower blocks in south London?'

'Those were his favourites.' She reached for Logan's phone, closing her hands around it. 'He loved the security, the *idea* of security. He'd have had us living like that if I'd let him, in a tower block. But I hate heights and we couldn't afford the sort of place he wanted. One of those brand-new blocks going up by the river.'

'Was there a place in particular that he liked? Somewhere he'd worked recently?'

'Brigantia Gardens.' No hesitation. 'Best views in London, taller than the chimneys at Battersea, better security than Fort Knox . . .' She eye-rolled, then hugged herself, Logan's phone tight to her chest. 'He'd have moved us in there before they'd finished building it. Not that they *did* finish. It's one of those places where they ran out of money. London's littered with them. But to hear Cal talk about Brigantia Gardens, you'd think that didn't matter.'

She looked away, at nothing, her eyes grieving. 'Cal's idea of a dream home, never mind the fact that it's standing empty, no sign of it ever being done. Never mind that there's no family now. That was it. His dream home.'

59

Loz was the youngest at the table, and the ugliest. Dirty hair, gritty armpits, chewed fingernails. She pretended she didn't care about that stuff, but she did, she really did.

Christie's face was super-smooth and her hair shone. Nothing freaked her out. She knew how everything worked in here, and outside. She knew how to get you to come back with her, and how to make you stay. She was scary, but not as scary as *him*.

He looked so . . .

Normal. Nice.

Loz tried to imagine how it was when the others were here, Grace and Ashleigh and May, all in the same uniform, squeaky clean. May with her hair shining and her words hidden. She'd hidden at home too, but she'd never looked like a Barbie doll without the boobs. Loz hated it. Hated the stupid clothes and the smell of baby soap under the cooking. Hated the *sameness*.

Harm said softly, 'We don't say grace here. Unless you'd like to?'

Loz shook her head. When Harm picked up his fork,

Christie did the same. As if the blackout blinds and candles were normal – as if all of this was *normal*. Eating off camping plates in the dark, the candles making everyone's shadow spooky. It wasn't dark outside, not yet. Was it?

Panic made her feet kick under the table. She didn't know what time it was outside. She squeezed her knees together, focusing on staying calm, on making them think she was calm.

'Eat up,' Harm said, smiling at her.

Loz loaded her fork obediently. Her mouth was flooded with saliva because she hadn't eaten in so long. When she opened it, spit squirted out like juice from a lemon. The curry tasted funny, made her thirsty. Her feet kicked again. What if it was poisoned?

May was strangled, *stupid. He doesn't poison you, he strangles you.*

She ate the curry, stopping to drink water whenever she could.

'This is nice,' Harm said. 'All of us together. It's good to have you with us, Loz.'

'Thanks. It's nice to be here.'

She could do this, play along, even though her stomach was tied in knots and she wanted to pee really, really badly. It was like being back home, pretending she wasn't sad, that she didn't care about being the ugly one, whose clothes were too big, who looked stupid in a dress, whose hair was a black lump of knots. The one who couldn't open her mouth without putting her foot in it, and who didn't want a hug at bedtime or any other time thanks, glad they'd stopped saying *We love you*, because how old was she anyway – eight? *Glad* that was all over.

Christie handed her a paper towel. 'Your nose is running. And your eyes.'

'It's the curry.' She wiped at her face. 'Thanks.'

Harm brought a fresh glass of water from the barrel, setting it down by her right hand. 'Here,' he said gently. 'It's okay. It feels funny at first, of course it does. Everyone's the same here. We've all been through something bad, or horrible. It's all right to be sad. You don't have to talk about it, but you can if you want to. You can be yourself here. Just . . . be yourself. We understand.'

He was good. Most people would've made that speech sound puke-worthy, teachers or counsellors or parents. But he made it sound like a thing anyone with any sense would say, like if you had a voice in your head that spoke sense instead of just the other voice, the one that hated you. He made it all sound okay, and suddenly Loz understood why May had liked it here. Why she'd wanted to be here instead of home, why she'd stayed.

Harm looked good, and he sounded good. Most psychopaths did. Loz had read enough to know that. They were charming, lovable even. Some of the stuff she'd read made psychopaths sound like pets, like you could pat them on the head or feed them biscuits under the table and they'd stick by you no matter what. A lot of what she'd read was bullshit. A lot of the *world* was bullshit. Loz wasn't stupid, not in that way, but he was good. Not just creepy, not even with the candles sliding his shadow around the room, not even knowing what he'd done. She could see why May had liked him. She understood why her sister had wanted to be here. What she couldn't understand was why he'd killed her. If it was him. It could've been Christie. Or Eric. Loz didn't think it was Eric, unless he was crazier than he looked, but she could believe it was Christie. Listening at doors, handing out phoney keys, looking at Harm like she'd do anything for him, crawl over broken glass, kill . . .

362

Spit filled Loz's mouth. Her feet wouldn't stop kicking under the table. She was afraid she was going to puke up the food, because her stomach was one big knot. She needed to find out who'd done it. That was why she'd come here. To know what had happened to May, find her sister's killer. Except now she felt stupid and scared and wished she'd stayed away, wished she'd phoned DI Rome or Noah Jake, and her mum and dad must be freaking out . . .

'You're not eating,' Harm said. 'Are you sick?'

She shook her head.

'Perhaps you need to wash. It's nice to be clean. We can get you some better clothes, too.'

He didn't like her smell. Didn't like the dirt under her fingernails or the way her hair was matted up on one side of her head. He wanted her to look like the others. A stupid plastic *doll*.

She didn't know why she said it.

Didn't know she was *going* to say it.

Just came out with it, opening her mouth as usual, words falling out:

'I'm pregnant.'

60

'Calum Marsh drives a white van for Resa Electrical. I've logged the registration. No recent sightings, but at least it's in the system now. He knew the layout at Battersea because he'd been there as part of the team in charge of wiring.'

'He was injured,' Debbie said. 'In the crash. He had a neck brace, broken arm—'

'Collarbone,' Noah corrected, 'and it wasn't broken, just badly bruised. His injuries weren't debilitating, not if he was determined. He knew how to get on site, knew exactly where the loopholes were in the security system. His sister Neve went missing when he was fifteen.'

Noah pinned up a photo of a teenage girl, her dark hair cut into a blunt fringe, her mouth straight and unsmiling, eyes fixed over the photographer's shoulder.

'Gina says he spent four years looking for her, part of his dad's search party. Homeless shelters, the streets, anywhere a teenage girl might go. Four years of searching. Neve was smart, independent, ambitious. She'd been talking about leaving home since she was twelve. Calum kept persuading her not to do it because he was terrified of being left alone with their dad and his rages. After she went, everything was much worse.'

'Cut to the chase,' Ron grumbled. 'He didn't get enough attention when he was a kid and now he's a psycho? Fine. Let's get him and put him behind bars. Now we know where he is.'

'We need to understand what we're up against,' Marnie said. 'If we storm in, we could get Loz killed. Better to talk him down, if we can.'

She looked to the hostage negotiator, Toby Graves, for his agreement.

'The more we know, the better.' Graves nodded. 'But we're against the clock, so I get that too. Two at-risk kids in there. Tell me about them, specifically in relation to Calum's psychosis.'

Noah said, 'Aimee's his favourite. He's convinced she's sick, needs his protection. He doesn't know that Aimee is actually Eric. He thinks he's found a lost girl like his sister.'

'If Aimee's Neve,' Debbie said, 'why does he need the others?'

'He's worked around homeless shelters for years. Gina says he was always looking for someone to save. Doing what he couldn't do for Neve.'

'So why'd he start killing them?' Ron demanded. 'Apart from he's a nut-job.'

'We don't know, but the timing's significant. He killed May on the day his son died. He was out the night of the accident looking for Grace. He might blame himself for the crash, but it's just as likely he blames Grace. Maybe he started blaming the others, too. He'll have been angry about May's pregnancy after all the warnings he gave the girls, the morals he tried to enforce. From what Grace says, there's a lot of shame in the mix. They all felt it, but they didn't all understand it. I think Calum was made to feel ashamed as a child. As a brother and a son. That sort of shame can be dangerous.'

'Maybe he was warning them about himself,' Debbie said. 'He was a teenage boy once, and an unhappy one. Maybe that's when he first realised something was wrong with him.'

'We know he finds the outside world a hostile place. Gina says he went through periods when he was very anxious, and bewildered. When they were buying their first home, he wouldn't consider anywhere with open access at the back. Always scoping out the exits, she said. And he was fascinated by prisons – four walls, locks everywhere. Gina says he watched programmes about prisons the way other people watch property shows.'

'He's made this place into a prison,' Ron said. 'Locked them all up for their own safety.'

'They're happy, Grace says. He makes them feel loved and valued. Useful.'

'So it's a cult. They're worshipping him in there. Until he kills them.'

It was a cult, Noah thought, of a kind. Toxic, peculiar. The family in thrall to Harm, who was in thrall to Aimee. 'We have eyes on Brigantia Gardens. We're checking the access points and the security. The danger's if he realises we're closing in and panics.'

'He's panicked twice already,' Ron said. 'If by panicking you mean killing.'

'Who's holding the balance of power in there?' Graves wanted to know. 'Calum, or Christie?'

'It's unclear, but we have to assume Calum's the killer. The size of the bruises on the girls' throats, and May was carried into the penthouse. There's a good chance Christie's helping him. Grace says she's in love with him.'

'The fact that he calls himself that,' Debbie said, 'tells us everything, doesn't it? He's not Calum in there, with those girls. He's *Harm*.'

'Do the girls see it that way?' Graves asked. 'From what you've told me about Grace, she's struggling even now to see him as a bad guy. We need to know what kind of reception we're going to get in there, whether they want to be rescued or if they'll fight with him, *for* him.'

'Loz won't,' Noah said. 'Christie and Eric, maybe. But not Loz. For one thing, she's angry.'

'Not too angry, I hope.' Graves shook his head. 'From everything you've said, putting this man on the defensive would not be a smart move.'

61

Christie was the first to stand up.

Slowly, putting back her chair, no need to hurry. She knew that the key in Loz's pocket wouldn't open the door, and that there was no signal on her phone. She'd let Loz keep the phone to make her feel safe, like the handing-out of the key to make her feel she was in control. As if a thirteen-year-old was in control of anything.

Christie tucked her chair under the table, making it neat, resting her hands on its back. Big hands, square wrists. Evidence – that was what they needed. To make an arrest, bring a conviction. No evidence on May. Crime scene too clean. That was why Loz had come here. To get evidence.

Across the table, Harm blinked at Loz, his fork still in his hand.

The table rocked, water tilting in the cups, shadows crawling the walls.

Loz said, 'What's wrong?' She reached for her cup.

Funny – she knew she should be scared, but she wasn't. Not any worse than before. As if she was watching this on a screen, as if it wasn't real. *May* – that was real. Not this.

'It's okay,' Christie said. 'I'll take her back. I'll take her away.' Her hands squeezed the chair, her eyes on Harm, watching him the way you'd watch a car that was coming down a road you were crossing, hoping it wouldn't speed up. 'I'll take her. Don't—'

'How old are you, Loz?' His voice was the same, soft, but his face had changed.

Loz heard Christie's breath coming in short bursts.

'Thirteen,' Loz said. 'Fourteen in July.'

'How are you . . . pregnant?'

Loz rolled her eyes like she'd seen other girls do, the ones with the fake tans and hair extensions, the ones who boasted about abortions. 'I can draw you a picture if you like.'

Like May's pictures. Everything in them. Fear and tears, and love and Eric.

'Who's the father?' Harm's face was stiff as a mask.

Had he looked like this when May told him about her baby? Like he wanted to break . . . everything?

Loz said, 'Eric.'

'Who's Eric?'

'No.' Christie grabbed her by the arm, hauling her up from the table. 'I'm taking her. It's my fault, I should have checked—'

'Eric's upstairs,' Loz said. 'He's upstairs—'

Christie wrenched her arm and Loz bit her tongue. Shut her eyes for a second against the pain, opening them to see Harm right *there* in front of her, his face like someone was dragging at it from behind, skin pulled back, eyes slitted. Teeth . . . she could see his teeth.

'Who's upstairs?' he demanded.

Two sets of hands on her. Christie's and his. Like they

369

were going to fight over her, pull her apart.

Good. Evidence . . .

If she was all over the floor, there'd be *evidence.*

Harm leaned in, red between his teeth and in the whites of his eyes. *'Who is upstairs?'*

'Aimee!' she shouted in his face. 'Eric is *Aimee,* up there in your stupid *special* room! That's *Eric,* pretending to be Aimee. You *idiot*! He got my sister pregnant and then you killed her. You killed my sister for *that* – for nothing! Your special girl is a boy . . . He's a *boy*!'

62

'Calum's credit card was used at Vauxhall tube station an hour before Loz went missing. It's not been used since. CCTV gives us this.' A face, female. 'Grace has identified her as Christie Faulk.'

Christie's face was grey. Eyes hooded, mouth flat. She could have been anyone.

'Vauxhall's the nearest tube to Brigantia Gardens,' Noah said. 'No local sightings of Calum, but his credit card was used to buy bottled water and a lot of liquid fuel. Long-life food, the kind Fran found in May's stomach, and Ashleigh's. Chemical toilet cassettes. You name it.'

'So he's with the girls in Brigantia Gardens,' Graves said. 'With a lot of liquid fuel. What else?'

'Knives. Kitchen ones mainly, but Grace says he's got a folding knife. And an axe.'

'An axe,' Graves repeated. 'Three cheers for Bear Grylls' product placement.'

Armed Response was on its way, putting guns in the mix.

Loz was in a tower block about to be under siege.

Noah's teeth ached with worry for her.

Marnie's phone buzzed. 'DI Rome.' Her face changed, its lines coming into focus.

'Mr Ledger.' She stood up, meeting Noah's eyes. 'Yes, we are looking for you. Where are you?'

She listened, then said, 'Stay on the line, please.'

'He's in Brigantia Gardens.' She nodded at Graves. 'And he says he's got eyes on where Calum's holding the girls.'

63

They dragged her up the stairs, fighting over her, one arm each, Christie's face spitting rage, Harm's like a rock with a crack running through it. Up the stairs to Aimee's room . . .

Threw her at the bed, Christie warning, 'Stay down!'

Harm left the room, but not for long, coming back with an axe.

An axe.

Loz scrabbled backwards over the bed, getting tangled up with the sheets, and Eric. Blinking upright, pale-faced, hissing, 'What did you do?' More scared than she was.

Harm was at the windows with wood and nails, blocking out the light, boarding them in.

Christie was at the foot of the bed, shoulders heaving, tears blotching her cheeks. Eyes swinging between them and Harm, always back to Harm.

'Stop him,' Loz said. Begged. 'You can make him stop.'

Christie laughed, her face breaking, showing her empty hands. 'No.'

'*Yes*. Stop him. Help us.'

'How can I?' Shaking her head, her eyes swinging back to Harm. 'How can anyone?'

64

Jamie Ledger looked like a hunted man, the scar above his left ear livid white. Dirt beneath his fingernails and speckled under his eyes, hunger hollowing his cheeks. 'I didn't know you were looking for me until now . . .'

'Tell us what you've seen in the building,' Marnie said. 'The rest can wait.'

'Marsh and at least one girl, plus the one who brings them back for him.' Ledger trained his eyes on the tower block. 'Sometimes on the top floor, mostly on the floor below that.' He pointed. 'Where the blackout's up.'

Brigantia Gardens was planned as luxury living. The developer's website showed an artist's impression of a curved glass and steel spine. In reality, the tower block was no less brutal than the ones on the Garrett estate, its glass skin covered in places by protective plastic. The 'lush communal garden' was a wasteland of broken bricks and skips.

'I didn't know what he was,' Ledger said. 'Until two days ago. He used to come to the hostel with the volunteers, that's where we met. I knew he was struggling. Didn't know how badly. Took two bodies for the penny to drop.' His lip curled. 'I used to be quicker than that.'

'Focus on the building,' Marnie told him. 'How are they getting in and out?'

He told them. Rex Carter from SCO19 briefed his team before asking, 'What else have you seen?' The edge in his voice made Ledger square up like a soldier. 'What're we up against?'

'He's schizoid. Passes himself off as a good guy. He fooled me, and I'm not dumb – seen stuff most people wouldn't believe. Maybe he was a bit weird with his son, a bit *off*, but not so most people would notice.' He moved his mouth, lips cracked with thirst. 'I saw the kit he was packing back at Paradise House. That's when the alarm bells started. I've seen men go to pieces out in the field. He was like that, on edge all the time. Walking the line . . . He thought it was a big deal me being in the army, said I reminded him of his dad. Bollocks. I told him it was all bollocks, but he kept saying it. Crap about paying tribute to men like me. Making the world a better place for us to come back to. Cleaner, tidier.' His stare was haunted. 'It's like he left her for me. It's like that psycho did it for *me*.'

'You've been following him for two days,' Marnie said, 'because you thought he might be our killer. Why didn't you call us sooner?'

'No proof. Might all've been up here like the rest of it, the nightmares.' Tapping the side of his head, strung out, wet-eyed with lack of sleep. 'I thought if he did it for *me*, if he'd got it into his head that he was . . . tidying up. *Paying tribute*. Shit. I couldn't live with it. Had to find him, find what he was doing. If he was doing what I thought he was, if I wasn't just imagining it . . .'

'All right,' Marnie said. 'We'll take it from here. You can stand down.'

'Talking to me like I'm a soldier?' A laugh rocked out of him. 'That'll work. Just wind me up and point me in the right direction? I stopped taking orders when I left the army.'

'Or I can arrest you.'

'For what? Keeping my eyes open?'

'Trespass in Mitcham, breaking and entering. Obstructing a police officer. You choose.'

His stare was wild on her face.

'Stand down,' she repeated quietly, 'and let us take care of these girls.'

Ledger went with Noah, to the waiting police car.

'No phone signal inside the building,' Toby Graves told Marnie. 'And they're high up, which limits negotiations. Ten hours since Loz was taken. That's moved us into the next round. I'm thinking we treat this as a kidnapping and send in SCO19. But it's your call.'

Marnie looked up at the unfinished tower block, the stab vest heavy on her chest.

Sixteen flights down to the ground.

Too far to survive a fall if someone jumped, or was pushed.

So many ways this could end in disaster.

Sean and Katrina Beswick already had one daughter in the morgue.

This was her job. It was what she'd chosen to do.

She nodded at Graves, and Carter. 'Tell me where you want me.'

65

Harm had a hammer. For boarding up the windows. A hammer and nails, bits of old wood and an axe – he'd got a fucking axe. He wouldn't look at me, his eyes everywhere but the bed. I was right where he wanted me, but he wouldn't look. Scared of seeing Aimee.

Aimee was safe. Aimee had everything . . .

He was going to let her die because he loved her so much. He hated Eric. I knew he would, it was why I'd stayed hidden, why I was never *Eric* with him.

Christie was watching him work like she'd put her favourite movie on repeat. He was snarling, deep down in his chest. All the touching he never did, all the *pretending*, boiling inside him. I could hear it boiling. He should never have pretended. He should've taken what he wanted right from the start. This was what we got – he and I – for waiting. For faking.

'We are what we are,' I whispered. I'd've shouted it if I'd dared.

Where was his happy family now? Where was his sick little girl?

He stooped and put the axe on the floor. Switched his

stare to Loz. She was wedged in the corner of the room, white as the walls. Trapped. She didn't look like May, I couldn't see any trace of May in her, but Harm could. He got her in his sights, his stare slowing to a stop on her face.

She was the one who'd told him about Eric, about me. She was the one who'd done this – brought the real world storming in here. Killed his dream, its blood all over the floor. Shoved a mirror in his face, showed him what he was. She was going to pay for that.

I yelled from the bed, 'I'm here! I'm right here!'

His head snapped round.

We are what we are . . .

'I'm right *fucking* here!'

But it was Christie who came for me.

Stopped him in his tracks, almost too fast for the pair of us. Almost.

Christie.

Most of the momentum was hers. I just got my fist in the right place so that when she swung me up from the bed, I punched her as hard as I could, twice.

She was stronger than me, serious muscles, but I had her. Because of where I hit her, and with what.

She tipped backwards, shouting.

I did it again, directly over the heart.

Harm came for me then, but I showed him my fist – red with her – and he stopped short, teeth snapping, seeing what I'd done, what *he'd* done. And he knew I'd do it again, hit her again . . .

You can't be too careful. *He* taught me that.

Christie was on her knees, staring at her chest, wild-eyed. Two dark spots spreading on her shirt. She ripped at it, making a strangled sound, disbelieving.

My fist was dripping.

The wire from May's sketchpad was cutting into my knuckles, its sharp end an inch shorter than before. It must've snapped off inside her, between two ribs.

She ripped at her shirt with her fingers, trying to locate the source of the pain. I kept my fist where Harm could see it.

Secure the perimeter.

She tipped sideways, stopped moving.

Lay like that, with the axe an extra arm at her side.

The wire was wrapped round my fist, what was left of its point facing outward. Still a decent weapon, although the axe was better, now I came to look at it.

Go for the wide-open spaces.

I looked at the axe. Then I looked at him.

Christie wasn't moving. I thought:

I've done her.

Just him now.

Me, and him.

66

Adrenalin made Marnie's fingers fidget, the stab vest sitting like a slab on her chest. The stairwell to the tower block smelt wet and incendiary as she followed Rex Carter's team up past half-painted walls where wiring coiled unfinished and windows of toughened glass were cross-hatched by safety tape. Thick dust had closed over everything, collecting their palm prints as they climbed.

On the sixteenth floor, Rex signalled them to a halt. They huddled to consult the floor plan and to hear the report from the team with eyes on the flat where Jamie Ledger had seen bodies moving behind the blackout.

'Five rooms,' Rex's man reported. 'Plus the one on the mezzanine level. Front door's locked, but we can fix that. We're not picking up any sound from inside.'

Rex looked at Marnie. 'Your call.'

'We go in. One room at a time, secure each room as we go.' Sweat stabbed everywhere on her body. 'The mezzanine's where he keeps Aimee. It's where I'd hole up, if I was him.'

Rex nodded at his team. 'You heard her.'

The front door was the easy part.

Inside, the dark swallowed them up, blackout blinds at every window.

Thermal imaging cameras clicked on. No bodies on this floor. At a gesture from Rex, Marnie hung back, letting the team complete their sweep.

On the table in the kitchen, the remains of a half-eaten meal.

Water barrels bounced sound back at her as she followed Rex through the half-furnished rooms, up an interior staircase to the room Grace had called the loft.

Aimee's room.

Two SFOs stood guard outside, shaking their heads at Rex and Marnie. A third and fourth were waiting on the stairs, weapons pointed at the floor, eyes trained on the door.

No lock. Just smooth wood and a brass handle.

From inside the room, silence.

This place, his safe place, reeked of Harm. A sharply resinous smell like split wood. The walls were too tight, the whole place packed and explosive.

Marnie lifted her hand and rapped on the door. 'Armed police. I'm Detective Inspector Rome. I want to speak with Loz, and Eric.'

A slow, winding silence. The room breathing on the other side of the door.

'I'm coming in. I need you to stay calm. Can you do that?'

The SFOs stayed back, weapons shouldered, waiting. They wouldn't move without a signal from Rex. Marnie was in charge, he'd made that clear. Her case, her call.

Silence. Then:

'You can come in.' Loz, sounding calm. 'Just you.'

Loz. She's alive.

'Just me?' Marnie waited, wanting the girl to give her

381

more, some clue as to what was happening inside the room. Behind her, the creak of an SFO's gloves gripping a gun. She ignored it, focusing on the sounds from the other side of the door. 'Loz?'

'They're dead,' Loz said clearly. 'It's safe. There's just me and Eric, but Eric's scared. He's really scared. If it's just you, it'll be okay.'

'If he's scared, it's better that I bring help.'

'No, it's not. He's . . . If it's just you, it'll be okay.'

'We're here to help you.'

'You said armed police. You had to, I know, but it's freaking him out. If it's just you . . . *Please*.' Tears in her voice, under the calm. 'Please.'

Marnie met Rex's eyes. 'All right. Okay.' She gripped the brass handle of the door. 'Just me.'

The door was heavy. She put her weight into it.

It sucked shut behind her on a hinged chain. Snug to the door frame, shutting out the SFO team on the stairs, and the light.

The split-wood smell was the only bright thing in the room.

Boarded windows at either end, a dredge of daylight but not enough to see, not properly, not straight away. Her eyes struggled, sending a stab of panic to her feet and fingers.

Two bodies on the floor to her right. To her left . . .

A bed shoved against the wall, its sheets in a snarl.

'Loz?' Marnie kept her back to the door. One shout from her and Carter's team would be through it. The stab vest kept her grounded, like an extra helping of gravity.

She looked to where the bodies lay on the raw, unfinished floor of the room. Some blood, but not much. Not enough light for her to be sure, but the bodies were too big to be children.

'Loz, I'm sorry it took me so long to get here.' The room swallowed her words. 'But I'm here now. Tell me how I can help.' She took a step nearer to the bed. No other hiding place that she could see. Bright dart of light behind her—

Dressing table bulbs, trapping the trickle of sun through the boarded windows.

Two of the bulbs were missing.

'Talk to me.' She should check the bodies. It was her job to check the bodies. 'What happened here? I need someone to tell me. Loz, can you tell me what happened?'

Crouched in the corner of the room, half wrapped in a sheet from the bed . . .

Two narrow figures, so tightly bound together they looked like one. Brambly black curls, bony white elbows, the jut of a jaw. Impossible to see where Eric ended and Loz began. Was he holding her down? How long had he been up here, in the dark? She had the sense that he could see her better than she could see him.

'Loz. Are you hurt?' Neither child was moving. 'I need to know if you're hurt.'

Dust danced through the dark, trapped in the thin funnels of light from the window. She couldn't hear them breathing, not quite. The floor creaked under her feet. Heat coming from somewhere. It pushed at the walls, shrinking the room, making it shudder.

'I need to see if you're hurt. If either one of you is hurt. But it's all right. I can promise you it's all right now.'

Movement behind her.

Rearing upright from the floor, dragging a shadow as solid as a wall—

Harm.

She opened her mouth to shout, but he slammed his

hands into the dressing table, shoving it across the door, leaning his weight behind it.

Looking at her. Right at her.

Carter's team was beating at the door, shouting her name. Stupid, *stupid* not to have checked the bodies first. She called out, 'I'm okay. It's okay.'

Harm moved his head at her, like an animal getting her scent, fixing her in its sights.

He stepped over the other body, ignoring it. Christie Faulk. It was Christie on the floor, but he was standing between Marnie and the door.

'I'm sorry,' Loz said, out of breath. 'I had to. He made me. I'm sorry . . .'

'It's okay.' She didn't take her eyes off the man. 'Calum. Mr Marsh. You remember me. I'm Detective Inspector Rome. We met at the hospital. You came to the police station.'

He didn't look like Calum Marsh, not like the grieving father she'd met. This man was taller and broader, bigger everywhere. The trickle of light showed blood on the front of his shirt.

'You're hurt. What happened?' She stayed between Harm and the children crouched against the wall. It was the room making him look different. The dark, the closed door behind him. It was her fear making his shoulders broader, casting its shadow alongside his. He was just a man. One man. 'How badly are you hurt?'

He shook his head slowly from side to side. The way a snake does before it strikes.

'I'd like to bring a paramedic in here to take a look at you.' Marnie stayed very still, speaking loudly enough for Carter and the others to hear. 'Would that be all right?'

'I'm not hurt.' His face made the shape of a smile. 'It was an accident.' His voice was calm, confident. 'No one

384

meant to hurt anyone.' He kept smiling at her, like no smile she'd ever seen.

His hands hung empty at his sides. No weapon, but his hands were weapons. He'd killed May and Ashleigh with those hands.

Should she shout for Carter's team, let them smash their way in here and take him down? The dressing table looked heavy, but Carter had four men out there, all armed and trained to do this.

No. Loz had seen enough violence in the last two hours.

Marnie would shout as a last resort.

'All right. That's good you're not hurt. But I'd like a paramedic in here in any case. To look at the children.' She put the smallest emphasis on the last word, watching for his reaction.

His stare reached into the corner of the room. 'Where are they?'

'They're safe. You want that, I know. You want them to be safe.' Her left shoulder took the brunt of his stare, bruisingly hard. 'I'd like a paramedic to make sure they're okay. And you too. I need to be sure everyone's okay.'

'Everything's fine. I wanted you to see that. You can go now.' Dust rose like smoke behind him. 'I'll look after everything.'

'I know you will, but I need to do my job. It's my job to be sure everyone's safe.'

'No. That's my job.' That smile again. 'The children are my job.'

Movement behind her, in the corner of the room. Feet scuffing at the floor.

Harm's stare shoved at her shoulder, wanting to get past.

'Mr Marsh. Calum. I need you to stay calm.'

'I am calm.' Breathing through his nose, the smile like a long splinter in his face. 'This is my place. This is my family. Let me take care of it.'

Six months ago, Marnie had been trapped in an enclosed space with a dangerous man. Raging, grieving for his family. She'd thought that was frightening, but it was nothing like this. *That* man could be reasoned with. His pain had a shape she'd recognised. Harm had buried his pain too well.

'Let me take care of my family,' he repeated.

'I can't do that. I'm sorry. I can help you to do that. But too many people have been hurt already, and it's my job to make sure no one else gets hurt. You understand that.'

'Loz.' He put his tongue to his top lip, showing the red inside of his mouth. 'Come out here.'

Marnie put a hand behind her, warning Loz not to move. 'Stay where you are.'

Harm's head reared back, his eyes like discs in the half-dark. 'This is *my* house.' Bubbles of froth between his teeth. 'My rules.'

'But it's not your house, is it? This place belongs to a property developer. The house in Chiswick belongs to you.' She held his stare despite its heat. 'Why did you move here?'

'Safer . . .'

'It *is* safer,' she agreed. 'We want these children to be safe. You and I want the same thing. To make this a safe place. So let me open the door and get help.'

'I don't need any help.' He took a step closer. 'Why would you think I need that?'

'Christie needs help.' Marnie pointed to the body on the floor. 'Doesn't she deserve help? She was looking after the children with you.'

'Not all of them.' Did he have a punctured lung? The heat coming off him smelt sulphurous. 'She didn't look after Ashleigh.'

'Tell me about Ashleigh.'

'No.'

'Then tell me about your sister, Neve. You didn't want these girls to be like her, living on the streets. Lost . . .'

A laugh barked out of him. If he was afraid, or feeling threatened or isolated, it wasn't enough. Not for Marnie to work with. No foothold for her here. She was close to being too late.

'Talk to me. About your family. Tell me what you need to make this better.'

'I made a mistake letting you in here.' His face closed up. 'I wanted you to see what good care I was taking of these children, but you don't see. Anything. Tell you about Neve! You don't see *anything*. It's better you go now.'

As if he'd thought he could make her understand. But about what – May and Ashleigh? Or his sister? All that time Marnie was searching for May . . . Who had searched for Neve? And why did they fail to find her?

'Grace is safe,' Marnie said. 'She told us how you helped her. She's grateful.'

'And you think I'm a killer.' His voice dropped, softening. 'Isn't that the truth?'

Was this how he'd trapped these children? With his soft words and rhetoric, making you think – no, making you *feel* he understood, everything unmuddled, the world no longer rocking around you. Restoring order with his rules, smoothing all the rough edges. No splinters, nothing to catch your feet or fingers, the whole world wrapped in duct tape, made *safe*.

'Two girls are dead,' Marnie said. 'May Beswick and

Ashleigh Jewell. Two girls whose families are grieving, like your family did. Like *you* grieved.'

'Christie was dangerous,' as if he was agreeing with her, 'but that's taken care of.'

'Who took care of it?' She matched her voice to his, mirroring the body language. 'You?'

'Eric.' Smiling again. 'But it was an accident. A misunderstanding.'

Misunderstanding. That smile . . .

Stephen had smiled like that.

And Calum Marsh was lying.

He'd told them that he never saw Grace walk into the road that night, but he'd been out looking for her. That was why his son was dead, and May and Ashleigh. *A misunderstanding*.

'How did it happen?'

'You'll have to ask Eric.' Showing his empty hands, sure of his powers of persuasion.

He'd wanted Marnie in here. To listen to his alibi, plant a seed of doubt in her head. He was so sure of his powers of persuasion, so used to being believed, and obeyed. Christie as a double murderer. Eric as *her* murderer. Leaving Calum the untarnished hero of the story.

'Eric didn't put May in that flat. And it wasn't Christie either. You told Jamie Ledger you wanted to make the world a cleaner place. Well, May's death wasn't clean. It tore a filthy great hole in her family's life. Dead bodies are *never* clean. Dead bodies are chaos, *mess*. They make the world a worse place. Dangerous, dirty. Death is the opposite of order, the opposite of clean.'

'*Hers* wasn't.' His eyes like discs again. 'Her life was like that before I found her. She was unhappy, in pain. I made her *better*. If you saw her, you know that. She was quiet, clean . . .'

'Look at Christie.' Marnie pointed at the body on the floor. 'Does that look clean to you? Does it look quiet?'

'Move.' He spoke softly, as if he'd been indulging her but that had to stop now. 'Out of my way.'

He wouldn't look at Christie, his stare fixed on the corner of the room where Loz and Eric were huddled. Marnie had lost. She'd tried, and she'd lost.

'I know you're upset. You've been upset since Logan died. Your son would want you to—'

'No.' He flexed his hands at his sides, his face shutting her out as effectively as if he'd turned his back. 'Move out of my way.'

'There are armed officers outside that door.' Her breath was stacked in her chest like bricks. 'This is a very serious, very dangerous situation. You have put *these* children in serious danger. Loz is in danger. You need to stand down. Now.'

'Wrong. You're wrong. I took care of her sister and I'll take care of her—'

The corner erupted behind Marnie, a body streaking past before she could stop it, her hand grabbing at nothing, at white cotton and a whiter face, the flash of something sharp in his hand—

Landing on Harm like a sprung tiger.

Eric Mackay, going for the man's throat with a broken light bulb.

'Carter!' Marnie shoved at the dressing table, but it was too heavy. 'Carter!'

Harm swung Eric by the scruff of his neck, the boy's bare feet hitting the dressing table with a crack. Crunching, savage – and Marnie was breathing in blood, a wet spray of it from Harm's face as he swung the boy at the wall, not letting go of his neck.

She put her weight into the dressing table, another set

of hands helping her – Loz pushing with her until Rex Carter shouted for them to stand back.

Marnie grabbed Loz, ducking the pair of them out of the way as the SFO team powered into the room, taking down the hot mess that was Harm and Eric, the boy glued to the man's body, his hand grinding the broken bulb into Harm's throat.

Marnie turned away, shielding Loz with her arms.

The whole room stank of blood.

More dragging, sucking, Rex's team trying to prise the pair apart.

'Don't look.' She held Loz tight. 'Don't look.'

Feet on the floor, slowing. Stopping.

A thin chime of glass fragments, falling.

Marnie stayed crouched with the girl in her arms until the long silence was broken by the sound of Loz sobbing.

67

The light in the interview room exaggerated Eric
Mackay's cheekbones and the sooty length of his
eyelashes. A paper jumpsuit swamped his slight body,
a dressing on his right hand where the wire and glass
had split his skin. He shrank from the light, his eyes
shutting in protest. Too frail and pretty to be a killer,
but he'd finished what he'd started. Calum Marsh had
died at the scene from blood loss, his throat lacerated
by the broken lightbulb.

Eric's appropriate adult was a thin-faced man in a cheap
suit and shovel-toed shoes, with a lick of yellow hair and
a sunken mouth that suggested he wasn't going to speak
unless he had to.

'Can you tell me what happened earlier today?' Marnie
asked the boy.

'We got what we deserved.' A crack in his voice, as if
he hadn't used it in a long time.

'Who did?'

'Me and him. Both of us. It's what we deserved.' He
ducked his head away from the light, but he looked at
her when she didn't speak. Extraordinary eyes, and that

heart-shaped face. She could see where Aimee had come from. 'I'll go to prison, that's fine. That's good.'

'Good?'

'The same. Better. No Harm.' He moved his hands on the metal table, putting them in the way of the light as if he was afraid she might not see them otherwise. Harm's blood was in his nail beds.

'Tell me why.'

'He killed her. May. He killed our baby. And Loz. He would've killed Loz.'

'Her life was in danger. That's what you believed?'

'All our lives. You saw. We were all going to die up there.'

Marnie waited, then she said, 'And Christie? What happened to Christie?'

'I did it. She was . . . Self-defence.'

'How?'

'She'd have killed us. She killed Ashleigh, that's what she said when she was dying. She killed Ashleigh, for him.' Eric blinked. 'She'd have killed the lot of us for him.'

When he blinked, Marnie could see Aimee. It was like an optical illusion, one of those pictures that was simultaneously an old woman and a young girl. Did he miss his disguise? He'd need a new one for prison. How many did he have? He'd have to learn how to hide all over again.

He moved his cracked lips. 'You said he had a son.'

'Logan, yes.'

'When he died . . . that's when he killed May?'

'I'm not sure it's that simple. You were with him for a while. Why do you think it happened?'

'He was . . . insane.' His eyes shivered with unshed tears. 'It was my fault. I should never have touched her. I made her keep my secret, and *our* secret. It was too much.'

'Was she unhappy?'

'No. *No*. She was excited, we both were. We wanted the baby. I even thought *he* might want it.'

'You thought Harm might want your baby?'

'He was hurting, I knew he was hurting.' Eric looked down at his hands. 'He wasn't just a nutter. I felt sorry for him, until Loz told me what he'd done.'

Marnie waited a moment. 'You said Christie confessed to killing Ashleigh. How sure are you that Harm killed May?'

'It was him.' His hands flinched. 'Christie was home with us when it happened. The night May left. Christie was with us. She can't have killed her.'

'And the following night, when Ashleigh was killed? Did you see how it happened?'

He shook his head. 'I was in bed.'

'You didn't see anything that might make you a witness to either murder?'

'I saw *him*. Right from the start, I knew what he was. Just like May saw *me*.' Blinking at his hands on the table. 'She saw me. He killed her because of that.'

'May found a way out of that building. So did Grace. Couldn't you have left with them?'

'I was scared. Aimee . . . was scared.'

'But you're Eric.'

'Only with her. Only . . . now.'

He'd worn his disguise too well, lost himself inside it. Who was he really? Joel had spoken of risk-taking, casual sex with strangers. Just as Jodie had described a version of Grace that no longer fitted the girl who'd escaped from Harm. They'd played roles for that man, and the roles had reduced them. Eric Mackay had loved to dance in the rain. Now he was a killer.

'He taught us all about survival.' The boy's eyes were wet. 'But none of his tricks counted for anything in the

393

end. I used to think he was strong, invincible. But I killed him with a piece of glass. He was . . . nothing. I thought *I* was scared. But he was terrified. Of living. Of being who he was.' He clenched his hands together. 'His heart was like *this*. Like a fist. Like a stone. May . . .' He opened his hands slowly, spreading his palms on the table, facing upwards under the light. 'Her heart was like this. I was scared it would make her weak. I warned her to hate him. Hate everyone, be afraid of everything. But she wasn't. She couldn't be. She was braver than the rest of us – than anyone. Like Loz, like her sister. She stopped me doing worse. Before you came, I mean.'

He raised his eyes to Marnie. 'That's how I kept us alive. You should tell her that. Tell Loz that *she's* the one who saved us. The brave one. Just like her sister.'

'How was it?' Noah asked.

'He's ready to go to prison for killing Calum, and Christie. He says he was afraid for his life, and Loz's.'

'Loz says the same. I didn't ask her any questions, I know we need to wait, but she insisted on telling me. Christie was going to kill them, she's sure of it. She's blaming herself, because she told Calum that Aimee was Eric.' Noah paused. 'Her parents are with her.'

'Good. I need to speak with them.' Marnie turned her head when she heard her name.

Joe Eaton was standing in the hospital corridor. 'Ruth's here for a check-up. I heard you found her. The girl from the crash. Grace, is it?'

'Yes.' Marnie walked to where he was waiting. 'She's here, in fact.'

'In the hospital? Can I see her?'

'Can you . . .?' The request surprised her. 'I'm not sure. You could ask.'

'I'd like to see her, if it's allowed. She's okay, isn't she?'

'Yes, she is.'

'I keep seeing her.' Joe tapped his head. 'Up here. I thought if I could see her for real . . . Only if she's okay. I hope she's okay?'

'She's in good hands.'

'Good.' Joe nodded. 'I'm glad.' He headed back down the corridor.

Noah watched him go. 'Who's helping Grace?'

'Social Services, I imagine.'

Noah nodded, looking impossibly sad. 'And Eric?'

'Juvenile detention. With luck he'll find a decent defence lawyer.' She touched a hand to his elbow. 'You did a great job, connecting Logan to Paradise House. Without that we might still be looking for them. Good work.'

'There was Ledger's phone call,' Noah reminded her.

'Ledger didn't give me the inside track on what was happening in Calum's head.' She kept her hand on his arm until he smiled, accepting the praise. 'That was down to you connecting the dots.'

'It was down to Loz,' Noah said. 'I just followed her search history.'

'I'll tell her you said so.'

68

Loz was in a private room with her parents. Sean and Katrina sat close, holding their daughter's hands, their faces wiped clean with relief, and love.

'We're waiting for the doctor,' Sean told Marnie.

'He means the psychiatrist.' Loz swung her feet from the side of the hospital bed. 'There's nothing wrong with me, nothing physical, but I might have PTSD or some shit like that.'

Sean squeezed her fingers, managing to smile. He put his free arm around Katrina, who leaned closer, returning his smile. They looked ready to drop, but happy.

Loz looked wide awake, her bright stare sweeping the room. She was doing a good job of disguising her distress, but Marnie wasn't fooled. Less than two hours earlier she'd held the girl in her arms, listened to her sobbing, felt her heart thumping through her skin.

'I was hoping for a quick word with Loz before the psychiatrist shows up.'

'A statement, you mean?' Katrina looked up. 'We want to be with her for that.'

'You will be. No, this is informal. I wanted to thank her for her courage.'

Loz flushed. 'Thanks,' but her tone said, *Shut up*.

'Would it be all right if we chatted for a couple of minutes? No longer than that, I promise.'

'Loz?' Sean stroked the back of her hand with his fingers. 'Would that be okay?'

'Sure.' She swung her feet, nodding. 'Yes.'

Marnie waited until Sean and Katrina had gone. Then she took a seat at the side of the bed.

'Before you ask,' Loz said, 'they're not abusing me.'

'Why would I ask that?'

'Because of the sketches. Because the sketches made you wonder and you never found out why May left and because we don't hug.' Loz tipped her head at the lino-leum floor. 'We're not *tactile*.'

'Plenty of families aren't tactile.'

'There you go then. We're *normal*. No good reason for her to leave, or for me to leave.' Swinging her feet deter-minedly. 'Lots of people have it worse than us. That's what the school keeps saying.'

Marnie sat very still, waiting for Loz to catch the different rhythm in the room and slow down.

'So, no abuse. No mad *rules*. They can be a bit strict sometimes, but that's how stuff gets done. May under-stood that. She didn't run *away*. She ran *to* him. Eric. Because she was *in love*.' Her voice said that abuse made more sense as a motive. 'This was a *love story*.' Her stare landed on Marnie, blackly. 'In other words, I'll be okay. I'm safe with them. And out there too. I'm not like May.'

'Eric thinks you are. He said you two were the bravest people he'd met.'

'Great.' Her face didn't change. 'A double murderer

thinks I'm cool. What else did you want to tell me?'

'You asked if I'd forgiven him,' Marnie said. 'Stephen Keele. I didn't give you a proper answer.'

Loz blinked in surprise. She'd been expecting platitudes, some variation of whatever she was afraid the psychiatrist was going to say. PTSD. *Or some shit like that.*

'I haven't,' Marnie said. 'I won't.' She chose her words with care, needing Loz to listen. 'I think about it all the time. About what I'd like to happen to him, how I'd like him to pay for what he did. I thought no one else understood. I thought I couldn't say it out loud in case people decided I was dangerous, or crazy, or obsessed. But lots of people understand. You do. And your parents.'

'They don't,' Loz said bluntly. 'They loved her, of course they did, but that just makes it worse. All I am is what's left. And I'm not enough, I've never been enough.' Her eyes filled with tears. 'I'm stupid. Look what I did, going in there. Look what I put them through. I'm *stupid.*'

'You're remarkable. You helped save us. Eric said so. That was you.'

'Don't tell them that.' Her cheeks were pink. 'Please.'

Marnie understood. Loz had played the survivor for too long. She needed to be a kid again, to be allowed to stop pretending that she didn't care and that nothing hurt when everything, *everything* hurt.

'I won't, but I need you to do another brave thing. Tell them how it feels. Your mum and dad. Tell them how angry you are, how much it hurts, how much you need them to look after you.' She drew a breath, smiling at Loz. 'Give them another chance. Let them make up for the stuff they've got wrong, because we all get stuff wrong, all the time. They're hurting too. They're sorry. Don't shut them out.'

'Is that what you did?' Loz asked. Before answering

her own question with the sagacity that made her so remarkable. 'It's what you *wish* you'd done, when you had the chance.'

'It's what I wish I'd done.' Marnie nodded. 'You have that chance, and the courage to take it. Do what I wasn't brave enough to do. Tell them how much it hurts. Ask for their help.'

'I don't know if I can.' She shook her head, blinking. 'I'm the awkward one, remember? I don't do asking for help. They'll think I've lost it.'

'Try.' Marnie reached for the girl's hands. 'Please.'

'All right.' Loz stopped swinging her feet, sitting still at last, her hands in Marnie's. 'I'll try. But,' wrinkling her nose, 'it's your fault if they freak out.'

'I can live with that.'

They smiled at one another, then Loz freed a hand to scratch her cheek. 'One thing I don't get. He had a sister. That's what you said, when we were all in that room. He had a sister who was lost.'

'Yes.'

'How? What happened to her?'

'We don't know, just that she went missing when he was fifteen.'

'They never found her?' Loz searched Marnie's face with her big eyes. 'All that time . . . He never knew what'd happened to her?'

'No one did.'

'That's horrible. At least we know.' She shook her head, wise beyond her years. 'At least we have that.'

69

A bed of dead rose bushes, black with thorns, marked out the front garden of the house in Chiswick. Rubbish had been dumped over the shallow wall between the street and the garden, empty bottles and beer cans, polystyrene boxes, a sodden pink blanket from a child's bed. There was no one living in the house to stop the fly-tipping, just the ghost of a once-neat garden under the neglect. Over the front door, a rusted nail held the broken chain from a hanging basket, long gone.

'Home sweet home.' Tim Welland stood back for the forensic team. 'This'll sort out the rising house prices. I might even be able to afford a bedsit round here myself.'

'Too many nosy neighbours.' Noah nodded across the street. 'You'd hate it.' He handed Welland one of the coffees he'd bought, passing a second cup to Marnie.

'So what are we looking for here, exactly?' Welland sipped at the coffee, giving the clot of bystanders a filthy glance. 'Apart from a starring role in someone's YouTube video.'

'This was where he first hid the girls,' Marnie said. 'It's

the house he grew up in. The one his sister ran from when she was seventeen.'

'And Eric Mackay did the CPS out of a job, at least where Calum Marsh is concerned. Do we need more evidence than the blood and bodies in Brigantia Gardens?'

But Welland followed Marnie and Noah into the house.

Inside, it was cold and smelt of wax, like a church. Forensics had shrouded the windows in polythene, clouding the light as they moved from room to room. Stacks of boxes everywhere, an abandoned house clearance. Dust squares on the walls where photos had been taken down. Rugs rolled into corners to make space for sleeping bags. A clock ticking obstinately in the kitchen, where limescale had crusted the taps and the steel of the sink. The house had been empty less than six months, but it had the stale, settled chill of a derelict building.

The girls had stayed here, brought back by Christie for Calum, living among the boxes and the memorabilia of his parents' half-dismantled life. Not all the photos had been taken down. Some showed a boy and his dark-haired sister, her mouth unsmiling. Calum and Neve, holding hands.

One wall was pinned with lists. Harm's plans for the move to the tower block, the paper edges curling away from the wall like scales, or feathers.

Welland read a couple of the lists. Said, 'He can't have set out to kill them, or he wouldn't have left this handy confessional for us.'

Upstairs, one of the rooms was different to the others. At the back of the house, overlooking the garden. Furnished like a guest room, but self-consciously, as if no guests had ever used it. The bed was made, its pale-red covers pulled smooth.

That waxy candle smell. The carpet worn down by the side of the bed.

Noah's scalp prickled tightly.

Neve's room.

A rag doll on the pillows, marking her place.

He walked to the window, looking down at the garden, a half-dug plot of earth where weeds had trapped the litter blown from the street behind. A wet breath of mould on the glass. The window frame, burnt by the weather, listed to the left. If he set a marble on the floor, it would race from one end of the room to the other.

The whole house crooked by their loss . . .

All those long years of searching, grieving. Calum, fifteen years old, trapped with his parents' fears and hope, the wildfire of their imagination setting story after story spinning in his troubled head so that for years he caught glimpses of his lost sister in the faces of street kids.

Years and years of looking and hoping and fearing.

'Exciting opportunity,' Welland sniffed at Noah's shoulder, 'to acquire a fabulous family home in need of TLC.'

A dog barked below them.

'DS Jake?' Marnie was headed back down the stairs.

Noah followed her, through the kitchen, out into the garden.

The cadaver dog, a golden retriever, stood at the side of the half-turned plot of earth like an arrow, her whole body pointing.

'Another girl?' Noah measured the ground with his eyes. 'There's space here for a dozen.'

'Just one,' Marnie said. 'I think. There's just one girl buried here.'

He looked up, saw her shivering. 'Who?'

402

She turned towards the bedroom where Welland was watching them. 'Neve.'

A crow rattled from the roof.

The dog didn't move, her coat bristling along her spine.

The disturbed earth was less than ten feet from the house.

'Here?' Noah said. 'The whole time she was *here*? The rages, PTSD. You think her dad . . .?'

'Calum.' Marnie held Welland's gaze across the neglected garden. 'I think it was Calum.'

The dog barked again, before going still.

Marnie and Noah moved back, out of the way of the forensic team.

'May wanted a garden,' Noah remembered. 'She was digging here. She found something.'

'Or she suspected something, after he stopped her digging. When we found her, you said she looked like the killer's confession.'

May, laid out like a child on that bed.

Calum Marsh's confession.

To more than one murder?

'Neve went missing when he was fifteen.' Noah could taste the turned earth, rancid with litter. 'He killed his sister when he was fifteen? Why?'

'Any number of reasons,' Marnie said. 'Because he hated her. Because she wanted to leave him on his own in this house with their father's rages.' Her voice tightened. 'Because he loved her.'

The forensic team moved around the black pit of earth, erecting the tent. One of the team petted the dog's coat. 'Good girl. Good Missy.'

'Smart, independent, ambitious.' Marnie moved back from the perimeter, drawing her coat closer about her. 'That's how Calum described his sister to Gina. All the things he hated those girls being. Grown-up . . . Neve had been wanting to leave home for years. He'd talked her out of it more than once. What if that last talk ended badly? What if this,' she nodded at the pit, 'was their last talk.'

'He came to the station when we were investigating May's death.' Marsh sitting, looking beaten, under the station's posters. 'Did he *want* to be caught?'

'He was living with the secret of Neve's death for a long time. That kind of secret, the weight of it? I think he buried it as best he could. Maybe he'd half forgotten he was a killer. If he was still searching for Neve . . . Unless that was a lie he told to the girls. We know he made a decent life with Gina and Logan. He was a good father, or as good as he could be. Then when his parents died . . .'

Marnie looked up at the house. 'He had to come back here. To the photos, the memories, her room like that, untouched. He filled this house with the girls he found. He wasn't hurting them, not at the beginning. Grace said as much, and Eric too. He wanted us to see the writing on May, to understand the pain she was in. He left her in a place she loved. He was in pain too. That's how Eric saw it. And Eric understood about secrets better than anyone else in that place.'

She stopped, shaking her head. 'Maybe. Maybe I'm wrong.'

Missy had her ears back, still pointing at the black earth, the place where May had started digging until Calum made her stop. The forensic tent had flooded it with shadow.

'Maybe we're going to find more bodies,' Marnie said, 'more lost girls.'

It could be days, or weeks, until this place gave up its secrets.

Years until they had all the answers.

Or it could be never.

Noah stood at her side, shivering, as the team began to dig.

Author's Note

Tastes Like Fear is a work of fiction, but I found the following to be particularly relevant and/or inspirational when I was writing and later editing the book:

Dark Heart: The Shocking Truth About Hidden Britain by Nick Davies, Vintage, 1998

Paranoia: The 21st Century Fear by Daniel Freeman and Jason Freeman, Oxford University Press, 2008

Loud in the House of Myself by Stacy Pershall, W. W. Norton, 2011

Explore Everything by Bradley L. Garrett, Verso Books, 2013

'"If I move, he'll attack": Mastering Rage in Prisoners' by Jonathan Asser in *The Observer*, 9 March 2014

'A Victim's Tale' by Spencer Ackerman in *The Observer*, 17 December 2014

Acknowledgements

This one's for the brave people, especially the girls. For Deb the Punk, my friend when I was fifteen (where have all the punks gone?), and Jude. Everyone who's ever felt out of place in her own skin, or out of step, or out of time. Who's refused to fit in, or has raised her voice against the tyranny of sameness – who stood out and paid the price, but stood out even so. This is for you.

Thank you, of course, to Vicki, Elizabeth and Jo at Headline.

And to Jane, Stephanie, Claire, Mary and everyone at Gregory & Co.

To the bloggers, reviewers and most of all the readers – thank you.

And to Terence Waywell, who won the Get in Character auction in support of the CLIC Sargent charity for children with cancer. I hope you approve of your role in the story.

TASTES LIKE FEAR

Bonus Material

READING GROUP DISCUSSION QUESTIONS

Family is an important issue in the DI Marnie Rome series and we see many different forms of 'family' in this novel. What does family mean to Harm?

Loz mentions 'The Forgiveness Project' to Marnie. Where is forgiveness seen in the novel? And where is it withheld?

The topic of homelessness is at the forefront of this story. How are the ideas of home and shelter pitted against each other?

This book is also about identity, its expression and repression. How does Harm repress the identity of the girls in his care?

Do we see identity repressed or altered elsewhere in the novel?

The first girl is found with writing all over her, as a form of graffiti. What does graffiti help to communicate throughout the novel?

Family and betrayal are closely interlinked throughout. In both Marnie's and Noah's past, how do these two factors come into play?

Stephen Keele continues to appear in Marnie's life, seeming to prevent her from moving past her tragedy. How do you think their relationship will develop throughout the series?

What are you looking forward to in the next DI Marnie Rome novel, *Quieter Than Killing?*

Sarah Hilary interviews DS Noah Jake

So, Noah. I'm wondering what it's like working with DI Marnie Rome?
It's fun. Okay, that's the wrong word. Not fun, but fascinating. Rewarding. And it's worthwhile; I feel like we're making a difference. Marnie never goes after the easy answers; she makes us dig for the deeper truths. That's really important to me.

Can you give us an example?
When we were investigating the deaths of two young brothers last year, our boss thought we should go after a neighbour because he looked odd and acted suspiciously. Marnie made us search closer to home. The hardest thing I've ever witnessed is the damage done to the family involved. People don't always think about the way pain ripples outward, but Marnie does. She takes us into the darkest corners, but we trust one another. We're a good team.

Has it always been that way?
A couple of years ago, when I was first working with her, Marnie kept her cards very close to her chest. But that's okay. She didn't know me, and I understand how much she values privacy because of what happened to her family, apart from anything else.

How about your own family?

I'm lucky. My mum and dad are safe, and happy. My brother Sol is . . . tricky. I worry about him. He and my partner, Dan, get on, which is good. Sol needs to find his path. But when I think about Marnie's family, especially her brother, I know how lucky I am.

What do you admire most about Marnie?

That's easy. Her courage. She could've gone away after Stephen killed her family. Everyone would've understood if she'd done that – hidden herself away. But she doesn't hide. Not even from Stephen. When she makes mistakes she picks herself up and keeps going. She's not reckless, or showy. Lots of people don't see her strength straight-away, because she's so quiet. Steady. But she's the bravest person I know.

Does anything worry you about working with her?

Not about our work, but I worry about her relationship with Stephen. She's so determined to get answers from him. He knows how much she needs those answers and so he's playing her. He's not a kid any more, he's nearly twenty. He's dangerous. I wish Marnie could let it go, that part of her past. But I know she can't. Not yet anyway.

You've become friends. How's she different as a friend to the way she is as a boss?

She's loyal and smart and fun to be with. But she's all those things at work, too. Maybe when Dan and I get her out on the town we'll see another side to her. I'd like to take her clubbing. I have this theory she was a wild child and I want to see her dancing. I bet she's a great dancer.

WRITING THE FEAR

by Sarah Hilary

This story started with a princess. With once-upon-a-time, and a princess.

Whenever I'm in London, I like to walk by the water. Across bridges, along the Embankment, up canal paths. Even down onto the mean strips of pebbled mud that pass for the city's beaches. The Thames is thick with history: Saxon treasure, skulls and bones, silver cups and cannonballs. And not just the Thames; London is leaky with its own past.

We're encouraged to look up – at the dazzle of high rises, all those sharp shards and spindles that make up the famous skyline. But I like looking down – to where the city's packed in layers under our feet. Each time another cloud-kissing landmark gets underway, its construction stops temporarily to allow the archaeologists to move in. To make certain that what's uncovered by the new foundation isn't anything we've never seen before. All that machinery, all those man-hours, can be halted for a medieval child's shoe or a Victorian convict's ball and chain.

And then, there's Battersea Power Station.

How huge it was, once upon a time. Monumental, an

urban cathedral with those dirty-white chimneys, elegant red bricks. For years, in the back of my mind, I'd been writing a story set here. But it wasn't until I was gathering my cast for *Tastes Like Fear* that I realised this was the story. My twin themes of homelessness and the illusion of safety found a natural setting in Battersea Power Station, still so much a part of London's landscape despite standing empty for years; temporary home to art exhibitions and concerts. And to urban explorers for whom she is their 'Princess'.

How small she is, now. Surrounded by glittering new apartments, her chimneys being deconstructed (an expensive machine eats them, from the top down), destined to be penthouses for the very rich.

Standing on the Embankment, seeing my favourite monolith besieged by the ambitious ascent of new London, I suffered a pang of nostalgia – and fear. Just like the lost girls in this book, torn between staying and leaving, courage and trepidation.

London is never still, and it is never safe. Any more than life is still and safe. Yesterday's monoliths are today's building sites, and tomorrow's exclusion zones. The lost girls in *Tastes Like Fear* believe they've found a place of safety. Marnie knows better, because she knows London. How its layers can swallow you whole. How the past rubs up against the present – catlike – throwing sparks.

Battersea's Princess, with her changing shape and her strange new shadows, reminded me that everything's a matter of perspective, and nothing is just what it seems. People as much as places; we all have our once-upon-a-time. And that was how this story started.

Keep reading for an extract from the next
spectacular DI Marnie Rome novel

QUIETER THAN KILLING

Coming Spring 2017

Six years ago

He's washing the car – slapping water, sloppy. She's in the kitchen, cutting. Not meat and not bread, something that chunks under the knife. Carrots or onions. The sounds soak up through the house to where Stephen is sitting in the bedroom with the red wall.

Her room. Marnie's. The shelf over the bed is full of her things. Books and pictures, and the dark blue box with its snarl of bracelets. His favourite is the horseshoe charm, silver, curved like a half-finished heart. He wears the bracelet under the sleeve of his pyjamas, in bed. They said they'd put her things away into the attic if he wanted but he said no, he didn't mind. He likes looking at her things; it makes him feel safe. He sleeps with her books weighted around him like stones.

She painted the red wall herself. He can see the places she had to stop and stand on a chair to finish, stretching her arm to reach the ceiling's right-angles. She was angry when she did it. The paint is too thick and too thin and where it's too thick it's full of holes where air bubbles burst.

She's not been here in years, but it's her room.

1

Marnie Rome's room.

He finds the shape of her in the bed at night and it's his shape, narrow. He wriggles down into it, imagining a trench she dug in the mattress, a place to lie low. Her eyes tracked these same shadows across the ceiling, and watched the sun crouch outside the cracked window.

The crack's at the top corner, in the shape of a hand. He measures it most weeks, to see if it's grown. Stands on a chair and reaches until he's touching the tips of his fingers to it. The last time, it drew blood. He climbed down and stood looking at his red fingers, like hers after she'd painted the wall. The fingers tasted rusty, old. He shut them up in a fist and set its flat side to the window, thinking about punching, thinking of the noise it would make and the feet that would come running, arms open, mouths lopsided, words worrying at him. Just thinking it makes him tired.

He's lonely. If it wasn't for her here with him, he'd have gone crazy by now.

'Marnie Rome.'

He says her name when he's held down by her books, the horseshoe charm biting at the inside of his wrist. They have the same wrists, thin and square. They're the same shape, lying together in the narrow bed, counting the holes in the red wall, all the places pricked by her anger. And not just anger. Sadness, too. She was lonely here, like him. Hurting, the way he hurts.

The slop of water from outside.

He's making the car shine.

From the kitchen, the smell of onions frying in butter.

She's making a casserole.

Stephen had never eaten a casserole until he came here. He was eight then. Now he's fourteen, 'a growing boy,' she says. In the other place it was all scraps and

2

mouldy sandwiches made with whatever was left in the fridge. Here, they won't stop feeding him. Proper food, she calls it.

'Let's get a proper meal inside you,' as if she can see his emptiness.

He's so empty it hurts.

Food doesn't help, stretching his stomach until he has to get rid of it to make more room for her, for Marnie. Food just gets in the way.

He's whistling as he washes the car. Stephen can hear water running onto the drive. He used to help when he first came here, when he was scared, wanting to please. He's not scared now. Not of them, not of anything, thanks to her.

'Marnie Rome.'

He counts the holes in the red wall, starting over.

From the kitchen—

The yellow smell of onions frying, and the slow chunking of the knife.

3

THRILLINGLY GOOD BOOKS
FROM CRIMINALLY
GOOD WRITERS

CRIME FILES BRINGS YOU THE LATEST RELEASES FROM
TOP CRIME AND THRILLER AUTHORS.

SIGN UP ONLINE FOR OUR MONTHLY NEWSLETTER AND BE THE FIRST
TO KNOW ABOUT OUR COMPETITIONS, NEW BOOKS AND MORE.